Forgotten Women

OTHER TITLES BY FREDA LIGHTFOOT

HISTORICAL SAGAS

The Amber Keeper
Lakeland Lily
The Bobbin Girls
The Favourite Child
Kitty Little
For All Our Tomorrows
Gracie's Sin
Daisy's Secret
Ruby McBride
Dancing on Deansgate
Watch for the Talleyman
Polly's Pride
Polly's War
House of Angels
Angels at War
The Promise
My Lady Deceiver

THE LUCKPENNY SERIES

Luckpenny Land
Wishing Water
Larkrigg Fell

THE POOR HOUSE LANE SERIES

The Girl from Poor House Lane
The Woman from Heartbreak House

FREDA LIGHTFOOT

Forgotten Women

LAKE UNION

PUBLISHING

Text copyright © 2016 Freda Lightfoot
All rights reserved.

Published by Lake Union Publishing, Seattle

www.apub.com

Amazon, the Amazon logo, and Lake Union Publishing are trademarks of Amazon.com, Inc., or its affiliates.

ISBN-13: 9781503934214
ISBN-10: 1503934217

Cover design by Debbie Clement

Printed in the United States of America

PROLOGUE

My dearest love,

Let me assure you that I am well. The silence in the prison cells as thousands of women prisoners wait for the call they dread is deeply distressing. Every night is the same. The guards come in the hour before dawn to select the next victims to be shot by firing squad. The only crime of many of these poor women is to have supported their husband by not revealing his whereabouts, or simply to raise funds for the Republican cause. Even failing to follow the teachings of the Catholic Church with sufficient diligence can result in execution, particularly if the family is of the wrong political persuasion.

Sometimes I feel that anticipating one's death is almost worse than the actual event itself, rather like waiting to be sacrificed to ancient pagan gods. The agony becomes so intense that desperation grows inside me to get it over with quickly.

Each night, when the call finally comes, the eyes of the women being taken go instantly blank, as if they've already departed this world and are looking beyond the grim walls of the prison to a life of peace in the hereafter. They walk to meet their fate with pride and courage, dressed in their best, heads shaved.

I confess to breathing a sigh of relief each time I am passed by, even if my heart bleeds for those less fortunate than myself. An emotionally charged silence generally follows, as those of us who have been spared listen for the sound of the shots that mark the end of yet more innocent lives.

Some prisoners have had their sentence commuted to anything from ten to thirty years. I can't recall how much of my five-year sentence I have served here in Ventas prison, or La Pepa as some call it. I've lost track. But then time no longer seems relevant. I do hope you are still safe, my darling. I live in hope for the day when this dreadful war is over and we'll be together again.

Sorry, my love, but I had to stop writing this letter and have returned to it a night or two later. I was interrupted by a heart-rending scream, then forced to watch in agonised silence as a woman frantically fought a guard who was dragging her child from her arms. He strode away with the screaming infant tucked under his arm as if it were no more than a rabbit. Silence descended upon everyone as the poor woman fell into a stupor, realising she had but hours to live. Perhaps she no longer cared, having lost the battle to save her child. The lack of facilities is such that many babies don't survive birth. Nor do their mothers.

The conditions here are unbearable: fleas, lice and bedbugs, with very little water to drink or wash ourselves. Yet we endure it all without complaint. It's the safest way. I've grown accustomed to battling hunger, dysentery, food poisoning, malnutrition and rat bites, even the regular beatings. But living with the fear of torture, rape and execution is another matter altogether. I try to be brave, as always. Did I write to tell you about the interrogation I had to endure, once I'd recovered from the trauma? Can't quite remember. I do hope you receive all my letters. I'm so grateful for yours that R brings to me. Reading them daily gives me the will to battle on.

Must hurry to finish this one as letters are already being passed to friends before the guards come for their next victims. Wedding rings, crucifixes, earrings and other jewellery are also being handed over. I have none left, as I've given them all away in payment for food and other necessities. Mothers are whispering a loving farewell to their children, preparing for the worst as they struggle not to shed a tear, fearful of frightening them. Babies are put to the breast to silence them too.

Ah, a small voice has started to sing. This happens often, almost as if the women feel the need to indulge in some light relief to make their last hours on earth joyous. I'm singing along with them. Can you hear me in your heart, my darling?

Sadly the singing has stopped almost instantly at the sound of footsteps clomping on the stone paving that leads to our cells. My heart is racing. The sound of breathing too has almost ceased. Fists are clenched. I hear soft whimpers and cries. The guard has entered and is reading out names. The women called rise at once to their feet, knowing there can be no delay in obeying or more will be taken in retaliation. Five are now standing in line. I am safe. Oh no . . .

PART ONE

ONE
SCOTLAND — SUMMER 1986

THE VISITOR gazing at the picture for the last twenty minutes had hardly moved an inch. He seemed riveted by its beauty, or the message it gave out with its images of clenched fists, soaring aeroplanes, flags, soldiers toting guns, and an injured woman holding her child to her breast, all randomly inserted into a beautiful Spanish landscape. Was he moved by the memories it evoked, Jo wondered. No, that wasn't possible. He was far too young to remember a war that ended nearly fifty years ago.

A bell sounded, indicating the art gallery was about to close, and she sighed with relief. This first day of the exhibition had been exciting but long and tiring, as they'd started preparations nearly twelve hours ago. Jo's mind instantly leaped ahead, wondering if Felix would be late again this evening, then she bleakly remembered their relationship was over. It was going to take time for her to adjust to life without him.

The lingering crowd was rapidly thinning as people made for the exit, but still the man didn't move. He was tall with black curly hair, formally dressed in a grey suit, a loosely knotted silk scarf hung around his neck despite the warm summer evening outside, and he had a certain tension in his powerful shoulders.

'Are you going to ask this fellow to leave, and deal with the old lady on the banquette who seems to have nodded off?' a voice demanded in her ear.

Jo smiled at the director with resigned patience, knowing he considered it beneath him to assist with such a mundane task. 'The old lady is my grandmother, waiting for me to take her home, but, yes, I'll see the gentleman out.'

Normally when she approached a visitor they'd instantly get the message and leave. Not this time. He didn't even glance at Jo as he began to speak in grumbling tones. 'You do appreciate this picture is a forgery. Someone is attempting to pass this piece off as the work of Ramón Peña Barros, no doubt in a bid to increase its value. That could be the fault of a fraudulent artist, or the gallery itself.'

Jo snapped her gaze from the picture to take in the ferocity of the man's expression, a frown creasing his brow. 'I assure you we do not exhibit forgeries in this gallery, nor do we commit fraud,' she retorted, the shock of his accusation resonating in her voice. 'The exhibition is to commemorate the year when local Scots joined the International Brigade at the start of the Spanish Civil War. The identity of this artist is not a major factor as the painting is very evocative of the era. The gallery has not attributed it to any particular artist.'

'I take it you are not familiar with Peña Barros, then?' the young man said, a tightness to his jutting jaw.

'I'm afraid not. What makes you so certain the picture is a forgery? Is this simply a guess on your part?'

He glowered, his dark eyes glittering with fresh anger. 'I do not make a *suposición*. I know what I am talking about. The work is quite well executed but lacking his usual finesse and style, among other things that are plainly wrong. For a start it doesn't bear a signature, just a smudge of paint as if someone has scrubbed out the name.'

Jo had to agree with him there. She'd been concerned about that too, and badly wished to know who the artist was. But she'd fallen in love with the painting on sight, with its bright colours and the political aspect it gave of the war. 'I assumed the name was rubbed out because of the danger the artist might have found himself in by producing such a picture during the conflict,' Jo said, her curiosity alerted as she realised the man must be Spanish. 'How did you come to hear of this exhibition?'

He brushed this question aside with a flick of one hand. 'I do not think that is relevant. This picture should most definitely be checked out, the paint and canvas analysed.'

Aware of the director rattling his keys by the door, Jo dreaded to think what his reaction would be if the gallery were indeed charged with fraud. Highly ambitious and hugely controlling, Mark Carter did not allow his staff much freedom to explore their own ideas. Discovering the picture had been the inspiration to hold this exhibition. Gran had obviously been less impressed with it as she'd dumped it in her attic. But then she was not an easy woman, and Jo had found it necessary to battle hard to win them both round. Offering a polite smile, she hastened to reassure this visitor she'd no reason to doubt that the paint and canvas were of that era. 'Appropriate checks were made.'

'Did that include an x-ray? Sometimes a forger will paint over an existing picture in an effort to prove authenticity.'

'I'm afraid not, but we'll certainly get that done as you've made me curious to know if it is by this Peña Barros. We made no claims for it to be a famous work of art, merely an exhibit to illustrate the war.' Indicating that he should follow her, Jo began to lead the way to the exit. 'Now I must ask you to leave. It's closing time.'

Glancing about him at the empty gallery the man looked slightly startled. '*Lo siento*. I'm sorry, I didn't realise. But someone has clearly copied the original, or more likely a photograph of it, and chosen to add certain items as an embellishment. I assure you there is no woman and child in the original. Also, the house is viewed from a slightly different perspective and . . .'

'You know it?'

Jo was startled to find this question being asked by her grandmother, who had come over to join them and was regarding the young man through narrowed eyes, her face having gone even paler than usual.

'Indeed, I am most familiar with it. Not simply the house, but the picture itself. Known as *Casa Oliva*, it hangs on the wall of my family's *finca*. Here's proof,' he said, handing the old lady a photograph. Then turning back to Jo he said, 'You are welcome to come and see it for yourself should you wish to compare the two, although it is in Spain.'

Her grandmother was staring at the black-and-white photograph, an expression of stunned disbelief on her wrinkled face, almost as if a host of memories were flooding into her head. A tear slid down her cheek and Jo quickly put an arm about her to give her a warm hug. 'What is it? Don't upset yourself, Gran. I'll deal with this.'

Ignoring her granddaughter, she lifted her troubled gaze to meet that of the young man, and speaking with measured calmness asked, 'Who are you?'

He gave a slight bow of his head. 'My name is Anton Quintana Méndez.' Then he turned to address Jo. 'I am only here for a short time, but you can reach me at the Almere Hotel. I look forward to hearing the results of your investigation. In the meantime, I recommend you remove this picture from the exhibition. Otherwise, I may feel obliged to sue the gallery.' Upon which threat he strode out through the door, head held high.

Jo had wasted no time in having the picture examined, which fortunately confirmed her assumption that the canvas, paint and style were entirely in keeping with the era. The director, however, had been far from happy when Jo showed him the photo of the alleged original and pointed out that this young man had threatened to sue the gallery.

'Sorry, Mark. I did admit at the time that we had no idea who the artist was, but didn't think that mattered. You agreed that it is a beautiful picture, painted in a style evocative of the period, and gave permission to display it.'

'Do not attempt to put the blame on to me. It was *your* choice, *your* decision, *your* exhibition,' he dismissively remarked, making it very clear that any charge of forgery would be directed against her entirely.

Jo winced, feeling slightly irritated that her boss wasn't prepared to support her. Had she messed up on this project because of the traumas life was throwing at her right now? She pushed all of that from her mind as she sat in the bar with Anton Quintana Méndez at his hotel, and prepared to relay the results. He'd ordered afternoon tea, but before the waitress had finished setting out the teapot and cups and saucers, together with a plate of scones on the table before them, he began firing questions at her. His expression grew increasingly sceptical as Jo gave her explanation that all was as she'd expected.

'So you have nothing new. *¡Nada!*'

'Not about the authenticity of the picture, no. Unfortunately, our expert has no other work by Ramón Peña Barros to compare this picture with, in order to check such matters as brush strokes or choice of palette colours. He could find no record of him, so who he is remains a puzzle.'

'It might prove your expert's inefficiency. Peña Barros is an artist known for painting posters of the Spanish Civil War. Not as famous as Picasso, or Salvador Dalí, but he most certainly had a following.'

Jo felt her cheeks grow warm with embarrassment as yet again she was being accused of failing in her job. It made perfect sense that the artist had painted posters, not pretty pictures or similar works of art, so why hadn't her expert checked that out? Why hadn't she asked him to? She really seemed to be losing it. Setting aside any hope of a cup of tea, as Señor Méndez made no move to pour her one, she reached for her bag to pull out an envelope. 'He did, however, discover something of interest. When our expert took the painting out of the frame he found a letter tucked into the back. It's fascinating, if somewhat distressing.'

Señor Méndez was instantly alert. 'May I read it?'

'Of course.' Jo handed it over, then picked up the teapot and filled his cup before attending to her own needs. She'd missed lunch, having been called to the director's office to receive a reprimand, rather like a naughty schoolgirl.

'Would you mind reading it to me?' he asked, handing the letter back to her. 'It is very squiggly writing and my English may not be up to the task.'

'Your English sounds impressively fluent to me,' Jo assured him, 'although I do agree parts of this letter are not easy to decipher.' With a smile she took one quick grateful sip of her tea. 'I'd guess it was a letter to the lady's lover or husband.

Ventas prison, 1938.

My dearest love,

Let me assure you that I am well . . .'

Jo continued to read the letter with great sensitivity, struggling to blink away her tears as she had done every time she'd read it. 'It ends with *The women called rise at once to their feet, knowing there can be no delay in obeying or more will be taken in retaliation. Five are now standing in line. I am safe. Oh no . . .* I suspect her name was called at that point.' She glanced up at him expecting a cool reaction, but was surprised to see that he was looking equally moved.

'I would very much like to know more about this lady, including her name,' he quietly said.

'The letter bears no signature. It would seem that whoever this poor woman was, she did not have time to write it. It's hard to imagine how one would feel faced with the prospect of death by firing squad.'

'That's how it was during the Civil War. People were arrested, kidnapped and sometimes executed for no reason whatsoever, other than politics. That part about the person who delivered her lover's letters, will you read it again, please?'

Jo flicked her gaze over the letter to find it. *'I'm so grateful for yours that R brings to me. Reading them daily gives me the will to battle on.* Unfortunately she doesn't give the full name. Are you thinking it could be this artist, Ramón?'

His eyes narrowed in deep thought. 'It's possible, I suppose. I was thinking that my grandmother's name also begins with R.'

'Really? What a coincidence.'

'Her name is Rosita.' After a thoughtful pause he cleared his throat and said, 'It would appear that this picture does have a genuine connection with the war, whoever the artist might be. I'd like to apologise for my earlier reaction. It was perhaps wrong of me to accuse you, or the gallery, of forgery. I should have made more of an effort to discover the full facts before making such an accusation. *Lo siento.'*

'Apology accepted,' Jo said, feeling a flicker of interest in the way his face lightened and became quite handsome when he gently smiled at her. 'As I said, we made no claim about the artist, and had no wish to pass it off as the work of this Peña Barros.'

'I accept that now, but something is not quite right. This letter raises more questions than answers.'

'Not least why it was tucked into the frame of a painting hidden in my grandmother's attic, which is where I found it.'

He stared at her, his dark amber eyes wide with surprise. 'So you didn't buy the picture at auction, then?'

Jo gave a little shake of the head. 'I came across it when clearing out Gran's belongings when she moved house. She's lived in Kirkcudbright all her life, and was most reluctant to leave the house by the river where she'd lived for so long. But now well into her sixties I helped her to find somewhere smaller and easier to maintain, and conveniently close to the centre of the village. I hoped my mother, or more likely my father, would help with the move. Now living in London, Mum had no wish to return to Scotland, and, as always, Dad claimed he was far too busy even to assist his elderly mother shift all her stuff. So it was all down to me. The reason is more likely that my parents were reluctant to meet up again. They're divorced, so no longer speak to each other,' she said with a wry smile.

'That can't be easy.'

'It certainly isn't. I feel like a referee at a wrestling match where those two are concerned. Anyway, I do what I can for Gran in the little spare time I have available, as I love her dearly, although she can be as equally stubborn and difficult as her son. Very distant at times.' Taking another sip of tea to prevent herself from divulging more of her personal problems, Jo gave an apologetic smile. 'Sorry, you didn't come all the way from Spain to hear me ranting on about family issues. Nor, I dare say, simply to visit this exhibition.'

He let out a sigh. 'As a matter of fact I did. Would you believe I came at *mi abuela*'s request, or rather her instruction? My grandmother read about the exhibition in a local newspaper, and sent me here in the hope of discovering information about old friends. She too is approaching seventy, and having been diagnosed with cancer, thinks this might be her last chance to find them.'

'I'm sorry to hear that.' A small frown puckered Jo's brow as she considered what he'd just told her. 'But why would *your* grandmother imagine she'd find her old friends at *this* exhibition?'

'It was because they were Scottish members of the International Brigade who went out to help the Spanish people in their hour of need. I very much doubt she's heard anything from them since the war ended. It has long been a taboo subject. No one was permitted to speak of it. Spaniards are only now discovering the truth of what happened, and beginning to demand that the bodies of their lost relatives be dug up from the areas where they were shot, so they can be reburied in the *cementerio* with other family members.'

'Oh, that must be so painful. I wonder if any of these friends of your grandmother's are still alive? Do you know their names?'

'I have them written here,' he said, opening up his notebook to show her.

When Jo read the first name she gave a puzzled frown. 'Charlotte McBain. That's a name I recognise, although I'm not certain who this lady is exactly. I've never heard her mentioned before, but the surname is most familiar. Oh, my goodness, Libby Forbes. That's my gran, whom you recently met. Did she really take part in the Spanish Civil War? She's never said a word about that.'

'Which doesn't surprise me. The Fascists continued to pursue their quarry for many years after the war ended. It was not an easy transition to democracy following Franco's regime.'

'But why didn't she tell *me*, her own granddaughter?'

'The silence inflicted on survivors could well be the reason, but it also worked as a means of security.'

A new thought struck Jo. 'What if this letter was from Gran, then she was fortunately released? Maybe that would explain her reluctance to speak of it. I'd love to learn more about her early life, over which she is remarkably silent. And as the x-ray has proved this picture to be of that era and we've found this intriguing letter tucked behind it, I would like to compare it with the original version, if you wouldn't mind? Once this exhibition is over, of course.'

'You'd be most welcome.'

'Thank you.' Jo made the impulsive decision that she really had nothing to lose by going to Spain to investigate these issues more thoroughly. In any case, she felt badly in need of a holiday in view of the fact that her life was in complete turmoil. 'I'm also keen to learn more about this alleged artist, Ramón Peña Barros. Perhaps he was the lover this poor lady was writing to. Maybe your grandmother has the answer.'

'I'm sure *mi abuela* could tell us a great deal, if we can but persuade her.'

༄

'Were you upset because that young man assumed the picture to be a forgery, Gran?' Jo asked with concern as they enjoyed Sunday lunch together at a local restaurant by the marina, the sun glinting on the blue waters of the River Dee. 'How did you come by this picture? You never did tell me. I was completely unaware that you joined the International Brigade. Unbelievable! How did that come about? You must have had to endure so much during the Civil War. What a brave young woman you were.'

'The painting was left tae me by a friend,' Libby said, ignoring all other questions.

'Who is this friend?'

Libby made no attempt to answer this question either. Being sent this picture some years ago had taken her completely by surprise. She'd locked it away in the attic, not wishing to look at it or recall the horrors of the past. But confronted by that young man, an all-too-familiar fear had sparked within her, as she realised his possible connection was only a small part of the puzzle. Could he provide the answers she'd so longed to find? Somehow Libby doubted it. Then why was he here? Did he know the artist, or had he come to Scotland for some other reason? If so, what would that be? She could hardly bear to think.

Her troubled thoughts were halted as Jo went on to explain how the young man's grandmother had sent him here. 'She's called Rosita and is apparently a friend of yours.'

'Nae real friend o' mine. Never was, and never will be.' Libby spat out the words with a hasty venom she instantly regretted, wishing she'd held on to her silence. 'I have nae wish to discuss the subject any further. Let's put it tae rest.'

'Sorry, but I'm intrigued to know more, so thought I'd go to Spain to investigate this picture.'

Libby stared at her granddaughter wide-eyed with dismay. 'No, no, dinna ever go there.'

'Why not? The exhibition will be over by the end of the week and I could do with a break, as well as to organise a comparison between this alleged forgery and the original. Anton has invited you too, Gran. It would be wonderful if you came with me.'

Libby felt the lump of fear expand inside her chest. That was most definitely a road along which she had no wish to travel. Having been persuaded to allow Jo to put the picture on public display, despite the risks involved, it was clear to her now that she should have thought things through much more carefully. But how could she stop her from going to Spain? She was a grown woman with a mind of her own.

'There's something else you might like to see,' Jo was saying. 'We found a letter tucked inside the frame.'

Now Libby's heart began to pound as her granddaughter slipped it into her hand. Dear lord, what might this reveal? Tears flooded her eyes as she read it, but she handed it back without a word.

'Have you any idea who this woman might be? Did you know her?'

Libby pressed her trembling lips together, making no comment.

'Did she go with you to Spain, or did you perhaps meet her there? I'd love to hear what made you decide to go and fight in the war, and how you coped with the battle.'

'We went tae help the Spanish people, no tae fight,' Libby wearily remarked, then stared out across the river, watching the fishing boats come in, feeling as if she was slipping back in time to another world. In 1936 the Spanish Civil War had felt like not only a worthy cause but also a great adventure, one they were all willing to grasp, being young and each struggling with personal problems. But the results of that decision had been shocking and changed their lives forever. Would her worst fears now erupt all over again, proving she should have remained a forgotten woman?

TWO
SPAIN — 1986

JO FOUND settling into her holiday home, situated on the edge of a quiet mountain village with stunning views, really rather exciting. It felt such a lovely place for a summer break. This ancient *cortijo* was small and basic, but idyllically set in a cleft of hills amidst rolling acres of ancient olive trees, most of them on land belonging to Anton Quintana Méndez. It possessed its own little olive grove and several almond trees packed with nuts waiting to be picked. A huddle of white houses with their red tiled roofs glinted like a blob of paint on the mountain opposite, with peaks of grey rocks and cliffs towering above. The perfect hideaway for a peaceful rest. If only Felix was still around to share the joy of it with her.

Despite having lived together for nearly three years, their relationship had entirely fallen apart. In the beginning it hadn't greatly bothered her that having suffered the grief of losing his beloved wife he'd been reluctant to marry again. But some months ago when she'd found herself unexpectedly pregnant, Jo had started to dream of a possible wedding. But all hopes of a happy-ever-after were later buried along with the child, although the doctor assured her there was no reason why she shouldn't have more children.

Felix did have a daughter, dear Sophie, a troubled teenager, but he longed for more of a family. And with grief escalating in him once more had turned to a colleague at work for consolation. Because a part of her still felt some love for him, Jo had been ready to believe his claim that the affair was over. When later she discovered they were still very much involved, she'd instantly called an end to their relationship and moved into a small rented flat, feeling utterly desolate.

Now determinedly putting these problems from her mind, Jo set off to explore the *cortijo*. The property had two bedrooms, plus two tiny bathrooms, each simply furnished and with white painted walls. The living room was long and narrow with a sofa, easy chair, built-in bookshelves and an open fireplace set in one corner. Beyond this lay a small terrace carefully shaded from the sun, with a dining table and four cane chairs. Adjoining the living area was a pretty little kitchen with yellow blinds and shining white units.

To her great delight Jo saw the house also had its own pool, and feeling hot and sticky after the long flight she wasted no time in peeling off her clothes, grabbing her swimsuit and diving in.

'Oh, this is wonderful,' she murmured to a swallow, which stopped skimming the surface of the pool to watch from a nearby tree as Jo took her turn in the water.

It really was time to make a new beginning. She would make an effort to rebuild her life, even as her heart bled with renewed anguish every time she thought of Felix, and her lost child. This holiday in Spain could be the opportunity she needed to make some decisions for her future.

༄

The next day it had been arranged for Jo to join Anton Quintana Méndez and his grandmother for lunch. 'I'm longing to hear more about what my gran did in the war, and yours too,' she said as they walked the short distance together to his family home.

He gave a little shake of his head. 'That's not a question I can answer. She's sixty-six, so was only sixteen when the war started. Persuading her to talk about that time isn't easy. All I can tell you for certain is that she married young, and had one son, my father, although who her husband was at that time I cannot say for sure.'

Jo was shocked. 'You don't know?'

'We know his name, nothing more. Demetrio Quintana López. You should be aware that Spanish names work differently to the British. A married woman is not required to change her name. A child will have one surname from his father, and one from his mother, as is the case with me. There must have been some problem with their relationship as she refuses to speak of him. He's most definitely a taboo subject.'

Jo frowned. 'How very sad. He must have caused her great pain in some way or other.'

'I dare say he did, or else she simply didn't love him. There may have been other romantic attachments since, but the Spanish consider it improper for a widow to remarry. She's a very determined and independent lady with a mind of her own and quite firm opinions, so I doubt she was easy to live with, whoever her husband might have been.'

'As was my grandmother,' Jo said with a grin. 'And if by that you mean she didn't feel she should obey his every word, then I'm with her on that one.'

Anton had the grace to smile by way of apology. 'I beg your pardon. I wasn't meaning to imply that a woman *should* obey her husband without question, but I'm quite certain that Rosita was involved in some important operation or other. Why I think that I really couldn't say. It's just a feeling I have.'

'If she remains reluctant to speak of it, how will we persuade her to tell us about these old friends of hers who were in the International Brigade, or to help me find out more about this picture, not to mention my grandmother?'

He gave a little shrug to his broad shoulders. 'We can surely assume that having sent me all the way to Scotland to seek them out, and with her life now slowly coming to an end, she is at last prepared to do so.'

Libby too had refused to speak of the war, claiming she and Rosita were not friends when something in her eyes seemed to say the exact opposite, which was odd. But then as an unsociable and self-opinionated lady who very much liked to be the centre of attention, she never revealed her true feelings about anything.

Jo recalled how her father complained that as a boy he was never allowed to go anywhere without her permission, not picnics, days out with friends, or even to join any sports teams. 'She very much kept me confined to quarters, and would watch me like a hawk,' he'd say. 'Mum might enjoy staying largely in the house, but why should I? I was a young boy eager to get out and about, play cricket and football, have fun.' He'd left home at the first opportunity in order to be free to do his own thing, but poor Libby had become even more of an agoraphobic in her old age, for which her son showed little sympathy.

Could this war have been the cause of her condition? And had it affected Rosita in some way too?

Rosita proved, in fact, to be a lovely lady, looking much younger than her sixty-six years and utterly charming and friendly. Her English too was remarkably good, considering she'd lived all her life in Spain. As lunch wasn't quite ready, she offered to show Jo around her garden.

Typically Spanish, it was set within a walled courtyard, the beds blooming with cactus, aloe vera, plumbago, oleander, hibiscus and bird of paradise flowers. Huge fan palms towered above, and in the centre was set a beautiful fountain off which protruded a long rectangular channel of water that was alive with goldfish. The air was laced with the beautiful scent of jasmine that climbed the walls of the house, a spacious and elegant villa. Beyond the courtyard was row upon row of olive trees stretching out across the *campo*.

'How very lucky you are to live in such a beautiful place,' Jo said, filled with admiration. 'I'm hugely impressed, and very jealous.'

Rosita laughed. 'It wasn't always this grand, or so beautiful. It's years of hard work, not least my son's business and property skills, that have lifted the family out of poverty and provided the means to extend this *finca*. There was a time when we were suffering near starvation, surviving on *pimientos* and *patatas*.'

'That would be because of the war, I take it? It must have been a very difficult time for you.'

Rosita gave a sad little smile. 'It certainly was, but I had friends to help me through it, many from your part of Scotland. The men came to fight, and the women to nurse the wounded at the front, as did your grandmother. She's called Libby, *sí*?'

'She is,' Jo agreed.

'I hoped she would come with you. That was partly my aim in sending Anton to the exhibition. I am not well enough to travel, and with little time left in this world, would love to see her once more.'

Jo felt deeply saddened at again being reminded of this grim fact. 'I'm so sorry to hear that. Unfortunately, she has no wish to visit Spain ever again.'

The old lady looked so upset by this news that tears ran down her cheeks. Jo helped her to a marble bench where she sat with her head in her hands in silent despair for some moments. 'It is fear gripping her, *sí*?'

'Do you think so?' Jo felt alarmed by this suggestion. Fear of what, she wondered. 'Actually, she rarely sets foot outside the house.'

'That is sad. I can understand why she would not wish to visit Spain. Life continued to be difficult throughout the Franco regime, long after the war ended. He died in 1975, an event welcomed by many as they waited in the plaza in Madrid with bottles of champagne in anticipation of celebrating his death. Yet just a few years ago we feared we were facing yet another coup d'état. Fortunately, one that was resolved by King Juan Carlos. Libby and I did have the odd quarrel or *las diferencias*, but remained friends, so I hoped she would come, now all these problems are over.'

Rosita was so distressed that this didn't seem quite the moment to produce the letter from the woman about to be shot. On hearing footsteps approach, she lifted her head and managed to smile at her grandson. 'I am sad to learn that my old friend is not prepared to revisit *España*.'

'I dreaded your reaction to hearing this news,' Anton said, then turning to Jo introduced her to the older man standing beside him. 'This is my father, Gregorio. And this is Joanna, the young lady I told you about, *Papá*.'

Jo held out her hand but as he slightly bowed his head and did not take it, she quickly dropped it again. 'Pleased to meet you.'

'You must be the granddaughter of Elizabeth Forbes,' he said, his brown eyes regarding her with open curiosity.

'I am, yes, although Gran was generally known as Libby.'

'A name that indicates the kind of woman who wishes to be free.'

'No longer the case, I'm afraid. So sorry I failed to persuade her to come.'

'Perhaps it is just as well.'

'Really?'

'You might not care for what you discover about her.'

'Why, what might that be?'

'Not now, Gregorio. Come, lunch is ready,' Rosita said, and quickly getting to her feet took her son's arm to lead him away to the dining terrace.

As they walked away, Jo turned to Anton with a puzzled frown. 'What was that all about? Have I offended him in some way by not persuading Gran to come?'

He gave a little sigh. 'I should perhaps have warned you that *mi abuela* did once admit that her husband was not his father. Gregorio assumed he must be illegitimate, a shocking thing to be in Franco's Spain. But as she refused to say any more on the subject, he went to ask the nuns at the convent, which is where babies were generally born. They suggested he could have been adopted. His birth mother would have given him away, as commonly happened with women unwilling to risk damaging their reputation. They would toss babies into a hospital basket for anyone to take. And they told him a Scottish woman did give birth around that time, so it could have been her.'

Jo felt shocked to the core. 'Is he implying that was my grandmother? I don't believe it. She would never do such a dreadful thing. Libby adores children. Does he have any proof?'

'Not that I know of, but it makes sense if Libby was Rosita's friend. *Papá* has put two and two together and made—'

'Five,' Jo sternly remarked.

'I'm afraid so,' Anton agreed. 'Rather than see himself as illegitimate, he now assumes he was adopted. *Mi abuela* will say no more on the subject, save for the fact it was common practice to adopt in those days, and not wrong in any way.'

Despite her eagerness to investigate Ramón Peña Barros, the famous artist, Jo realised there was a much bigger problem hovering in the background. How dare anyone accuse Libby of such a thing when she adored children, and was most protective of her only son? A heart-rending thought. And as Jo knew from personal experience how painful it was to lose a baby, she could not believe for one moment that any mother would willingly give up their child unless pressure was put upon them to do so. She made a private vow to ring her father and ask if this charge could have any truth to it. She really hoped not.

ᐯ

Jo found the atmosphere over lunch with Anton's family rather chilly and fraught with tension. Gregorio sat opposite with his wife, Dolores, by his side. They would frequently cast curious glances in Jo's direction while conversing quietly in Spanish. She felt uncomfortable until Anton's great-aunt Marta, a sweet-looking lady in her fifties with a plump wrinkled face and frizzy white hair, happily settled beside her. Nothing was said about her grandmother having supposedly tossed away her child, although Jo felt herself burning with anger inside at such an assumption. But as she knew very little about Gran's early life, she didn't have the first idea how to set about defending her. She concentrated instead on the paella, a delicious mix of chicken, shrimp, rice and chorizo.

'This is wonderful,' she said to Rosita. '*Muy bien*. Sorry, but my Spanish is not very good.'

'Then perhaps you should learn,' Gregorio drily remarked, in almost perfect English, blinking at her yet again as if trying to decide whether or not they were related.

'I shall do my best, but as I'm only here for two weeks I doubt it will improve much. I intend to spend a good deal of my time investigating the authenticity of this picture.'

'Why does that matter?' he asked.

'It was my idea to hold the exhibition in the first place, so I'm curious to know whether or not it is genuine. I feel it's very much my responsibility to do so. I also hope to learn more about my grandmother's life in the Civil War,' she added, deliberately avoiding his probing gaze. 'But I agree that my lack of Spanish will not help.'

Marta gave her hand a gentle little pat. '*No pasa nada.*'

Anton smiled. 'My great-aunt is telling you not to worry. We are all happy to act as interpreters in your quest.'

'Thank you. Most generous of you.' Jo said no more, nervous of causing offence. The conversation reverted to Spanish while she chatted a little with Anton.

Once lunch was over, she and Anton sat with Rosita and her younger sister Marta, the rest of the family having gone their separate ways, and after a friendly chat Jo finally found the right moment to risk a question: 'Surely my grandmother didn't come alone to Spain? Were any of her friends or family with her?'

Rosita smiled as she poured them each a cup of coffee. 'She came with a lovely group of friends, including Lady Charlotte.'

'Ah yes, I believe she must have been related to Alexander Ross McBain, the local laird. Gran worked as his housekeeper for a number of years when he became old. I often used to stay with her at Craiklyn Manor when I was young, helping Gran with many chores. But I never heard this lady's name mentioned once.'

'I could tell you what I know about her,' Rosita said, drifting her gaze to look at the distant hills, which were peaked and barren. 'Dear Charlie told me her life story, little by little over the period of our friendship. I think it helped her at times when she was at a low ebb to re-examine the problems she'd once had to endure as a young woman, and how she'd coped with them. It may have given her the strength required to deal with the ones she was then facing. It also helped her to understand the reaction and behaviour of the people in her life. She shared her pain with me, as did I with her. Libby too eventually revealed anguish of her own past as the three of us would sit chatting over breakfast together,' she said with a smile. 'But it was not easy.'

Wondering what she meant by this remark, Jo felt an eagerness to ask more questions, but holding herself in check gave a polite smile. 'I'd love to hear more.'

'It is a complicated and painful story.'

Anton reached for his grandmother's hand to give it a gentle pat. 'Isn't that the reason you sent me to that exhibition in Scotland, because you wished to find your old friends? If you tell us your story that could help us find them.'

The old lady was silent for a moment, then glanced across at her sister, who gave a little nod. 'We agreed it was time to speak of the war, Rosita, and as I was only seven at the time, I can remember very little, so tell them all that you know.'

Rosita nodded. 'Very well. It is rather long, so we'll have to do it a little at a time. We'll begin with Lady Charlotte and your grand-mother.' And settling back in her chair, hands knotted firmly in her lap, she took a breath and began her tale.

THREE
SCOTLAND — SUMMER 1936

THE SUN was rising over the River Dee as Charlotte McBain sat at her window gazing out over the estuary, the shining beauty of its golden orb lighting a pathway over the waves. How she longed to step out along that glorious avenue into a magical world, one not ruled by money, power and controlling men. The sails of a fishing boat heading out to sea were glowing red in the far distance, as if joyously lighting the way. Closer to shore a flock of oystercatchers was searching for food in the mud flats, bringing her firmly back to reality. There would be no escape today, not even a walk through her beloved woods or along the beach with her dear friends, Libby and Laurence. She was locked in her room yet again.

How wrong people were to imagine that as the stepdaughter of a Scottish laird she led a charmed life. Nothing could be further from the truth. In reality she'd endured a neglected, somewhat cloistered childhood. From an early age she'd viewed the outside world as the key to her happiness. It not only represented a happy diversion from her lonely life, but was filled with the possibility of wonderfully exciting adventures. Charlotte dreamed of a time when she would be free to explore it more widely, and had believed for one glorious moment that she'd finally achieved that goal.

Then yesterday, over lunch, she'd learned how wrong she was.

The meal had been salmon salad, as chilled as the atmosphere in the unheated dining room. Craiklyn Manor, with its fortified tower dating back to the thirteenth century, arched windows and domed turrets, might be set in a beautiful estate that included woodlands, farms, stables and a small harbour on the banks of the river, but it possessed stately drawing rooms full of dust and woodworm, freezing cold bedchambers, a library alive with silverfish, and countless rooms covered in dust sheets. Not at all the warm loving home Charlotte had always longed for.

Gathering her courage she'd taken a deep breath and revealed her news in a calm, matter-of-fact tone. 'You may be interested to hear, sir, that I've been offered a place at the Glasgow School of Art.'

Setting down his knife and fork with a clatter, the laird had glared at her. 'I beg your pardon? What are you talking about? Why would they offer *you* a place?'

'You know how much I love to draw and paint and . . .' A small beat of anxiety flickered in Charlotte's breast as it occurred to her that this was the moment she must reveal her long-kept secret. Without doubt art was her passion, and as a favourite haunt of artists, Kirkcudbright was the ideal place for her to live. Raymond Dunmore, who occupied a studio on High Street, had agreed some time ago to allow her to join his class. But Alexander Ross McBain had refused to give permission, as he did not consider it appropriate for the stepdaughter of a laird to be associated in any way with bohemian artists.

It was as if she'd asked to join a brothel.

But Charlotte had been so excited that such a famous London artist was willing to take her on, as well as entranced by his handsome good looks, that she'd stubbornly disobeyed the order. The moment had come to reveal that fact.

'Actually, I've been attending art classes for some months, and my tutor submitted some of my pictures to the Glasgow College.'

The laird's face had turned purple with rage. 'How *dare* you defy me! You are a most rebellious and obstinate child.'

'I am no longer a child, sir. I'm only a few months short of my twenty-first birthday.'

'Do not argue with me. I am your father!' he snapped.

'You are my stepfather,' she'd calmly corrected him. Charlotte's own father had died just after the Great War. She still had a few memories of him, and he would ever remain a hero in her eyes, something the laird would never be.

'Nevertheless, you must do as I say. How dare this man interfere in your life without my agreement?'

Aware of her mother fidgeting anxiously beside her and with no wish to exacerbate a relationship that had not quite lived up to expectations, Charlotte elected to concentrate on the issue at hand. 'Mr Dunmore believes I show potential. He has faith in me.' Which is more than you have, she thought with some degree of irritation. 'I attended an interview in Glasgow and they offered me a place. I assure you I did not accept there and then. I explained that I would have to ask for your permission.'

'Which you will never get. I arranged that trip to the city in order for you to buy elegant new clothes for the season, not to attend an interview for a career as an idiot artist,' he roared. 'You will write a letter forthwith and refuse their offer. This very day, or you will live to regret it.'

As always when she obstinately clung to her independence and refused to obey him, her stepfather had marched Charlotte to her room, insisting that was where she would remain until she retracted from this latest show of rebellion. Her throat had gone dry with fear, hot anger pulsating through her body as she found herself locked up like some prisoner in a cell, as had happened so often in the past. She was allowed no rights to speak her mind. Nor live her life as she would choose.

Being the local laird, he was a law unto himself, volatile, unpredictable, and given to explosive fits of temper when crossed. Charlotte had rarely seen a smile soften the harsh lines etched into his sallow skin from the tight-jawed scowl to his beak of a nose. Even his short beard seemed to bristle with temper. If he wasn't lashing out at one or other of the servants he would turn, almost with grim pleasure, upon her.

She'd long ago grown accustomed to her life being ruled by a strict daily routine, one controlled down to the last detail. He would present her with a list of required tasks each morning as if she were one of the enlisted soldiers in his old battalion. And woe betide her if she failed to clean her shoes to the necessary degree of polish, or didn't fold her clothes correctly when she put them away. The laird seemed to resent the fact she'd survived when his own two sons by her mother had died at birth, as if she were in some way to blame for that tragedy.

Turning to her mother for support rarely helped as she too lived in fear of her bullying husband. This was a fact of life Lady Felicity McBain kept to herself, possibly out of shame for ever trusting him. Her marriage might be a sham but she'd become obsessed with appearances, concerned only with what the neighbours might think.

Charlotte had never understood what had attracted her mother to this cruel, arrogant man. She could only suppose that having lost her husband and young son to the Spanish flu in 1919, she'd married him out of desperation at being left largely alone in the world, and believed in his love for her. Charlotte remembered her own excitement on the long journey north to beautiful Scotland in 1921. Having been nearly six at the time she'd fallen in love with her new home, but within months had lost all hope of affection for her new parent. Her mother, too, soon discovered that his reason for marrying her had been money and nothing at all to do with love. Not only that but his treatment of her had done further damage to her already fragile mental state.

Sighing, Charlotte returned to gazing out upon her beloved view, imagining herself walking over the headland and escaping into the glorious dawn of a new life. Yet that was not about to happen.

⁓

After two days on a meagre diet of bread and water Charlotte finally succumbed to the laird's demand and wrote the required letter. She despised herself for giving in. It went against every cry for liberty that reverberated in her soul. But what choice did she have?

Late the previous evening she'd heard a gentle tap on the door and her mother's soft voice whispering to her. 'Darling, don't make things any more difficult for yourself. Write the letter.'

She'd felt a strong desire to remind Lady Felicity of the agony and pain this union had brought her, but thought better of it. As always, she would explain away her husband's unpredictable temperament by listing his injuries inflicted by the Great War: a shattered kneecap, burns to his hands as a consequence of trying to save his best friend from a fire, and the nightmares he still suffered after coming too close to death himself. There were occasions when the laird would lapse into long periods of silence, shut himself in his study and refuse to speak to a living soul for days on end. These times almost came as a relief to the entire household.

Charlotte strived to be more understanding of his behaviour since the war had clearly damaged him mentally, as well as physically, but it wasn't easy.

Now he paced back and forth as he dictated what she should write. Handing the letter over so that he could check she had indeed done exactly as instructed, Charlotte rose to face him, chin held high while striving to adopt an appealing smile. 'Actually, I have an art class this afternoon. Am I allowed to attend one last time, if only to thank my tutor for his efforts on my behalf?'

Her stepfather pensively stroked his beard as he considered her request. 'You may, so long as you deliver the letter and inform this allegedly famous artist that it will be the last time he ever sees you.'

'Thank you, sir.' She felt weak with relief that he'd agreed, and, deciding it wise to make no further comment, quietly turned to leave.

'Wait one moment.' Reaching for the bell he summoned the chauffeur. When the young man appeared, the laird issued a string of instructions. 'Take my stepdaughter into town, and make sure she is home by five o'clock at the latest.'

Charlotte inwardly groaned. She usually cycled to class while her stepfather was absorbed with estate duties and her mother had yet again retreated into her own private world to play her piano in the drawing room for hours on end, or entertained her friends at little tea parties. Now she felt deeply humiliated, as if she were being treated like a child.

The laird's next words, however, stated the complete opposite. 'You should bear in mind that you have little time left for such trivialities. Before long you will be a busy wife and mother.'

This was by no means the first time he'd made such a remark, one Charlotte viewed as a serious threat. It brought to mind her eighteenth birthday party when her stepfather's pursuit of a husband for her had first become apparent. He'd attempted to pair her off with a local baron she really did not care for, being more than twice her age, short and plump with a large bulbous nose. Presenting herself in the ugliest dress she could find, the laird had insisted she change before the gentleman in question arrived. When she'd bluntly refused, Charlotte had been locked in her room for the entire night and all the following day.

A punishment that soon became a regular occurrence.

Unwilling to create further argument by protesting that marriage and babies would not be on her agenda for some years to come, Charlotte gathered up her satchel of pencils, paints and brushes from the hall table and left without saying another word. The chauffeur stood waiting, patiently holding open the door of the shining new Alvis 3.5-litre saloon that her stepfather had recently purchased at goodness knows what cost. No doubt with her mother's money.

Obediently climbing into the back seat, Charlotte made a private vow that the moment her much-longed-for twenty-first birthday actually dawned, she would grab her freedom with both hands and pursue her own dreams, with or without her stepfather's approval. Women had rights too, and she fully intended to exercise them and to be free of his control.

FOUR

THE ART class had started by the time Charlotte arrived, which earned her a frown of amused disapproval from the tutor. 'Kind of you to spare us the time from your busy social life,' he teased, as she hastily set up her easel with the still life she was currently painting.

'I'm so sorry, only my stepfather . . .' Not wishing to embarrass herself further before the curious stares of her fellow students, Charlotte paused. 'May I explain later? I do hope I haven't held up anything important.'

'Not at all. We're very relaxed here. My time is yours, *milady*,' he murmured with a slight bow, then playfully tweaked her dark curls as he smiled into her dove grey eyes.

Charlotte felt the urge to protest over the way he addressed her. She really had no wish to be defined by her class as she was no blood relation to the laird. But catching the wry expression of her friend Libby, seated on a couch dressed in a Victorian costume as she acted as model for the group, she instead started to giggle. They all recognised that as a gifted artist Ray Dunmore was an excellent teacher, but he did love to tease and flirt, and at times was a little too free with his hands.

Charlotte began squeezing out small dabs of oil paint from various tubes on to her palette. Selecting a brush she was soon busy with her painting, so engrossed that she didn't hear him approach until he again coiled a strand of her hair about his finger, giving it a little tug to capture her attention. 'Oh dear, how very dull. Why are you not trying out primary colours? I've pointed out countless times that you use a far too restricted palette.'

Quickly fastening her hair up into a knot, so that he might not be tempted to touch it quite so much, which she found very distracting, Charlotte studied her painting. It was of a bowl of fruit, with a blue jug set beside it. 'I'm nervous of mixing strong colours and prefer more earthy shades for a still life. With this one I've used burnt umber, ultramarine, cadmium yellow, a little vermilion, and of course titanium white and ivory black. These are my favourites. Is that a problem?'

'In normal circumstances, no, but you could have chosen brighter colours and a more lively picture to paint. The figure of Libby here, for instance, like the rest of the class.'

Charlotte glanced with apology at her friend. 'Sorry, but I'm still not very good with anatomy. Can't quite seem to get the curves and shapes right.'

'Tut tut, that is essential for any artist, as is experimenting with colours.'

'I know, but I do try to vary the tone. Am I failing with that too?' At times Charlotte felt completely inadequate. There was so much to learn she wondered if she ever would paint a picture that satisfied her and her tutor. Dunmore remained very critical of her work, and any confidence she might have felt at having been offered a place at Glasgow quickly began to evaporate.

'Cool tones are all very well, but you need to learn how to use warm ones too.'

'I am not very familiar with those,' she said with a wry smile, and he laughed out loud, knowing how she frequently complained of living in a freezing cold house.

'This shadowed section beside the bowl should be much darker to give it more depth. And the fruit does not look good. The apples are too dull, not at all appetising. No gloss or glow. Which colours did you use for those?'

Charlotte explained how she was having trouble mixing the right green. 'I thought I just needed to mix yellow and blue, but I agree they are dull. I tried adding more yellow, then white, but it just went grey.'

He came closer to whisper softly in her ear. 'Would you like my assistance?'

She glanced up, meeting the shimmer of his tawny brown eyes and felt a stir of desire deep inside her. Was this where her passion for oil painting was derived, from her growing fascination with her tutor? She'd started drawing as a young child with pencil, chalk and pastels, then moved on to watercolour. Now she was anxious to try oil painting. Was she falling for him, or simply flattered that he found her attractive? There was no denying that he was a handsome man, and as her stepfather declared, bohemian in his manner and style of dress. Even indoors he always wore a straw hat of some kind, and a silk scarf tied about his neck. Perhaps it was this lack of convention in him that so appealed to her, but her heart would flutter every time she looked at him. 'Your advice is always welcome, Mr Dunmore.'

'Ray,' he softly reminded her. 'No necessity for you to be formal with me, Charlotte.'

Then turning to address the class and clapping his hands to gain their attention, he ushered Charlotte from her seat and took charge of her palette. 'You can take a little break, Libby, while we consider the mixing of colours. Now everyone watch and learn,' he said, beginning to rummage through her tubes of paints. 'We are going to mix green. Ultramarine has too much red in it so we'll choose cerulean blue instead, to which we will add yellow ochre, or you could use cadmium if you prefer.'

Dunmore proceeded to demonstrate while Charlotte and the rest of the class watched, fascinated, as he started work on the apples. She'd learned so much under this man's tuition that she always listened carefully, striving not to think of the effect his touching and smoothing of her hair had upon her. It saddened her deeply to think that this could be the last class she'd be allowed to attend. The laird had made it abundantly clear that he would be keeping a much closer watch on her activities in future. A worrying thought.

The afternoon passed in blissful contentment. By the time it was over she felt much happier with the apples in her picture, which now glowed quite appetisingly green with a sweet blush of red. Libby quickly praised her efforts before dashing off home to catch up with her farm chores.

'See you soon,' Charlotte called after her.

Once brushes and palettes had been cleaned and packed away, she waited until the rest of the students had departed before handing him the letter of rejection. Ray Dunmore stared at the missive with a puzzled expression. 'I don't believe this. Most people would give anything to be offered such an opportunity. Why are you refusing to accept it?'

Clasping her hands, Charlotte decided to be completely open in the hope that it might salvage the offer of a place for her to take up at some point in the future, maybe when she turned twenty-one. 'It's not *my* choice. The problem is that my stepfather refuses to grant his permission.' She did not explain why. Dunmore gave a sympathetic shake of his head as if he guessed already.

'That's a great pity. You might have made a good artist one day, with the right sort of tuition and effort. Unfortunately, that won't now happen. Your problems with colour mixing, composition and perspective, and the mistake you keep making by placing objects in the centre of your picture, will no doubt continue.' Then he winked at her, as if to prove he wasn't being too serious, which made her laugh out loud. Charlotte liked this man's wry sense of humour.

'I'll do my best to remember everything you've taught me, and keep practising at home,' she promised.

'I'm glad to hear it. You're such a sweet girl.' Reaching out, he pulled at the pin that held the knot of her hair so that her pretty brunette curls fell loose, tumbling to her shoulders. 'I have to say that I'll miss teaching you, Lady Charlotte. But if you can't go to Glasgow, can we at least find a way to carry on with our arrangement here?'

Her heart leaped. It would be quite against the laird's orders, but then it had been for all the months she'd been coming thus far. And then Charlotte thought of a further problem. 'I'd love to, but unfortunately I've used up most of my savings, so I doubt I could afford to continue.'

He moved a little closer, his breath warming her cheek as his mouth came to within inches of hers. Charlotte cast a sideways glance up at him from beneath her lashes, and couldn't help wondering what it might feel like were he to actually kiss her. Her heart raced at the thought.

'I'm sure we could come to some arrangement that would satisfy us both. I'd be happy to carry on tutoring you, in return for you acting as a model. Libby, being busy on the family farm, is not always available when I need her. No money need change hands. You were a pretty wee lass, as the locals say, when you first came. Now you're a stunning beauty. Perfect for a model, so what do you say?'

'Oh, my goodness, that would be wonderful,' she cried, flattered by these remarks. She had never thought of herself in such terms.

Lady Felicity was the one everyone agreed was elegant and beautiful with her golden fair hair and blue-grey eyes, the perfect society belle. Adoring and admiring her mother as she did, Charlotte saw herself as plain and inadequate, not the least bit attractive. Gazing up at him in astonished gratitude, she asked, 'What would I have to do?'

'Just sit still and smile. Why don't you peel off that frock and we could make a start right now.' His gaze drifted over her, lingering upon her breasts as one hand slid over the silky skin of her neck and shoulder.

Suddenly aware of the intensity of his gaze as well as the shiver that ran through her at his touch, which seemed to have passed beyond mere flirtation, Charlotte took a quick step back. Goodness, she was actually being propositioned by her tutor! What would her stepfather say to that?

'That's very kind of you, Mr – er – Ray. I'll give your offer serious thought', and turning on her heel she walked briskly away. Smothering a smile, she could only hope he hadn't noticed the glitter of anticipation that must have lit her gaze at the prospect of a kiss from him.

At least Ray Dunmore viewed her as a woman and not a child. He seemed to be more than ready to continue with her lessons, if also tutor her in other ways, which Charlotte had to confess held a certain appeal. There was something about this man she found really exciting. But whether it would be wise for her to accept such an offer, however flattering it may be, was another matter altogether. She'd talk to Libby about it first. Her friend's advice was always helpful, and she'd acted as a model for him on numerous occasions, although hopefully always fully clothed.

Charlotte was chuckling to herself as she climbed back into the Alvis, much to the puzzlement of the chauffeur, who'd no doubt been expecting floods of tears after this, her last art class.

That night as Charlotte snuggled into bed, she dreamed of how it might feel to be held in a passionate embrace by Ray Dunmore, his mouth upon hers, his hands caressing her breasts. She could barely sleep as her imagination stoked her desire with fresh heat, making her feel rampant with need. Pouring herself a cooling glass of water she resolutely set these emotions aside, reminding herself that the most important thing she must concentrate on was a future free from the laird's dominance.

The following morning over breakfast came yet another command, quite out of the blue. 'Ah, Charlotte, I'm sure you'll be delighted to hear that you've been blessed with a proposal of marriage, which I've happily accepted on your behalf.'

FIVE

THE TOAST dropped from Charlotte's hand, splattering marmalade over the white damask tablecloth as she stared at her stepfather, open-mouthed. 'I beg your pardon. Did you say a proposal of *marriage*?'

'I did indeed.'

Hastily dabbing at the smears of marmalade with her napkin, she struggled to keep her voice calm. 'What right have you to accept a proposal on my behalf without so much as mentioning it?'

'It is my duty to secure a good future for you. I seem to recall that I've already made my rights on the subject of your future perfectly clear, and I'm mentioning it now.'

'What about *my* rights?' Charlotte ground her teeth with frustration. 'From whom did you receive this so-called proposal?'

'Laurence, of course, who as you know is a fine young man. He came to see me yesterday afternoon while you were at that stupid art class.'

'*Laurence?*'

'I knew you'd be pleased.'

'Why would I be?' Aware of how easy it was to upset the laird and bring forth yet another storm of fury raining upon her head,

Charlotte took a steadying breath. 'I understand that you want the best for me, sir, but I'm far too young to consider such a drastic step.'

'Nonsense, darling,' intervened her mother in gently soothing tones, casting her scowling husband an anxious glance. 'I was only eighteen when I married your father.'

'But you were in love, Mama. I am not.'

On seeing her mother blush bright pink at the memory, and bite her lip as she recalled the pain of losing the love of her life, Charlotte put her arms about her to hold her close. 'Sorry to upset you, but it's true.'

Charlotte was fully aware that her stepfather had married her mother for the money she brought to the marriage, although her beloved mother had naively believed in his love for her, and no doubt it would be considered her duty to do the same. Charlotte kept her tone remarkably calm as she responded. 'I do appreciate that the question of marriage is bound to arise eventually, but please, not just yet. As you are both only too aware, I have other plans with regard to learning more about painting.' At times like this Charlotte wondered if she ever would be free to make her own decisions. But this was one battle she couldn't afford to lose. 'If I'm not allowed to go to art school, I'm certainly not interested in marrying Laurence.'

'Why on earth not?' the laird barked. 'You've never shown interest in anyone else.'

She met his glowering gaze with every ounce of courage she possessed. 'What other young men have I met? We don't exactly live in the heart of town, and there never seem to be many at the social functions you insist upon my attending. What opportunity do I have to meet anyone of interest?'

'I will not allow any stepdaughter of mine to go gallivanting about town like some cheap hussy. Laurence is a good man, and you've known him all your life.'

It was true that dear Laurence had been her best, at times her only, friend, apart from Libby, for as long as she could remember. With bad weather fairly common in Scotland during the winter months, Charlotte would find herself largely confined indoors with no companions other than the servants. And as her mother disliked being distracted from her music, Charlotte would feign a headache to avoid the endless lessons imposed by her governess. Then with the help of the housekeeper, Mrs Murray, she'd sneak out through the back kitchen and go and help Libby and her parents on their farm, being tenants of the laird. If the weather was too bad for that, she'd cycle over to Laurence's and they'd play chess or draughts together. Anything to escape the boredom of her stepfather's imposed regime.

'Laurence is the perfect gentleman,' her mother gently reminded her. 'He's never been anything but kind and generous towards you.'

Charlotte stifled a sigh. 'I do not deny that he is a sweet man, not to mention fun to be with, and quite good-looking.' Some might describe him as not so much handsome as beautiful, with his smooth pale skin, bright sea-green eyes and a tousle of fair hair. What woman wouldn't be proud to be seen walking out on the arm of such a gorgeous man?

On summer days they used to climb trees together, build dens and dam up streams to catch fish, coming home covered in mud, much to her mother's disapproval. In recent years they'd taken to hill walking, cycling and canoeing, happily arguing, sweating and giggling as each tried to outshine the other's efforts and win whatever challenge they'd set themselves. Libby would join them whenever she could be spared from her farm chores.

But none of this explained why he would ask for her hand in marriage.

'A childhood friendship is one thing, love and marriage quite a different emotion entirely. Fond as I am of Laurence, I don't nurture those sort of feelings for him.'

Charlotte considered it unwise to admit the direction in which her emotions were leaning at present.

Ripping the napkin from where he'd tucked it beneath his chin and tossing it furiously aside, the laird rose to his feet to tower over her, his temper clearly about to explode. 'The offer has been made and accepted, so stop complaining and start appreciating your good fortune. The ceremony will take place on your birthday at the end of October.' Upon which announcement he strode from the room, leaving her rigid with shock.

⟶∿

The laird's departure at least provided the opportunity for her to speak with her mother. Surely the much-neglected Lady Felicity would understand how her daughter must be feeling about this ludicrous marriage proposal, and be prepared to help her find happiness. It became instantly clear that the very opposite was the case.

'You would be hard put to find a better husband, my dear,' Lady Felicity declared, gently patting her daughter's hand.

'I cannot believe this is happening. Why are we women treated with such callous disregard?'

'Because it is our lot in life, my darling, to marry well. A duty we must accept.'

Never, Charlotte promised herself in silent fury. 'Why would the laird be so set upon this marriage, and why would Laurence make such an offer in the first place? There has never been the slightest flicker of romantic interest between us, neither on my part or his. Nothing more than a fleeting kiss at a Christmas party once when we were about eleven or twelve. More by way of experiment than for any other reason. He's like a brother to me, not a prospective husband.'

Charlotte smiled as she recalled her romantic dreams of finding a handsome hero, her knight on a white charger. As a young girl she used to imagine how it would feel to kiss the butcher's son, who was more delicious than the sausages and cutlets he sold. Now such dreams were associated with quite another man entirely.

'I want you to be happily settled with a lovely kind man from a good family. It is important to maintain your status in the community, and behave like the lady you are.'

'Oh, don't start all that again, Mama.' When Charlotte had turned thirteen, Lady Felicity had decided that the only way to make her daughter behave like a proper lady, instead of the tomboy she was turning into, was to send her away to boarding school. The governess had been dismissed and the young honourable Charlotte McBain had been duly dispatched to the auspices of a highly regarded girls' school near Castle Douglas.

She'd gone with some trepidation, fearing she would be facing more control than the rules laid down by her domineering stepfather and society-conscious mother. But to her surprise Charlotte discovered that she was able to do largely as she pleased, so long as she kept quiet about it. Naturally, she'd selected her friends carefully, choosing only those she could trust with knowledge of the secret life she led.

The staff had presented few problems, soon recognising in her a brick-wall stubbornness that was hard to break. If Charlotte said she was not going to join the netball team but play tennis instead, eat the meat but not the dumplings, say the prayers in church but not go down on her knees, nothing the teachers said or did would make her change her mind. When the pupils were instructed not to leave the school buildings on any account, Charlotte continued to sneak out at lunchtime and walk over to Carlingwark Loch, where she'd sit and draw. And she would frequently climb out through the pantry window of an evening to join in the dancing at the local village hall. There was nothing more fun than a Scottish reel. No one was any the wiser as she managed to sneak back in without waking a soul.

To throw people off the scent of such rebellious behaviour, Charlotte always behaved with perfect decorum, not arguing with anyone or allowing them to see what her true opinions were. To all outward appearances she obeyed the rules to the letter, and smilingly agreed with whatever she was told to do, while in reality doing exactly as she pleased. Some of the staff recognised this spirit of independence in her, and privately admired it.

With this current problem, however, any show of obedience could be disastrous. Mama was looking pensive and sad, then after a long silence quietly remarked, 'Marriage, particularly for people like us, is not just about love, my darling.'

'Why, because we're rich we must breed with the right sort of people?' Charlotte asked, her tone one of caustic disbelief. 'Are we not allowed the joy of loving someone?'

There was a slight pause before her mother answered. 'No, I'm not saying that. We all ache for love, of course we do. But we can seek it elsewhere.'

Charlotte was shocked. 'You mean by taking a lover?'

Lady Felicity met her daughter's probing gaze without flinching as she nodded.

'Are you saying that *you* have a lover?' The moment she saw the expression on her mother's face, Charlotte instantly regretted the question. What daughter would wish to know the secrets of a parent's sex life? Her cheeks blushing bright red, she quickly said, 'Never mind, forget I asked.'

'What I am trying to explain is that, as you do not always find the love you seek in marriage, the primary reason should be to choose a good and honourable man, and carefully consider prosperity and heritage, as well as securing the future of the estate.'

Charlotte stared at her mother in dismay, eyes glittering with unshed tears. 'So despite us now living in modern times, not medieval or Tudor, my happiness and opinion count for nothing? All that matters is that our two neighbouring estates are joined.'

'I'm afraid that has to be taken into account.'

༄

Unable to tolerate any more argument, or risk upsetting her mother, who seemed to have lost all sense of independence as a result of being bullied by the laird, Charlotte marched off in a huff. She went in search of Laurence to tell him what she thought of this stupid offer, only to discover that he wasn't at home. The butler answered the door, telling her that the entire family was out. What a strange thing to do the day after he'd made this proposal via her stepfather. Could he be deliberately avoiding her? And why hadn't he made the proposal personally?

Where are you, Laurence? I need to speak to you now!

A sense of gloom descended upon her. Striving to shake it off, Charlotte strode briskly along the beach, splashing through pools of seawater, kicking at pebbles with her wellington boots in quiet fury. A few moments later she paused for breath, calming herself by gazing out upon the unspoilt beauty of the estuary, the pockets of gorse, sea rocket, globeflowers and scurvy grass.

How she loved the coast of Galloway, this particular stretch of the beach having been privately owned by the laird's family for generations, no doubt since Robert the Bruce had been a wee laddie. It was a place Charlotte loved to escape to as it always brought a sense of tranquillity to her heart, but she felt precious little of that emotion this morning. The sight of a gloriously yellow rockrose, which would normally have had her reaching for her sketchbook and paint box, did little to alleviate her sense of depression.

Why was her stepfather attempting to force her into marriage instead of allowing her to pursue her dreams? But when had he ever paid any attention to what she wanted? Admittedly, she might never develop the kind of skills Ray Dunmore possessed, or ever make it as an artist, but surely she deserved the right to try? And why wouldn't her mother support her instead of stubbornly shutting herself away? The poor lady seemed to have lost all her courage to stand up to her husband. Living with the laird's determination to treat her like an errant five-year-old had never been easy for Charlotte either. Now she felt utterly sick at the prospect of being married off without being permitted any say in the matter. She most definitely would find the necessary courage as she had no intention of allowing that to happen.

Charlotte quickly came to the decision that if she couldn't find Laurence she'd speak to Libby instead. In any case, she needed a word with her friend over the issue of acting as a model for Dunmore. Turning on her heel, she set off along a path that led over the headland, to emerge hot and sweating in the farmyard where she slowed her pace at last on a sigh of relief.

SIX

NEARLY TRIPPING over the hens clucking happily about her feet, Charlotte rubbed the ears of the old farm collie dog. He'd bounded over to greet her, as he always did, the moment he heard her coming along the path, wagging his tail with joyous enthusiasm.

'Morning Champ, where's your mistress? At the milking, I suppose.'

Minutes later Charlotte was seated beside Libby on a milking stool, her head pressed into a cow's flank as she gently squeezed each teat with her finger and thumb, squirting milk into the bucket she held between her knees. Whether it be milking the cows, feeding the sheep and hens, digging potatoes or chopping logs, Charlotte loved helping out on the farms of the laird's tenants. It was much more fun than idling away her day socialising, as her parents seemed to expect.

But what would he say if he could see his stepdaughter with muddy boots and her hands covered in milk? She chuckled to herself at the thought.

At least on this occasion she wasn't dressed in one of her fancy gowns. Charlotte would frequently call on her way home from some social function or other, and Libby would tell her off for sweeping out the hen hut in a frilly satin party frock, or tossing her fur coat on to the hay rack before feeding the lambs. But Charlotte was forever heedless of the messy farmyard and the damage that clods of mud and cowpats could do. There were, however, times when she became aware of a twinge of envy in Libby as her friend never would be granted the privilege of wearing such glamorous items of clothing. The cost of one dress would have kept the Forbes family in food for a month or more. Today Charlotte was more sensibly clothed in a grubby Aran sweater and old slacks and boots, her glossy dark hair tucked up in a tatty woolly hat. 'How are you this morning, Libby?'

'Quite well, and you?'

'Oh, don't ask. Not good, to be honest.'

'I'm sorry to hear that, milady. Nothing serious, I hope.'

'*Milady?*' Charlotte said, rolling her eyes in despair. 'Don't start all that again, Libby. Didn't I make it clear years ago that you should never address me as such? I get enough of that attitude from Ray Dunmore. Have I offended you in some way?'

Libby shook her head as she gave a whispered response. 'Course not, only Da says it's no appropriate for me tae call ye Charlie any more.'

'Libby Forbes, how can he suggest such a thing? Haven't we known each other all our lives, right from when we were wee bairns?'

'Aye, but we aren't wee bairns any longer, are we? Da says things change when people grow up and duty calls, particularly for an aristocratic young lady such as yerself.'

Charlotte knew she'd be heartbroken if that were to happen. Despite their differences in so-called status, which caused Libby to be a bit prickly at times, she loved her friend dearly. On numerous occasions the laird had attempted to put a stop to their friendship for this reason, but now they were no longer children they could surely please themselves. True, rich gentlemen were queuing up to dance with her, not to mention making frequent offers of marriage. Problems she'd preferred to ignore. Until now. 'We are still friends, aren't we?'

'Friends forever, Charlie *milady*,' Libby said, and both girls collapsed into giggles.

'Thank goodness for that! How could I get up to any fun and mischief without you?' Charlotte said, as the two friends happily wiped the cows' teats with disinfectant and saw them out into the pasture. 'And survive this ongoing battle with my stepfather.'

'I wondered why I hadna seen ye for a few days. Been serving another sentence, have ye? What did you do to offend him this time?' Libby's small elfin face creased with sympathy as Charlotte told how she was not to be allowed to attend the Glasgow School of Art. 'Och, I'm sorry ye canna accept that offer, although I would have missed you if ye'd gone off to Glasgow. But are ye sure it's a good idea to act as a model for Ray Dunmore? He can be a wee bit – overzealous in his attentions.'

Charlotte hid her private thoughts on this with a carefully orchestrated giggle. 'I do know that, which is why I am asking if he's ever made a pass at you?'

'Och noo,' Libby said. A flush appeared upon her cheeks, seeming to indicate she was telling a fib.

'Well then, if you managed to hold him off, why shouldn't I?'

Giving a casual shrug of her shoulders, Libby turned away to busy herself filling milk cans, saying nothing. Charlotte came to help her stack the empty buckets ready for washing as she went on to tell what had happened over breakfast that morning. Her friend stared at her, wide-eyed.

'Nae, ye surely have some say over whom ye marry? Who is this man the laird has chosen for ye?'

Charlotte pulled a face. 'Would you believe, Laurence?'

The shock on Libby's face was a delight to see. '*Laurence?*'

'Isn't that ridiculous? We may be old friends, but nothing more than that. I certainly don't love him in *that* way. And I don't believe for one moment that he loves me. I'd be mad to accept, don't you think? How and why this proposal came about, I really cannot imagine.'

Frowning slightly as she scrubbed out the milk buckets, Libby appeared to be struggling to take in what Charlotte was saying. 'There has been something odd aboot Laurence's mood lately, he's no his usual jolly self. But he's a lovely man, handsome and rich, and a good friend, so why refuse such a wonderful offer?'

'You think I should bite the bullet and marry him as duty demands? I could instead act as a model for Ray Dunmore and pursue a career as an artist.'

Libby didn't respond until they were kicking off their boots and washing their hands together at the kitchen sink. 'I think ye should first ask Laurence why he didna go doon on one knee and make a proper proposal to ye?'

'Ah, good question, and one I fully intend to ask. But what about the art classes?'

Libby met her friend's gaze, unwavering. 'It wouldna be wise to play at modelling for Ray Dunmore. He did make a pass at me, but I'd rather not speak of what happened next.'

Charlotte grabbed her hands. 'Oh, Libby, do tell me more.' Their conversation was interrupted by a call from Libby's mother, busy in the kitchen.

'Mebbe later, breakfast is ready.'

ᘒ

Breakfast for the Forbes family always took place after the early morning chores were done, and the family all sat down at the scrubbed pine table. The kitchen was warm from the fire burning in the grate that heated the oven beside it. A delicious smell of oat-cakes and bacon filled the room and Charlotte felt her stomach churn with hunger. She'd failed to finish her own breakfast, being too anxious to escape and give herself time to think.

Mrs Forbes started dishing out the porridge, serving Charlotte first as she always did even though her husband, James, had been working since long before dawn. Charlotte did not, however, pick up her spoon until the entire family of three sons and four daughters had been served, although they all waited politely for her to begin eating first. Much as she hated this deference to her status, she'd learned long since that there was nothing she could do about it.

'Will ye be going tae the meeting tonight?' Mr Forbes asked his eldest son as he tucked into the bacon, egg, sausage and black pudding his wife had placed before him. Charlotte had hastily declined when offered the same, knowing money was tight. The farmhouse possessed neither an indoor toilet nor running water. Charlotte considered this quite shameful when she thought of all the laird wasted on gambling, his far too regular drams of whisky, smoking his precious cigars, and other foolish pastimes. Money which could be put to much better use improving the housing conditions of his tenants. Mrs Forbes took in washing to make ends meet. But in spite of all their hard work the family would sometimes get behind with their rent.

'Of course,' Nick said. 'Will ye be coming with me, Da?'

'Aye, I'm told the talk'll be aboot agricultural matters, so I might as weel.'

'Who is giving this talk, Mr Forbes?' Charlotte politely enquired.

He gave a shrug, again casting a sideways glance at his son. 'I canna say for sure.'

'A member of the BUF,' Nick explained, his sneering tone revealing his opinion of them. Being Libby's twin brother he had the same dark hair and brown eyes, and as an intelligent young man with a lively and adventurous nature, he spent a great deal of time listening to the news on his crystal set.

'And who might they be?' asked his mother as she pulled towels and sheets from the rack to stand folding them while her family ate, occasionally scolding Libby's younger siblings for not sitting or eating correctly.

'They'd be the British Union of Fascists, Ma.'

'If you remember, Nell, last February back in thirty-five, William Joyce, Oswald Mosley's deputy, addressed a meeting here in Kirkcudbright. Mosley himself has given talks in Dalbeattie and Dumfries. The BUF has raised quite a bit of money for the towns through whist drives and jumble sales, football matches, dances, and suchlike events.'

'I do remember a busload of folk going, now you come tae mention it. Some of the ladies from the chapel were quite excited about seeing him.'

Nick gave a snort of derision. 'The BUF aren't raising money out of love or charity, Ma. More likely as a bribe to recruit for their revolutionary movement.'

'You could be right, son, but not everyone would agree,' James Forbes pointed out. 'They have provided life-saving patrols all along the shores of the Solway, which has gone down well locally.'

'I don't believe these so-called Blackshirts are as good for Britain as some people might imagine,' Nick protested. 'They're nought but over-controlling Fascists.'

'I can see why you would say that, in view of what is happening in Spain.'

Charlotte frowned as she listened to this conversation, wishing she was better informed on such matters. 'I'm not very knowledgeable about politics,' she said, 'but I believe that when Mosley gave talks in London, it led to riots. Might that happen here? He's reputed to be very domineering with a contempt for the middle classes and strong anti-Semitic views. Even my stepfather does not approve of him, despite the fact he's pretty right-wing himself.'

'I'm glad to hear that, milady. The BUF does tend to attract quite a number of disaffected Conservative voters as well as former soldiers. Can't say I care much for the fellow either.'

'The laird says Lord Rothermere was on Mosley's side for a while, but then changed his mind following a BUF rally at Olympia last year, which apparently got pretty nasty. But why would the BUF come here to Kirkcudbright, a small town in the middle of nowhere?'

James Forbes set down his knife and fork to take a sip of milk, fresh from the cow. 'We may have a water-powered mill in Gatehouse of Fleet but little in the way of coal in this region. We've never enjoyed the kind of industrial revolution they had in north-west England or the Midlands. We're dependent almost entirely upon agriculture, which is suffering badly at present, so require all the help we can get if we are tae survive. As far as I can see, there's precious little o' that coming from the landowners.'

A small silence followed this statement, finally filled by his wife. 'Are you sure you wouldna like a little scrambled egg, milady?' she asked, clearly thinking the discussion was entering dangerous territory.

'No thank you, Mrs Forbes, the porridge was quite sufficient,' Charlotte said with a kind smile. 'I agree with you on that last point, Mr Forbes. But I do want to understand what is going wrong with my stepfather's tenants, and help if I can. I wonder if I might attend the meeting with you?'

The old farmer raised his bushy eyebrows in surprise, rubbing an ear and frowning as he considered her request. Libby and Nick exchanged startled glances. 'You must do as ye think best, milady, but I doot ye'll find it a pleasant experience. As you said yourself, there could well be riots. There was certainly trouble at the last one they held in Dalbeattie, between the Blackshirts and the Communists. I wouldna like anything to happen to ye.'

'I'm sure I'll be fine. I can look after myself.' Charlotte quickly changed the subject by asking Mrs Forbes when the next ceilidh was to be held at the church hall, as she did so love to dance.

Charlotte spent the rest of the morning in perfect peace attempting to sketch Libby as she fed the calves and churned the butter. But her friend refused to say anything more on the subject of modelling for Dunmore. Having become utterly absorbed in her work, Charlotte suddenly noticed the time and began to hastily wash brushes, palette and paint rags, bundling them away in her satchel.

'Goodness, must dash. Need to change before lunch.' Her parents were always insistent upon punctuality.

'I'll be interested tae hear what Laurence has tae say when ye catch hold of him,' Libby said, unlatching the gate for her.

'So will I,' Charlotte agreed. 'Probably I'm worrying unduly and nothing will come of the laird's stupid plan. I do hope so. See you at the meeting, Libby. I'm really keen to learn more about the problem facing the people of Spain.' And quickly making arrangements about where they would meet, she broke into a run along the path leading back over the headland.

SEVEN
SPAIN — 1986

'HOW STRANGE that Gran never told me any of this, or that she was friendly with an aristocratic lady of great talent, beauty and fun, by the sound of it.'

'They were good friends but did have something of a complex relationship, due to their difference in status. Class was sadly very much one of the causes of the Civil War, along with over-controlling men,' Rosita said with a wry smile. 'But these two ladies remained good friends at heart, despite all the problems that arose between them over time.'

Jo frowned. Was that the reason Libby had never spoken of her? So what had happened to distance them? She would love to hear more. But this part of the story could wait for now as she was keen to hear Rosita's own tale, since she was Spanish. 'The war must have come as a horrendous shock for you and your family. Anton tells me you were only sixteen when it began. How on earth did you cope?'

'Not easily. It was utterly devastating, and not something I've ever wished to bring to mind,' she said, glancing at her grandson with anguish in her expression.

Putting his arm about her, he gently kissed her cheek. 'We have agreed that the time has come to speak of it, and I am here to offer support.'

Jo felt herself quite moved by the kindness of this man. 'Me too, and do say if there's anything you wish to keep private. Do you now feel able to speak of it?'

'I do.'

❦

I remember when the war reached my family only too well. It had been a long day with a multitude of tasks and young and fit though I was, I felt deeply weary. I'd spent most of the morning doing the washing at the *fuente-lavadero* over in the village. After that an hour checking the *riego*, clearing out the irrigation channel along which the water ran as it had become blocked with too much sand and soil built up by the wind. Such chores seemed to take twice as long as normal in the summer heat, but were necessary to make sure the melons, tomatoes, lettuces, and peppers were properly watered. We did have a small water wheel, operated by Taco, the family *burro*, who helped to bring up the water from the well then carry it out into the olive grove. I also had to refill the water jars for the household. Our mother was most particular about the quality of the water the family drank.

Taco the donkey helped with much of the work, and was my best friend. I clearly remember the day he'd been born, as well as the sad day a few years later when his dear old *madre* died. It broke my heart, as to lose a mother so young must be so painful, even for an animal.

On this particular day I was glad of a siesta in the long hot afternoon, sleeping curled up in the shade beneath an olive tree. The olive harvest didn't begin until November, which we dealt with as a family. But this was August so the almond trees were already bursting with nuts that would soon have to be picked. Yet another hot and tiring job to look forward to, in addition to the myriad of domestic chores I was expected to do as a girl.

My brother, of course, was spared such tasks as washing and ironing, cooking and cleaning. To be fair, at nineteen he was busily engaged helping *Papá* on the land. But that's what he had always wanted to do, although he could have done anything he wished. No doubt Fernándo would once have become a miner as our father had done when he was a young man, but those days were gone. The mines had closed a decade earlier following a disastrous period and famine in the Great War, from which the industry never properly recovered. *Papá* was at least fortunate to have some family land that fed us and brought in a little money. The vast majority of the hundreds of unemployed miners had been forced to emigrate. We were thankful to be able to remain in Spain, as we loved our home dearly.

But at that time, girls and women were not permitted to take a job outside the house without the permission of their father or husband. It always irritated me that I'd been legally obliged to leave school at twelve, despite my love of books and learning. Who knows what I might have chosen to do? Maybe become a teacher or a nurse, had I been allowed to consider a career. Boys were permitted to stay on much longer, while for girls school was used merely as a means for teaching domestic duties.

Strangely enough the war initially brought a change in the status of women, at least until Franco took over. Once he came to power in 1939, women were yet again cloistered. Education was limited, and every effort was made to prevent women from attending university. We were denied divorce, contraception, abortion, not even allowed to open a bank account, apply for a passport or hold a job outside of the home once we married. Laws were set up to ensure that women acted only as good wives and mothers. Fortunately, when I was young I loved being out in the open working on the land, and enjoyed the glorious panoramic views of the *sierras*. I liked working with animals too, and my father always thanked and praised me for my efforts.

'What a beautiful, hard-working daughter you are,' he said, when I woke from my siesta an hour later, giving me a piece of *turrón* by way of a reward. 'I know Demetrio will be calling in to see you later, but if you could find the time to feed the hens and goats, I would appreciate it. I have some walls to mend, and to prepare for the almond harvest.'

'Of course, *Papá*,' I told him with a smile. 'You know I would do anything for you.'

'And I for you, *querida hija*,' he said, planting a kiss on my brow.

The family farm and *cortijo* may have been small and simple, with not much in the way of comfort or money to help us through these difficult times, but I never failed to appreciate how very fortunate I was to have such a loving father and mother. Many parents would say that a sixteen-year-old girl was far too young to have a *novio*, but my own were far more tolerant and free-thinking.

'Don't forget to let your *madre* know if he is staying for supper. The boy is most welcome, but food is particularly precious right now, so she cannot risk wasting any if he is not.'

'I don't think he will be staying tonight, *Papá*. We'll just be taking a walk before supper, then he has to leave as he must be up early tomorrow for a job he's doing.'

Cupping my face between his hands, he smiled into my innocent blue eyes. 'Do not wander too far, my sweet, or stay out too late. I do not want you to fall into any trouble.'

I almost giggled, knowing that much as *Papá* liked Demetrio, he did not entirely trust him, as it was quite clear we enjoyed a strong attachment. But I had no intention of allowing my boy-friend's caresses to go too far, not until I was ready.

'I will take great care, *Papá*,' I assured him.

'*Bueno*, and no talking to strangers. Spain is breaking into turmoil and rebellion, strikes and uprisings. It is not a safe world at present. There's a madness erupting, over which we have little control.'

Coming to sit beside me under my favourite olive tree he went into one of his political rants, which had become all too common in recent weeks. *Papá* carried a huge chip on his shoulder as a result of the poor conditions he and his fellow miners had suffered in the final days of the industry, which had resulted in many union disputes. Now he was complaining about some general called Franco I'd never heard of before, who had brought an army of Moors over from Morocco to create rebellion in various cities on the mainland. He spoke of towns such as Burgos and Salamanca falling too easily to the rebels, of a siege taking place in Toledo, and of miners and other working men heading for Madrid and Barcelona to help those two cities do battle against the Falange party. I understood little of what he was saying, but guessed that were he still a young man, he would be joining them.

'There are reprisals from supporters of the Republican government, particularly in this area. We will not give in easily. Those right-wing rebels have a fight on their hands, you can be certain of that.'

I nodded, only half listening, as my young mind was preoccupied with more personal matters. I was accustomed to my father holding strong views. Small and stockily built, with powerful shoulders from his years of work on the farm, Manolo García Díaz was a determined character. But he was also the kindest and gentlest of men. I loved him dearly. I also adored my mother, only too aware that both parents would give their lives for their beloved children, as we would for them. Not that it would ever come to that, poor as we were, I told myself. Why would it? There might be strikes and unrest in parts of Spain, particularly in the north, which troubled *Papá* greatly, but why should that affect us here in the south? We were miles away from such dreadful places, living in the middle of nowhere.

'In any case, this so-called coup d'état is bound to fail, according to *mi papá*,' I announced to Taco the donkey later as I fed him hay and water after seeing to the chickens and goats. 'So we have nothing to worry about here in La Colina de Arboledas, our lovely quiet *pueblo*. And I have no intention of taking the risk of producing *un bebé* at this early stage in my life. Although I might well allow Demetrio to kiss me a little,' I confessed to my old friend with a soft sigh.

Leaving Taco to his much needed refreshment and rest, I hurried to my room tucked away at the back of the *cortijo* to wash and change. Demetrio would be here soon and excitement brought a strange feeling in the pit of my stomach at the thought of his kisses, almost like sickness yet far more pleasant.

Slipping out of my work clothes, I stowed them neatly away in the wooden box by my bed, then sponged myself down with soap and hot water from the bowl I'd filled from the kitchen range. Choosing what to wear from the small selection of clothes I possessed wasn't easy. With a sigh of resignation I pulled on a well-worn cotton skirt and a blouse that was becoming tight around my breasts. I felt this to be shaming as I wanted to look my best. Much as I loved my parents and the land, I also loved Demetrio, if in a different, far more exciting way.

I was so besotted that were he to ask me to marry him, which I so longed for him to do, I knew I would not hesitate to accept. If that meant leaving my beloved home and moving into the next village with him, I would gladly do so. As always, I could hardly wait for him to arrive.

I sat waiting for him at the end of the track that led to the farm. I perched myself high on a pile of rocks. This gave me an open view of the huddle of white houses forming the village on the mountain opposite, and of the path leading down the hillside along which he would come. The silence of the summer evening was broken only by the sound of the cicadas, as well as my own soft breaths of excitement. The scent of lavender was strong in the air and as the sun began to slip down behind the mountains, turning the sky into a fiery red, I did begin to worry a little. He really should be here by now. Then, as if in response to my anxious thoughts, I heard the familiar sound of his Norton motorcycle clattering over the stony path below, which brought me leaping to my feet.

Moments later his arms came about me, holding me close against the beat of his heart. How I revelled in the tender touch of his mouth upon mine, the burn of desire strong within me as his kiss deepened. I had longed for this moment all day. I adored Demetrio, believing without question that he felt the same way about me. When the kiss ended I met his gaze with a smile as happiness soared through me, weakening my limbs to a trembling mush. But remembering *Papá*'s warning, I dutifully linked my arm firmly into his and began to walk. This was the moment for our evening *paseo*, not lovemaking.

'Sorry I'm late, my sweet,' he apologised, squeezing my hand. 'Have you been waiting long?'

Giving him a teasing smile and a little shrug of my shoulders, I airily remarked, 'Why would I? You think I have nothing better to do all day than lounge about dreaming of you?'

Laughing, he stopped walking to pull me into his arms again. 'I wish that were true. I can't get you out of my mind. Dreaming of kissing you keeps me awake half the night.'

I too suffered from the same problem, and would love to have been by his side through those disturbed nights of his to offer comfort.

I cringe now at the memory of such stirring thoughts, although fortunately was not so foolish as to admit it. He was, however, extremely good-looking: quite tall, if not particularly muscular, but lithe and athletic with dark hair that sprouted haphazardly from his head, very much in need of a good barber. He wasn't too good at shaving either as there was nearly always some shadow of growth about his chin and mouth. Yet I found all of that quite attractive. Demetrio seemed to me to be a quiet, thoughtful young man. I could also sense a tension in him, an edginess in the way he moved, seeming to be needy in some way, perhaps out of love for me, I thought.

At that stage he hadn't revealed his true feelings, yet I sincerely believed that one day soon he would pluck up the courage to do so. His charcoal grey eyes certainly regarded me with an intensity that thrilled me to the core. But then I'd loved him from the moment I first set eyes on him two months before, when he'd come knocking at our door seeking work.

He'd asked my father if he had any jobs he could help with, explaining how he was good at building work, and could drive. As he'd watched *Papá* herd the goats, he'd freely confessed that he wasn't very good with animals. My father had no work to offer, and Demetrio failed to find a permanent job. I didn't see nearly as much of him as I would have liked, as he lived a few kilometres away in the next village. He spent much of his time dashing about doing odd tasks here, there and everywhere.

'We'll have no more kissing right now,' I told him that evening. 'We are taking our evening promenade, and should prove to *mi papá* that we can be trusted to behave with the utmost propriety.'

'Of course!' he agreed with all due seriousness. 'You will ever have my undying respect, no matter what your father might think or say about me.' As he'd used the word respect and not love, it wasn't quite what I longed to hear. But in my innocence it felt like a step in the right direction.

'He doesn't disapprove of you, Demetrio,' I explained.

'I agree that your father has been most kind and welcoming, even if I don't share his political persuasions.'

I giggled. 'I don't understand half of what *Papá* complains about either, but it's the way he is. He says the political upheaval between the right and left we've been suffering from for years is driving the country into chaos, and that the election in February achieved nothing at all. Of course, he also grumbles about the depression affecting the price of crops, the value of olive oil having gone down greatly, and the lack of other work available. It is a worrying time for him, and money is tight.'

'But he has succeeded in producing a beautiful daughter with satin skin and glossy black hair, whom I find utterly irresistible.'

These words brought a flush to my cheeks and new hope to my heart. Tucking my arm back into his we set off along the track across the *campo*, the sound of the cicadas going about their own courting business loud in my ears. Why would my father not trust him, when I most certainly did? I adored him, and genuinely believed it to be possible to walk out with Demetrio in the fiery glow of a beautiful sunset and not resort to kissing him again. I soon realised that I'd been entirely fooling myself. Nevertheless, I took great care to limit his caresses. Finally came his farewell kiss. He'd stayed far longer than expected that evening. Twice I'd reminded him that I should return home for supper, but on each occasion he'd persuaded me to walk a little further and kiss him some more. Now he was leaving, promising to return the next evening if possible, depending on how long his job that day took.

Hugging myself with happiness I hurried back up the farm track. The family never ate early, but would no doubt be sitting down to supper by then and I'd apologise for being late. I was surprised to find the front door open. My parents rarely bothered to lock it, but *Madre* liked to keep it closed when we were eating to ensure we weren't infested with too many flies or wasps. Swallows loved to fly in and startle everyone, and geckos would settle themselves on the walls above the oil lamps to catch any passing mosquitoes. Was that why the door was open? My mother, Estela, who was very fussy about the cleanliness of her home, could well be in the process of chasing out a lizard or something with her brush.

The scene that met my eyes caused me to almost faint with shock. I was expecting the familiar sight of my father, young sisters and brother seated at the table, chatting and laughing as *Madre* served them *patatas a la pobre* or more likely *gazpacho* on this hot evening. Instead, the kitchen table was bare, while the floor was littered with broken crockery. Every surface in the room had likewise been swept free of items usually kept there. The table in the corner where the bread was cut carried only a few crumbs while beneath it was a trodden heap of broken loaves. The kitchen range was stripped of its pans, dishes, racks and earthenware jars, its surface splashed with what appeared to be the remnants of a rabbit stew.

The sound of sobbing brought me spinning round to find my mother huddled in a corner, clasping my two sisters tightly in her arms as she wailed and sobbed. I ran to her in dismay, shocked to find her face a mass of bruises.

'*Madre, Madre*, what is it? What's happened?'

It took several moments before I managed to calm her down sufficiently to get any sense out of her. Fetching a mug of water I held it to her lips, tears of fright already beginning to slide down my cheeks. My two little sisters, Marta and Catrina, were strangely silent, not even whimpering as I begged them to tell me what had happened.

Marta at last spoke up, her pale face yet more ashen. 'They came for him, for our *papá*. They took Fernándo too.'

I was horrified, unable to take in what I was hearing. 'What are you saying?' I asked. 'Who came? Took them where?'

Catrina looked up at me, wide-eyed with terror. 'Fernándo fought them. Our brother was so brave. But there were too many of them.'

'Your father too struggled to resist. I tried my best to help him, but then one of them beat me.' *Madre's* voice broke on a sob as her hand rested upon her swollen jaw, which had obviously been punched by some man's large fist. 'We could do nothing.'

'But who were these people? *Where* and *why* did they take them?'

'I assume they are Fascists. *Papá* has kept saying how he is not on the side of Franco, this general who means to take over *España*, perhaps rule the world, who knows? These young men came to punish him for such beliefs. They kidnapped him.'

I recalled the conversation I'd had that very afternoon with *Papá*, how he'd gone on at length about military troops who were being mobilised to take over government institutions. How the Fascists intended to seize power and that a nationwide rebellion was very much in the air. Why hadn't I properly listened, and taken his concerns more seriously? Instead, I'd been too busy dreaming of love and Demetrio. 'I know *Papá* is very interested in politics, but why take Fernándo too?' I asked of my mother.

'The poor boy was given no choice. He was told that he must either join them, or . . .'

The shots rang out before *mi madre* had time to finish the sentence. The war had arrived on our doorstep.

EIGHT
SCOTLAND — 1936

CHARLOTTE SLIPPED quietly out through the conservatory to be picked up by the Forbes family in their farm truck at the end of the drive. She'd made no mention to either parent of her intention to attend the meeting, held in the Town Hall on St Mary Street, very much feeling it necessary to avoid them both. She was surprised to discover how well attended it was, packed to the doors with farmers and their families.

She smiled and nodded at people she knew, although as the stepdaughter of the laird she didn't always receive answering smiles back. Charlotte guessed that feelings were running high against landowners with the kind of selfish attitude they demonstrated towards tenants. If only they knew that she shared their dislike and distrust of her stepfather. She always listened with sympathy to the worries and tales of woe from his tenants, wanting to help them in any way she could. He really had no right to ruin their lives, let alone use her as a tool to supply himself with yet more wealth. The very notion made Charlotte feel sick with shame.

Glancing around, she wondered if Laurence would be here, as she desperately wanted to talk to him. Was she too to be denied any say over her own destiny? There was surely plenty of time for her to find a husband, hopefully one she truly loved. Seeing no sign of him, she took her seat next to Libby, Nick and Mr Forbes, chiding herself to stop worrying about her own problems and concentrate on what the speaker had to say.

He began by talking about the situation in India but as agriculture was the major topic of concern in this region, soon moved on to stating that this was an important part of the BUF's campaign. 'We need complete reorganisation in order to put men back on the land, and to create stability within the economy,' he said, waving a fist in the air.

'Ye canna end this depression by raising prices any further,' shouted one farmer.

'Och no, ye should get rid of the middlemen who take too big a slice of our profits,' said another.

'And how do we do that, by closing down wholesalers and retailers, thus destroying more jobs?' challenged the speaker. As people began to whistle and jeer he put up his hands, calling for silence. 'We want a government with the courage to put an end to foreign imports. Surely we can produce enough food for our own use, without needing to buy any in from abroad.'

'If that's what ye're expecting then every farmer would have to double the amount of land he farms, and rents are too high for that to happen, were land to be available.'

This last remark came from Mr Forbes himself and Charlotte cringed, lowering her head in shame as she recalled how the laird had raised the rents of his tenants yet again on the last quarter day. In her opinion he should reduce them in order to help his tenants survive. His motivations were entirely selfish, using everything to his own advantage. The laird couldn't claim to be in poverty, not like the hundreds of unemployed in Scotland desperately seeking work, or farmers no longer able to make a decent profit from their land.

She didn't manage to follow everything that was said as it seemed quite political and complicated, but every now and then another member of the audience would call out a comment, people would cheer and applaud, while others would heckle or hiss. It seemed quite a noisy gathering and there were several groups of men at the back of the hall, moving about in a threatening manner.

'There seems to be quite a bit of ill feeling here. What's going on? Who are those people hovering at the back?' Charlotte whispered to Nick, who was sitting on her right.

'Blackshirts, brought over from Dalbeattie tae control the Communists. But the protesters are mainly ordinary men and women simply trying to speak up for themselves, and for Jews. There've been any number of strikes and protest marches, particularly in Glasgow. Plenty of folk are sick of the dole queue and the soup kitchen, so is it any wonder if they have nae wish to be ruled by Nationalists operating a totalitarian regime.'

'I agree with them on that. I'm very much a believer in freedom and democracy.'

'We can but hope that the BUF will be beaten in the end by this strong anti-Fascist movement.' Nick lowered his voice to keep their conversation private. 'But having said that, Spain too has been suffering from similar problems over land reform and issues over pricing tending to favour the land owners. Now there's the threat of a military coup d'état led by Francisco Franco, a monarchist turned Fascist after King Alfonso XIII decided to abdicate. He has something of a tough reputation from when he was in charge of an army who inflicted harsh treatment upon coal miners on strike in the Asturias, a year or two back. Now he's leading a revolt against the government.'

'Aren't they doing anything to stop him?' Charlotte felt a surge of shame at her own ignorance. Nick was eighteen, more than two years younger than herself, yet a young man with firm opinions. She rather liked him and greatly admired his knowledge.

'Elections were held in February but there remains fierce disagreement between left and right wing, and the Popular Front, who are now in power, largely seem to have lost control. Several politicians from both parties have been murdered as a result. Then in July, Calvo Sotelo, a leading figure of the right, was abducted and killed. I'm sure Franco was planning this conspiracy all along, but the death of Sotelo gave him the excuse he needed tae take control. Now he's leading a military rebellion, which is rapidly turning into a Civil War. I dinna care tae think what might happen next. Spain is a democracy and should remain so. We also have tae ask ourselves, what if the same thing were tae happen here?'

'Goodness, do you think it might?' Charlotte asked, stunned by this last remark.

Nick nodded, his expression grim. 'It could, if fascism spreads and Mosley gains the same sort of control. The BUF is in sympathy with Franco, and with Mussolini, who both have the support of the Catholic Church. Of course, many Scots see that as a plot to damage Protestantism, so hopefully these sort of protests will pay off.'

They both watched as the latest protester was frog-marched from the building by a couple of the Blackshirts. 'Democracy or no, ye canna say something the BUF might disagree with,' Nick snarled.

Ignoring the growing pandemonium, the speaker raised his voice above the din and repeated Mosley's cry: 'Hold high the head of Britain, lift strong the voice of Empire.' Then he ended his talk by encouraging young men in the audience to join the British Union of Fascists. 'Write to our headquarters in Chelsea and help to resolve Britain's problems,' he cried, once more waving his fist in the air.

'If folk see Mosley as the saviour of Britain, they're fooling themselves,' yelled a loud voice from the back of the hall.

'Bloody Communists. What would you know?' came the swift response.

At which point a fight broke out between the two groups at the back. Many members of the audience immediately leaped to their feet and ran to join in, while others fled for safety.

'Quick, we can get oot by the side door,' Mr Forbes urged. Charlotte grabbed Libby's hand and the two girls and Nick were quickly ushered out by their father just as they heard whistles and the clatter of boots.

'It's going tae be all right. I think we've been saved by the polis,' Libby said. No sooner had she spoken than someone lashed out, sending her flying. Banging her head against the doorpost, she fell unconscious to the floor.

'Heaven help us, who did that?' Charlotte cried, rushing to gather her friend in her arms before she could be trodden underfoot. Nick hurried to help and between them they carried his sister safely out to the farm truck. Libby soon came round, although complaining of a headache. They felt no small degree of relief when Mr Forbes climbed in and drove them all safely home.

❦

The next morning, Charlotte wisely made no mention of her attendance at the meeting, not wishing to annoy her stepfather any further by challenging him over his authoritarian behaviour. He may not be as bad as this Franco person that Nick had been telling her about, but the laird's treatment of his tenants, and of herself, was grossly unjust.

The moment breakfast was over, she again went in search of Laurence, heading for the woods where she knew he loved to walk, but still could find no sign of him. Pausing to skim a few pebbles over the gently lapping waves, she counted the number of bounces achieved with a small glow of pride. If she suffered from a neglectful family, she was at least a fit young woman with stubborn pride and a degree of courage, and a risk-taker. She'd always had the full support of her best friends, Libby and Laurence, who had helped her stand up to her stepfather, and build her own strengths.

Now, as she planned a new future for herself, she should take into account the skills and accomplishments she'd acquired over the years as a result. As well as drawing she'd turned out to be quite good at languages. Thanks to excellent teaching first at boarding school and then at finishing school in Switzerland, she'd acquired a decent smattering of French, German and Spanish. How that would help a career in art she had no idea, but at least it boosted her confidence.

It felt vital that she maintain faith in herself and find the strength to stand up to her stepfather's continual harassment. Dear Mama might give in to his every whim, but Charlotte had no intention of making the same mistake. She had no desire to replicate their loveless marriage.

Why would her parents, or Laurence for that matter, be so determined to bring this match about, and in such a hurry? It didn't make sense.

She supposed that marriage to the heir of a Scottish aristocratic estate might explain his parents' motivation. Like her own family, no doubt the Cunninghams believed love to be largely irrelevant in comparison with increasing their wealth, and linking the family land with that of their rich neighbour. Was Laurence being bullied into this marriage as much as she was, and was that why he'd gone into hiding, out of guilt?

Yet money did tend to slip quickly through her stepfather's greedy fingers, mainly because of his love of gambling. He'd always been fond of betting on the horses, and had taken to blackjack and poker with a passion when he'd given up hunting, since he was no longer able to tolerate the sound of gunfire. Her mother, of course, consoled herself by attending glamorous parties with her society friends, which must cost a small fortune. Could that be the reason? Were her parents suffering from a loss of income? They'd certainly spent little on the house of late, which was looking a shabby mess, or was that simply because her mother had lost interest in it?

Charlotte asked herself if she was prepared to sacrifice her own dreams to save her parents from so-called destitution. Highly unlikely.

She spent the entire afternoon sitting drawing in a glum glaze of misery, worrying over how on earth she was going to resolve this problem. Charlotte was very fond of Laurence, but not for a moment could she imagine herself in a loving clinch with him. Quite out of the question.

As dusk began to fall and hunger kicked in, she packed away her sketchbook and pastels to take one last stroll across the beach before heading home. Despite her mother's suggestion, the notion of marrying Laurence and finding herself a lover, perhaps in Ray Dunmore, felt equally obnoxious to her.

She reached the far end of the beach where the cove ended in a circle of rocks and a path curled upwards over the headland towards Craiklyn Point, marking the boundary of the McBain estate. Not a challenge she wished to face at this time of day. Aware the tide would be starting to creep in soon, she was about to turn back when she heard a groan. It sounded as if somebody was in pain, followed by gasping, breathless little sobs, sounds she soon recognised as not agony at all, but more like ecstasy.

Dropping silently to her knees Charlotte peered over a jutting rock, and, in the golden rays of the setting sun, gazed wide-eyed at the two figures locked together in the shelter of the headland.

She could see a familiar thatch of fair hair topping the naked back that was pounding up and down with a powerful rhythm. Charlotte had no trouble in recognising the person receiving the benefit of this amorous attention, his face turning to look up at her with a stunned expression in his eyes. It was Gowan Clarke, Laurence's old school chum. Clapping a hand to her mouth, she tiptoed speedily away over the soft sand.

Only when she reached the privacy of the woods again did Charlotte allow the laughter that was bursting in her chest to be released. She felt no shock, only amusement and a burst of happiness. No wonder Laurence had never shown any interest in kissing her. His desire for marriage was not romantic at all, or about maintaining noble estates. More likely a requirement for respectability forced upon him by his parents and society.

Tears came to her eyes but from joy not dismay, and an immense sense of relief. She bore Laurence no ill will over his proclivities. We were all different creatures after all, all lovable in God's eyes, and he would ever be her friend. Oh, but this could be the perfect solution to her dilemma.

NINE

'I'M SO SORRY that you should find out this way, Charlotte,'
Laurence said, his face wreathed in sadness. 'When Gowan told
me you'd seen us, I couldn't believe it. I hope you aren't too
upset, or angry with me.'

'Why should I be?' It was the following morning and they were
sitting by the harbour wall watching one of the fishing boats unload
its latest catch of trout and salmon. Gazing into his gorgeous sea-
green eyes her heart melted with pity for him. 'Oh, Laurence, I
don't mind in the least if you love Gowan. He's your best friend,
but that doesn't mean that you and I can't still be friends, if in a
different way.'

'I thought you wanted us to be married? The laird said as much,
and that I must do the right thing by you. We are apparently a perfect match, and I'd never find a more wonderful wife.'

Charlotte rolled her eyes in despair. 'He said very much the
same to me. But isn't this a decision for you and me to make, not to
be bullied into a match by my stepfather?'

He stared at her in surprise. 'I say, so it wasn't your idea, then?'

'No, not at all! I have other plans. You know how passionate
I am about my drawing and painting. I was hoping to go to the

Glasgow School of Art but the laird put an end to that dream.'
Making no mention of what she may have to do in order to keep
the dream alive, she told him how she'd cycled into Kirkcudbright
to pursue the idea of continuing with her art classes, determined to
do something positive with her life.

For once ignoring Libby's advice, however well meant, she'd
happily agreed to act as a model for Dunmore, although firmly
declined to pose for nude pictures.

'Anyone would think you didn't trust me, dearie,' Dunmore
had said, accepting her decision with a low chuckle, as was his
way.

Was that the reason, she wondered, or was it herself she didn't
trust? Since she'd never seen him without his straw hat on, Charlotte
had little idea what colour his hair was but judging by the smoothness of his flushed skin, the smattering of freckles across his promi-
nent cheekbones, and his bushy eyebrows, she suspected it would
have a reddish cast to it. The urge to remove his hat and run her
hands through his hair had been scarily strong in her. Most of all his
tawny eyes had radiated a light that sent shivers of longing rippling
down her spine. Becoming close to him artistically might well be
exciting, but could also present problems of a different nature.

'It's part of a model's job, just as studying the human form is
part of an artist's task,' he'd said. 'I must say I'm pleased that you
aren't going to Glasgow after all and that we can continue as we are.
I shall do my utmost to teach you all that is necessary for the task.
And I live in hope that you'll change your mind once we become
better acquainted,' he'd finished with a wry grin.

'I appreciate your help,' Charlotte had coolly responded, feeling
slightly breathless at the possibility of ever appearing naked before
this good-looking man. But when she again failed to agree to this
request, he gave an amused shrug.

'I'll start with your face, then. Painting a good portrait can be tricky, but you have a lovely skin. I shall use titanium white, yellow ochre, cadmium red and perhaps a little raw umber to begin with.'

He'd stroked her cheek with the back of one hand, and a small fire had lit within her. Was she mad to agree to this? Yet what was the alternative? If she possessed some skill with painting, however small, she should pursue it, not sit about allowing herself to be used and taken advantage of by her stepfather.

Now Charlotte heaved a sigh, pushing these thoughts aside to meet the query in Laurence's gaze. 'Boys have so much more freedom than girls.'

He gave a snort of derision. 'Absolute piffle! Don't you believe it, old thing. Only if we obey the traditional roles laid down for us by society, which I clearly don't. I'm a misfit in every conceivable way. I was bullied dreadfully at school so have little education to speak of, and no particular talent or skills, unlike you with your facility for art and languages, which I admire enormously. My only interest is in politics, which is no doubt terribly boring of me. I may, when the time comes, be content to inherit the family estate and spend my free time fishing and sailing. But I'm dashed if I'm in any hurry to rush into marriage.'

'Me neither,' Charlotte agreed with fervour. 'Pay no attention to society or tradition, Laurence, just live your life as you please.'

'That way I could end up in jail. We both could, Gowan and I, were the truth ever to come out.'

She looked at him in dismay. 'Oh, I hadn't thought of that. But plenty of people do break the rules. What about the clever lady artists who live in Greengate and Fisher's Close here in Kirkcudbright. Some are happily married, but others have left their husbands to engage in affairs, while some are apparently not interested in men at all, but do have a love life.' She smiled. 'You aren't alone in being different, Laurence.'

He shook his head, an odd sort of sadness in his eyes. 'I wish everyone were as understanding as you, Charlie.'

'What I admire most about those lovely women is that they are following their dream, whether it is in art or relationships. They produce wonderful pictures, do sculpture or silver metalwork, and in addition make a valiant stand for women's rights. We only have one life and should surely be allowed to live it the way we choose.' There was a confidence to her tone that she didn't quite feel, yet she was determined to stand firm in her beliefs.

'The thing is, Charlie, most people aren't as tolerant or as caring as you. Marriage would of course provide me with the necessary aura of respectability, and save me from possible prison. Have you considered that it could also provide you with the freedom you crave? I wouldn't put any bounds or restrictions upon you.'

She took a moment to answer, as the notion had indeed crossed her mind. 'Mama did point out that true love can be found elsewhere. However, I would like to think that one day I might find both the love and happiness I'm seeking within marriage,' she said, smiling sheepishly at him.

'I hope you do, dearest Charlie. But let me know if you change your mind.'

She shook her head. 'I'm afraid it simply wouldn't work for us. However, both sets of parents . . .'

'. . . are adamant that it's a good idea. I know,' Laurence sighed. 'But their focus is fixed entirely on the land, property and possible increase in wealth, with no thought to our happiness.' He gave a mocking little laugh. 'They might change their minds if they realised I couldn't guarantee them an heir.'

'Oh, Laurence, don't torment yourself over something you can do nothing about. Look to the future. If politics is your interest, then you should pursue that. You'd make an excellent politician, very much the kind of person Westminster needs, particularly as a representative for Scotland. Don't worry about me, or what our parents or society might think. As I say, you must choose your own route through life, as I fully intend to do. We'll remain friends forever, you and I, no matter what, but marriage between us is out of the question. Agreed?'

'Agreed.' He grinned at her, and Charlotte beamed back at him with affection in her soft grey eyes.

'That's more like the Laurence I know and love, like a brother, you understand. Now, we just have to find a way to persuade my stepfather to cancel this stupid wedding.'

'Without revealing the true reason,' Laurence added, more soberly.

'Indeed!'

'Never mind damaging your reputation.'

'Oh, my goodness, I hadn't considered that either. There has to be some way out of this mess without risking either disaster.'

They were both silent for some moments before finally he spoke again. 'I think the decent thing would be for me to jilt you. Gowan and I could elope, or run away together to live a discreet life of lies and secret happiness.' He smiled.

'I could simply politely decline your offer, and stand up to my stepfather for once in my life.'

It was Laurence's turn now to gaze upon her with deep sympathy. 'Take care,' he warned. 'I am well aware that you've already tried that many times before, and he is not an easy man to cross.'

Charlotte really had no wish to contemplate what the laird's reaction would be were he ever to discover she was planning to take private sessions with a bohemian artist, and act as his model. His response to an absolute refusal of his plans for her marriage would be far worse. She could find herself locked up indefinitely in that darned bedroom of hers.

Taking a deep breath, she managed to smile. 'I will not allow myself to be bullied. I must learn to stand firm, no matter how difficult it might be. But don't worry, your secret is safe with me, Laurence. I promise.'

୬

On her return to Craiklyn Manor, Charlotte asked to speak to her stepfather, only to be coolly informed by his valet that the laird was too fully occupied with estate business at present to speak to anyone. Charlotte thought it more likely he'd taken the train to Ayr to attend a race meeting, since he was thoroughly addicted to the sport.

She repeated her request several times over the course of the following days, but to no avail. He didn't join them for breakfast, lunch or dinner, locking himself away in his study. This was exactly how he behaved whenever one of his tenants wished to discuss their problems with him. He would refuse to listen, just as he now had no wish to hear Charlotte's very reasonable objections to his plans for her.

Panic was beginning to set in as she faced what must be the shortest engagement in history, with the wedding ceremony barely weeks away. If she didn't find a good reason to call the whole thing off, she might find herself walking down the aisle and married before she could blink.

By the end of the month it became perfectly clear that arrangements were well underway. Her mother had engaged a dressmaker, who arrived promptly at ten one morning to measure Charlotte and show her various designs of wedding gowns.

This was so typical of Lady Felicity. There were occasions when she would overwhelm her daughter with gifts: strappy shoes, stylishly cross-cut evening gowns, wide-brimmed hats with bows and ribbons, fur wraps, all the very latest fashions, whether Charlotte wanted them or not. It had been Mama who had bought her the bicycle, which she'd called 'a gift of freedom', with a beaming smile. Right now Charlotte would have preferred a motor car, since that held a greater prospect of freedom, although such a thing would be shamefully self-indulgent. Mama, however, felt no shame in being obsessively hedonistic, and would smother her daughter with attention. This was how she expressed her love. And possibly out of guilt for her inability to defend her daughter against the laird. Then she'd quietly slip back into her own secret world. Lady Felicity no doubt considered devoting hours to the preparation of Charlotte's wedding to be a complete delight. She also seemed to imagine that by marrying her off to dear Laurence, all would then be well in her daughter's life. She couldn't be more wrong.

'Mama, I'm not yet prepared to go through all of this process,' Charlotte protested, already beginning to lose the necessary courage to confront the laird, and find a sufficiently good reason to call the wedding off.

'Nonsense, darling. Time is short, so we must make decisions.'

'I haven't agreed to accept Laurence's proposal. Don't you recall what I said about my feelings for him, or lack of them?'

Cancelling the wedding had seemed perfectly straightforward when she'd talked things through with Laurence down by the harbour. Now, as the dressmaker lifted her arms to run a tape measure over her breasts and hips, her mother fussing excitedly over designs and fabric, Charlotte couldn't seem to find the right words to put an end to this farce. No one was listening to her.

'I like this style with the frilled collar and long swirling train,' Lady Felicity was saying. 'The veil, too, is delightful with its pretty little flowered cap. Now let us consider which would be the right fabric. Should we have satin or lace?'

'Satin is very much in fashion at the moment, milady,' the woman responded, opening up her sample book.

It seemed, as so often had been the case throughout her life, that Charlotte's opinion was of no account whatsoever. She might as well be invisible for all the notice anyone was paying her.

The morning passed in a blur, decisions made with her scarcely saying a word. The next day the caterers arrived, and once again Charlotte was obliged to sit in silence through an endless discussion, this time over the number of tiers for the wedding cake, the choice of menu, wine and dessert, the design of place cards, and whether there should be a Scottish pipe band playing. Her mother was clearly in her element, choosing the very best of everything without a care for the cost, and certainly no thought of any consultation with her darling daughter. She might imagine this to be a caring thing to do, but completely missed the point.

Charlotte took a breath and resolutely broke into the conversation. 'Mama, I must go soon, as I'm attending one of my classes in oil painting with Mr Dunmore.'

Lady Felicity regarded her daughter with pure panic in her blue-grey eyes. 'Didn't Papa refuse your request?'

This choice of name always irritated her, as Charlotte had never succeeded in thinking of her stepfather in such terms. 'He would not allow me to accept a place at the Glasgow School of Art. This class is local, in Kirkcudbright, so hardly the same thing. In any case, if I am old enough to marry, I am surely free to choose how I spend my leisure time.'

'You'll have none to spare with a wedding to organise,' her mother fussed. 'So forget it.'

'Why should I? You know how much I love painting. Even if I never will be as famous as Picasso or Monet, it's a wonderful way of expressing myself, of enjoying life and reflecting the beauty I see around me. You have your music, so why can't I have my art? It brings me great pleasure.' Charlotte tactfully made no mention of the pleasure it brought her being taught by a handsome, charming man.

Lady Felicity gazed upon her daughter in deep distress. 'Darling, my private obsessions have done me no good at all. I would not recommend you repeat my mistakes.'

There was certainly one Charlotte had no intention of repeating, if she could but find a way.

❧

It had been some time since Libby had last seen Charlie, and she wondered if her friend had succumbed to Ray Dunmore's request. She feared that she might have done, as he could be very persuasive. Libby was trying to decide whether she should have revealed the truth about her own relationship with him. But that could have involved revealing more than she wished to divulge.

She'd agreed to act as a model for Dunmore in order to earn a little extra money, as her father was in no position to pay her much for the work she did on the farm, and jobs were few and far between. She'd once been offered the post of parlourmaid by Lady Felicity, but Libby had politely refused. Working as a servant at Craiklyn Manor would completely destroy her friendship with Charlotte. The difference in their class was best not thought about too closely, although there were occasions when Libby would feel envy at the privileges her friend took so much for granted. Not least her beauty, talent and riches.

Libby had been flattered by Ray Dunmore's request, and the attention he'd paid her. She'd also quite enjoyed the fun of dressing up and preening herself, as well as adding to her savings. Having quickly become captivated by his good looks and charm, she'd offered little resistance to his teasing kisses, which had become increasingly passionate.

The first time he'd asked her to pose naked her instinct had been to refuse. But as he'd slid the silk regency gown she was wearing from her shoulders and bared her breasts, all her senses had flared at his touch. She'd been too breathless and excited to object, her desire for him beyond denial. Before Libby realised what was happening he was inside her, making love with an urgency that set her alight with joy.

Relations between them had advanced at a pace after that. But it was not until a few weeks later, when she'd realised the consequences of their coupling, that the foolishness of such reckless behaviour had finally sunk in.

She was with child. According to her diary she'd missed two of her monthlies already. However much she might choose to deny it, there was little doubt that she was now a fallen woman! A devastating thought. Much as she loved him, Libby was fully aware that to Dunmore the attraction was purely sexual, not involving his heart at all. She was filled with shame for being so stupid. Libby certainly had no wish to confess to Ray about her condition, or beg him to do the decent thing by her, as he'd be unlikely to agree. What her parents' reaction would be when they learned their daughter was about to present them with an illegitimate grandchild was too dreadful to contemplate.

Charlotte might imagine that she had a problem because of an unexpected and uncalled-for offer of marriage, but Libby would welcome such an opportunity with open arms.

As if all of this wasn't enough to send her mad with worry, Libby was also concerned about her brother. Nick had been unusually quiet of late, which troubled her greatly. She hadn't seen him at all today, not even at breakfast. She guessed he'd taken himself off into the hills to brood over the situation in Spain, which was becoming something of an obsession with him. He'd been telling her all about the International Brigade, which would be going out there soon to help the Spanish people, clearly itching to become involved. The thought of her twin brother thousands of miles away, getting caught up in a war, was a terrifying prospect. Libby decided that she must do her utmost to talk him out of it.

But right now she had a more urgent problem to deal with.

TEN

LIBBY MADE a decision to find Laurence and invite him to join her and Charlie to see Robert Donat in the film *The Thirty-Nine Steps* that evening at the local village hall. Charlie too was coming. Did he truly love Charlotte? If so, why hadn't he gone down on one knee and proposed to her properly? What Libby wouldn't give for him to do that to her, particularly considering the mess she felt herself to be in right now. Nick was coming too, and she could but hope that it might take his mind off more serious issues, and relieve hers of her own problems too. She was looking forward to the film, rarely having the opportunity to enjoy such a treat, but felt anxious to have a wee chat with Laurence.

Later that afternoon, she chanced to spot him walking over the headland. Calling her dog to heel, Libby hurried over. 'Ah, there ye are, Laurence. I've been looking for ye.'

'Hello, old thing, I was hoping I might see you too. Chatting with a good friend might help lift my spirits right now.'

'Ye can always depend upon me,' she said, linking her arm in his and giving it an affectionate squeeze. They walked for a while in silence, content with each other's company, commenting on the cool September breeze coming over the headland that was a welcome relief after the heat of summer. A blue butterfly lighted on a patch of heather and they instinctively paused, not wishing to disturb it. At length Libby posed the question that had been troubling her for some days.

'Might I ask if the reason ye feel so down has something to do wi' Charlie?'

He glanced at her, studying her flushed cheeks, the brightness of her chocolate brown eyes beneath winged brows, and her firm rosebud mouth. 'You know, then. Did she explain that this wedding wasn't my idea?'

Libby's heart gave a little leap of hope. 'I did wonder if there was something more behind this proposal, mebbe a sense of honour on your part for years of friendship, or pressure from that controlling stepfather o' hers?'

'Something of the sort, yes,' Laurence agreed, giving a little nod. 'However, Charlie has made it very clear that she doesn't love me, not in that way.'

'Och, aye, she told me that too. Does that hurt terribly?' Libby's heart was singing. If Charlotte had made it clear that she didn't love him, then there was no reason to feel any guilt over the plan forming in her head. Assuming she could find the courage, and the right way to go about it. The alternative was to involve herself in strenuous activities in order to rid herself of this child. A prospect which shamefully occupied her thoughts at times, but also filled her with misery and guilt as she could never bring herself to do such a dreadful thing.

'To be honest, it's something of a relief.'

'Really? But Charlie is beautiful, and a lady, no less. Surely ye must be secretly heartbroken? Mind, I canna think why she doesna love ye. I doot any other woman would have turned ye down.' The declaration of her own problems hovered on the tip of her tongue but Libby managed to restrain herself, realising she must proceed with caution.

Putting an arm about her shoulders, Laurence gave her arm a gentle rub. 'It's very flattering of you to say that, Libby, although I'm not sure it's true. I have little prospect of making a good husband for anyone. Who would want to marry a lazy soul like me, with no skills or job to call my own? You wouldn't, would you?'

She gazed up into his sea-green eyes, heart pounding. 'Ye didna ask me,' she murmured, mesmerised by the sweet curve of his mouth. Why would she not wish to marry him when they'd been good friends for years, and he was a man of distinction?

A small silence, as if Laurence was startled or perhaps excited by her response. Then pulling her a little closer, he murmured, 'I might well have done so, had I thought there was any chance of your accepting.'

'Och, Laurence!' Libby felt quite unable to breathe as the conversation developed exactly as she'd dreamed of. 'It's no too late,' she teased, giving him her most seductive smile.

He had both arms around her now, his mouth hovering mere inches above her own. 'So what if I did ask? Would you be content, Libby, to be the wife of a no-good useless lump like me, rather wrapped up in himself?'

Something melted inside her at his modesty, and then the words were out of her mouth before she could prevent them. 'Laurence, dearie, don't I love the bones of ye? I'd give my right arm for the pleasure of being yer wife.' She did care for him, in a certain way, and would welcome marriage with him. But she made no mention of a more pressing reason.

Then his mouth came down upon hers, kissing her quite gently. Libby felt as if she were floating on a cloud of joy. Could this be the answer to her dilemma? Putting her arms about his neck she clung to him, responding with fervour till his passion increased a little to match hers. She thought an attempt to seduce him must surely be the best way to win him over. When the kiss ended he smiled into her eyes.

'Do I take that as a yes?'

'Och, Laurence!' All other words seemed to have deserted her as Libby struggled to control her emotions. She could hardly believe her good fortune. 'Are ye serious? This isn't one of your practical jokes, is it?'

Cupping her face between his hands he kissed her again, with more vigour this time. 'I would never do that to you, Libby. You're absolutely correct, old thing. I'm not in love with dear Charlie, we're just good friends. And her refusal didn't trouble me in the slightest. As you rightly guessed, it was her father who pushed me into making that proposal. Had I known your true feelings for me, I would never have allowed that to happen. I was contemplating escaping down to London to pursue a career in politics.'

'Is that what ye wish tae do?'

'Not necessarily. I'd prefer to stick around with my friends here.'

'So what are ye suggesting?' Heart racing, Libby could barely wait for his answer.

'That I'd be honoured to make you my wife. Although I can't promise to be the best husband in the world, I'd do my utmost to make you happy, dearest Libby.'

'What about yer parents? They'd never approve. I'm a farmer's lass, and your family is – well – rich.'

Laurence gave a careless shrug. 'What does that matter? The world has changed since the Great War. It's true that Mater and Pater were carried away with the idea of my marrying a titled lady, but I'm over twenty-one so don't need their permission. And they are keen for me to wed, so I'm sure they'd come to accept you, given time.'

She gave a troubled little frown, beginning to worry about how this might be achieved. 'My parents might no be so happy, in view of the class difference between us, and I *do* require their permission, being only eighteen.'

He grinned at her. 'Not if we elope. What would you say to us popping over to Gretna? It wouldn't take more than a day or two to tie the knot. They'd all come round soon enough after that, once the deed was done.'

'Och, do ye mean it?' Excitement sparked within her at the thought.

'I most certainly do. But in the meantime, it must be our secret. Not a word to anyone.'

Any doubts or further worries Libby might have felt about the immediacy of this decision were lost in the kisses that followed, mainly instigated by herself as she was overwhelmed with relief that her problem had been so easily resolved. Hadn't she loved this man all her life? Although whether it was the right kind of love to sustain a marriage was admittedly open to question. Not one she wished to ask herself right now. But if he wanted to marry her, and wasn't concerned over what his parents might think, what could possibly go wrong?

❧

Laurence did come to see the film with them, but Libby made sure that they didn't sit together. Charlie seemed quite happy to be seated beside him, the pair of them chatting like the old friends they were. Libby was struggling to contain her excitement, mingled with a touch of jealousy as she watched them happily laughing together. If only she could tell Charlie what had taken place earlier, but Laurence had insisted it be kept a secret, a request she fully intended to obey. Besides, nothing would persuade Libby to risk losing Laurence now. This was the only solution she could think of that would save her reputation.

The local village hall, used for ceilidhs, concerts, meetings and as a reading room, was quite small. The projectionist was standing at the back of the room, and there were one or two hiccups before he managed to get the equipment working properly, which created some laughter and a few heckles from the audience. Nick arrived just as British Pathé News was starting with images of people in Spain fleeing for their lives. He sat there grim-faced throughout, as did they all.

There were boxes, mattresses and rolls of clothing strapped to the roofs of cars. The sound of honking horns, trucks thundering along, children crying, all quite heart-rending. The scene changed to one where a procession of people were walking in the dusty, empty landscape, loaded down with their worldly possessions; many items obviously abandoned because of their exhaustion and the heat littered the road behind them. The clump of their weary feet was suddenly interrupted by the roar of planes overhead, and screams of fear as people dropped everything, snatched up their children and ran for cover. Some were not so fortunate and were struck by falling bombs or shells from the planes.

Libby's hands flew to her mouth in dismay. She heard Charlotte cry out in agony, saw Laurence pat her shoulder in comfort, and a fresh surge of jealousy overwhelmed her. But as the newsreel ended with the camera focused one last time on the dead bodies lying everywhere, she was filled with shame at her own selfishness.

However painful the problem she was now facing, it could not be compared to those being suffered by the Spanish people.

An eerie silence spread through the hall, broken at length by her brother, speaking quietly but with a firmness in his tone that reverberated over several rows of seats. 'The Duchess of Atholl, a staunch member of the Conservative Party, sees victory for Franco as a serious threat to Britain, and the spread of fascism in Europe as a danger for the British Empire as a whole. We should pay heed to her words.'

No one argued with this statement, in fact there were several murmurs of agreement. Libby was so used to Nick's political ranting that she'd never paid much attention. Now, after watching this newsreel, she began to see why he was so distressed by the news, and so anxious to help. He'd never been the kind of person to tolerate bullies, and always helpful to those less fortunate than himself. But what would she do if he carried out this ambition of his to go out to Spain to fight?

The pair of them had never been separated since the day they were born, so should she go with him, or would that be too dangerous? And how could she go in her condition?

Charlotte whispered, 'Isn't this dreadful? Are you all right, Libby? You've gone quite pale. You've been looking anxious ever since we sat down, in fact.'

'I'm as well as anyone can be after watching all of that,' Libby said, unable to admit that she'd also been keeping a close eye on Laurence, just to make sure he really didn't have any regrets about marrying her instead of Charlotte, and she too had made the right decision by persuading him. Libby glanced across at him now, aching to be the one whose hand he was holding in comfort. Catching her eye, he winked at her. Libby could have wept with relief. He was telling her it was all right, that he was only going through the motions and his promise to her held good.

❧

In the days following, Charlotte felt at her wits' end. What on earth could she do? The church service had been booked, invitations ordered, cousins selected as bridesmaids and their dresses were already being furiously stitched, together with the bride's gown, by the diligent dressmaker. There were barely more than a few weeks left before her dreaded wedding day actually arrived. Yet no matter how many times she might protest, no one paid the slightest heed to a word she said. The whole performance was turning into a living nightmare.

Worse, not only had she still failed to speak to the laird, she'd quite lost her nerve to do so. Charlotte's entire courage seemed to have evaporated, leaving her shaking with fear at the very thought of confronting him.

She elected instead to spend her time hiding in her small studio in the back garden, painting roses, lupins and penstemons to keep her mind off her coming fate. The latter, with their foxglove-like flowers in fiery pinks, purples and mauves, were colours she was having great fun mixing. Would Ray approve of this picture, being much brighter than the still life he'd so disliked?

One morning her peace was shattered as the laird came storming across the garden, burst into her little wooden hut and slapped a letter down on the table beside her. Judging by the expression of fury on his face it clearly did not bear good news.

'Would you believe the fellow has had the audacity to *reject* you! How dare he? I've a good mind to sue the young fool for breach of promise.'

Charlotte's heart began to race with new hope as she picked up the letter and began to read.

Dear Sir,

It is with sad regret that I must inform you I am obliged to call off the wedding due to a change in circumstances. Fond as I am of dear Charlotte, I realised that I was making a bad mistake in making such a proposal. I'm afraid it wouldn't work for us as I love someone else, someone I have just married. I may well decide to go to London and seek a career in politics. My sincere apologies to you and your family, sir, for any inconvenience caused. I send my heartfelt gratitude to Charlotte for her continued friendship and belief in me.

Yours sincerely,

Laurence.

Charlotte could hardly believe her good fortune. Dear Laurence had done the decent thing. He'd taken it upon himself to call off the wedding and pursue his own dream, so there would be no necessity now to challenge the laird, or face being locked up in her room ever again. Not for a moment did she believe his excuse that he loved someone else and had married this alleged person. That was simply an excuse he was making to get her off the hook. Bless him. Setting aside the letter, she gave a pragmatic little sigh as she looked up at her stepfather.

'Don't fret, sir, this was only to be expected. We really are not suited. I have no wish for you to sue him on my behalf. I don't see this as a rejection, more a realisation on Laurence's part that a marriage between us simply wouldn't work, as we're more like brother and sister than potential husband and wife. I have been trying to explain that to you for some time.'

'Don't talk nonsense! He would never have made such a decision had you not refused him, you stupid girl!' the laird shouted, waving a fist in the air.

'We discussed our feelings quite openly together, and realised that although it would please you and the Cunninghams to see us married, *we* would not be happy. Laurence and I are not in love,' she patiently repeated. 'So there's an end to the matter. And as I have said countless times, marriage is not on my agenda at present.'

'It most certainly is.'

Charlotte struggled to maintain her calm. 'You have to understand, sir, that I intend to concentrate on my art.'

'You selfish, uncaring child. It's time you learned to appreciate the financial difficulties we are in and what a difference it would make to our lives if you stopped thinking of yourself, and gave some consideration to others for a change.'

Charlotte was stunned by this remark. 'How can you say that? It's *you* who is selfish and uncaring, not *me*! I've seen the callous way you treat your tenants, who are near starving.'

'The survival of this estate is far more important than that of a few idiot farmers who can't make their own farms pay.'

Charlotte took a moment before answering, her throat dry as she gathered the courage she desperately needed to stand up to him. 'Has it occurred to you, sir, that the reason Craiklyn Manor is in financial difficulties, if that is true, could be because you have wasted too much money on your own personal entertainment? No doubt to pay for your fancy car, your gambling debts and racehorses. Not only that, but by imposing too high a rent upon the tenants you could damage the estate income even further, as they simply cannot produce the necessary profits. As for selling me off to some rich husband in order to save yourself, I will never allow that to happen.'

His hand shot out to slap her across the face, sending her sprawling from her chair. Then kicking the easel after her, he stamped on the picture she'd been painting, breaking it in two. Charlotte lay crumpled in pain, shocked rigid by his attack.

'You will do as you're damned well told! I most certainly *will* find you a rich husband! Make no mistake on that score.'

ELEVEN
SPAIN — 1986

JO HAD SPENT most of the previous afternoon listening avidly to Rosita tell more of Charlotte's story as they sat in the shade of an ancient olive tree in the courtyard, and felt equally fascinated by what she had learned about Libby. This morning they were enjoying a *café con leche* together, Anton being busy with the almond harvest. 'It must have been quite devastating for Charlotte that no one paid any heed to what *she* wanted from life. Even worse to have been facing marriage with a man she didn't love. It's certainly not a situation I would relish.'

Rosita gave a sad little smile. 'Nor did she.'

'But your problems were surely far more serious and dangerous than being forced into marriage with the wrong man. As for Libby, I knew a little about Gran's life on the family farm and as housekeeper for the laird, but not her time as an artist's model. I'd no idea she'd fallen pregnant and married that young man. Poor Gran, how shocking and humiliating it must have been for her.'

'That is the story of how Laurence and Libby got together,' Rosita said, pouring out a glass of fresh cold lemon juice for her guest.

Jo was feeling slightly bewildered. 'My grandfather was called Robert Hendrick. I remember him as a stocky, bald-headed little man, always with a big grin on his round jolly face. He died when I was quite young, about five or six, in the late sixties. I'd no idea Gran had been married twice.'

'It could be a part of her life she prefers not to remember. Marriage and relationships are not always easy.'

'So true. My own parents split up when I was only ten years old.' Wrapped in an emotional war, they'd treated her as a ball to bat between them, or more accurately a weapon, with neither prepared to take full responsibility or proper care of her. By the time the divorce came through, Jo had been twelve, and her mother, being a social creature, decided to head south to London and take a job as a waitress in a grand hotel. She'd been a good mum to her in many ways, but it meant she left home at the crack of dawn in order to serve breakfast, returning only for a few hours each afternoon before going back to the hotel for some function or other most evenings.

And as Gran refused to leave Scotland, or visit them in London, that had left Jo entirely alone, a latchkey kid. They would write to each other regularly, and Jo spent weeks with her in Scotland every school holiday. Fortunately, she hadn't been as over-protective and controlling over her granddaughter's activities as she'd been with her son. Jo could remember Gran actually encouraging her to join a dance club and go on outings with the local church. They'd grown ever closer although Libby could be quite reserved, sharing little of her personal life. She'd certainly never mentioned that she'd been a member of the International Brigade, or the fact that she'd once married because she'd found herself pregnant. Probably because she considered it too shocking to discuss.

'What of the secret Charlotte vowed to keep for Laurence, to save him from possible arrest? Having been brought up in London, I didn't realise it was a criminal offence to be a homosexual in those days. How very sad and cruel that was. Did she ever break her promise to tell Libby?'

'As you can imagine, it was not a dilemma that Charlie found easy to resolve. A promise is a promise. In addition, she still felt very much under the control of her stepfather so rather wrapped up in her own problems.'

'I know about neglectful fathers, though thankfully mine was not a bully.' Jo had contact with him only on birthdays and at Christmas, when he would send a present and a card. At first she'd blamed her mother for keeping them apart, but when Jo had asked if she could live with him he'd dismissed the idea, saying she was better off with her mother. Jo's relationship with her father had not been an easy one since, as he was clearly far too involved with his new wife and children to be interested in a daughter from a previous marriage. Now she'd lost Felix and an all-too-familiar sense of loneliness washed over her. Why was it so difficult to find anyone who truly cared for her? 'But what of your own family problems? Do tell me how you coped with the loss of your father and brother.'

෦

That first night my mother was a shattered wreck. I too was shaking with emotion but doing the best I could in difficult circumstances. I put my weeping sisters to bed, said a little prayer for them before re-joining *Madre* out in the courtyard. We sat in silence throughout that long night, not able to think of a future without *Papá* or Fernándo. Dawn was almost breaking before the two of us finally crawled into our beds to fall asleep out of sheer exhaustion.

The next day I was shocked to discover that dozens of other men in the village had suffered the same fate. La Colina de Arboledas, like several other villages in the area, had been invaded by gangs of Fascist youths who had taken it upon themselves to act against alleged 'enemies of the state'. They captured not only men thought to be anarchists, Republicans or Communists, but also anyone considered not to be of the right. This seemed to include men who belonged to a union, were members of a local political party with fairly moderate leftist views, and even freemasons, all of whom were lined up and executed. It seemed that such horrific acts were taking place across *España*, and in our own province of Andalucía.

Some men were shot in the cemetery, while others, like *mi papá y mi hermano*, had to be carried there before the day was out. The sight of rows of coffins with women and children screaming and crying over them is something that will haunt me forever. The village was in mourning, filled with ghosts. A deep sense of anger and hatred against the perpetrators was growing inside me. I was tempted to find a gun and go hunting for them. We did have rifles in the *cortijo*, but that would not have been a sensible thing to do. Keeping a low profile was much safer.

The day after that, Demetrio returned, as promised, and I fell into his arms, sobbing against his chest, utterly heartbroken.

'Don't worry about telling me, I know what happened,' he said, patting my shoulder in an effort to soothe me. 'I'm sorry that your family were taken too. I did hope they would have been spared.'

'I understand none of this,' I told him, as I wept. 'My father, and particularly my young brother, did nothing to deserve to be . . .' The word *murdered* rang in my head, but I couldn't bring myself to use it. '*Mi madre* is devastated, as now we are all alone.'

When he offered to marry me and care for our farm and family, I could hardly believe my good fortune. 'Oh, Demetrio, do you love me enough to take that risk?' I asked.

'Someone needs to look after you. Women are not able to cope without a man around to guide them and tell them what to do.'

I might have argued against that remark had I not been so young, and he was kissing me, assuring me that we could work well together. 'So long as you agree to look after the goats and hens,' he finished with a smile. 'And the donkey, of course.'

I almost laughed, but then the tears started again and I gave myself up to receiving his kisses and loving caresses to counteract my grief.

Days later we were married by the priest, with *Madre's* permission, necessary as I was so young. It was not at all the kind of wedding I'd once dreamed of. My mother wept throughout the ceremony, and my heart bled from having no father or brother to stand beside me and offer their blessings. My dear little sisters seemed entirely bemused by the tragedy that had changed their young lives. I could feel a silent anger pulsating out of Catrina. At just turned eleven she understood enough to feel the pain of loss as well as the desire for revenge. Little Marta at seven was too locked in a numbed state to comprehend anything, while our mother seemed to have lost all interest in life. No one in the village was in the mood for a celebration of this kind, so it was a very quiet wedding and quickly over.

Marriage to Demetrio was what I'd dreamed of from the moment I first met him. And on our wedding night when he made love to me, my heart almost burst with happiness, although afterwards I sobbed in his arms as the reality of my situation overwhelmed me yet again. Living with our loss was difficult for us all, and the responsibility for running the farm, for everything in a way, seemed to have fallen upon my shoulders. At least now I had Demetrio to love and help me to cope. But snuggling close, I felt I wanted to express something of the anger churning inside me.

'I don't understand. Why would anyone wish to harm my dear brother?' I said. 'He was a fine young man with all his life before him. How could they do such a thing?'

'It was no doubt because Fernándo refused to join the Falangists,' Demetrio explained.

'Why would he, when they were threatening to kill his father? And why would anyone want to kill *mi papá*? He was such a lovely, kind man.'

'I'm afraid his political views did not coincide with today's world.'

'But he wasn't in charge of any political party, or any longer involved with the miners' union. Nor was he on the local town council. He was a farmer, nothing more.'

'Ah, but he also acted as an agent at the last election in February, working to persuade people to vote for the Popular Front.'

Pulling myself from his arms to sit up in bed, I stared at him, confused. 'How would you know that? You never lived in this village and hadn't met him then. In any case, why would it matter?'

'I keep my ear to the ground, and it matters what your father did because this new government is a failure and a farce. Fortunately, much of the south and west is now under the control of the Falange party, who we should look upon as the new Nationalists. Granada is facing a bloody battle with shelling and bombs, so that city too will fall to us soon, as will Madrid ultimately, despite its strong resistance. Then we'll have a new government in Spain who will manage things much better.'

His choice of words, the tone of satisfaction in his voice and the smile upon his face caused something inside of me to freeze. 'You speak as if you are a part of this group.'

He gave a wry smile. 'Have you only just realised that, my love? Of course I am. Why do you think I kept you out late that night? I wanted to keep you safe.'

I felt as if I'd been stabbed through the heart. 'Are you saying that you knew these rebels were coming to take *mi papá y mi hermano*?'

'This is war, Rosita. There are always victims. I knew they were coming to the village, but it was unfortunate that members of your family were taken. I hoped they might be spared, but the decision was beyond my control.'

My heart seemed to contract with a new kind of pain as the implication of this remark sank in. 'You *knew* they were coming! Yet you did *nothing*!' Throwing back the covers I leaped from the bed to gaze upon my new husband in shock and horror. 'How could you be so cruel? I *trusted* you! *Papá* trusted you.'

My last conversation with him again sprang to mind and it came to me with a jolt that perhaps my father hadn't entirely trusted Demetrio. *Papá* wasn't simply worrying about the possibility of my becoming a fallen woman but of this growing rebellion. I'd taken little interest in his rants and complaints, and never thought to connect them with Demetrio. But something clearly had been concerning him and, to my shame and foolish naivety, I hadn't properly listened or understood. Had *Papá* guessed that my boyfriend possessed strong right-wing tendencies? Surely, if he had, he can't have taken them too seriously or he would never have allowed me to go on seeing him. Although why would he expect a difference in their political views to escalate into murder?

Trying to scrub the agony of these thoughts from my head I turned to my new husband, my voice loud and condemning. 'Why were you not honest with me about your political persuasions?'

Demetrio gave an exasperated sigh. 'There's little point in keep going over this issue. What's done is done, and cannot be undone.'

'But you could have warned us about the coming attack. If you had, they could have escaped to hide themselves high in the mountains, in a cave, or one of the mining tunnels. How dare you do *nothing* to save my family, when you were aware of all that was about to happen?'

'Stop nagging, woman, and get back into bed. We have work tomorrow.'

'But . . .'

'Enough! This is our wedding night.' Then grabbing me around the waist he pulled me back into bed. This time as he mounted me, he made no attempt to kiss or caress me. Holding me down with the weight of his body, one arm pinned across my breast, he pulled my legs apart and thrust himself into me with a powerful vigour. As he pounded into me, uncaring of the agony he was causing, I could hardly believe this was happening. I'd never known such pain, and would have screamed had he not slapped his hand over my mouth. It came to me then in that terrifying moment that Demetrio had never really loved me. He'd simply wanted me in his bed.

Afterwards, as I mopped up the blood seeping from me as a result of his brutal assault, I quietly wept. Deep in my heart was born a hatred for the boy I'd felt besotted with for months. What a fool I'd been not to get to know him better before committing myself to marriage.

∾

'I would call it a naive trust in human nature, perfectly reasonable in a young girl,' Jo softly remarked, her heart filled with pity.

Rosita met Jo's horrified gaze with a sad smile. 'True, my once unshakable love for this man had been completely destroyed. In just a few short weeks I'd changed from an innocent sixteen-year-old girl with her head full of dreams, to a married woman with a whole heap of problems. My world had changed forever.'

'How dreadful! I used to dream of marriage, now I feel like I've completely gone off the idea, thanks to Felix's betrayal,' Jo quietly said, receiving a sympathetic smile in response. 'I do hope my grandmother's marriage changed her world in a more positive way.'

TWELVE
SCOTLAND — 1936

LIBBY WAS LYING in bed at the hotel in Gretna Green, happily reflecting upon the fact she was now Mrs Laurence Cunningham. How amazing! Admittedly the elopement had not turned out to be quite as romantic as she might have hoped. The drive to Gretna in Laurence's Renault sports car had seemed quite long and tiring, with autumn rain sheeting down the entire time. The ceremony itself, which had taken place in the now famous Blacksmith's shop, had been over in minutes. But Laurence had presented her with a beautiful gold ring and gently kissed her the moment they were declared man and wife.

She felt sad in a way that her family had not been present to share this special day with her, but Libby knew that her parents would have strongly disapproved, warning her of the class difference between them. Yet they couldn't be more wrong. Laurence had always treated her as an equal. He didn't boast or show off in any way about his rich heritage, or expect any special attention or privileges. Quite the opposite. He insisted that he was really quite ordinary and unprepossessing.

Not that Libby saw him in that way. True, he was modest, but with a stately elegance about him. She loved his golden fair hair, his sea-green eyes that smiled so softly at her and the perfect symmetry of his face with its aquiline nose and chiselled chin. Maybe she really did love him in the right way, after all. Excitement buzzed within her as she heard the door open and he came towards her, his face lit with that bewitching smile of his.

'Hello, my love. How beautiful you look in your nightgown.'

Libby fingered the stiff cotton she'd carefully starched and ironed to make it look respectable. 'It's a wee bit old and plain. I wish I could have had time tae buy a new one,' she said, assuming she could have found the necessary money.

Taking off his dressing gown to reveal his own nakedness, he laughed. 'It's very pretty, although I'm sure you'll look lovelier without it.'

Libby could feel her heart pounding. Was that love, or nerves? As he peeled the nightdress from her, she could feel his hands shaking a little. Perhaps he too was feeling nervous, wondering how it would feel to make love to an old friend. She so wanted to please him, to make him happy and love her forever. This was their wedding night and the sooner they made love, the better. That way he wouldn't question her condition when finally she revealed it to him.

He smelled of Lifebuoy toilet soap and the cigarette he'd just smoked. Libby suspected that he'd also treated himself to a dram or two of whisky. Not that this troubled her in the slightest. Curling her hands into the tousled locks of his fair hair, she arched her back to meet him as he straddled her.

She'd loved having sex with Ray, as he'd always brought her to a glorious pitch of fulfilment. Laurence's lovemaking might feel different, but she really mustn't compare her new husband with her past lover. Putting Dunmore firmly from her mind she softly stroked him. 'You feel wonderful,' she murmured.

She began to kiss him, eager to feel a response, which was slow in coming. But as she moved his member to assist him in finding the right position, as he seemed to be having trouble in that direction too, he suddenly rolled off her.

'I say, old thing, would you mind awfully if we postponed this for another night. I don't know about you but I'm bone weary. It's been such a busy few days, first driving all this way, and then going through the performance of organising the wedding, dealing with the paperwork, finding accommodation and so on. Not to mention the ceremony itself and all the celebrating we've done today. I think I've had far too much food and whisky.'

'Och! I hadna realised.' Disappointment bit deep in her. Had she failed him in some way, or expected too much?

'I'm exhausted. I'm sure you are too. So let's get some shut-eye, eh?'

'Aye, of course, if that's what ye wish.'

'Good-oh.' And heaving a sigh, he turned over and fell instantly asleep. Feeling oddly embarrassed and with an uncomfortable sense of rejection, Libby searched for her nightgown and pulled it quickly back on. She really mustn't let herself worry about this. It wasn't a rejection. As he said, he'd probably had far too much to drink. Even Ray was not the best of lovers when in his cups. And for all she knew, Laurence might well be a virgin. She almost giggled at the thought, then remembered he would expect her to be a virgin too. Had she been a bit too eager? She should remember her own hesitation the first time it had happened, and replay that emotion.

Nevertheless, it was vitally important they consummated this marriage soon, as there would soon come a time when she'd have to tell him she was expecting. She would worry later about explaining away what would appear to be a premature birth. Right now, all that mattered was that they were married, and Libby felt extremely content and relieved about her situation. This was only their first night together, so surely things would get better, once he was properly rested. Within moments, she too was asleep, equally exhausted.

Come morning, Libby woke to find herself alone in the bed. Laurence was already up and dressed, saying something about leaving straight after breakfast.

'So soon?' Yet again she felt a flicker of disappointment. This was not at all the honeymoon she had imagined.

'You know that your parents will be concerned about where you actually are, old thing. We mustn't upset them more than we have to.'

'Of course, ye're right.' Now she felt beset with guilt. Libby knew it wouldn't be easy persuading her parents that this marriage was a good thing. She certainly had no wish to reveal her condition, and could only hope they would eventually come to welcome their new son-in-law into the family.

The moment she walked through the door it was to find her mother in floods of tears and her father sitting grim-faced. Then seeing the letter in his hand, Libby recognised at once that her worst fears had been confirmed. The letter was from Nick, stating that he was on his way to Spain with the International Brigade.

She felt devastated. What would happen to her beloved twin brother? Would he be safe? Her parents were equally traumatised. Revealing her own news came out rather flat, feeling of no importance as they clung to each other in fear for Nick. It was only later that they began to express doubts, although they appreciated it was far too late to object, and wished for them to be happy. As Laurence kindly explained, the deed was done and they were indeed happy.

Nick's situation, however, was entirely different. Libby's instinct was to run to Charlotte and pour out her concerns. But then she remembered that her friend would not be aware of her marriage either, and that was the first thing she must deal with. It would not be easy, but she agreed with Laurence that the news would be best coming from her.

❧

The next morning Libby found Charlotte seated at the easel in her studio, painting a picture of the garden sundial surrounded by a glorious range of pansies and petunias.

'Och, that's lovely. How very clever ye are. Very talented lady.' Libby pulled up a stool to sit beside her. 'I wonder if I can interrupt ye for a moment, as there's something I need tae tell ye.' She was worrying over what her aristocratic friend's reaction might be to her news. Had Charlotte simply been playing hard to get over Laurence's proposal? If so, then she could well be furious at being rejected. She was a lady, after all.

Charlie barely paused in her work, casting Libby only a quick smile as she darkened the shadows in the centre of a petunia she was painting. 'If you're going to tell me that Laurence has declared the wedding is off, don't worry, I know that already.'

'Och, did he call tae see ye?' Relief washed through her. So it wasn't going to be difficult, after all.

'He sent a letter explaining that he'd changed his mind.' Charlotte chuckled, which Libby took to be a sign of relief.

'So ye know all about it then?'

'I do.'

'And ye aren't angry?'

'Why would I be? My stepfather was, naturally, but I did point out that the choice is ours. I reminded him, yet again, that Laurence and I are free to make our own decisions in life and not have his wishes inflicted upon us. Generally for entirely selfish reasons. Laurence can do as he pleases, as will I.'

'So ye don't mind that he chose to marry me instead?'

The sable brush Charlotte had been using fell with a clatter on to a pot of linseed oil, knocking it to the floor. Ignoring the mess of paint-streaked oil spreading across the floorboards, she stared at Libby open-mouthed. 'He did *what?*'

Libby's heart sank. 'Ah, he didna mention *who* he'd married then, in this letter?'

'No, he didn't. Are you saying he's married *you?*'

'I'm delighted tae say, aye, he has.' Libby managed a smile. 'I hope ye're pleased for us, because I couldna be happier. I've loved Laurence for as long as I can remember,' she lied, waiting and hoping for a positive reaction from her friend. Charlotte seemed stunned into silence. Eventually, after what felt like endless moments, Libby tentatively asked, 'You didna want him for yerself after all, did ye?

'No, of course I didn't.' Charlotte quickly put her arms about Libby to give her a warm hug. 'Sorry, I was just stunned. I'm so pleased for you.'

'Aye, well, Ma and Da are a wee bit confused too. They're no sure how tae react. He's a fine young man, but very rich, and I'm as poor as the proverbial church mouse. Which does beg the question that mebbe I married him for his money,' Libby admitted with a smile. 'Folk are bound to accuse me o' that, d'ye no think?'

'It's nobody's business but your own. I hope you'll both be very happy. *Are* you happy? Is everything – working out for you?'

'Aye, we're absolutely fine,' Libby said. 'Considering it's only been a few days.' A part of her longed to confess that there were a few problems, not least that she was carrying another man's child, and that her new husband had shown no interest yet in making love to her. Could he suspect the reason she was beginning to feel slightly unwell? Much as she valued her friendship with Charlie, Libby kept reminding herself that she was actually *Lady* Charlotte McBain, a person with strong opinions and high status. Libby had always taken care to tread carefully in her company despite their long friendship, and she certainly had no wish to cheapen herself in her friend's eyes. Although now she'd surely raised her own standing in society a little. 'Why would we no be happy?'

Charlotte was frowning as if not entirely convinced. 'No reason. I suppose this has come as something of a surprise because you're my best friend and I would very much like to have been forewarned. I would love to have bought you a present, and attended your wedding.'

'Och, I'm so sorry aboot that. I would have loved tae have ye there too, mebbe as my bridesmaid. But as we knew that our respective parents would be bound to object, we decided it had to be an elopement to Gretna Green. I must say it was quite exciting. Laurence insisted we keep it a secret, until we'd tied that wee knot, as he called it.'

'He's very good at keeping secrets,' Charlotte drily remarked, then quickly added, 'What I mean is, he never revealed that he'd made a proposal of marriage to me via my stepfather, or one to you. But I'm so happy for you, Libby,' she said, giving her friend another hug. 'So long as you are happy too.'

'Och, I am indeed. We're fine.' She then changed the subject and began to talk about Nick.

გდ

Charlotte went to speak to Laurence. 'Did you tell her the truth? I don't see how you can have done, or Libby would never have agreed to marry you. Why on earth would she want to do such a thing? And what about Gowan, is he still around? What was his reaction to this hasty wedding?'

'Which question would you like me to answer first?' Laurence asked with a gentle sigh.

Being far too wary of her stepfather's reaction were Laurence to come to the house, they were meeting in the woods, as they had done so often in the past. Seated uncomfortably upon a log, they were watching a red squirrel busily scrambling back and forth up the trunk of a beech tree, no doubt storing his nuts away for the coming winter.

'Answer all of them, and fast, before I break my promise and introduce a touch of reality to this alleged honeymoon of yours.'

'There's nothing alleged about it, Charlie old fruit. We are married, albeit by elopement to Gretna Green, and therefore man and wife. If you're interested in more details, and consider it any of your business, I'll admit we have not yet consummated our union, but that's by the by. Libby is really quite erotic in bed, and I almost fancy her. Who knows, I may turn out to be bisexual.'

Charlotte found herself blushing, filled with embarrassment at having broached the subject. 'Sorry I asked. You're right, it really isn't any of my business. I do hope you'll play fair with her though, Laurence, that's all I'm saying. Do try your best to love her.'

'I do love her, in every way but that one.'

'And what was Gowan's reaction to this news?'

'Gowan left for London some time ago, following that little incident on the beach when you came across us quite by chance,' Laurence admitted. 'He just walked away, deciding it was over between us. He believes that I should do my duty to my family and marry. So I see no reason why Libby and I shouldn't enjoy a happy union. I do hope that you won't upset her by revealing that private little moment to her. I'm trusting you to keep your promise, Charlie.' His tone had changed, with a much cooler resonance to it.

Picking up a stick, Charlotte began to doodle in the sandy earth, not wishing him to see her concern. 'Your secret is safe with me, Laurence, so long as you make Libby happy. But may I suggest that you don't mention your marriage to the laird at this stage. He will not be happy to discover that you've chosen one of his tenant's daughters in place of a titled lady such as myself.' She gave a wry little smile. 'He does tend to think in those terms, I'm afraid. I'll try to find an appropriate moment to break the news to him.'

'Thank you. I'm sorry in a way that it couldn't have been you, dear Charlie. But I do appreciate your assistance in this matter. I'll make sure that I keep well out of the laird's way until you do, as I have no wish for you to suffer any unpleasant repercussions. And I assure you that I will do everything in my power to make Libby happy. You have my word on that.'

As she watched him stroll away Charlotte couldn't help thinking what a kind and caring man he was, wondering if she did nurture any regrets over refusing his offer? Marriage to Laurence would surely not be unhappy, in spite of his secret preferences. But then she thought of Ray Dunmore, and a different emotion encompassed her. No, she'd made entirely the right decision. She could only hope and pray that her good friend Libby didn't regret hers.

Charlotte soon discovered that all mention of Laurence was banned at Craiklyn Manor simply because he had rejected her. Much to her dismay, her stepfather turned his attention to inviting yet more potential suitors to the house. These gentlemen were of all ages from eighteen to what could easily have been eighty, judging by their appearance. Many had titles, and without exception they were rich.

She pointedly ignored every single one of them, refusing to engage in conversation, or sit down to a meal with them. Charlotte would claim to be on flower roster duties at the local Baptist chapel, feel unwell and need to retire to her room, or would simply decline to meet them, saying, 'Since you are a friend of the laird, I will leave the two of you to talk in private.'

Such excuses never went down well, but it worked so far as Charlotte was concerned. She really had no interest in any of these men.

Ray Dunmore, however, was another matter entirely.

THIRTEEN

MEETING LAURENCE'S parents proved to be more difficult than Libby had feared. Mr and Mrs Cunningham sat stiffly erect in their respective armchairs in the library of their stately home, frowning disagreeably upon their son. They paid not the slightest attention to Libby, not even to wish her good morning or offer her a seat. Dear Laurence, however, fetched a straight-backed dining chair for her, placing it a little distance away from his sour-faced mother before seating himself beside her.

'I can hardly believe what I'm hearing. Are you saying that you have turned your back on doing the right thing by your family, and eloped to Gretna Green with this absolute nobody?' his father barked, casting a grimace of distaste in Libby's direction.

Libby winced, knowing his parents' reaction would worsen were they ever to become aware of her condition. She glanced anxiously at her new husband, wondering if he secretly shared his father's low opinion of her, but Laurence seemed entirely unmoved by this caustic remark.

Taking her hand to give it a comforting squeeze, he said, 'I am doing what I believe is the right thing for myself, sir.'

'You imbecile!' Mr Cunningham growled as his wife began to weep into her lace handkerchief. 'I'll make sure that you live to regret this decision. How could you be so selfish as to let us down in this way? You are perfectly well aware how the connection of the two estates would help us to prosper, not to mention the honour and glory. What are we supposed to do now, eh?'

'I'm truly sorry, sir, if you are disappointed in me, but there is more to life than money and estates. Surely personal happiness counts for something.'

'*Not in the real world!*' roared his father. 'Paying the bills and living well is far more important than whether or not you are in love with the woman you marry, damn it!'

Mrs Cunningham wailed all the louder at this, clearly hurt by her husband's callous disregard of love and marriage, in addition to the alleged misbehaviour of her son.

Libby felt a surge of pity for the woman and almost reached out to hug her, but was thankful she'd resisted when Mrs Cunningham turned upon her son with equal venom in her tone of voice, despite the apparent reasonableness in her choice of words. 'We do want you to be happy, Laurence dear, but why would you not wish to marry Lady Charlotte? She's a lovely girl as well as being a titled lady. What could you have against her?'

'Nothing,' Laurence said with a sigh. 'Except that she rejected me. Quite rightly, as we don't love each other in that way. Darling Libby, however, is my soul mate. Has always been so, for as long as I can remember. Now, if you'll excuse us, I think it best if we go. You both require a little time to grow accustomed to the idea. We'll call again, in a little while.'

As they walked away, Libby felt her heart quiver with newfound joy. She had done the right thing, after all, in marrying Laurence, no matter what his parents might think.

In the Forbes household, all talk of Libby's marriage was set aside in the light of Nick's decision to join the International Brigade. His parents were deeply concerned for their son's safety. Showing the more practical side of her nature, Libby tried to put forward Nick's point of view.

'Ye should be proud of your son,' she told them. 'The cause of the Spanish Republic is striking a chord with many here in Scotland, no just with men but women too. I've seen some mothers using prams to collect food for them. They're knocking on doors and folk are being very generous, despite the hard times they're suffering. They see fascism as authoritarian and wrong, whether it be in Caledonia or Catalonia, and there's no denying Nick was speaking the truth when he said the people of Spain are desperate for help.'

There was a long silence as her parents digested these comments. Her father was the first to speak as his wife quickly wiped the tears from her eyes. 'Aye, ye may well be right, Libby. I am indeed proud of our laddie, and there's no reason to suppose anything dreadful will happen tae him. I've fought in a war meself and came home in one piece. Let's drink a wee dram to his health, and wish him well.'

She hadn't been feeling too good lately, and not simply because of worries over her brother. Libby knew she really ought to consult a doctor, but couldn't quite bring herself to take the risk. The family doctor would instantly realise that she must already have fallen in the family way before she married Laurence, a fact she'd much rather keep to herself. Not least because they still hadn't consummated the marriage. He must have some problem or other, although she'd really no idea what it might be. Could it be the disapproval of their respective parents, and the fact that he had to live here at the farm instead of in his own fine home?

'Dinna ye love me?' she asked him one night when yet again he turned from her, making some excuse to avoid her caresses.

'Don't even think such a thing. I adore you, my angel. I'm just feeling emotionally stressed right now.'

'I can understand that when your parents are so disapproving. And are ye fearful my family might hear us through these thin walls?' she asked.

'I confess that is a concern,' he whispered, looking almost relieved. 'Best to get some sleep, old thing. You've not been looking too well lately. Don't worry, we'll get going on the – you know what – just as soon as we can find the time, place and energy. There's really no rush, is there?'

Libby felt she had no option but to agree. It was vital they made love soon, and build a good relationship. How she missed Ray. But now that she was married, Libby knew she shouldn't be thinking of him at all, despite the problem he'd left her with. The thought of him still set her heart wildly beating. Why would it do so when he'd deliberately taken advantage of her? She really ought to hate him.

Later that night she felt a terrible pain in her belly and came to the shocking realisation that she was wetting the bed. Dashing outside to the lavatory at the bottom of the farmyard, she was shocked to find that within minutes she was also covered in blood. What was happening to her? The pain was growing worse, seeming to drag her down. Only then did it dawn on her that she must be having a miscarriage. Crying out, she sank to her knees in agony. She might well have secretly longed to be rid of this problem, but the pain was horrendous.

An hour later as Libby washed herself down in the silence of a dark kitchen, she was heartily thankful that since it was long past midnight there was no one around to witness what she'd just gone through. It took some time for her to clean up the mess of blood everywhere. Then finding herself a clean nightgown she sat in a state of shock at the kitchen table, drinking a mug of warm milk.

It would seem that her marriage to Laurence had been entirely unnecessary. If she'd waited a little longer there would have been no necessity to persuade him into marrying her, although she did still feel quite fond of him. But something wasn't right between them. Either he didn't truly love her, or else he believed that she didn't love him. Every morning when she woke she'd felt the urge to vomit, and would quickly dash outside so she could do it quietly behind the cowshed, or better still in the woods beyond. She'd hoped he wouldn't notice but he might well have guessed her condition and taken offence at being tricked. Oh, what a mess she'd made of her life. Was it too late to save their marriage, or had she thrown away all chance of happiness by rushing headlong into tying this wee knot?

჻

'I always said that I'd go with Nick if he decided to join the International Brigade in Spain,' Libby admitted to Charlotte a few days later as they sat having tea and cakes after the art class. Now that she was no longer expecting it was something she could consider. A part of her felt devastated at losing her child, but Libby now felt free to do something different with her life.

'As twins, Nick and I were inseparable when we were growing up, so I feel that I should be there tae protect him.'

'It could also work the other way around. If you joined him, he may feel obliged to protect you,' Charlotte warned. 'In any case, as a woman how could you join the International Brigade?'

'I'm no suggesting I take part in the fighting, but when Nick first mentioned going tae Spain, I started a first aid course. I'm actually quite enjoying it, so surely I could be of some use in tending tae the wounded?'

'That would be most courageous of you, old thing. But you should appreciate that injuries are not just about cuts and grazes,' Laurence pointed out, having joined them for the tea, if not the art class.

Libby felt her mouth tighten, as it tended to do when she was irritated. Did he imagine her stupid enough not to understand what she'd be dealing with? But wary of starting their first marital row, she paused before answering. 'I do realise what I'll be facing, but feel the need tae do something useful with my life,' she muttered, with restrained patience.

'Me too,' Charlotte said, as if sensing the tension between them. 'I'm wondering if we could help here in Scotland, perhaps by fundraising. These young men must require food and clothing, and, as Libby rightly points out, bandages and first aid equipment. We could surely raise some funds for the International Brigade, as well as for the residents of Republican Spain fighting for democracy.'

'We could indeed.' Libby clapped her hands with enthusiasm. 'Bless you, Charlie, what a clever lady you are. According to what Ma once told me, women worked hard to make a good political case during the strikes a decade ago, startling the male-dominated trade unions with their efforts, so they were no longer simply thought of as wives of striking miners, but campaigners in their own right. If women could do that back then, we can surely do it even better now.'

Laurence grinned. 'I agree. And if the BUF can raise money from whist drives and dances, so can we. How do we set about it?'

'We could start by holding a rummage sale, which is easy to organise. I'm sure we'll manage to drum up support. There were plenty of women protesting at that BUF meeting we attended, and people were horrified by the newsreel we saw. We could hold a *rastro*, that's a Spanish market, or a *fiesta*. Then we could have a ceilidh, which are very popular.'

Nodding in agreement, Libby said, 'How about a tug-of-war, a marathon walk along the river bank, or a tennis match?'

'A fishing contest would be good too,' Laurence put in.

They each went on to suggest a whole host of events they could hold. Pushing aside her cup and saucer, Charlotte pulled a sheet of paper from her sketchpad. 'Since we are in agreement, let's make a list.'

They worked hard over the coming weeks, holding many events from dancing, walking and fishing, to games of football and cricket, just as they had planned. They went begging door-to-door. Libby happily pushed a wheelbarrow around collecting donations of food and clothing, while Charlotte and Laurence called upon all their rich friends. Charlotte also painted dozens of posters declaring: *Save Spain, and you'll save Britain.* This became their constant cry, one that was taken up by the many volunteers who offered to help.

At the art class Libby was keen to create a traditional, patriotic image, which went down well with the budding artists. Her modelling costume comprised a kilt, a plaid wrapped around her slender shoulders, and a black Scottish beret trimmed with a matching band of ribbon on her head. Charlotte admitted she enjoyed dabbling with colours for the tartan.

The students too became increasingly involved in the campaign, and wishing to remind them of his fame as a London artist, Ray Dunmore offered to donate some of his pictures to sell at auction, which brought in a fair sum of money. Libby felt she was at last doing something to support her brother.

᷈◐

Charlotte was greatly relieved that the line of suitors had finally reduced to a trickle. No doubt because the laird was running short of likely candidates. Fortunately, he raised no objections to Charlotte's fundraising efforts, viewing charity work as the kind of activity a young woman of her class should involve herself in. This was a great relief to her, as the thought of what she'd seen on the British Pathé News had haunted Charlotte ever since. Spanish refugees turned out of their homes must be in desperate need of food and clothing.

The laird did, however, occasionally ask what else was taking up so much of her time, as she was rarely home these days. Charlotte obstinately avoided telling him the truth, making all manner of excuses. The last thing she wanted was more interference, or for her life to be turned into a web of lies awash with secrets. The most important one being her modelling sessions for Ray Dunmore. The laird must never find out about those.

'I believe I have sufficient portraits of you now, Charlotte dearie,' Dunmore announced one afternoon, quite taking her by surprise. 'If we are to continue with this arrangement, then I'm afraid it's time for you to offer me something a little more – shall we say – challenging.'

Charlotte could feel her cheeks growing warm with embarrassment at what he was implying, a quiver of anticipation stirring within her. Adopting an expression of pure innocence, she politely enquired, 'Challenging in what way?'

He chuckled. 'I think you can guess my meaning. A fascination with the human form is in the soul of all artists. Yet you might as well be wrapped up tight in a blanket for all I can see of your figure.'

Following Libby's example Charlotte had chosen to dress in a kilt and plaid, which had not received the kind of appreciation from him that she'd hoped for. 'You don't think it's a good idea to be patriotic, then? Besides, I'm too busy with our fundraising to find time to keep dashing home to change into a more suitable gown.'

'Then take it off.'

Charlotte gasped. 'Goodness, no, I can't do that.' She might find it secretly exciting to be admired by this fascinating man, but there were limits to how far she was prepared to go. Flirtation was one thing, an affair quite out of the question. Even being with him here alone, without a chaperone, was against all etiquette and decorum. Not only her stepfather, but her mother too would be appalled. They would no doubt declare that such behaviour would ruin her reputation and all hope of finding a husband. But as Charlotte had no immediate plans for marriage, why shouldn't she allow herself to be introduced to the fruits of pleasure? Would that be so wicked? Dunmore really was most attractive with those sparkling tawny eyes, full lips and gleaming white teeth.

He came to stand beside her, his gaze roving over her while she kept hers firmly fixed upon the top buttons of his shirt, attempting to mentally shut herself off. Sensing her withdrawal he suddenly turned on his heel and strode to the door, pulling it open. 'Very well, then, we'll call the whole thing off. Time for you to leave, milady. I have no further use for a model who refuses to do her job properly.'

Disappointment flooded through her. That was the last thing she wanted. Why couldn't she do what he asked? Why didn't she trust him? Was it shyness or cowardice on her part, or a lack of trust in herself? If she didn't go some way towards satisfying his demands, it was possible she could lose everything she'd ever dreamed of. And he was making a valid point. Anatomy in art was important. Steeling herself to face reality, she made what she hoped would be an acceptable offer. 'What if I simply reveal my bare back? Would that do? I'm sorry, but I really have no wish to display myself fully, keen as I may be to continue with my art classes.'

He paused to consider, then a smile lit his face. 'That would do nicely. For now. Go behind the screen and get yourself ready.'

Charlotte had begun to regret the suggestion long before she'd unpinned her kilt. She must be mad to take such a risk. Yet if she wished to continue enjoying his tuition, and not least his attention, wasn't it only fair that she did the job correctly? She must think of it as playing a role, as if on stage.

Wrapping her plaid about herself she went to sit on the couch, feeling distinctly awkward as she attempted to adopt a pose, keeping her back towards him. When she felt reasonably comfortable she took a steadying breath and allowed the plaid to slide down to reveal her naked back, carefully keeping the more private parts of her body covered. A shiver ran down her spine as its protection slipped from her, though whether from desire or nervousness she couldn't quite decide.

'Beautiful!' he sighed. 'The slope of your shoulders is divine. Your neck gracious and elegant, and your waistline wonderfully slender. Now keep sitting straight and still, your chin raised a little with your head turned slightly to one side. That's it. Perfect.'

What a fusspot she'd been to assume that appearing naked before Dunmore would be difficult, or rude. Not that she had any wish to turn round and reveal any more of herself to him. This way he could see only her naked back, which surely wasn't too shocking.

Silence fell, the only sound that of his brush dabbing paint on to the canvas, and Charlotte began to relax. Time passed, and her back started to ache from keeping it in this rigid position, but she resolutely maintained her elegant pose. The room was not cold, so she felt perfectly comfortable and really quite safe, if a little tired. But then they had all been working hard lately, and there was still much to be done if they were to achieve their aim. It wasn't an easy task they'd set themselves but by the end of November they'd raised sufficient funds to buy not only food and clothing, but also a load of bandages, medicine, and other essential first aid equipment.

'The question now is how do we get all of this stuff to Spain?' Charlotte had put this question to her friends, brow creased in thought.

'I would take it myself, if I had a car and could drive,' Libby had replied.

'Me too,' Charlotte agreed. 'It's rather old-fashioned of me, I suppose, to only be able to ride a bicycle.'

'I could teach both of you to drive my Renault,' Laurence had offered.

'Really? Oh, that would be wonderful,' Libby cried, giving her husband a grateful hug.

'I'd be happy to drive you to Spain, but as it's only a sports car it wouldn't be big enough to carry such a huge load. Could we raise enough money to buy a second-hand truck, old fruit, as you're the exchequer here?'

'Not sure, but I'll investigate the costs involved and let you know.'

The last two weeks had been filled with driving lessons, which involved a great deal of scraping of gears, jumping and lurching in Laurence's car, plenty of strong language and a surprising amount of laughter. The two girls had learned how to change tyres, check the oil and crank it up when necessary. They loved driving up and down the quiet rough lanes of Scotland. Spain, however, was a foreign country, so driving into an unknown world would not be so easy.

As she patiently held her pose, Charlotte's mind began listing tasks still to be done, adding up the various profits in her head to check if they were anywhere near the amount needed to buy a truck, or to pay someone to take everything out for them. She became so engrossed in her thoughts that she did not notice the door had opened, nor hear a sound until a voice rang out, 'What in damnation are you doing, girl, behaving like a whore?'

FOURTEEN

THIS TIME she was not locked in her room. Her stepfather at once ordered her to pack her bags and leave. 'You're throwing me out?' Charlotte almost laughed out loud. 'You can't be serious. Where am I supposed to live?'

'Wherever you damn well choose, but it won't be in *my* house. You have destroyed your own reputation and I certainly will not allow you to destroy mine. Get out!'

Her mother was begging him to calm down and not be angry. 'Dearest, she was only acting as a model. I'm sure nothing dreadful was going on.'

'Absolutely not!' Charlotte cried. 'I had to do that in order to pay for my lessons. As you could see, I took care only to present him with my bare back.'

At that, it was her mother now who turned upon her in shock. 'You revealed your *bare back*, while sitting alone with this man? How dare you behave like a hussy? Hasn't your Papa done his best for you, finding you a respectable husband whom you carelessly tossed aside? And yes, we did hear that Laurence has married Libby Forbes instead. The whole town is now talking about it. What kind of young woman are you? One with no sense in your head, so far as I can see.'

Charlotte hated her stepfather for his callous treatment of her, but adored her mother, and couldn't bear the thought of her disapproval. She could but assume that the laird had destroyed all Lady Felicity's confidence in herself as she was far too used to following his dictates. Charlotte might feel outraged and angry at her parents for their treatment of her, but tears still rolled down her cheeks as she walked away.

∽

The Forbes family welcomed her with their usual degree of respect and friendship, and nobody asked any awkward questions, not even Libby. Charlotte said little about her own situation, save that the laird had thrown her out as punishment for continuing her art classes without his permission. She made no mention of the half-naked pose, or the insinuation by him that she'd behaved like a whore. She was simply grateful to have somewhere to stay.

Now Charlotte lay in the cold bed usually occupied by two of the children, who'd moved out to make space for her. Battling with her emotions she struggled to sleep. So much had gone wrong with her life in recent months. Her stepfather's treatment of her seemed entirely unfair. As for throwing her out over such an innocent act, it was utterly ludicrous!

Not that she cared a jot about leaving Craiklyn Manor, but losing daily contact with her beloved mother would be a high price to pay for this unexpected independence.

She'd paid the Forbes family something for her keep, but it wouldn't be right to impose upon their generosity for too long. Where was she going to live, and how could she support herself? Would the laird continue to pay her allowance? Possibly he would, if Mama asked him to. These were questions yet to be resolved. How Charlotte longed for true independence, for paid employment of some sort, however modest, as well as the chance to do something positive with her life. If that were to happen then she'd no longer have to request support from the laird, even if most of the money in his coffers had been brought into the marriage by her mother. And it was beginning to look as if he'd wasted most of it. But it wasn't her responsibility to pull him out of whatever financial difficulties he was in. Sighing, she turned over and closed her eyes, ordering herself to stop worrying and get some sleep.

There was also the question of Laurence having married Libby. Something was troubling her friend; Charlotte was convinced of it. She wasn't at all her usual cheerful self, which seemed to indicate Libby must be experiencing marital problems, which was no surprise.

When Charlotte had again asked Laurence if he'd confessed the truth to his wife, he'd given a virulent shake of the head.

'Libby hasn't been too well lately, but she does seem to be improving. And as I've already told you, our marital situation is really none of your concern. So don't make things worse by interfering. I'm trusting you to keep my secret.'

Charlotte had felt very much put down by this remark, but what could she do? Laurence was right. How their marriage was conducted was really none of her business. Much as she cared for Libby and wanted her to be happy, cared for them both in fact, seeing her husband sent to jail for such an unfair reason would surely not help in any way.

But as Libby knew nothing of his predilections it could be Laurence's parents who were the problem, having expressed disapproval of the match. That might be the reason the newly-weds were still living on her parents' farm. It made Charlotte feel more determined than ever not to marry. She'd really quite gone off the idea.

Her troubled thoughts were interrupted by a light tap on the door, and Libby herself popped her head around it. 'Can I come in for a moment?' she whispered.

'Of course.' Pulling back the blanket Charlotte invited Libby to snuggle in beside her, as it was far too cold for her friend to sit in her nightclothes on top of the bed. 'What is it, darling? Do you have some problem you wish to talk about? Laurence told me you haven't been too well lately. Is that what's bothering you?'

Libby shook her head. 'I'm much better noo, thanks. It's Nick,' she murmured, her tone grim. 'As ye know, Charlie, he left for Spain nearly two months ago. At first we received regular letters from him, several a week in fact. But we have nae heard a word from him in nearly a month. It's very worrying as it's no like him at all. Why doesna he write?'

'Oh, Libby, I hadn't realised. How dreadful!' This was the last thing Charlotte had expected to hear, but then she'd been far too wrapped up in her own difficulties. This news worried her more. Whatever her own problems, they were nothing by comparison with the possible loss of Libby's brother. 'Have you any idea where he might be? Where was he when he last wrote?'

'Heading for Madrid, and from what I hear, there's something of a battle in progress there, and a siege starting up.'

'That doesn't sound too good.' Both girls were silent for some moments, then Libby started to quietly weep.

'I wish I'd gone with him. Not knowing where or how he is, is agonising. At least if I was there with him I could help in some way.'

'Then why don't we all go?' Charlotte said, the suggestion popping out of her mouth without thought. Yet the idea felt like a natural instinct as she did feel eager to do something useful and positive with her life. 'We have the food, clothes and equipment ready to take out there. We could do that ourselves, as Laurence suggested.'

Libby looked at her in astonishment. 'Oh, Charlie, do you think we could?'

'Why not? Let's see if he still thinks it's a good idea.'

When Libby put the suggestion to her husband the following morning over breakfast, Laurence instantly agreed. They all three felt more than ready to do their bit for the brave men willing to fight to protect democracy, as well as helping the Spanish people. The Forbes family too were not against the idea, as they were deeply concerned for their son.

'Bring my laddie home,' Mrs Forbes urged them.

'We will, Ma,' Libby promised. 'Safe and well.'

Laurence bought an old farm truck from one of Mr Forbes's farmer friends. Then they started to load it up with the bandages, medicine, first aid equipment, clothing and food they'd acquired, plus several sacks of potatoes, carrots and turnips donated by Libby's father, and prepared to leave.

'Before we go, I would like to make one last visit home to say goodbye to Mama,' Charlotte said. 'I know she was deeply upset by the laird's decision to toss me out, despite her scolding. But I can't bear the thought of us parting like this.'

'You go,' Libby said. 'We'll finish loading and wait for you here.'

❧

Lady Felicity was standing looking stony-faced when Charlotte was shown into her parlour. The lid of her beloved grand piano was firmly closed, as if she hadn't felt up to playing her favourite music in the days since her daughter had left. Charlotte remained by the door, feeling cautious of intruding any further upon her privacy without an invitation.

'Mama, I'm so sorry about all of this, but may I speak with you in private for a moment?'

Lady Felicity regarded her daughter with an expression of cool disapproval. 'If this is to be a confession, then you'd better sit down. So will I, as I suspect more bad news is about to be rained upon me.' Sinking into the sofa by the fire, she clasped her hands together as if in an attempt to gather strength.

Charlotte propped herself on the edge of a stool at her mother's feet, feeling the need to be close but in a position to flee yet again, if necessary. 'I expect it was irresponsible and stupid of me to do what I did, but I assure you, Mama, that nothing immoral or unseemly took place between us. If the laird had not been so against my art lessons in the first place, none of this would have happened.'

'Don't blame your stepfather for your own foolish behaviour. He may have his problems, but it is your responsibility not to create more for him by parading yourself naked before that dreadful man.'

Charlotte stifled a sigh, feeling very much the wicked child. 'I do realise that, and I apologise for offending you, Mama. But believe me when I say that Ray Dunmore treated me with absolute decorum. He was simply doing his job as an artist, and so was I as his model by displaying my back. Nothing more.'

'That is some comfort, I suppose.'

'Then you believe me, Mama?'

A small smile flickered in her eyes. 'You are my beloved daughter, of course I believe you.' Gathering her hands to give them a small squeeze of affection, she asked, 'Where are you staying, my darling? I've been so worried.'

'As the laird made it perfectly clear that I am no longer welcome here, I'm with Libby and her parents. They've been most kind to me. However, this issue isn't the only reason I have called to see you, Mama. I've also come to say goodbye.'

Lady Felicity looked startled. 'Goodbye? Why, where are going? And why would you leave when you can stay with them for now? I can certainly make sure you continue to receive your allowance and keep your future secure. Alex has agreed that I should be responsible for paying that from now on. I accept that I've had little control in this marriage, but I do insist upon having some say over my own expenses.'

Charlotte gave her mother a grateful kiss. 'That's so kind of you, Mama. But as you know we've been busy these last months raising funds for the International Brigade. We've now made the decision to take the supplies we've collected and purchased out to Spain ourselves.'

'What!' Lady Felicity put her hands to her mouth in shock, falling back against the sofa cushions as if she was about to faint. 'Oh no, that is a most dangerous thing to do.'

Charlotte quickly went to sit beside her, gathering her close in her arms to offer comfort. 'Don't worry, Mama, we'll be quite safe. Laurence is coming too so we won't be alone. We've volunteered to join the Scottish Ambulance Unit. Both Libby and I have recently completed a course in first aid, so we are well prepared.'

Charlotte watched in dismay as her mother's face turned ashen with horror. 'Are you saying you intend to stay and serve the wounded?'

'I am.'

'Your Papa will *never* allow you to enter a war zone.'

Charlotte kissed her mother's cheek. 'Please don't call the laird that. *My* papa was a stalwart hero who did his bit in the last war. I believe the part of me that misses him so much wants to honour his memory by doing my duty too.'

'Oh, Charlotte.' Her mother's eyes instantly filled with tears.

'All I ask, Mama, is that you don't tell the laird until after we've left. This is a good thing we're doing, something my beloved father would have approved of. People in Spain are starving, their children dying, and the British government is doing nothing to help, or to stop the Fascists from taking over. We can't simply stand by and not offer to help. I love you, Mama. Please let me go with your blessing.'

Tears were rolling down Lady Felicity's cheeks now as she enveloped her daughter in a warm hug. 'My darling child, I love you too, so very much. I'm aware I haven't always been the best of mothers, not nearly as attentive as I should have been. Tending to lock myself away from reality. But I see this as one truth I cannot ignore. You are very much your father's daughter, a loving, caring girl who feels the same obligation John did to help humanity, before he sadly caught a disease which ended his life. I promise I will say nothing to the laird of your plans for as long as is necessary. And if you need help with anything, just let me know. Please do take care, and write to me every week.'

'Oh, I will, Mama, I promise.' This was the closest Charlotte had felt towards her mother for some considerable time. After one final embrace she walked away, blinded by tears as her heart sang with joy. She was not only free to do something worthwhile with her life at last, but taking the much longed for love of her mother with her. Come the dawn, they would embark for Spain.

PART TWO

FIFTEEN
SPAIN — 1986

THE DAY was sultry and hot, the cicadas noisily chatting, far removed from what those three friends must have faced crossing the Pyrenees in the winter of 1936. Jo's head buzzed with questions. She was anxious to hear how things had turned out for them once they reached Spain and became embroiled in the war, as well as eager to learn more about Rosita's life in Spain. But she felt she should proceed with caution, as the old lady was again looking tired, no doubt as a result of her illness.

Giving a little smile Rosita lifted a bell to summon Maria, the housekeeper. 'You must be hungry. We Spanish like to enjoy a substantial luncheon around two o'clock, but I'm aware you British prefer to dine earlier.'

'You really shouldn't feel responsible for feeding me.'

'I'm enjoying your company, Joanna, so please do stay.'

'Thank you, that would be lovely. But it's barely twelve, and I'm really in no hurry to eat. Could I see the original of this picture that I'm supposed to be investigating?'

'¡Muy bien!' Turning to Maria, the old lady asked her to call Anton.

Standing before the large canvas that took up a considerable portion of one wall in the main salon, Jo felt utterly spellbound by its beauty. She could see at once why Anton had challenged the much smaller, more confused version that she'd found. Brightly coloured flowers and the soft green of olive trees surrounded the white *cortijo* with its red tiled roof. A small brown donkey was tucked into one corner busily drawing water from the well, a young girl standing beside it. This must be Rosita happily chatting to her friend Taco. The painting seemed to represent a typical summer's day cultivating the land. Except that the beautiful blue sky was littered with black planes, and creeping in from all sides upon this peaceful landscape were images of soldiers bearing guns.

'It's a very moving image,' Jo murmured.

'It certainly is,' Anton agreed. 'I'm delighted to see your reaction.' The twinkle in his bright eyes warmed her even more.

'That must be Taco, and is the Olive House depicted here the one I am currently staying in?'

He nodded. 'This picture was painted in the thirties, decades before we built the large villa.'

'Ah yes, I remember Rosita explaining how poor the family had been at the start of the war, and how your father's efforts in business have improved the situation. He must be a clever man.'

'He is very much a financial wizard, an expert on the stock exchange, while I am content working the land. It is my task to produce the olives, almonds, oranges and lemons. A full-time occupation if not a particularly glamorous one.'

'Sounds a pretty good life to me. Better than working in an office in cold, rainy Scotland,' she said with a chuckle.

He laughed. 'My father is also something of a neurotic, and a bit obsessive about detail and facts, always asking questions, seeking or offering information on whatever is currently occupying his mind.'

'Gran is the complete opposite and reveals little if anything about herself. Before I left, I searched again through the boxes of stuff she's throwing away, looking for anything that might indicate how she came by this painting. To my astonishment, apart from an album of old photographs and what appear to be love letters from my grandfather, which I probably shouldn't read, I found nothing of any significance. No birth certificates, no school records, family bible, diaries, scrapbooks, no personal memorabilia of any kind. I'd always assumed that everyone has keepsakes; details of themselves and their family tucked away someplace in their personal treasure chest. It's as if she's deliberately destroyed all record of her past life.'

'She might have considered that to be a wise move in the circumstances, choosing to become a forgotten woman in order to survive.'

'You may have a point there. Fortunately, I did find some photos. Look at this one.' Jo dipped into her bag and drew out a small black-and-white snapshot of a young woman. She was dressed in a ragged-looking dress, her head shaved, staring into the camera with an expression of blank indifference on her face. 'Do you recognise her, by any chance?'

Taking the photo, Anton studied it with great care for some moments before answering. 'No, but could this be the unknown lady who wrote that letter from prison?'

'I was wondering the same thing. But why would there be a photo of her, taken just before she's shot?'

He shook his head. 'I have no idea, unless it was for propaganda purposes to prove the power of the Falange party.' Handing the photo back, he gave a pragmatic smile. 'You could show this to *mi abuela*. She might know who the woman is. But we must carefully choose the right moment so as not to upset her.'

'I agree.' Jo turned to study the painting again. 'I also see that the viewpoint is slightly different. There's no woman with a baby, and no flags in this original version. Is that because the one we have was meant as a poster, not a work of art to be hung on a wall?'

'Possibly, but yours is much more roughly painted. Is it by the same artist? That is the question.'

Stepping closer, Jo searched for a signature on the canvas, locating it without difficulty in the bottom left-hand corner. 'As we know, there's no signature on Gran's picture. I'd really love to know who this Ramón Peña Barros is, and if my version of this picture was painted by him too.'

'Consulting an expert is the answer.'

Jo nodded. 'I agree. If you direct me to the nearest art gallery, I could ask them for advice on who to contact.'

'I have a friend who works at a local museum and would be only too pleased to help. We could go later in the week, Wednesday or Thursday, if you like. I would welcome a little break from the almond harvest by then. Afterwards we could perhaps enjoy a meal out.' Something in his tone of voice as he made this suggestion brought a quiver of excitement within, quite taking her by surprise.

Rosita was waiting for them when they returned, happily seated in the shade of her favourite old olive tree, and listened with interest to what Jo had to say. 'What a wonderful picture it is. Whether or not my grandmother's painting is genuine, we'll have to wait and see what the local expert has to say about that. I do hope it is. This artist, Ramón Peña Barros, seems remarkably gifted. Unfortunately, I've managed to discover very little about him so far.'

'Me neither,' Anton said.

Rosita looked startled by this. 'Didn't I explain who the artist was before you left for Scotland?'

He gave a puzzled frown. 'Not that I recall. Why would you? You were intent upon finding your Brigader friends, not checking the authenticity of a picture you didn't even know existed.'

'Ah, of course. So it wasn't that I forgot to mention it because I am growing old?' Rosita said with a chuckle.

Anton met her smile with a grin. 'I don't think so, but who is this man? Do you know him?'

'Not a man at all. That was the name Charlotte used for her work, partly to keep herself safe and also because she insisted women were not highly regarded in the art world. She judged it wise to pretend to be a man. She quite liked to be called Charlie, but chose this name instead as it means jutting rock, mud or clay, which had some relevance to her.' Rosita laughed. 'She apparently loved nothing more than getting into a muddy mess while working on the land, and saw it as a perfect choice.'

'Oh, how fascinating!' Jo cried, clapping her hands with joy. 'And this talented lady was a local Scot. Wonderful! I must look out for more of her work.'

∽

Following a delicious lunch, for which Maria produced *salmón ahumado*, followed by *tarta de queso*, Jo slipped back to the *cortijo* and considered ringing the director to tell him what she'd just discovered about the picture. But that would involve walking into the village to find a telephone box since she hadn't got around to buying herself one of those new mobile phones. Besides, why bother speaking to him until she had some genuine information to share. It would be good to ring her mother, but perhaps she could do that later too. Definitely not Felix, she thought, blocking him again from her mind. Instead Jo settled down for a siesta, wisely avoiding the heat of the midday sun.

When she woke, she enjoyed a swim in the pool to cool herself down before returning, as invited, to hear more of Rosita's story. This time she found her in the garden clad in an apron, gardening gloves and a large straw hat. Jo gave her a fond kiss on each cheek along with grateful thanks for her generosity. As it was cooler in the late afternoon she offered to help Rosita water the plants.

'We do have a watering system for the garden, but it doesn't quite reach everything, and the plants in pots and jars require a little more care.'

'Then I shall help fill and carry the watering cans for you.' It felt good to be doing something useful. How she loved it here. When that task was completed they returned to sit on the terrace. Rosita took a moment or two to recover her energy, her eyes gazing out into the distance as she began to speak, picking up the story from where she left off.

☙

Relations between Demetrio and me became increasingly strained over the coming weeks. His patronising attitude made me feel like a piece of mud caught on the heel of his boots. My mother would glance at him in dismay whenever he addressed me with barely disguised contempt. Thankfully, seeing a plea for silence in my desperate gaze, she would bite her lip and make no comment. I dreaded her questioning the reason our marriage had gone so badly wrong. Discovering that my new husband could have saved *Papá y Fernándo* would only upset her further, and hinder her recovery from the terrible grief that swamped her. The result of that decision to keep silent meant I had no one with whom to share my troubles. I felt more alone than ever. The only way I could cope was to fill my days with work.

I was the one who must now take the goats out for their daily *paseo* so they could feed on grass and herbs on the *campo*. I looked after the chickens and ducks while *Madre* tended to the vegetable garden. Demetrio was rarely around, or found any time at all to help with work on the land. He nearly always had some job lined up that he must attend to. His frequent absences were something of a relief. The love I'd once felt for him had changed to a burning hatred. The prospect of spending my entire life with this ruthless, uncaring and selfish man filled me with despair. How foolish of me to rush into marriage at such a young age and the most difficult time of my life. If only I'd paid attention to what *Papá* was telling me, or asked more questions of Demetrio, then the truth might have dawned.

Now it was too late, and all I could do was to focus on my family's survival.

My biggest worry at that time concerned the coming olive harvest, which was about to begin. The trees were heavy with black fruit. But how would we cope with such a huge task without my father and brother, and few young men left in the village available to help, as they were generally happy to do. Those who had been fortunate enough to survive the recent attack had either gone to fight the Fascists or were hidden away deep in the mountains, making secret attacks of their own upon the rebels. It was a changed world for us all.

Madre had picked some of the olives while they were still green, which she stored in a huge jar in the larder, changing the water every day to soften them. After thirty days or so, she would preserve them in small jars with anchovies or herbs to add flavour. But picking the main crop of ripe black olives was a huge task that must be done quickly. They would then be sold to the local *cooperativa* in order to provide the necessary *pesetas* to live on, which would be little enough.

With no one to do the work but ourselves, we set about the job with resolute determination. I brought out the various stepladders and buckets which *Papá* kept for the purpose, and spread nets to catch any fallen fruit. Then using our fingers we began forking the olives from the branches. The satisfying rattle as they fell into the buckets, the sacks and crates becoming quickly filled, created in me the belief that we could indeed cope. Having taught me how to do this from being a small child, *Papá* would have been proud of me. The big fat ones always seemed to be just out of reach, but Catrina was very good at climbing trees so she picked the olives from the highest branches. Little Marta crawled over the ground gathering up those that fell, while *Madre* and I worked our way around each tree from branch to branch. It was a long and laborious task, resulting in aching arms and necks from all the reaching and stretching. Just when I thought I'd cleared a branch of fruit, I would look up, or move to a different angle, and a whole lot more olives would be revealed. It was a seemingly endless task.

'Can't you come and help us?' I asked Demetrio one morning, as he pulled on his coat to leave the house as usual.

'I have more important things to do,' he coolly remarked.

'More important than earning us sufficient money to live on?'

'*You* look after the land which brings in the money. *I'll* help capture the country.' With a snort of laughter he walked out the door, climbed onto his motorbike and rode away. How I hated him! How naïve I'd been to trust in this man and believe in his love, when he'd only wished to use me as a sex object and gain ownership of our land and farm.

Madre came to put her arms about me. 'Do not fret, my love. We'll get through this together.'

Two weeks passed, filled with hard work, leaving us feeling exhausted yet there were still a dozen or more trees to deal with. Each evening at dusk, cousin Pedro, who lived in the village, would come to load the sacks of olives we'd picked that day on to his two donkeys. He'd then transport them to the village *cooperativa* for pressing. I was so grateful for his help as lifting those huge sacks was not easy. I think he was equally grateful to be busy as it kept his mind from worrying too much about his big brother, Guillermo, who'd gone off to fight.

'He's on his way to Madrid to join the International Brigade,' Pedro told me, a mix of anger and pride in his young eyes. 'Our lives are in ruins, thanks to this dratted war.'

'At least he wasn't slaughtered along with your father and mine,' I said, attempting to console him.

He looked at me now with fresh anguish. 'But will he come home alive? That is the question.'

'I'm sure he will. Guillermo is a strong and determined young man.'

We said no more on the subject as it was far too painful, each of us privately praying for an end to this devastation. That was not to be the case. I was holding his *burro* one evening while he fastened a heavy sack into place when a great droning sound filled the sky. Looking up, we were shocked to see a squad of aeroplanes flying over. It was then that the bombs began to fall. Terror shot through me, and little Marta screamed. Pedro dropped the bag of olives he'd been holding, scattering them all along the path. I yelled to Catrina, *Madre* scooped Marta up into her arms, and we all turned to run.

But where were we running to? I had no idea. My mind was a complete blank as I stumbled over the root of an olive tree and fell to the ground. *Madre* came running back to drag me to my feet. 'Quick, to the cave.'

Paralysed with terror I found myself unable to move, and just stood staring out across the hillside, the sound of explosions ricocheting through me. 'They're attacking the *pueblo*, not us,' I cried. Then I pointed in the opposite direction. 'Look, they are bombing other villages too, as well as the towns beyond.' We stopped running to watch as far-off buildings crashed and crumbled, fires sprang up everywhere and the night sky glowed red.

'Come, *mis queridas*,' my mother urged us. 'You too, Pedro.' And gathering my sisters in her arms, *Madre* led us out of the olive grove to a cleft in the mountainside in which was located a cave.

Caves are quite common in this area, some of them turned into cosy homes, but this one on our own land had been a favourite place for me as a small child. I would bring my rag dolls and little sisters to play school in it, and sometimes hold a secret midnight feast. Now I found myself trapped inside in the dreadful knowledge that many innocent people I knew and loved may at this very moment be dying all around.

Where was Demetrio when he was most needed? What was it that my husband got up to during the time away from the farm, and why was it more important than protecting us from the bombing? Like it or not, my marriage had turned into a complete disaster. I could not rely upon my husband for any support and made a private vow during that endless, terrifying night, that I would find some way to protect myself and my family, and learn to be much more independent.

℘

As Rosita rubbed the tears from her tired face, Jo felt filled with admiration. 'I have made a similar promise to myself,' she said with heartfelt sympathy, recalling how Felix would treat her with equal disinterest. Yet her problems were as nothing by comparison with Rosita's. 'How brave you were.'

'I had little choice.'

'And what of people like Charlotte and my grandmother, setting out for Spain? Did their support give you the hope and assistance you were badly in need of?'

Rosita smiled. 'Yes indeed, as with all the volunteers and members of the International Brigade. They too were brave but did not have an easy time of it crossing the Pyrenees, the war catching up with them far sooner than expected.'

SIXTEEN
SPAIN — 1936

THE MOUNTAINS of the Pyrenees were cloaked in thick cloud, blocking out all sight of the snow-covered mountains, and at times the road upon which they drove. The journey had been long and slow due to the icy roads, and they'd frequently been compelled to climb out of the truck to dig away snowdrifts, battling against a freezing northeast wind as they did so. Not for a moment had Charlotte expected the crossing to be an easy one, yet despite the bad weather and bitter cold, she felt a surge of joy as she took her turn driving the truck.

Entering a war zone was not how she'd planned to spend her life. Art remained Charlotte's passion, not battles or marriage. But she was filled with excitement by the prospect of at last doing something useful with her life, in spite of the unknown dangers awaiting them across the border in Spain. At heart she felt very much a pacifist, with a strong belief in communication and compromise instead of fighting. But the people of Spain surely had a right to freedom and democracy, to fair wages, education and an equal society, all now being destroyed by Franco. She looked across at dear Laurence, seated fast asleep beside her with his arm about Libby, and smiled. If the only way to defend those rights and their country was for young men to fight, then the three of them could at least do their utmost to offer support and help where necessary.

In her own small way Charlotte understood perfectly the wish to defend one's rights. How many times in the past had she been forced to protect herself against the arrogant laird? But unlike darling Mama, who had fallen prey to his constant harassment, Charlotte had won her freedom at last, if not quite in a way she'd expected.

As the sun came up over the mountains, lighting the snow-covered slopes into a sparkling brilliance, her heart lifted with it. The winter scene reminded her of once sliding her sledge down Brown Willy on Bodmin Moor, a pimple compared to these mountains. But it had been a glorious day spent with her beloved father just before he died. He'd been the kindest and jolliest of papas. Charlotte could still remember the scent of cigar smoke on his coat whenever she snuggled up on his lap, and the warmth of his breath when he kissed her brow. How she had loved him. On his return from the war he'd brought her a small stuffed toy donkey, a shiny silver bracelet, and a pretty enamelled box in which to keep it. She still had these private treasures safely stowed away among her possessions back home in Scotland, apart from the bracelet, which she always wore.

Now she would honour his memory by doing her bit in this war, hopefully with a better outcome than the fate he'd met with. She'd missed him badly throughout her life, and would miss dear Mama too in the months ahead. But now Charlotte knew she must set all of these personal issues aside and concentrate on helping others, and on the reality of war she was about to face. At least she still had her dear friends to rely on.

As they approached Saint-Girons they spotted a Republican poster with the words: *Madrid and Barcelona today, Paris and London tomorrow.*

'Not a happy thought,' Laurence muttered, now back in the driving seat.

'No, but it makes the point why it is so important for the International Brigade tae come to Spain,' Libby said. 'And for us to bring this equipment and do what we can tae help.'

'We'll definitely do our bit,' Charlotte agreed. 'It's a long way to travel, and it will be tough. But no matter what we have to deal with, we must remain strong, positive and cheerful. Agreed?'

'Agreed.' As of one accord they all three began to sing: 'It's a Long Way to Tipperary', followed by 'Pack Up Your Troubles in Your Old Kit Bag', and 'There's a Long, Long Trail A-winding'. Songs that were not necessarily relevant, being melodies from the Great War, but brought a smile to all their faces.

Pausing to eat at a local bar, they came across a group of Scots who had trekked over the mountains, an arduous journey that had taken them days. They carried bagpipes not rifles, but their aim was to reach Albacete in the south, where they would receive the necessary training, and proper equipment with which to fight.

'I can't imagine walking across the Pyrenees, particularly in this weather,' Charlotte said, on a gasp of astonishment. 'You must all be very fit and strong.'

'We Highlanders are accustomed tae a mountain landscape so had nae trouble. Lowlanders are no so robust, and city types often give up and settle for the train or bus,' one young man, introducing himself as Fergus McKenzie, told them with a laugh. Tall and robust with powerful shoulders and strong thighs, he had dark brown hair and eyes, and a bright cheerful smile.

Charlotte laughed. 'I don't blame them. I can see some men boarding that line of canvas-topped charabancs. They face a long and tortuous journey. I do hope they're all aware of what they are letting themselves in for.'

'Dinna fash yerself,' he said, puffing on the cigarette he was holding between his thumb and fingers. 'They are very determined young men. The bombing of civilians they saw on the news really got tae them. But tak' care what you say in these towns. Local Fascists are quite likely to "shop" those they suspect of being against Franco's forces. So remember tae keep yer voices down if ye're saying anything they might interpret as being against them, for fear of being overheard.'

'Oh, we will,' Charlotte said, glancing over her shoulder in case anyone should be listening to them right now.

Laurence added with a wry smile, 'We're very cautious, and do try to keep our heads down whenever another vehicle passes us on the road. We've no wish to be stopped and questioned.'

Fergus regarded Laurence with an interested gaze, as if taking in his stylish appearance in his tweed jacket and breeks. 'That happens all the time. Some folk are deported, although they often secretly return.'

'You didna meet with a young man called Nick Forbes, by any chance?' Libby asked. 'He's my twin brother who I havna heard from in weeks.'

Fergus's gaze rested upon Libby with sympathy. 'I'm sorry no, we didna. But I'll keep my ears and eyes open, in case I do. He too may have been captured and returned to Scotland. Fascist guards at one checkpoint questioned our group as we're heading out to join the International Brigade. They locked us up in a filthy old hut, asking why we'd come to Spain and would we return if they released us?'

'What on earth did you say in answer to that?' Laurence wanted to know, looking anxious.

'That we'd come out here seeking work because of the low state of the economy in Scotland,' Fergus blithely replied with a twinkle in his brown eyes. 'Unfortunately, they weren't satisfied with our answer and kept on coming each morning to question us some more. "*Esta tarde, todos ustedes van a morir*," they would say.'

'Meaning what?'

'This afternoon you will all die. They then took some of our men out and we heard a burst of machine-gun fire.'

Libby gave a gasp. 'Oh no, could that have happened to Nick?'

Fergus gently patted her hand. 'Dinna fear, the laddie could be just fine. When my turn came I was marched out, thumbs tied together with wire. Striving not to reveal my fear I was convinced this was the end, and I was about to meet my maker. To my amazement and great relief I found all my comrades lined up and still alive. It was then that the guards released us with the warning that next time, if we returned to Spain, they really would shoot us.'

There was silence for some moments before Charlotte spoke. 'Yet here you all are, on your way back to Spain.'

'Aye, still fighting for a just cause.'

Tears had come to her eyes as she'd listened to this man's story, and his declaration to continue fighting. Could she be equally resilient were she to find herself in a similar situation? The possibility of being captured and held by guards was not something she'd ever considered.

Laurence ordered a glass of cognac for everyone. 'I reckon we are all in need of a little "Dutch" courage.'

He also bought them each a substantial meal of lamb cutlets, cooked in the delicious French way, which went down a treat, particularly with the group of Brigaders. Who knew when they might get another meal as good? Ahead they still faced crossing the high mountain route into Spain, one that had been carefully chosen to avoid too many official checkpoints. Charlotte could only hope that they would be more fortunate than this group of fellow volunteers.

As they got up to go on their way, Fergus paused, placing a friendly hand on Laurence's shoulder as he offered him a puff of his cigarette. 'Do tak' care, I'd hate anything to happen to ye all.'

Laurence met his concerned gaze with a grateful smile. 'We'll be fine. You take care too.'

Courage, Dutch or otherwise, would most definitely be in demand.

It was as they were preparing to leave that Charlotte again happened to glance across at the line of charabancs upon which new Brigaders were embarking for the last section of their journey. As she did so her eyes widened with shock. Grabbing Libby's arm she spun her round to show her what she'd seen.

'See that man over there in the hooded jacket. Do you recognise him? It can't be, can it?'

Libby gasped. 'Oh, my goodness, it's Ray!'

❦

'What on earth are you doing here?' Charlotte cried as he strolled over to them.

'How did you come?'

'Why didn't you tell us you were coming?'

'Are you planning to join the International Brigade?'

'Did you know that we were coming to Spain?'

The string of questions fired at Dunmore came randomly, from each of them all at once. His initial response was to chortle with laughter. 'Whoa, one at a time. I did hear that you'd left for Spain, so thought I'd follow, but chose to come by train. I purchased a weekend return ticket to Paris, travelling on a tourist train, which meant I didn't have to produce a passport. Just as well since I don't own one.'

'How very daring of you to take that risk,' Libby said, sounding completely in awe.

'It was quite a pleasant trip, actually. The ticket cost twenty-eight shillings and sixpence, and included the crossing on the Newhaven–Dieppe ferry. I was, however, obliged to wait in Paris overnight, but found a decent hotel where I met many Scots, Austrians, Czechoslovakians, Dutch, Danish and English of course. We ate at a cooperative restaurant in Paris. I must say some of the volunteers looked so young they'd clearly lied about their age when accepted as a Brigader. Those who couldn't afford the train fare were taken south by bus, issued with *alpargatas*, rope-soled sandals, to be led over the Pyrenees into Spain. Goodness knows how long that would take them. I chose to take the "red train".'

Charlotte listened to his tale in stunned disbelief. The memory of her art teacher had been hovering at the back of her mind ever since they'd left home, Dunmore being one of the people she knew she would miss. But meeting him here in the Pyrenees was the last thing she'd expected. Charlotte wasn't sure whether it pleased her or not. Her feelings towards this man were still a total confusion in her head. He might be devilishly attractive, but she suspected there could in fact be a devil lurking in his soul. There was something about him that unnerved her. Perhaps it was the way his eyes would narrow whenever he glanced at her, then roam over her body as if stripping it in his mind, and not for some picture he might be painting. She'd noticed he did the same to Libby, or any other woman for that matter.

His manner was always devious, flippant and flamboyant, and completely vain. Her heart would skitter whenever he touched her hair, while a part of her shied away as if she didn't entirely trust him. Yet he'd behaved like the perfect gentleman when she'd acted as a model for him, even when she'd presented him with her naked back, despite her stepfather believing otherwise.

She finally found her voice. 'You knew we were busily engaged fundraising for the International Brigade, and donated some of your pictures for us to sell. So why didn't you let us know you were interested in joining, then you could have come with us for nothing.'

Smiling at her with that mischievous sparkle in his eyes she recognised so well, he shook his head. 'I was too late, milady, you'd already left. It might have helped if you'd considered mentioning your plans, and offered me the opportunity.'

'I'm afraid it was a last-minute decision,' Laurence admitted. 'It never crossed our minds that you would wish to come, Mr Dunmore.'

'Ray, please.'

Laurence nodded, although Charlotte noted his expression was not entirely friendly, his brow marred by a disagreeable frown that was most unlike him. Not wishing Dunmore to notice, or start an argument, she quickly intervened. 'Now that you are here, you're welcome to travel with us the rest of the way.'

'At least as far as Figueres,' Laurence put in. 'We understand that it is a base for British volunteers, and where initial training takes place before men are transferred to Albacete for more training.'

Libby had remained silent throughout most of this conversation, gazing at Ray transfixed. He now turned his slightly amused gaze upon her. 'Your wife might object.'

Laurence frowned. 'Why would she? My *wife* is a most kind and thoughtful lady.'

'Of course she is. I wasn't suggesting otherwise. But she may prefer to keep this trip between close friends, rather than – business colleagues,' he finished, pausing a second as he appeared to search for the right word to describe their relationship. Libby flushed bright crimson as Laurence put his arm about her.

'Fortunately, it is too cold for modelling here, and for standing about talking as time is passing. So let us press on, shall we?'

Nothing further was said as they all climbed aboard the truck. But as it would be too much of a squeeze to fit four instead of three people on the front seat, Libby and Charlotte tucked themselves among the boxes of food, clothing and first aid equipment in the back of the farm truck, and fell asleep almost instantly.

಄

They were stopped and questioned much later that evening at a small town close to the border. Because of the non-interventionist agreement, the guards asked to see their passports, as in theory the British were not allowed to enter Spain. Libby was worried because, like Ray, she didn't possess one, but Charlotte created a distraction by chatting cheerfully to the guards in French and Spanish, using all her charm. Taking a tip from the group of Brigaders they'd spoken to earlier, she insisted they were not coming to fight but delivering first aid equipment to help all concerned in the war, and would be returning at once to Scotland. Laurence backed her up, making it very clear that they had no intention of staying. The guards seemed willing to believe them, appearing to be reasonably sympathetic. They did not trouble to check their papers too carefully, eventually waving them on their way.

'I suspect they were secretly pleased tae see us here,' Libby said, drawing in a breath of relief.

'They were certainly polite,' Laurence agreed.

'I'm relieved to see that you three aren't entirely against Fascist sympathisers,' Ray drily remarked.

'Is that what you are?' Laurence snapped.

149

It took a moment for Dunmore to answer, a twist of a smile upon his full lips. 'I do tend to be rather right-wing. If that's a problem for you, I'd better catch that train after all.'

'No, that's fine,' Libby burst out, ignoring the scowl on her husband's face. 'It really isn't for us to judge anyone.'

'Just as well,' he remarked.

This enigmatic remark was left hanging. And in a valiant attempt to lighten the atmosphere, Libby began to sing 'Take Me Back to Dear Old Blighty', which made them all chuckle and join in, as no one had any desire for the conversation to develop into an argument.

SEVENTEEN

THEY ARRIVED IN FIGUERES to see volunteers being issued with khaki uniforms, Balmoral-style caps, strong boots and, of course, food. The supplies that Charlotte, Libby and Laurence delivered were received with huge cries of gratitude, as they'd been running low for some time. The three friends were pleased with the response they received, and thankful for a few days' rest after their long, bitter-cold journey. On that first evening Libby handed out sausages and apples she'd bought earlier from a market stall, and the four of them chatted comfortably together as they ate, discussing what they hoped to achieve.

'My priority is tae find Nick, as well as helping wounded soldiers,' Libby said, her distress still evident in her tone of voice.

'We'll help you with that, old thing,' her husband assured her.

Charlotte agreed. 'For me it's about being free to make my own choices in life, and to do my bit to help.'

'Good for you. I am naturally interested in the politics of it all,' Laurence stated. 'What about you, Dunmore?'

Ray gave his sardonic smile. 'Hopefully I can find some interesting subjects to paint.'

Nothing was said in response to this selfish remark.

After they'd eaten they were directed to their respective sleeping quarters, the women in one tent, men in another. The temperature was a little warmer south of the border here in Catalonia, and feeling in need of a breath of fresh air Charlotte expressed the wish for a short walk before turning in for the night.

'Don't ye go too far now,' Libby warned.

'I won't.'

As dusk began to fall she marvelled at the sight of the Castle of Sant Ferran, an eighteenth-century military fortress built atop a hill that overlooked the town. How Charlotte wished she could explore further as, being the birthplace of the famous artist, Salvador Dalí, whom she admired enormously, Figueres held a certain charm for her. She loved Dalí's surrealist style, one of her favourite paintings being *The Persistence of Memory*, which showed clocks and watches melting, implying that time is not fixed.

'Were you thinking of Dalí?' said a voice in her ear, making her jump.

Turning to face Dunmore, Charlotte attempted to calm her flustered breathing, irritated with herself that he should still have this effect upon her. 'How did you guess?'

He chuckled. 'It's Dalí's town and you're a would-be artist. Are you aware that his own father dislikes his work, and disapproves of his relationship with Gala? Dalí too was thrown out of the family home.'

'How difficult men can be at times, although I believe his father changed his mind when the couple eventually married in a civil ceremony a couple of years ago. I could never see the laird agreeing with anything I did.'

'Mine neither,' Dunmore admitted. 'My father did nothing to help when I was assaulted as a child by my elder sister's husband.'

'Oh, my goodness, that must have been dreadful! Why didn't he protect you?'

'Because by the time I plucked up the courage to tell him what was happening, he didn't believe me. Father was convinced I was making it all up because I wanted all her attention for myself, my mother having died when I was a baby.'

'So was it a lie?'

'Don't *you* believe anything I say either?'

'I never know what to believe where you are concerned.'

He gave a caustic little laugh. 'I won't inflict specific details upon you, but it involved interference of a sexual nature, which went on for some time and was completely demoralising. I did finally retaliate by punching the fellow on the nose, breaking it in fact, once I grew big enough to stand up for myself.'

'Good for you.'

'As a consequence, I'm afraid I became something of a tyrant myself, although hopefully not as bad as Franco,' he said with a laugh.

'I do hope not.' Had she learned more about him, she wondered, or was he making this story up?

As if reading her thoughts, he said, 'You can certainly believe me when I say that Figueres remains loyal to the Republican government.'

'That's a comforting thought.'

'Ah, so you are a Republican?'

'To be honest, I have little interest in politics. I do, however, support the rights of women. I admire the Republican government for at least attempting to do something for women by improving their opportunities for education, making it compulsory for girls as well as boys. Spanish women have long been considered subordinate to men, kept at home as wives and mothers. The Republicans were considering changes in the law to allow divorce, so long as it was for a just cause such as domestic violence, surely a right all women should have? But if Franco takes control, I suspect that would all change.'

153

'You obviously know more about politics than you realise. I'm glad about that as I adore and admire women, although how much power they should be given in relation to their husbands is another question.'

'Really?' She glared at him now in open annoyance, not sure whether he was serious or teasing her, as was his way. 'Many men think that way, out of fear that women are actually more articulate and intelligent.'

He burst out laughing. 'The needs of men and women will always be in opposition to each other, like the beliefs of the left are very much at odds with those on the right in politics.' Taking her arm he hooked it into his as he walked her towards a small copse of trees.

Infuriated by these remarks Charlotte attempted to free herself, with little success as he kept a firm hold upon her. 'I believe in democracy, which is surely why we are here. And the Republicans offer that, don't they?'

Dunmore gave a snort of derision. 'It's far more complicated than that. Spain has also been hit by the recent depression. Wages rose despite factory owners insisting they couldn't afford to pay more. There are other issues, including big estates being taken over by the government. You can surely sympathise with that as you might have lost your own, milady, had you been Spanish.'

'I don't have an estate. Craiklyn Manor belongs to the laird,' Charlotte sharply reminded him.

'From whom you've finally achieved your freedom, I'm delighted to note. Well done! Catalonia and the Basque region here in northern Spain sought independence too. Had they achieved that, it could well have led to the break-up of the entire nation. It's a long-standing battle, with many sides to it. But you should appreciate that a large section of the population see the Fascists as Nationalists working for the good of Spain, not battling against it.'

'I doubt Nick would agree with you, were he here. He does not see them as a good influence, or kind, caring people. He explained it all to me once at a meeting we attended in Kirkcudbright.'

'Nick is entitled to his opinion, but you should also take into account the fact that the Republican government is considered by many to be incapable of running the country, suffering from its own internal war between anarchists and Communists.'

Charlotte took a calming breath, wondering how on earth they'd got into this political argument. It was a long way from Dalí, art and neglectful fathers. 'I'm greatly impressed by your knowledge. However, I prefer to keep my thoughts private as the rights of any individual fighting in a war mean that neutrality is essential when nursing injured soldiers. We were told during our training as first aiders for the Scottish Ambulance Unit that no matter who the patient is, or which side they fight for, they deserve to receive medical assistance and help. I agree wholeheartedly with that principle.'

'How sweet of you,' he said, brushing her cheek with the back of his hand, and allowing it to slide down her neck. 'So you aren't entirely anti-Fascist, then?'

Charlotte turned her head away, wishing he wouldn't touch her as it had such a disturbing effect. 'Since I'm British, not Spanish, what right do I have to take sides? I freely confess that I don't fully understand the politics of Spain, or the different factions involved in this war. I'm saying we are here to serve and help people, not judge.'

'You are such a lovely lady, so kind and beautiful.' Pausing to push her gently up against the trunk of a pine tree, he smoothed his hands over her arms, sliding one perilously close to her breast. 'You must know that I adore you.'

The pale oval of his face was temptingly close and Charlotte was beginning to feel increasingly vulnerable even as her heart rate quickened. She felt trapped by him against this tree, but his flattering remarks lit a spark of excitement in her yet again. She'd never thought of herself as beautiful. Such a compliment was more appropriate for her mother, the elegant Lady Felicity. Charlotte saw herself as a plain, obstinate and independent woman. Striving not to give in to his charm, she held fast to her argument.

'What you say proves my point. Working out who should govern the Spanish people is not our concern. We must keep our opinions private and concentrate on helping those in need, no matter what their political views. Now it's dark. Time we went back to the camp.'

He moved closer, pressing himself against her. 'I do love to hear you stand up for yourself, milady.'

'Don't call me that.'

'What would you prefer? Charlie, Charlotte, dearie, or my love? Because that's how I see you.' Then he was kissing her, his mouth devouring hers with a passion that stunned, his tongue pushing its way between her lips, and despite her earlier resistance Charlotte found herself responding to a pleasurable embrace that shamed but also thrilled her, desire soaring within. Why shouldn't she have some fun and happiness in her life? Just scenting the maleness of him set her senses on fire. He might be an irritating and seriously disturbed man, but he was also dangerously irresistible.

Charlotte carefully avoided Dunmore in the days following, not wishing to become involved and much more interested in watching the training. It soon became clear that equipment was in a worse state than they'd expected. The exercises were conducted using wooden sticks, not rifles. Real guns of any sort seemed to be in short supply, although boxes of weapons had arrived recently from Russia, presumably being kept safe in readiness for the next battle.

The new recruits appeared to have little if any experience of warfare, seeming to be overwhelmed by it all. They certainly showed little skill in holding a rifle, even if it was only a piece of wood. Seeing how they shuffled and fumbled, Charlotte was filled with pity for these young men. Thanks to being taken out on hunting trips with Laurence and his father, Mr Cunningham, although never by the laird as the Great War had damaged him too much, she was fairly familiar with the workings of a gun. Charlotte sincerely hoped that she would never be called upon to use that skill.

Fergus McKenzie arrived, again with a cigarette dangling from his pert mouth, together with his buddies. They appeared to be much more skilled, probably because those in the group who had previously served in the Great War helped to train the younger ones. Laurence explained this to her as he and Fergus chatted, having become quite friendly.

Dunmore, she noticed, did not take part in any of the training as he was too busy sketching the Brigaders. Clearly more interested in his own fame.

Later, the men were split into different units but within a week or two of arriving in Spain a halt was called to the training. The new recruits were informed they were to be dispatched into battle to fight. Many looked anxious, not expecting the call to have come quite so soon. Where they were being sent wasn't stated, but Charlotte, Libby and Laurence resolved to go with them.

'We could find ourselves close to the front line,' Laurence warned.

'Then I could paint even better pictures and sell them to newspapers and magazines, which would be excellent for my career,' Dunmore blithely remarked, as always his attention focused entirely upon himself.

Charlotte chose to ignore this comment and only answer Laurence. 'That's why we're here, to help nurse the wounded. If the other medics are going, we should join them.'

'Agreed,' Libby said. 'And with a wee bit of luck we might also find Nick.'

EIGHTEEN

ON REACHING MADRID they found the city in a state of shock and utter panic. Bombs were raining down everywhere, but despite Madrid being under constant attack the government had departed for Valencia. Was that a deliberate desertion on their part, Charlotte wondered, or did they feel it necessary to retreat to a safe place while they considered how best to protect Madrid? Having failed so far in his efforts to conquer the capital, Franco was attempting to capture it by crossing the Jarama River. He now had the support of both Nazi Germany and Fascist Italy, who were providing air cover and armoured units, the kind of sophisticated weapons he wanted. There were constant air raids from the German Condor Legion, and although anti-aircraft guns forced the planes to fly higher, making them less accurate, bombs continued to blast the city day after day. And incendiary devices started fires everywhere, doing untold damage. Lives were lost as buildings were destroyed and people ran screaming to the nearest shelter, not all managing to find one.

The first of the International Brigade had arrived early in November, and despite their lack of equipment and training, were proving to be a valuable support for the Republicans guarding the city.

'*¡Salud camaradas!*' the people had cried, waving their fists in joy as they'd marched along Gran Via, a busy shopping street in the city centre. At first many people had been under the illusion that they were Russian, who were supportive of the Republicans. But when they discovered that this was a mixed bunch of foreigners come to help, they still welcomed them with open arms. '*Vaya usted con Dios.*' Go with God.

Now, as this new battalion entered the city, they too met with cheers. Young children jumped up and down with excitement, which brought joy to Charlotte's heart. A hospital was soon set up in one of the educational establishments, quite close to the university district where much of the battle was taking place, as well as in former hotels, churches and similar buildings. By the morning of the second day many of the volunteers were brought back from the fighting on stretchers.

Charlotte, Libby and Laurence were soon fully engaged in caring for the wounded, working day and night alongside the doctors, constantly digging out shrapnel and attending to broken limbs. They found themselves caught up in a cause they felt passionate about, giving all the support they could, although soon discovered that however genuine their motivation it came at a price. They suffered a great deal of privation, freezing cold and discomfort. The sights confronting them were horrendous: limbs blown off, stomachs and ribs protruding, faces seared or burned beyond recognition. And the putrid stench of blood and decaying bodies at times was utterly nauseating.

Charlotte had never experienced such terrors and horrors in her entire life. Whether she was nursing a wounded soldier back to health, holding his hand and praying for him as he slipped away, or embracing a crying mother who'd just lost her child from starvation or a bomb, it broke her heart every time. On one occasion boxes of chocolates fell from the sky, which starving children ran to grab in great excitement. Tragically, these proved to be packed with small grenades. Opening them resulted in children being left handless or burned in some way.

'As someone has said, this is a "bastard of a war",' Charlotte said, nursing yet another deformed child. In her opinion, all sides were to blame. Why weren't men prepared to sit down and find an answer through discussion, instead of going to war and creating mayhem and death?

Despite the hard work and devotion of the doctors and nurses at the various hospitals, medical centres and ambulance units, remaining neutral was not an easy option. Arguments frequently took place between those who were in favour of the Republic, and those supporting the Nationalists. There were also a fair number who wished the next government to be neither.

Charlotte made a vow not to discuss the issue any further, particularly with Dunmore. He might be good fun and quite a lively character in his way, and she had some sympathy with the sad tale he'd told of his own childhood, assuming it to be true. But she could not decide whether he was deliberately provoking her for his own amusement, or attempting to make light of principles he ardently believed in that could well prove to be dangerous. He did seem to have a politically dismissive attitude towards women.

Following the incident in the woods back in Figueres, she was making every effort to resist his charms. She would often find him lingering close by, creeping up behind her to slip an arm about her waist, or give her a quick kiss on the cheek, as he was doing now.

'Please don't do that,' she protested. 'I'm busy.'

'Then tell me when you'll be free.'

'I won't be free. Not for you, ever!' Charlotte had made that very clear when she'd eventually managed to brush him off in the woods. Thankfully, she'd kept her head on that occasion, despite the temptation, and not allowed him to go too far. 'Do please leave me alone.'

'Ooh, milady, I love it when you sound so fierce.'

Charlotte stormed away, hating herself for actually wishing she could come to like this man, instead of just finding him sexually attractive. But the following afternoon he caught her in the pantry where she was brewing coffee for her patients, pinning her up against a wall in an attempt to kiss her, as he had done before. This time she was having none of it.

'What the hell do you think you're doing?' she cried, slapping him. Much to her dismay, her heart again raced with excitement when he came close. Taking no offence, he merely chuckled and strolled away, hands in pockets, whistling happily to himself. Ten minutes later she spotted him in a clinging embrace with one of the pretty Spanish nurses.

'I'm beginning to really hate that stupid man,' she announced to Libby, as they sneaked a moment to grab a cup of coffee together.

'You've no been having an argument with my husband, I hope?' she asked in surprise.

'Of course not! Dear Laurence will ever be a good friend. I'm talking about Ray Dunmore. That man doesn't seem capable of keeping his hands to himself. He's like a loose cannon where women are concerned.'

Libby stared at her in stunned silence as some minutes ticked by. 'Are ye saying he did something to ye?'

'I most certainly am. I've just slapped him for attempting to kiss me in the pantry, which he seemed to find very amusing.' Charlotte made no mention of the night she had not slapped him but instead responded to the thrills of his embrace. 'What do I do to make him leave me alone?'

Yet again Libby seemed to sink into silence. Tired of waiting for a response, Charlotte sighed. 'Come on, haven't you any notion how I can make him behave?'

Libby gulped down the last drops of her coffee and stood up to leave. 'I think we have far more important matters to concern ourselves with than the odd silly kiss from Ray Dunmore. If you are dreading another marriage proposal, I doubt ye have anything to worry about, milady. Sometimes, Charlie, you think far too much of yerself.' And she walked away, head held high, leaving Charlotte frowning in puzzlement. What on earth was wrong now?

❧

Later that day, finding Ray painting the image of a soldier holding a gun, Libby challenged him with what Charlotte had told her. He'd done very much the same to her the previous evening, only they'd soon gone beyond kisses. Fortunately she hadn't allowed herself to reach the ultimate moment of surrender, although she'd been seriously tempted and had loved his caresses. But why shouldn't she enjoy herself a little, since her husband still wasn't interested in making love to her? Libby had believed Ray when he'd told her that he was falling in love with her. But if that was the case, why was he also making a pass at Charlotte? 'So ye fancy milady more than me, is that how it is now?'

He glanced up at her in surprise. 'Of course not! You are my angel, my beloved, and my soul mate. You and I are meant for each other. Why you ever married that Laurence chap I really cannot imagine.'

'Shall I tell ye the reason?' Libby said, struggling not to break down in tears. 'Because ye took advantage of me and left me wi' a serious problem.' By the time she was done telling her tale, his face, she was pleased to note, was ashen.

'Are you saying that you deliberately rid yourself of the child you were carrying? *My* son, or daughter!'

She gave a little gasp. 'Nae, it wasna *my* fault. I did nothing except suffer from a miscarriage. It was just one o' those things.'

'But why didn't you tell me? I could have helped.'

Libby gave a little laugh of disbelief. 'In what way? By offering tae marry me? I very much doot ye would have done so. Ye'd made it very clear that you were no interested in any sort of commitment. Laurence, however, was.'

He frowned. 'That surprises me. He really doesn't look the type to marry.'

'Now ye're being ridiculous. 'Course he is. He's a fine young man and heir to a large estate, so why wouldna he wish to marry and have a family of his own?' Hearing herself say these words in her husband's defence Libby again wondered why, if this were true, he wasn't interested in making love to her. Could it be because he suspected she was in love with this man here, womaniser though he undoubtedly was? Laurence certainly hadn't looked pleased to see Ray when they'd met up on the Pyrenees. Could he be jealous of him, just as she was so often jealous of Charlotte, despite their long friendship? If that was the case, she shouldn't be talking to Dunmore like this, which could only make things worse.

Ray was still speaking, of which she caught only the last part. '. . . so from what I hear his family strongly disapprove of his marrying you, and may well disinherit their only son.'

Libby was aghast at this news. It was true that the Cunninghams had made no effort to welcome her into their family. The disastrous meeting with his parents was something she preferred not to remember. But she had not been aware that they might go so far as to disinherit him. That would be dreadful, more so for Laurence's sake than her own, as he loved his home with its surrounding woodland and acres of pasture. 'Where did ye hear that nonsense?'

'The jungle drums of Kirkcudbright, where else?'

She felt flustered, as if her world was cracking beneath her yet again. 'At least he *loves* me, so that is *their* problem. Why should I complain?'

'Had you not been in that condition you might never have married the fellow. I assume that to be the case. And having lost your child, the marriage has proved to be entirely unnecessary.'

Misery seeped through Libby at the truth of these words. 'I'm afraid so. But I'm very fond of Laurence, and always will be.' Whether it was true love she felt for him was still open to question. And did Laurence truly love her, or had he agreed to marry her out of disappointment over Charlie's rejection of him?

'It's a shame, though,' Ray said. They looked at each other then, with pity in his eyes and heartbreak in hers. 'I reckon you and I could have made a good team, but there it is. You made your decision and must stick by it. I still adore you, so why would the fact you tied that knot be a problem for us? I'll be here for you always.' And with a smile he drew her gently down on to the grassy turf and began to unbutton her blouse and slip his hand over her breasts. Letting out a gasp, Libby wrapped her arms tight about his neck and gave herself up to pleasure. How could she resist?

With Christmas almost upon them the battle in Madrid was easing a little, as if the rebels were realising that they had a bigger fight on their hands than they'd first appreciated. Where would they all be by Christmas and how might they celebrate it, Charlotte wondered. She had no idea, but felt no desire to return home. Helping the wounded and working in the wards was so important to her. There might be an acute lack of medical staff and equipment but the hospital was well organised, efficiently run and most friendly.

In spite of their wounds, injuries and loss of limbs, the soldiers would chat happily together. Charlotte was content with her work. And though she missed the green hills of Scotland, she was coming to love Spain and had no wish to leave just yet. Besides, they'd still had no word of Nick. Then one morning Libby came running in, her face alight with joy.

'I've heard news of my brother. Remember that young man, Fergus, the one who smokes all the time? He's sent a note, passed on via various people and finally handed to me by Laurence. It says that he's *alive*.'

'Oh, Libby, that's wonderful!' Charlotte cried, grabbing her old friend in a warm hug. 'So where is he? Somewhere safe, I hope.'

The happy smile slipped from Libby's face. 'I'm afraid he's been arrested, accused of having looted the bodies of dead soldiers. Nick has denied it, of course, as my brother is no criminal. He's being held in a local prison. I must go and see him, find out how I can get him released. I'm going now, this minute, if that's all right with you.'

'Are you sure that's wise? You could find yourself charged with being an accessory or something equally dreadful. In any case, you can't go alone, Libby, it's far too dangerous out there.'

'I'm going with her,' Laurence said, coming to put his arm about his wife in his typically protective manner. 'I've found a lawyer to help, and as the Spanish police have no proof, he is fairly optimistic we'll succeed. See you soon, hopefully with good news.'

'Oh yes, and do bring Nick back with you.'

Charlotte watched them leave with her heart in her mouth. What if they too were arrested, or injured? She could hear the rattle of machine-guns, the fury of heavy artillery shells and mortar bombing. The chilling sound of explosions going off across the city. In addition to street fighting, the bombing had continued relentlessly day and night, save for in the Salamanca district, a region in which many Nationalist supporters lived. Franco seemed intent on frightening the local people into surrender. So far the Republicans were managing to hold their ground, but there were heavy casualties. The thought of something dreadful happening to her friends didn't bear thinking about.

Charlotte felt filled with admiration for Libby. She was a very brave lady, as were the women here in Madrid.

'*¡No pasarán!* They shall not pass.' This was a slogan announced daily on the radio by Dolores Ibárruri, more famously known as 'La Pasionaria'. She said it in an attempt to rally support, and to urge women to help do battle with the rebels.

People were starving, babies dying for lack of milk. Mothers would be out on the street before six each morning to queue for food to feed their children. They would then take lunch to their husbands, fathers and brothers, whether they worked in a factory, down in the trenches, or at the barricades. Many women ran soup kitchens and childcare centres, while others worked with the militia, carrying a gun to fight side by side with the men and looking every bit as much of a soldier. A women's battalion had defended Segovia Bridge, and engaged in a battle at Getafe, one of the most populated and industrialised parts of the city. Charlotte had dealt with many women militia casualties, all so strong, and some looking remarkably sprightly and well groomed. Now she prayed that her equally brave friends would succeed in rescuing Libby's brother, without any risk to their own safety.

It was later that afternoon while Charlotte was assisting in the operating theatre, the doctor probing one young woman's leg, without anaesthetic, for a bullet lodged there, that the bomb dropped.

NINETEEN
SPAIN – 1986

JO FELT STUNNED as she drove the rental car down to the *playa* the next morning. Poor Charlotte! How on earth did one cope with being bombed? It didn't bear thinking about. Thankfully, Rosita had assured her that she did survive, but that everything changed for her. Jo couldn't wait to hear in what way. Needing cash to pay for meals in the week ahead as she had no wish to be entirely beholden to Rosita's generosity, Jo went in search of the nearest ATM. Pushing in her card she glanced about her, taking in the hazy blue of the Mediterranean stretching out across the horizon, palm trees waving gently in the summer breeze. How beautiful it was, and so peaceful, apart from a few tourists lazing upon a golden sandy beach. She found herself falling in love with Spain, not only with the sea and beaches, but the mountains and white villages, olive groves and scent of rosemary and thyme. Spain was not simply about sangria and sun at all. It had a fascinating history being told to her by Rosita. And the light and space it offered to someone like herself, who loved art and painting almost as much as Charlotte had done, was wonderful. It had a great deal to offer. Not to mention a handsome neighbour, with whom she would soon be enjoying a day out.

Lifting a finger ready to punch in her PIN Jo was shocked to discover that her card had disappeared. 'What on earth . . . ?' Oh, no, she was new to this ATM system so had she used the wrong card? She and Felix had a joint account from which they paid the mortgage and bills on the flat they still owned together. But Jo did have a personal account too, which was important now that their relationship had ended and she'd moved into rental accommodation. Once they found a buyer for their flat, which was on the market, she fully intended to buy an apartment of her own. No more sharing. Now she would have to go into the bank and ask for her card back, using her dreadful Spanish.

Fortunately, the lady who offered to help did speak good English as so many of the Spanish did, but was unable to return the card.

Feeling slightly irritated, Jo was at least allowed to ring the bank in England, only to discover that their joint account had been frozen. The official she spoke to was not prepared to explain the reason, and clicked off before she could argue the point with him. She instantly rang Felix from a call box nearby, making a mental note that she really ought to buy herself one of those hideous mobile phones, even if they were the size of a boot and twice as heavy. Receiving no reply, not even from the office where he ran his finance company, she rang her mother instead. Before Jo could get a word out, spending no time on pleasantries and sounding very slightly distressed, her mother instantly asked, 'Has Felix been in touch?'

'No, why would he? We've split up, remember.'

Jo listened in stunned silence as her mother explained that his business had crashed. 'Felix has been declared bankrupt. He rang to ask me to pass this information on to you. I haven't heard from him since, but the bank has now repossessed your apartment.'

'What! But it's for sale.'

'Not any longer, at least not by you, and no one has any idea where Felix is. I'm so sorry to be the bearer of bad news but you seem to have lost everything. Not only the man you loved and trusted, but also your share of the property you bought together.'

Heart pumping, Jo felt a sickness spread within her, making her quite unable to respond or find the words to express her emotions. Felix had never been particularly thrifty where money was concerned. He loved to socialise, go to the theatre and the opera, and possessed a wardrobe crammed with quality suits. She'd thought that was fine since he was running a successful business. But it seemed that wasn't the case at all. She felt utterly devastated by this news.

'Don't worry, love,' her mother was saying. 'They surely can't take your share as you aren't married to him. It may take a while, but I can lend you some money until it all gets sorted. I'll put some in your personal account today, shall I?'

'You don't have to do that, Mum. Thanks for the offer but this month's salary has just been paid in, and I do have some savings.' Most of which were invested in that apartment, she bleakly reminded herself. Promising that she'd ring again soon, Jo drew some money from her own account then treated herself to a coffee and *tostada* at a local bar by way of compensation.

As she sipped her espresso, Jo wondered how Felix could justify not warning her about his financial difficulties. It was beyond belief. Jo felt she'd done her utmost to set the problem of his betrayal behind her and make a fresh start, but hadn't found it easy to forgive and forget. Felix's dismissive attitude and his reluctance to spend time with her had made it increasingly obvious that either he no longer loved her, or else he wanted more of a family and didn't believe she could produce one. Jo had worried about that too, but as they hadn't made love for months how would she ever know? It never seemed to enter his mind that she too was grieving for her lost baby. How stupid of her to be so trusting.

Now, looking out over the blue Mediterranean, her anger seeped away. Fortunately, she thought of him less and less. And bearing in mind what that dear old lady had suffered during her lifetime, Jo felt she really had no right to complain about her own problems, which were minuscule by comparison. Unlike Rosita, who'd rushed into marriage far too young, she was still a single woman in possession of the freedom both Rosita and Charlotte had desperately sought.

A fresh start was indeed called for. There was no reason why she couldn't rent an apartment here in Spain, and perhaps start a business of her own teaching painting. Jo certainly wasn't obsessed with returning to work at the gallery, and felt no great loyalty to Mark Carter, the director. She fully intended to give this possibility serious consideration.

In the meantime, Rosita had promised more of her story. Jo paid the bill and set off back to the *cortijo*, eager to hear of how Rosita dealt with that brute of a husband of hers, and how she sought to achieve her own independence.

⌒◞

The raids continued, coming regularly two or three nights a week, sometimes at dawn when we least expected them. I stocked our cave with blankets and cushions, food and water, as that was where we now spent most nights, cuddled up together to keep warm. Sometimes Demetrio would join us, issuing orders as if he were General Franco himself. More often than not he was away working with his Falange compatriots on some raid of their own, much to my disgust.

This being a Monday, I was at the *fuente-lavadero* doing the washing. Catrina and Marta were at school, while *Madre* was busy cleaning the house and cooking. Demetrio was yet again absent.

As I scrubbed the sheets on the washboard, my mind kept turning over the list of jobs waiting to be done. The olive harvest was finished but the trees now had to be pruned. I must speak to cousin Pedro to see if he was willing to help with that task too, otherwise it would take weeks to deal with the sixty or more trees. I couldn't afford to pay him a wage, but he was young and kind, and we could at least offer to feed him.

As I began to rinse the sheets in fresh cold water, I couldn't help but listen to the chatter of the women working alongside me. The village was in utter turmoil, many of the houses damaged by the bombing, adding to the trauma they were already facing. Having lost husbands and sons, and with no employment available to them as women, many were desperate for money. Friends spoke of burning furniture in order to keep warm; mothers were starving themselves so that their children could be fed. And far more cities had fallen to the rebels than my father had feared, including Seville, Cordoba and Granada.

But from all accounts, whatever we'd suffered in this region was nothing compared with the bomb damage being done to Spain's capital city.

'Madrid is clinging on,' one woman was saying. 'How much longer it can hold out against the insurgents is uncertain. I've heard that half the country is now in the hands of the rebels.'

'Someone told me that Franco has already declared himself head of state and set up a government in Burgos,' said another.

'I don't rightly care who is head of state, so long as I can feed my children,' cried one young mother, and everyone went to hug her, or to offer a share of their own food if her children were hungry.

'Be careful what you say, and to whom,' I warned. 'The Falange band of mercenaries could come again, any night, and execute more people if they think we're against them. I've heard they are now seeking out doctors and teachers. Who knows, it could be mothers and children next, if they decide we are of the wrong political persuasion. Some women, I believe, have already been killed.'

Gasps of fear and whimpers of distress echoed among my friends and neighbours as they gathered beneath the shelter of our washhouse.

'Listen to her, she's right,' agreed Lorena, a lovely young woman who was an old friend of mine. She went on to describe how she made sure the door of her *casa* was firmly locked and barricaded each night, particularly when her husband was out fighting. 'Fortunately, it's a good solid door with large bolts, and hopefully the *rejas* will stop those thugs from breaking in through my windows.'

'I do the same,' another woman agreed, and there were murmurs of agreement all round. Others, who had never troubled about locking their doors, began to see the benefit of doing so.

Forgetting to wring out the sheets, I began to tell them of something I'd recently learned. 'I've been doing some reading up on how to deal with these horrors that are happening to us. We could join the *Mujeres Libres*. The group aims to represent women's liberation. They don't do battle with men, but neither do they believe that women should be ruled by them. They claim we are equal and should have the same education and opportunities as men, be their partners, in fact. What do you say to that?'

A great cheer went up as my women friends eased their aching backs to wave their fists in the air. I laughed, delighted with their response, and the washing was completely abandoned as everyone gathered closer to hear more details.

'Some view them as anarchists as they want what is right for everyone, not just an exclusive minority who rule through an authoritarian state. They are providing day-care centres, setting up classes for women to train as nurses at the front, and an emergency clinic to treat those injured in the fighting. They are also teaching those women who missed out on education to read, in a bid to empower them.'

'Is there a group in Almeria?' my friend Lorena asked.

'There is. I could ask if someone would come and talk to us. I believe they are holding target practice sessions for women who want to learn how to shoot. I've no wish to do that, but I'd like to know how we can help our militia in what is rapidly turning into a civil war. And supply food or clothing to the soldiers on the front line. Is anyone else interested in helping?'

Hands shot up all round, including the older women who were willing to offer their support in some way, even if they weren't prepared to nurse at the front, or brandish a gun. I was suddenly filled with new hope. It felt good to believe I could do something positive for those men who had escaped execution and were fighting for the Republic. Would this be the way to take revenge upon the devastation that had hit our village, and fight for the women and children of Spain as well my own independence?

ᕲᕫ

'Oh, my goodness, what a challenge that must have been,' Jo said. 'And did you succeed? Please tell me that you kept safe and none of your family were injured.'

'Fortunately, we did, but let us take a little walk as I feel stiff with sitting so long.'

ᕲᕫ

They took a stroll over to the almond grove where Anton was checking the state of the nuts. 'How beautiful they are,' Jo said, admiring the long rows of trees. He looked pretty handsome himself too, came the thought at the back of her head.

He gave her a bewitching smile. 'Even more so at the beginning of the year when they herald the start of spring with their blossom. In Greek mythology the *almendros*, as we Spanish call them, are said to represent a beautiful princess who was abandoned at the altar by her fiancé on her wedding day. After dying of a broken heart, the gods turned her into a leafless almond tree. When her lover returned and found what had happened to her, he embraced the tree and it burst into bloom. Ever since, the almond tree is considered to be a symbol of hope.'

'Oh, what a sad but lovely story,' Jo said, thinking how she would not be against enjoying an embrace herself from this man. 'I'd love to come again in the spring to see them in bloom.'

'We'd love to have you,' he said, his amber eyes sparkling. There was something in the way he looked at her which set her pulse racing. Steadying her breathing, which for some reason had quickened, Jo concentrated on asking a more practical question. 'So how do you know when they are ready for picking?'

'When at least three-quarters of the hulls ripen sufficiently to split and reveal the almond shell, within which is the nut. We can't leave them too long otherwise the birds will get there first and steal them. As you can see, we put a tarpaulin beneath the trees and knock the nuts off with a pole. Then the hulls are removed by machine and the nuts left to dry. We start with the outer branches and work our way in over the coming weeks. It's a long and hot process.'

'Could I help?'

He smiled. 'If you wish, but as you are only here for a short time it would be more sensible for you to concentrate on your investigation. I think we could now show *mi abuela* the photo you found, as she seems a little better today.'

'What photograph is that?' Rosita asked, coming over to join them.

'It's quite a tragic picture of a woman. We were wary of upsetting you but wondered if you recognise her.' Pulling the photo from her bag, Jo was appalled to see all colour drain from Rosita's face.

'I wasn't aware this picture existed. Yes, indeed I do know this lovely lady. This is Charlotte facing the firing squad.'

'Oh no! I was so hoping it wasn't her. Is this letter from her too?' Jo asked, filled with sympathy as she handed it over. 'I didn't wish to upset you with this either, so kept putting the moment off.'

The old lady read the letter with tears in her eyes, avoiding meeting Jo's gaze, perhaps because the pain was all too much for her. 'I remember her letters well.'

'I assume you never discovered where her body might be buried. But if during the course of our investigation into the picture we find a clue as to where it is, I'll certainly let you know. Then you could give her a proper burial in the *cementerio*.'

Rosita looked away, sadly silent as she handed the letter back, and bidding them *buenas noches* returned to the house, claiming to be tired. She was probably too upset to talk any more.

Jo's heart too filled with sadness, if with very little hope of being able to fulfil this heartfelt wish.

Anton turned to her with a smile. 'Thanks for your patience and friendship. You're a very kind young woman, which is possibly why *mi abuela* seems to be willing to speak about a subject she has so long avoided.'

Jo found herself flushing at the compliment, relieved not to have caused any offence by asking Rosita to tell her story. 'Sometimes it's easier talking to strangers who accept what you are saying without question, rather than with family where there is often a great deal of emotion involved.'

He laughed. 'That may well be the case, certainly so far as my father is concerned. He can never keep quiet long enough to listen to anyone properly, not even his own mother or me, his son.'

Jo was laughing with him now. 'Mine is just the same. It must be a man thing.'

'I sincerely hope not. But thank you for helping her.'

'It's me who should be thanking Rosita. I'm most grateful for all she's telling me.' And as he gently took her arm and offered to show how they dealt with the hulls, a warm glow spread through her. What a lovely man he was. Jo began to feel that the *almendros* were proving to be a symbol of hope for her too.

TWENTY
SPAIN — 1937

CHARLOTTE COULD hardly breathe beneath the clutter of stones, dust and rubble, the stink of cordite, seared flesh and smoke almost choking her. The heat made her eyes burn and her vision blur. Was a fire starting up somewhere? Unable to move or escape, terror overwhelmed her as the building violently shook. Would she be burned alive in this pit of blasted bricks? Not that she could hear any flames crackling, but then the world around her had fallen completely silent. Had she gone deaf? She saw the charred outline of an arm mere inches away. Whether or not it was still attached to a body she couldn't tell. Could that be her own arm blown off? Clenching each hand in turn, Charlotte felt a surge of relief that she was still in one piece, or so she hoped. She felt something running down her leg, was it water or blood? Or had she pissed in her pants? How long had she been lying here trapped in this hole? If she wasn't burned to death she might die of internal bleeding or injuries caused by flying pieces of glass or stones. She opened her mouth to call for help but nothing came out, something seemed to be blocking her throat. Was it blood? Her tongue felt sore and swollen. Had she bitten it off in the shock of the bombing? But then darkness pressed in on her once again.

The sound of a voice calling to her from some far-distant place woke her the next time.

'*¡Digame! ¡Digame!*' And as Charlotte opened her eyes the voice said, '*¡Gracias a Dios!*'

Stones being lifted from her, the lessening of weight upon her pain-wracked body, and the feel of a fresh wind fluttering over her hot skin brought tears of relief running down her cheeks. Charlotte found herself gazing into the softest grey eyes she'd ever seen, the blur of a face smiling down at her. Could this be an angel? Then she was being lifted up – carried to heaven?

'Am I alive?' she asked in English, to which there was no reply.

Moments later she was being settled comfortably on a bed where friendly nurses and doctors at once began to check her for injuries. She thanked God too, and this wonderful man, whoever he might be.

❧

'*¿Quiere usted comer?*' It was that same voice again, the warm familiarity of it rippling through her, lifting her from a horror-filled sleep, just as it had done before. In spite of the sleeping tablets the doctor had given her, echoes of the bomb, the screams and crashes, the shock of stones falling upon her, heightened by the fear of being burned or buried alive, had caused her to yell out during the night, bringing the nurses running to waken her from a nightmare. The terror induced by that bomb still resonated within. Charlotte doubted it would ever leave her.

Now she opened her eyes to focus upon the face of the man who had rescued her. Not an angel, after all. His eyes were the soft grey she remembered. Chestnut brown hair, cut quite short, sprouted haphazardly above a face that was not classically handsome but held a definite allure, being beautifully toned and olive-skinned, his mouth quirked up at the corners into an appealing smile. He was studying her now with a slightly puzzled expression as she gently shook her head. Speaking in halting Spanish, too desperately tired for her brain to be working clearly, Charlotte attempted to answer his question.

'*No gracias, no quiero comer.* I don't wish to eat. The nurses fed me porridge some hours ago. All I could manage.'

'*Muy bien,*' he said. '*¿Qué tal?*'

'I'm feeling much better, thank you,' she said in English, and then again remembering her Spanish, asked his name in what she deemed to be a polite manner. *¿Cómo se llama usted?*'

'Guillermo Abana Martínez.' He grinned at her. '*Para usted, Guillermo, por favor.*'

'Pleased to meet you, Guillermo. I'm Charlotte, or some friends call me Charlie.' The conversation continued in simple Spanish as she thanked him for rescuing her, asking what had happened to the doctor and patient she was with at the time of the bombing. He told her the doctor had fortunately survived, but the poor lady on the operating table had not. The young man sorrowfully explained that many people had lost their lives, as the part of the education building used as a hospital was now a heap of rubble. 'I owe you my life,' she said, tears sliding down her cheeks.

He gently wiped them away with his thumb. '*Usted es una mujer muy valiente.*'

'Not brave at all.'

'*Tengo mucha suerte de haberte conocido.*'

There was a small silence then, as if he was meaning so much more than the fact he felt lucky to have found her. And wasn't she the lucky one? The intensity of the moment flickered through her, making her feel truly alive again. The young man got to his feet, speaking softly in Spanish. 'You have friends waiting outside. I was honoured to be allowed the first visit of the day, but I shall leave you now so they can come in.'

'You will come back tomorrow, won't you?' she asked, panic in her voice at the thought of not seeing him again.

His nod was brief but accompanied by a smile that warmed her. '*Sí, con mucho gusto.*'

She watched him walk away, a conflict of sadness and joy in her heart.

~

Libby rushed to put her arms around her friend, hugging her tight. 'Oh Charlie, we thought we'd lost you.'

'Never.' Charlotte smiled. 'I don't give up on life so easily.'

'You certainly haven't lost your sense of humour,' Laurence said with a chuckle, as he gave her a hug too. 'And you're looking pretty good, as beautiful as ever, old thing. Nothing seriously wrong, I hope?'

Watching the embrace Libby felt her usual prickle of unease. Charlotte did indeed still look lovely, despite the pallid appearance of her skin. Laurence had been utterly devastated when he'd learned of the bombing, and had insisted on buying her a bunch of flowers, which he was now handing to her, kissing her cheek most fondly as she smiled sweetly up at him. Did he love Charlie more than he was prepared to admit?

'Plenty of cuts and bruises but I am at least alive and beginning to feel human again. Well, almost,' Charlotte said, brushing away tears and giving a little shrug. 'I was fortunate to be rescued when so many others were not. I think it has made me yet more determined to do my bit to help people, to make a difference in this war. But tell me how you two got on. Did you find Nick?'

Pulling up chairs, Libby exchanged a glance with Laurence as if sharing a secret, and then leaning closer began to tell their story. 'The lawyer firmly told the authorities that they had nae decent evidence.'

'And as the police refused to investigate further we decided to do some of our own,' Laurence said. 'We talked to Nick's comrades and learned that after a drunken night at a bar in town, they'd witnessed a couple of fellows riffling the pockets of dead bodies found in the street following a bomb blast close by.'

'They were known tae be troublemakers,' Libby put in, 'and Nick and his mates attempted tae stop the thieving.'

Laurence nodded. 'Unfortunately, when the police arrived on the scene the two perpetrators and Nick's pals had fled. So Nick was the one arrested, as he was the only person still around.'

'That was because he'd been attempting tae revive someone he believed still tae be alive,' Libby said, in defence of her brother. 'Of course, the language problem prevented him from being able tae properly defend himself, and he wasna offered a lawyer.'

'We did, however, manage to find the names of the men responsible, whereupon the lawyer explained the full story to the police, and all charges were dropped. Nick is a free man.'

'Oh, that's wonderful,' Charlotte cried. 'Thank goodness for that, and it couldn't have happened at a better time. Had the pair of you not been out speaking to the lawyer and conducting your own investigations, you would both have been on the ward and might well have been killed.' Tears again rolled down her cheeks.

'Hush now, dinna fash yerself, Charlie. We know,' Libby softly murmured, deeply moved by her friend's anguish. 'We have been so lucky.'

In an attempt to cheer up both women, Laurence grasped their hands. 'Let's think positive. The number of casualties could have been far worse. The rebels are not finding it easy to conquer Madrid.

This latest battle hasn't achieved the success Franco wanted. I doubt the war is anywhere near over as he's bound to try again, here in Madrid and elsewhere, but we'll be there to help wherever and however we can. Right?'

'Right!' both girls agreed.

'Absolutely topping. All for one and one for all,' he brightly responded, making them giggle. And the three friends raised their hands in unison as if swearing a pact.

'Where that might be is still open tae question,' Libby said, gently easing her husband free of Charlotte's hold. 'Finding a safe place to move the hospital to will no be easy. But you stay right where ye are, Charlie milady, until ye're feeling better.'

'I'll be up and about in no time. You can be sure of that,' she stoutly responded. But then closed her eyes as exhaustion overwhelmed her yet again.

ᡣᠥ

Leaving Charlotte, with some regret, Libby kept a firm hold of Laurence's hand as they picked their way through the ruins of bombed buildings. They took great care to keep an eye out for Franco's Moroccan *regulares* who could suddenly appear out of nowhere and start a street fight.

It had been a great relief to see that Charlie hadn't been too badly injured, but a part of her almost wished she'd been the one caught in the bomb blast. Maybe then Laurence would have appreciated how much he truly loved her. She so wanted their marriage to work and be worthwhile, and for him to make love to her as was normal in a marriage. That way she could at least then try for another child one day. But sharing a tent had not been possible. Libby knew there was no hope of sharing a room with him either at the temporary accommodation allotted to them following the bombing. On impulse she decided to address the problem they'd ignored for far too long. She began by offering her heartfelt thanks for his help in finding her brother.

'I canna find the words tae express my gratitude. You were wonderful, Laurence darling. I could never have managed it without you. I do love ye, I hope ye know that.'

'And I love you, old thing.'

Pulling him into a doorway Libby grabbed his tousle of hair to draw his face to hers and start to kiss him, her mouth opening, longing for him to plunder it. But his kiss was brief, sweet and tender, not at all passionate. Looking up at him, her expression filled with disappointment, she asked, 'What is the problem, Laurence? Why will ye no make love tae me?'

'I say, old sport, this isn't the place for such intimacy,' he said with an embarrassed little laugh, glancing about him at the barbed wire hooked around broken buildings, and the sight of people rummaging through heaps of rubble searching for remnants of their lost possessions, or their dead children. 'In any case, how could we ever have managed it, surrounded by our friends?'

'Where is the right place, then? There's rarely any moment we're alone these days, and when we do have the opportunity, ye dinna take it. Ye've hardly touched me in all the weeks we've been married, not even when we *were* sleeping together back home in Scotland. Why? Are ye certain ye love me? Mebbe ye regret having tae settle for an idiot farm wench, instead o' beautiful Charlotte.'

'You know that's not the case. You weren't well when first we tied the knot, and then came this war which means we're both overloaded with work, exhausted, and never alone.'

Libby sighed with frustration. 'But once I'd recovered from whatever that sickness was, ye claimed tae be too tired even when ye weren't working. And judging by the visits some of the soldiers make to certain houses in the city, I'd say other men dinna allow war tae hinder their needs, so why do *you*? Can we no find some place, some time, tae actually give it a go? If ye truly love me, why would ye no wish to?' She was begging him now, such anguish and pleading in her tone that his face became suffused with a flush of what she could only assume to be guilt.

'To be honest, I think I must have some health issues. I don't find it easy to reach the necessary degree of . . .' He paused, as if searching for the right word.

'Desire?' Libby suggested, her tone icy.

'No, that's not what I meant. Erection. I must have a problem. We could try, I suppose,' he said. But the doubt in his tone made her curl up inside with fresh agony.

'You dinna love me at all, do ye?' she snapped. 'Ye just married me on the rebound because Lady bloody Charlotte had rejected you.' And spinning on her heel she marched away.

TWENTY-ONE

HAVING SET UP a new hospital in an old school building on the outskirts of Madrid, they were celebrating Burns Night on 25 January 1937. Christmas had been something of a damp squib despite the Brigaders and volunteers enjoying a special meal of roast chicken and mashed potatoes, followed by oranges, dried fruit, nuts and cheese. But as a result of the bombing no one had been in the mood for jollities. Now, feeling a desperate need to boost morale, this latest event was welcomed by everyone, not just the Scottish.

Charlotte smiled as she watched Guillermo sit tapping his feet in time to a Scottish reel.

'I'm really enjoying myself,' he said, his gaze flicking over her with warm affection, which made her heart quiver with happiness. 'Me too,' Charlotte said, looking around with pride and noting how the Scots were all beautifully attired in kilts and plaids. These were often connected with a particular clan to which the wearer belonged. Some of the women wore shawls over their skirts or dresses. And there was dear Libby clad in her favourite kilt and black Glengarry bonnet, although she'd replaced the tatty old army jacket she usually wore with a smart warm plaid on this occasion.

'My friend has made a huge bread and butter pudding for *postre*,' she told him. 'She so loves to provide hard-working Brigaders with a treat whenever she can.'

Guillermo grinned. 'I look forward to it, even if I don't know what it is.'

Charlotte laughed. It was proving to be a fun night with plenty of songs, Scottish reels and, of course, poetry, not least that written by Robert Burns himself.

Libby proceeded to explain the tradition to the English and foreigners present, and Charlotte quickly translated her words for their new Spanish friends. 'Usually the haggis is carried in to the sound of the bagpipes, and placed on the table while someone reads the ode "Address to a Haggis" written by the bard himself. Then it is ceremonially sliced and the meal begins.'

As they'd been unable to find any haggis, or the ingredients to make one, the Brigaders had to make do with sardines and mashed potatoes, or tatties as the Scots called them. So the piper played to the dishes of sardines instead, among much laughter and applause.

'Och, we havna had so much fun since we were bairns, have we laddie?' Libby said, giving her brother a hug. 'Go on, you read it, Nick, in honour of your recent release.'

Grinning, he stood up, wrapped his plaid about himself and began to recite the poem, carefully pronounced in clear English so that everyone could understand:

'*Fair and full is your honest, jolly face . . .*'

Many joined in, some in true Scottish dialect, their voices fusing into a glorious tumult of sound. The poem finished with an applause of joyful appreciation. Feeling great admiration for how her old friend had organised this event so well, Charlotte too joined in, managing to remember some of the words.

There was no Scotch whisky, and many of the English Brigaders would have preferred a pint of beer, but that wasn't available either.

For those who were not teetotal, they instead relished a glass of Spanish wine or cognac. Some indulged in a little too much wine as it turned out to be an uproariously lively celebration, which lasted well into the night. Charlotte kept safely to water.

'It is so good to be able to spend time with you, knowing that you are fully recovered,' Guillermo told her. His smile was tender but also exciting, seeming to indicate how their relationship was quickly developing into a deliciously close friendship.

'I'm just fine, thanks to your well-timed rescue.' Not that this was the only reason she was growing increasingly attracted to this man. He was kind and caring, and fun to be with, and really quite good-looking now she'd recovered sufficiently to see him properly. Spending time together seemed to be the most natural thing in the world, as if she'd been waiting for him all her life.

Whenever he was out fighting in some skirmish or battle, Charlotte found herself waiting anxiously for his return, her thoughts consumed by worry for him. The moment Guillermo was back at base, he would come right away to assure her that he was safe. At first she would simply nod and smile shyly by way of response, then she'd reach for his hand to eagerly shake it in relief.

On one occasion after a particularly dangerous battle when he was late returning, Charlotte had been so terrified she might never see him again that when he did finally appear she'd flung herself into his arms to give him a hug of delight. It had not taken long after that for those hugs to turn into a sweet embrace, combined with a tender kiss or two, if at first only on each cheek in true Spanish style.

He would take every possible opportunity to come and chat with her, if about nothing in particular. Generally in Spanish, although Guillermo was already picking up some English, with Charlotte's assistance. But just as she helped him, he corrected her

Spanish, sometimes with an amused chuckle when she made a mistake but always with patience and generosity.

Charlotte found him utterly fascinating, and could barely take her eyes off his uptilted mouth, which always appeared to be on the verge of a smile. And she ached to run her fingers through the tufts of his chestnut hair. He came from Andalucía, and was neither Communist nor Fascist, seeing himself more of a moderate, a man who loved his country and was passionate about democracy. He was political but at heart seemed to be a gentle, quiet sort of man.

'Tell me about your home and family,' she asked him now.

'I'm part of a large Catholic farming family who have suffered terrible tragedy already in this dreadful war. I could take you to meet them when we head south, those that are left, that is.' He told her then how his father and elder brothers had been massacred by the Falange party, along with many other men in the village. As Charlotte stared at him, speechless with shock, he took her hand and kissed it.

'That is why I am here, to fight on their behalf. I lost my uncle Manolo too, and cousin Fernándo, who were killed on the same night. My young brother Pedro helps my aunt and her daughters with the work on the farm whenever he can, although he's busy supporting our mother too. His childhood has abruptly ended.'

He paused, and unable to find the right words to express her horror, she gave his hand a gentle squeeze. 'I'm so sorry.'

'You'll like my cousin Rosita. As a young girl she was great fun but she too has had to grow up pretty quickly, and be very strong-willed in order to cope. She's working hard on the land as well as caring for her mother and sisters, and has joined the *Mujeres Libres*. I think her strong reaction to the tragedy proves how wrong the authorities have been all these years to treat women as inferior beings. From what I hear in letters from my mother, the only thing she did wrong, following the grief and panic of losing her father and brother, was to rush into marriage far too young. I'm sure she would welcome you as a friend.'

'I look forward to meeting her.' Charlotte was delighted to have learned so much about him.

He kissed her hand again. 'That is enough talk of the war and sad events. Tonight we must enjoy ourselves.' He nodded in the direction of the dancers, laughing as most of them were men, some tottering from the wine they'd drunk as they jigged about in the reel, but all having a jolly time. 'It looks fun, could you teach me how to do this dance?'

'I'd be delighted.' The rest of the evening passed in a blur of pleasure. It seemed that every day brought them closer together, whether they were sharing the agonies of war or just enjoying some fun and laughter.

Oh, but how she longed for so much more from him than that.

∾

The day came when finally he asked her out on a date. 'I wondered if you would you like to go into Madrid to the pictures some time?' he asked, with a slight bow of his head.

'Oh, yes please,' Charlotte said, seeing this as the answer to her dreams. 'Haven't been to the flicks since before we left home,' and she told him about the film, *The Thirty-Nine Steps*, they'd seen and how it had been the British Pathé News which had inspired them all into coming to Spain. 'It would be good to go out and be sociable for a change.'

Life as a Brigader was not easy, often dreadfully dull and boring. There was a small library of books available, and the men would play games such as chess and football, which were ever popular, patients and medical staff all happily joining in. A group had even formed a choir, encouraging everyone to join in and sing along.

Sometimes, the hospital would be visited by a travelling picture show or a lively band, actors would put on a play for them, or there would be a poetry reading night. Classes in Spanish were also regularly held. Every effort was made to keep morale high.

Brigaders were paid one pound per week, although there was little to spend it on besides booze and cigarettes. When they ran out of money they would try smoking leaves, which didn't always do them any good at all. On this evening a large group of them travelled into town in the back of an army truck, to sit among the local Spanish at the pictures. Even though Charlotte and Guillermo would not be alone, it was such a thrill that he'd asked her out.

The film was in Spanish. Charlotte could follow quite a bit of the dialogue, but lost track of the story as she was far more engrossed by the warmth of Guillermo's body seated close beside her. Taking her hand in his he stroked a thumb over her knuckles, which set her senses racing. And when he slipped his arm about her shoulders, something inside her skittered with desire. It felt wonderful to feel the brush of his thigh against hers, and his warm breath against her cheek, a wave of delight spreading through her.

Every now and then they would be reminded of reality by the clap and crash of shells going off outside the picture house. Nobody moved, the audience remaining completely absorbed by the film and amazingly pragmatic, as the defiant Spanish tended to be.

For Charlotte, simply being with Guillermo was like a golden ray of sunshine lighting up her life. Just the way he looked at her made her feel as if she was floating on cloud nine. As he gently tilted her face up to kiss her, with considerably more passion this time, Charlotte knew in her heart that she was falling in love with this man. But did he feel the same way about her? Oh, she really did hope so.

Days later it was Valentine's Day, and Guillermo came to her while Charlotte was making the patients' beds to present her with a posy of Bermuda buttercups. 'Sorry, but it's the only flower I could find. A wild weed that invades the heart of agricultural land everywhere.'

Smiling, she accepted the bunch of pretty yellow flowers with a shimmer of joy lighting her heart within. 'I think you've invaded mine too. I've drawn you a picture on a postcard, but haven't put any name on it, so that you won't guess who it's from.'

He grinned at her. 'Thank you, that's lovely. How talented you are. And I would have been very hurt had you forgotten me.'

TWENTY-TWO

USILY MAKING beds at the opposite side of the room, Libby watched in stunned surprise as her friend accepted the flowers and gave Guillermo a quick kiss. They were speaking in Spanish, so she wasn't entirely certain what they were saying, but the attraction between them was plain to see. As they walked away, still laughing and kissing, she felt filled with envy. She'd been hoping for a similar expression of love from her husband, preferably in physical terms. Following the bombing when she'd confronted Laurence over the lack of lovemaking in their marriage, he'd promised to at least try. One night she'd been thrilled when he'd taken her into his arms and led her to his empty tent, where they'd snuggled inside his sleeping bag. At last, she'd thought with delight as he'd begun to stroke and kiss her.

'You taste so sweet,' he'd murmured, as he licked her nipple with his tongue. 'I'd like to eat you all up.'

Libby had giggled with delight. 'I think ye'd find me a wee bit chewy. I'm a tough, hard-working, no-nonsense farmer's lass, remember.'

'Which is what I've always loved most about you. Don't ever change. But your breasts are deliciously soft, so I'll start with those.'

Her laughter, as he'd continued to smooth kisses over the flat of her stomach and downwards, soon changed to cries of ecstasy as Libby's emotions skittered out of control. Then he was inside her and within seconds, or so it seemed, it was all over. She'd cried out, from disappointment rather than sated passion, as she'd wanted it to go on for so much longer.

Had she failed him in some way, or expected too much? This might have been Laurence's first time since he'd led such a sheltered life, and it wasn't the most romantic setting as they were engaged in a war. If that was the case then he would surely improve with practice, and their lovemaking would last longer next time. He'd let out a sigh, presumably of contentment, and almost instantly fell asleep with his arm still around her. Libby had felt a huge sense of relief. It had not been perfect, but thankfully they had now consummated their marriage.

However, he hadn't touched her since.

She'd held great hopes that things would improve on Valentine's Day. She'd waited hours for some gift or card, hoping he'd come looking for her and suggest they take a walk for a little privacy. Thus far he seemed far more interested in chatting with Fergus and the other Brigaders, as well as sharing cigarettes with them. The sound of their laughter had haunted her for the entire morning. It was as if he'd forgotten all about her.

Was that because she did not possess Charlotte's beauty, still evident even when milady was dressed in scrubby overalls and muddy boots? Libby was wearing her usual kilt, thick woollen stockings and an old khaki jacket upon which she'd embroidered a few thistles. Did her appearance not excite Laurence in any way? She wondered if he even remembered what day it was.

It was Ray who sneaked up behind her to give her a quick hug and whisper, 'Happy Valentine's Day.'

'Behave,' she giggled. 'Someone might see us.'

'Then let's meet someplace. I want you, Libby.'

'How can we do that? And where?'

'In the woods just beyond the camp. No one will see us there. Please allow me to demonstrate how much I adore you.'

As his hands secretly explored her waist and back, sneakily brushing over her breasts, a wave of desire flooded through her. Why should she hold back? Who else could she turn to for such pleasures? Certainly not her own husband. Laurence might have finally done his duty that night, some weeks ago, but not once sought to repeat it.

Laurence or Ray Dunmore? Whom did she truly love? She really had no idea, but needed someone to lift her heart, particularly in the middle of this dratted war.

'I'll meet ye at three this afternoon, after dinner,' she whispered, walking away keeping her chin aloft, as if they'd just had a disagreement and not agreed to enjoy a romantic tryst.

⁂

The battalion was currently stationed south of Madrid in the Jarama Valley, facing machine-gun fire in yet another bloody battle. The result had been thousands of casualties on all sides, in both the Nationalist and Republican armies, as well as the International Brigade. The Fascists seemed to have achieved little by way of advance, thanks to the strength of their enemy, but life as a volunteer had become harder than ever.

More often than not meals comprised simply soup, beans or rice. Local Spaniards would often bring them food, out of gratitude, but the men would regretfully decline as they were appalled by the poverty these people were suffering. Fortunately, there was generally a good selection of fresh fruit growing nearby. Strawberries, oranges, tomatoes, peaches, plums or cherries, all of which could be picked from trees or the fields. Meat, however, was a rarity. There'd been none to eat for weeks now. Knowing how restless and exhausted the men were, and requiring some sort of excuse to leave the camp, Libby marched over to the cooks and spoke sharply to them.

'As a farmer's daughter I know it's vital that hard-working men be given plenty of protein, particularly soldiers. You canna fight a war on an empty stomach, so why do ye no do something aboot it?'

'How?' snarled the chief cook. 'Would you like me to start breeding pigs?'

'I perfectly understand that's no possible as we keep moving aboot, but mebbe some of the local farmers breed them. And this is wild boar country, so I'm sure many will go oot hunting too. Ye should go and ask them.'

The chief cook looked at her with the kind of shocked expression that indicated he thought her completely mad. 'Why would we consider venturing out of camp? It's not our job to take such a risk.'

Libby waved a furious fist in his face. 'Then I'll go and ask someone myself,' she said, and stormed away. Selfish cowards the lot of them, she thought. What was so difficult about visiting a neighbouring farm less than a few hundred metres away, just down the road? Didn't she meet their neighbour recently at a local market? She'd go and have a word with him right now. Then once she and Ray had enjoyed their little get-together, they'd go and speak to a few more local farmers and see if they could come to some sort of deal. A supply of pork, or eggs, would be wonderful. Something had to be done to improve the food, and who knew better than she how to go about it?

'Where's Libby?' Charlotte asked, some hours later.

Laurence looked startled by the question. 'I thought she was with you.'

Charlotte shook her head, suddenly feeling a stir of unease. 'When did you see her last?'

'Just after luncheon. She went to talk to the cook, but I haven't seen her since.'

It took only a few questions of the kitchen staff for them to discover where Libby had gone. Laurence's expression was one of complete horror, and he began to shake with fear. 'Did you hear the guns going off this afternoon? I assumed it to be another skirmish, but what if the Moorish mercenaries have captured her? We have to go and find her. *Now!*' He set off at a run, and it took both Charlotte and Guillermo to wrestle him to the ground and restrain him while a search party was rallied to help.

Dunmore also appeared shocked by this news, although said not a word as he quickly volunteered to join the search. Many other comrades also joined the group and they set forth fully armed. More than an hour later they found Libby lying in the woods, a bullet hole in her shoulder, surrounded by a pool of blood.

Having lost so much blood Libby remained sunk in a coma for some days. Charlotte sat by her bed in complete anguish, fearing her old friend might not survive. How they had suffered from being caught up in the terrors of this war. Could even worse happen, and would any of them survive? It was a horrifying thought. When finally Libby blinked and opened her eyes, Charlotte leaped up to kiss and hug her. 'Oh, thank goodness, you're back with us, darling.' She quickly sent this good news to the entire battalion, which brought forth huge sighs of relief all round. But everyone was still deeply concerned for her.

'She should go home,' Laurence anxiously stated, sounding unusually firm. 'We aren't able to give her the necessary care and attention here that she desperately needs.'

'You're quite right,' Charlotte agreed. 'A full recovery will take time. And as more equipment and supplies are necessary for the Brigaders and the hospital, I'll take her, if you like. I wrote to Mama some time ago asking if she'd be prepared to continue to raise more funds in our absence, and she readily agreed that she would. Let's hope she's managed to do so, then I'll take the opportunity to restock.'

Ray stepped in at this point. 'You women should not travel alone, nor drive back across the Pyrenees in the truck to transport supplies. It will be quicker and safer if I go.'

'My wife's safety is none of your concern,' Laurence snapped, and the two men glared at each other in cold fury. Now it was Nick's turn to intervene.

'She's my sister. I'll be the one to tak' her home.'

Charlotte rushed to support him, sensing an argument could erupt at any moment between these two rivals for Libby's affection. 'I'd say that's the best plan as he deserves a spell of leave too, having spent time in a prison. Why don't Nick and Laurence take her by train? We still need that truck for transport here. Hopefully Mama will have raised sufficient funds to buy another to bring back fresh supplies. Then you can drive back together when you're ready, leaving dear Libby safe in her parents' care. Your ma and pa would love to see you too, Nick. It's been so long, and they've been very worried about you.'

'Aye,' he agreed with a grin. 'And I'd love tae see them too.'

The thought sprang into Charlotte's head how much she would love to see her own mother, as she missed her dreadfully, although she really had no wish to meet up with the laird. Not ever. She could at least write Mama a letter.

So it was decided.

But when Charlotte explained to Libby what they'd arranged, her friend protested strongly. 'I dinna want tae leave,' she sobbed.

'I want to stay here with you, and Ray . . .' She glanced down the ward where he was standing talking to her husband. 'And Laurence too, of course.'

'Laurence will be with you, as will Nick. Think of the joy of taking your lovely twin brother home to your parents, having successfully rescued him from prison. Isn't that what they wanted you to do?'

'Och aye, they'll be so thrilled.'

'And why would you miss Ray? Is there something you aren't telling me, darling?' Charlotte asked, with a puzzled frown.

'I was meaning to name everybody, not just Ray. Guillermo, Fergus, everyone.' Then she added, as if as an afterthought, 'And there's work still tae do here. I dinna want to go home yet.'

'You must concentrate on getting well first, Libby darling. We'll all still be busily occupied doing our bit, you can be sure of that. I feel it in my bones that we'll all remain safe. And I'll be sure to write and let you know if we move on someplace else. But you must make a full recovery before you return to Spain. Understood?'

Libby gave a slow nod and Charlotte couldn't help noticing how her glance again strayed across to Ray as he stood by the door. As if by instinct he lifted his gaze to smile back at her. Was there something going on between them? This did not seem quite the moment to ask, not while her friend was so ill. On the other hand, maybe she should, bearing in mind she might not see Libby again for some weeks.

'There isn't still a problem between you and Laurence, is there? You two are happy?'

'Of course, we're fine and dandy,' Libby snapped, sinking back on to the pillow with a tired sigh. 'Why would we no be happy?'

'And there's nothing else troubling you? Are any of these men bothering you? You can always talk to me, darling. I'm a good listener and your friend.'

'If a wee bit bossy, milady,' Libby said with a low growl, pulling up the blanket and closing her eyes, as if wishing to shut herself away.

Charlotte took that to mean she had overstepped the mark yet again, which was so easy to do with Libby. She'd hoped her friend's sense of inferiority would disappear as they worked together in this war, but clearly it hadn't. And the accusation did feel slightly unfair, considering how she herself had battled against a domineering stepfather for much of her life, dear Mama still stuck with him. But Libby wasn't quite herself at the moment, and probably didn't mean it as an insult. Shrugging the criticism aside, Charlotte chose to respond with a good-humoured giggle. 'I remember my mother saying much the same to me countless times when I was growing up, that I was far too stubborn and independent-minded.'

'Mine would say I tended tae leap into a muddy puddle instead o' stepping round it with caution,' Libby murmured, then after a slight pause, added with a smile, 'Mebbe they were both right. The truth is I got meself into this mess. I was so cross with Laurence for no sending me a Valentine's Day card or bunch of flowers, I agreed tae meet Ray in the woods. But then I went off in search of food for our hungry soldiers, so stupidly put meself in danger.'

'Oh no, why on earth would you take such a risk? I know, out of generosity of heart,' Charlotte said, tactfully making no mention of the arranged tryst. 'You do love to make sure everyone is well fed.'

The two friends gazed at each other with an instinctive knowledge of the agonies each had faced in life and this war, even if they didn't feel able to speak of them in too much detail.

Charlotte gathered Libby in her arms. 'At least you're safe now, and will soon be on the mend. What a relief! We'll miss you, Libby darling, not to mention your bread and butter pudding.' Both chuckling, they held each other close for several long moments before wiping the tears from their eyes to prepare themselves to face whatever might happen next. 'Do take lots of rest as we need you back here with us as soon as you're fit and well. And do give Mama a warm hug from me please.'

'I will, and I'll miss you too.'

Nick and Laurence left for Scotland the very next day, driven to the nearest railway station by Fergus, with Libby tucked safely into a camp bed in the back of the canvas-covered truck. As she watched the vehicle bump down the track, Charlotte was filled with anguish. She would sorely miss dear Libby, and Laurence too. Perhaps she should have gone with them, instead of just sending Mama a letter to assure her that all was well. But then Guillermo's arm slipped around her waist, and leaning against him Charlotte felt a surge of joy that she hadn't left.

PART THREE

TWENTY-THREE
SPAIN — 1986

LISTENING TO THE DEVASTATING story of how those two brave young women had each suffered terrible injuries was heart-rending. Her grandmother's sounded much more serious, and Jo felt desperate to hear of her recovery. But why was Libby naïve enough to trust Dunmore? He was a real piece of work, always chatting up Charlotte, and apparently other women too. He must have constantly betrayed her. It had been a stupid suggestion of his for them to meet up in the woods, far too risky when they were living through such dangerous times.

Of course, Jo knew how easy it was to be fooled by a good-looking man. It had been equally naïve of her to trust in Felix. His self-obsession had not only destroyed their relationship but also deprived her of a considerable sum of money. A situation that presented enormous problems for the future. Her father too had left home with barely a backward glance, being a very restless man who could not stay in one place for more than five minutes. He had told her to concentrate on living life as she wished, and having suffered so much hurt that was something Jo fully intended to do. She would hang on to her independence and keep a safe distance from this Spanish fellow. But she really had no right to be sitting around feeling sorry for herself. These women had suffered far worse.

How badly did Dunmore's betrayal and the proclivities of her husband affect Libby? Did she truly love either of them or was she simply seeking happiness, wishing to increase her status in the community, or else demanding attention as she'd tended to do throughout her life? The local hairdresser was booked to call every week to wash and blow-dry Gran's hair. A beautician came once a month to deal with her finger and toenails, and a physiotherapist to give her a regular massage.

But young Libby did sound confused. Jo felt sorry for her ignorance over the cause of her marital problems, which must have made her far too needful. It was so wrong of Laurence to keep a secret of that nature from his wife. Highly unfair and selfish, although she understood he was nervous of being arrested. A dreadful law.

Yet, what courage those two ladies must have had. They were no doubt haunted with fear for the rest of their lives. No wonder Libby had objected to Jo coming to Spain and had refused to accompany her. How could one ever recover from the terrors of war?

It was Thursday and Anton had promised to pick her up around three o'clock to take her to see the art expert. As the time approached, she showered and dressed in a simple lemon cotton dress, not wishing to appear over-dressed. Then, fastening her long fair hair up into a knot to keep her neck cool, Jo rubbed more sunscreen over her skin, as the day was still hot. Last of all she added a touch of pink lipstick and mascara. Did she wish to look a little glamorous, after all?

They drove in companionable silence to the museum, where Anton handed over both pictures for comparison. Jo pointed out that she had no reason to believe hers was a forgery. 'I'm simply intrigued to know if these two pictures are by the same artist, and how my grandmother came by it.'

'Can't help with the latter issue, but can certainly compare them. Were it to be a copy or forgery, it wouldn't be the first,' the expert said with a sad smile. 'Salvador Dalí and Pablo Picasso, among many other famous artists, suffered from this same problem; works typically sold to private art collectors.'

'I'm sure that must be the case.'

'There are three types of forger: the would-be artist who replicates or modifies a famous artist's works. The person who tries to pass it off as genuine, and the idiot who buys the fake, realises their mistake but still sells it on as an original.'

'I assure you I am not any of those people,' Jo said, leaping to her own defence. 'I made no claim about who painted it, so don't believe I've done anything wrong. In addition, the x-ray proved the pigments and canvas were of the same era, and there was no underpainting of an earlier work.'

'I've no doubt you are innocent of such a charge,' he politely agreed. 'Do you have any provenance by way of paperwork that says where and how the picture came to be in your grandmother's possession?'

'I'm afraid not, and Gran refuses to speak of it.' Then remembering the letter they found tucked inside the frame, she pulled it from her bag to show him, watching how his face puckered with sympathy as he read it.

'Ah, so it may indeed have connections with the Civil War. Many artists used paintings to denounce the massacres that were taking place, and the attacks on Spanish cities. They also wished to share the solidarity and courage of ordinary men and women who fought for what they believed in, as well as promote their yearning for foreign aid.'

'So art was used as a form of propaganda?'

'Indeed it was, by both sides. The most famous being *Guernica*, painted by Picasso to show the horrors of aerial bombing and

slaughter of civilians by German bombers. He was appointed director of the Prado Museum in Madrid, which stored its art collection
in the basement for safety, but later they were obliged to send it to
Valencia and Geneva. All were returned to Madrid at the end of
World War Two. These two pictures, however, are much milder in
tone. Leave them with me and I'll see what I can discover.'

Thanking the art expert for his help, they left.

∽

Anton drove slowly over barren humps of mountains set against a
backdrop of the blue Mediterranean lit by the crimson glow of the
setting sun. Here and there Jo could see pockets of white houses
huddled together in a small valley. He pulled up at a restaurant
located in a tiny hamlet. 'Are you ready to eat?' he asked.

'I most certainly am.'

'¡Venga!'

A few goats were wandering about enjoying the evening breezes.
A donkey stood swishing its tail, watching with open curiosity as
they climbed out of the car. Jo couldn't resist going over to stroke
its nose, and the donkey nodded his head in appreciation as she
scratched his neck.

'Isn't he lovely?'

'He is indeed, and no doubt a seasoned veteran, a relic of Spain's
past. *Los burros* used to be everywhere, carrying logs or water jars,
working the land, as well as a means of transport. There are still
some around, if not as many as in the old days. He clearly likes you,'
he said with a chuckle, his own eyes bright with interest.

'Oh, I like him too.' Glancing up into his smiling gaze, Jo
thought how she liked this man, despite her vow to steer clear of
him. 'I can see why Taco was Rosita's best friend.'

'One she badly needed.'

Her first impressions of Anton when she'd met him at the exhibition in Scotland had not been good, but he was really kind and attractive. His skin had a sexy olive tint to it, and his amber brown eyes sparkled with good humour. The aquiline nose, heavy dark eyebrows and chiselled chin might give off a determined look, his voice deep and rasping when he became irritated, but on closer acquaintance she was coming to quite like him. Rather a lot, in fact. Oh dear, and hadn't she promised herself to show no further interest in men?

The meal was delicious. Jo had *ensalada mixta*, followed by *chuletas de cerdo con salsa de hierbas*. Beautifully tender pork chops with a herb sauce, which went down well as she found herself surprisingly hungry. Anton opted for steak.

Jo deliberately kept the conversation light and impersonal, largely confined to the weather, other holidays she'd enjoyed, and a little about her work at the art gallery. She made no mention of Felix, whom she'd totally dismissed from her mind. It was not until they were waiting for their *postre* of ice cream to arrive that she risked asking the question that had been niggling at the back of her mind for some time.

'Is your father still convinced that Libby gave birth to an illegitimate son who she tossed away in a hospital basket?'

'It would seem so.'

'What led him to make such an appalling charge?'

'He'd kept asking his mother for more information about his own father, but she always refused to speak of him.'

'Is that because her husband was very much a Fascist sympathiser?'

Anton gave a philosophical nod. 'Unfortunately it took some time before she explained all of that. Then in an argument they had, *mi abuela* finally confessed that her husband was not in fact his father. Since she had never remarried, *Papá*, who is actually quite a sensitive and morally upright person, preferred to believe the nuns' explanation. That was generally what happened with illegitimate babies, and they told him of this Scottish lady.'

'They could be entirely wrong, even if Libby did return to Spain, once she was well again.'

Anton scowled. 'Are you suggesting the nuns told him a lie?'

'How would they remember exactly what happened back then? They could just be making stupid guesses.'

'So you're saying Rosita committed adultery?'

'These things happen, particularly if you have a cruel husband. It's not a crime.' Attractive and pleasant though Anton undoubtedly was, he was beginning to irritate her.

'It would be so to *Papá*, and in Spain at that time. I really feel quite sorry for him.'

'Oh, for goodness' sake, Rosita is a lovely lady so what does it matter if she did make such a mistake? Your father has no right to put the blame on to my grandmother without proof. Why trust those nuns?'

'Because they are members of the Church,' Anton retorted, his face creased with a frown.

'I believe the Republic was quite hostile towards the Catholic Church, viewing it as a rich landowner with too many privileges in society. So the nuns' attitude could be equally superior and naïve, not necessarily reliable.'

'Are you accusing my father of being the same, simply by believing what they told him?'

'I'm saying that despite their so-called principles, that doesn't make it right for them to accuse my grandmother of something *without proof*!' She felt anger stirring inside her as they glared at each other. Taking a calming breath, she said, 'I wish to speak with them. Can you take me to this convent?'

'If you wish,' he coolly remarked. 'They told my father nothing more as silence is strong within the Catholic community, particularly over such issues. So whether they will agree to speak with *you*, is another matter.'

'I can but hope to persuade them to do so.' The resolution inside her head strengthened as a result of this disagreement. One way or another Jo was determined to prove Libby innocent of such a dreadful crime. And she'd been right to avoid any sort of relationship with a man ever again, she firmly told herself as they drove back in a silence that was far from companionable.

 ❧

Jo's next session with Rosita warmed her heart, making her feel much more relaxed. They sat in their favourite spot beneath the shade of an olive tree, the glorious pink of the oleander in bloom all around them. The peace and quiet of this walled garden in the late afternoon sun was so relaxing that Jo felt as if she could stay here forever. Yet she had little more than a week left in which to discover the results of the inspection of the picture, find out more about Gran's time during the war, not least her recovery, and speak to those nuns.

Anton was not with them today. Could that be because he was avoiding her, following their quarrel, or had he returned to work on the almond harvest? Jo couldn't help but feel a slight guilt over her valiant attempt to defend her grandmother, which might have been a little too argumentative.

'Thank goodness Libby went back to Scotland to receive proper care and treatment. The lives of these Brigaders did not seem to be easy and relationships were complicated. One moment she seemed to be filled with jealousy for Charlotte, and the next swearing to be friends forever, surely not helped by the situation they found themselves in.' Jo had a feeling it might get worse, once Libby learned the truth about her husband. Nevertheless, she felt nothing but admiration for all these forgotten women, including dear Rosita. 'You said you'd tell me more about how you achieved your own independence,' she gently reminded her. 'And as your grandson is not with us, we can talk woman to woman.'

The old lady gave a little chuckle. 'The pair of you do seem to be becoming good friends.'

Jo felt herself blushing. 'I think we are. He's a lovely kind man. Were you still having problems with your husband?'

'Indeed I was. It would be far more accurate to say how I attempted to achieve my independence, which was not easy for a woman in those days.'

'I'm sure it wasn't.'

'In Demetrio's eyes I was a complete failure as a wife. "Why have you still not given me a son?" he would roar at me. It's perhaps the wrong time of the month, I would tell him, which was entirely the wrong thing to say. "Then we'll make sure we find the right one," he snarled, thrusting himself into me with great ferocity each and every night.

'In all honesty, I took great care to protect myself as I had no wish to bear his child. Thanks to my dear mother I learned how to use a little lemon juice in a soft sponge, then a vinegar douche afterwards, a secret I carefully kept from my husband. But I feared that one day he might catch me out before I managed to do that.'

Jo's heart went out to her as she listened to this story. Yet at the back of her mind was the thought that if this smart lady had understood how to protect herself, how could she accidentally have fallen pregnant? Perhaps Gregorio really had been adopted. If so, and a Scottish lady had given birth around that time, could it have been Gran, after all? Presumably Libby returned to Spain at some point, so did she fall pregnant again, thanks to Laurence or Ray? She did hope not. Jo would then be related to Anton, which oddly enough was not a happy thought. But even if she had, Libby would surely never toss her baby away. Dismissing this concern, she smiled with sympathy at Rosita. 'It must have been so difficult to find yourself married to such a control freak. How on earth did you cope?'

'I began to work for the *Mujeres Libres*, without my husband's knowledge, of course. Fortunately Demetrio was generally absent, which was a huge relief to me. I happily provided food from our farm for the fighting men, begging many of our neighbours to donate fruit and vegetables from their own land. Some food was hard to find, but oranges, lemons, plums, tomatoes, peppers, lettuce and, of course, almonds, we had in abundance. I worked hard on the land in order to produce a sufficient quantity.'

'What about the women who didn't farm, how did they help?'

'Some trained as nurses and worked in local hospitals or health centres in place of the nuns who had previously been the only ones to provide nursing care. Friends minding their children while they were working would support them in this task. We all did what we could for our country.'

'I was hoping to go and speak to the nuns soon to ask why they would accuse Gran of tossing away her baby.'

'You'd find out nothing from them,' she quickly responded.

'Do you know the answer?'

Silence fell as Rosita chewed on her lower lip, her eyes focused on some distant place in her head. But when she spoke again it was simply to continue with her own tale. 'As the school in the *pueblo* closed when the teacher went off to fight, I set up an early morning class to teach children to read. To my delight some of their mothers came along too,' she said with a smile. 'I was so grateful to my father for teaching me when I was young. *Papá* had no prejudice against girls being allowed to acquire knowledge, and believed education to be a means of developing self-confidence. I think it also allows women to fight for their place in the world, as *Mujeres Libres* wanted, instead of being held subordinate to men.'

Jo realised Anton had been right when he'd warned her the subject of his father's birth was most definitely taboo. Rosita's silence on the subject appeared resolute. 'Did the Republicans support women's rights?'

'To some extent they claimed to believe in equality. But whatever they might say at meetings, in reality many of the men went home to their wives and forgot all about these so-called principles. Women were still largely ignored, their role in life only to be good wives and mothers, to cook and sew, knit or weave. The few women who did work outside the home were given the lowest-paid menial jobs, their role considered derisory.'

'That's appalling.'

'It's how it was in those days. Men and women lived completely separate lives. Many men were reluctant to be seen walking out with a woman.'

'No wonder you joined the *Mujeres Libres*.'

'*Exactamente*.' Rosita laughed. 'Young as I was, I became so infuriated by this male attitude that I resolved to help make a better world for us women. I took lessons from our leader on how to do that, and gave talks. Then my old friend Lorena and I began visiting factories and workshops to encourage women workers to be more resilient in choosing their own path through life, and build confidence in themselves. We believed that a woman's sense of worth should be encouraged. But then it all went wrong.'

Jo blinked. 'In what way?'

∾

One day Lorena and I were walking home together arm in arm, chatting happily about what we'd achieved that day, as we so liked to do, when I suddenly spotted a figure on the hill above. It was

Demetrio, standing legs astride, arms folded, like Goliath waiting for David.

I grabbed Lorena's hand in panic. 'Oh no, I wasn't expecting him home until tomorrow, but he's arrived early. Where should I say I've been?'

'Tell him you've spent the day helping me spin wool,' she said, giving my cheek a quick peck before scuttling off to her own home. How I wished I could go with her. Instead, taking a deep breath, I approached Demetrio with a smile, reaching up to kiss him too, as any good wife should. 'Sorry I'm a little late, but I'm doing what I can to help deal with this war.'

He flung out a hand and punched me, sending me rolling down the slope for some metres. Before I could recover sufficiently to get to my feet he was upon me, lashing out and beating me in fury.

'You should be at home,' he yelled. 'Why weren't you in the kitchen getting my meal ready?'

'I'm sure it is ready. *Madre* does the cooking while I look after the farm. But today I had other jobs to do. Don't I have that right?'

'You do what I tell you,' he roared. I started to add the tale Lorena had suggested, but he wasn't listening. He was far too engrossed in slapping and kicking me as I lay curled up on the ground, desperately striving to protect myself from his fists and boot. Then grabbing my wrist he dragged me along the path back to the *cortijo*, tossed me on to the bed and once more attempted to make me pregnant. Fortunately, although on that occasion I was not prepared, he failed yet again. For once it really must have been the wrong time of the month.

❧

Tears glittered in her faded old eyes. At that moment Anton arrived, and as he poured a glass of almond liqueur for his grandmother she smiled up at him. 'Ah yes, I could do with something a little stronger than coffee right now, as could Jo, I imagine.'

Jo quickly rose from her seat. 'Better if I leave you in peace, Rosita. I think a rest would be good for you, after such a heart-rending tale.'

'I'm afraid that's true. Come again tomorrow and I'll tell you of how a few days later my cousin Guillermo arrived with lovely Charlotte. What a charming lady she was.'

'Oh, I shall look forward to that.' And giving the old lady a kiss on each cheek, and a little smile to Anton, Jo quickly left. A part of her secretly hoped he might follow her to apologise for their disagreement, and felt disappointed when he made no move to do so. Men could be so stubborn and arrogant, she thought with a scornful sigh.

TWENTY-FOUR
SPAIN – MARCH 1937

CHARLOTTE'S FIRST GLIMPSE of Rosita was of a lovely young girl clad in baggy grey overalls, a bright red scarf wrapped around her head as she dug up potatoes with a spade that looked far too big for her. Taking Charlotte's hand, Guillermo led her carefully between the rows of plants to meet his cousin. Looking up, the girl gave a cry of joy, then flung herself into his arms. They instantly engaged in a rapid conversation in Spanish, far too fast and complicated for Charlotte to understand a word of it. Stepping back she felt a sense of wonderment at how delighted they were to see each other again. They were so fortunate to have such a loving family, something she'd missed out on. Oh, but she did miss her dear mother.

Eventually, Guillermo turned to her with a big grin on his handsome face. 'This is my cousin, Rosita García Díaz, who has kindly offered us shelter in her home.'

'*Gracias*, that would be lovely,' Charlotte said. 'And much appreciated by the Brigaders.'

Tossing aside her spade, Rosita gave her a welcoming hug. 'Guillermo *es hijo del pueblo*,' she said, proudly telling her that he was a son of the village. Charlotte wanted to say that he was also the love of her life, but thought it wise to keep such emotions private at this stage. Guillermo did seem to have a fondness for her, but was it quite the same as she felt for him? She lived in hope.

Tents were quickly put up in the olive grove and the men fell into their sleeping bags, exhausted, many wounded from the latest battles they'd fought. A fire was lit and a huge pan set upon it. Rosita's mother, Estela, began to cook a vegetable stew into which she tossed *bacalao*, dried salted cod. Her three daughters, Rosita, Catrina and Marta, scurried back and forth to fill the plates of the hungry volunteers. Charlotte helped too, since it was part of her job to care for the Brigaders.

As they sat eating together by the fire, Guillermo spoke of the recent traumas they'd faced. 'Feeling we'd done all we could in Jarama, we came south on hearing that with the support of Italian forces, Franco had also taken Malaga.'

'We are aware of that too,' Rosita said. 'Yet until now southern Spain does not seem to have been considered of any importance.'

He shook his head. 'Clearly it is. Many people managed to escape in a destroyer that took them to Gibraltar, but as the ship didn't linger long in port most missed the opportunity. Houses were looted, murder and crime were rampant but some managed to flee into the mountains with the aid of their donkeys. When we arrived the bombing raids were still going on, aircraft clouding the skies, and the roads leading out of the city were packed with refugees desperate to escape, the procession strung out for many kilometres. People were suffering from exhaustion and starvation, having been walking for weeks, their terror all too evident on their worn-out faces. Feet were wrapped in rags to stem the bleeding, children screaming at being flung onto the ground whenever the zoom of an aircraft was heard roaring towards them.'

Charlotte listened in silence, knowing the Brigaders had witnessed the reality of a scene she'd seen on Pathé News back in

Scotland. While she'd been safely hidden in the *sierras* helping to nurse the wounded, her fears for everyone's safety, Guillermo's in particular, had never left her for an instant. And the relief she'd felt when he'd safely returned would never leave her. Later, she'd helped tend the evacuees' wounds and drive them to safety. Her heart still bled at the memory of it.

'As if that wasn't bad enough,' Guillermo was saying, 'warships out at sea were also shooting at them. Whichever way they turned these poor folk faced danger. I rushed to pick up one child who fell when she was hit but she died in my arms.' He paused for a moment as the horror of the moment reverberated in his head. 'We did what we could to help,' he softly finished, 'saving hundreds of children's lives, as well as their parents'. We loaded them into lorries and ambulances and drove them to Almeria. Although how safe they will be in the city, I cannot say, as I believe the Fascists will continue making conquests in order to cash in on their recent successes.'

No more was said on the subject, as it was far too painful. To fill the bleak silence some of the Brigaders began to sing, as they so often did. Rosita and Charlotte joined in, a friendship already beginning to grow between them.

～

It was as they made their way to their tents for a good night's sleep that Charlotte went to put her arms about Guillermo and kissed him. 'It wasn't your fault that child died. I remember you telling me she'd lost a foot and bled to death. At least she was unconscious and didn't feel the pain. And you did find her mother.'

He bleakly nodded. 'She came running over, her other children clutched in her arms or clinging to her skirt. I prefer not to speak of her reaction at finding her baby girl dead. It was beyond words.'

'It's impossible to imagine how it feels to lose a beloved child,' Charlotte agreed. 'Losing anyone you love must be extremely painful.'

He gazed at her with open adoration in his eyes. 'I could never bear to lose you.'

'Nor I you, my darling.'

'If something ever happens to me, Charlotte, know that I have loved you from the moment I pulled you from that bombed building.'

Melting with love for him, she put her arms around his neck and rested her head against his chest, feeling the pounding of his heart. As they kissed, her desire for him exploded within her. Their love for each other was now without question, and aware that each day in this war could be their last, she led him to her tent, where they made love. They surely needed to enjoy each other while they could.

∽

The Olive House, little more than a battered old *cortijo* in the remote mountains of Andalucía, soon became their refuge and small haven. It felt like a sanctuary of peace, a place for the Brigaders to lick their wounds and relax. As well as feeding the men, Estela and her lovely daughters also helped to wash clothes and tend wounds, their assistance gratefully appreciated by all.

Within no time at all Charlotte and Rosita had become firm friends. Charlotte happily accompanied her to collect food from neighbours for the fighting men, drove her to do talks, and helped to dig and weed the land, which she so loved to do. Charlotte felt filled with admiration for her, and the many Spanish women who quietly and pragmatically coped with the difficulties of survival.

Rosita's husband, however, was not so welcoming. 'Do not encourage my wife to spend time away from the house. This is where she belongs,' Demetrio retorted one afternoon when they returned rather late from a meeting.

'We are all working for the same cause,' Charlotte said with a smile, damping down a desire to argue more firmly with him, as he sounded just like the laird.

'It is dangerous out there for women.'

'We're far more resilient than you might expect. Besides, we've only been training women in the village on first aid and how to nurse their wounded husbands. You must be very proud of your clever wife.' And she walked away, arm in arm with Rosita, head held high, all too aware of the fury creasing his face. 'Don't let him browbeat you,' she whispered to her new friend.

Rosita sighed. 'I try not to, but he's not an easy man to disobey.'

'I know the feeling,' Charlotte said with sympathy.

Life was indeed difficult, and really scary at times. There was always the worry they might be captured and find themselves facing possible torture and prison for associating with the Republicans. But at least she now had Guillermo's love to sustain her. Undeterred, and faced with the reality of her own mortality, and her dear friend Libby's too, Charlotte valiantly refused to reveal such fears.

'I have a friend who is being pursued by the local Fascists,' Rosita quietly told her one day. 'They are seeking to arrest her for supporting her Republican husband, who they've already executed. It won't be an easy task but I feel I must help her to escape Spain so that she is safe, and her children too.'

'What does she need?' Charlotte briskly asked.

'Money, food and warm clothing, plus transport down to the quay to find a boat.'

'Right. Are there others requiring help too?'

'Ah *sí*, there are plenty.'

'Then let's sit down and make a plan.'

Thanks to her dictatorial stepfather, Charlotte had long since learned to stand up for herself. Now she was happy to help others, regardless of the dangers involved. Although because of this strong sense of independence she did not find it easy to accept advice, or to ask for help herself. On this occasion as she busily set about organising an escape schedule, it didn't occur to her to mention what she was planning to Guillermo, until he asked what she was up to.

When she explained, he warned her to take care. 'Don't tell a soul what you are doing, and remember you should take some rest after all you've been through.'

'I can't just stand by and do nothing when women are in danger of being arrested simply for supporting their husbands,' Charlotte valiantly responded. 'I believe any so-called "friend" can denounce them just for having voted for the Popular Front. That's dreadful. So if Rosita and I can help them escape, we will.'

'Then I'll help too. Just let me know what you'd like me to do. You're such a beautiful lady, and so strong,' he said, kissing her cheek. '*Muy fuerte.*'

Thinking how much more supportive he was than Rosita's husband, Charlotte fell into his arms and responded to his kiss with vigour.

Not for a moment could she imagine life without him. A whole new future seemed to be opening up before her, one Charlotte could only hope and pray would eventually materialise, once this war was over.

༄

Their rest period did not last long as the Scottish Ambulance Unit was called out to collect many wounded men, women and children who were yet more escapees from Malaga. A large hospital tent was quickly erected and over the weeks following, Charlotte worked harder than ever tending to the wounded. Rosita and her sisters provided the patients and medical staff with water, helped by Taco, of course, and plenty of good food. Sometimes the volunteers worked in nearby towns or villages, rarely in a proper hospital building, more often some shabby old village hall, or a tent, and not all the victims were refugees. Many of them were fighting men from all sides. Following their firm belief in neutrality, the Brigaders never asked a patient to state which party they were a member of.

'I'm not a Republican,' one young man said to her as he lay on a stretcher, waiting his turn to have shrapnel removed. 'Does this mean I've been captured?'

Charlotte smiled at him as she wiped his brow with a damp cloth. 'Why would it? You have the same right to treatment as anyone else. Our supplies and equipment are at an all-time low so it won't be a comfortable procedure, but we'll do all we can to get you back on your feet. Then you can return to the front.'

He barely whimpered as she dug an instrument into his arm to remove the fragments of shells, his soft gaze quietly thanking her. When he departed some hours later, Charlotte gave him a slice of bread and cheese to help him on his way. Watching him go she could but hope that she'd done enough to help, and that the young man did not get an infection as a result of his injuries. Unfortunately, she'd been unable to offer any medication or ointment to help with that.

Not having received a letter from Scotland for some time, Charlotte found herself starting to scribble a list of items needed. She would send this home to her mother and beg her to do more fundraising. Hopefully, Libby would have arrived home safely by now, and be making a good recovery.

Homesickness welled within her, but quickly abated as she saw a young child with a missing arm being wheeled over to the operating table, his mother stroking his ash-white face as the doctor instantly set about saving the boy. Charlotte hurried to help, sending up a silent prayer that the child would survive. Sadly, he didn't, and her heart bled for his distraught mother.

Night had fallen, and despite a long exhausting day yet another young man was placed on the bed she was making. With a lurch of her heart Charlotte realised it was Guillermo. Seeing him lying there injured made her realise how very much she loved him.

'Don't panic, it doesn't look too serious,' a fellow nurse consoled her. 'It's a leg wound he received from machine-gun fire while he was trying to rescue the escapees. But he insisted on being the last to be brought in.'

'I'll be fine, my darling,' he murmured, as pain resonated in his face.

Charlotte instantly set about applying pressure to reduce the bleeding. 'Yes, of course you will,' she kept on saying, to herself as much as to him, as she cleaned the raw open wound with fear and horror in her heart. It seemed the International Brigade, as well as the refugees, were also considered to be a legitimate target.

She was at least able to give Guillermo the good news that a battle taking place at Guadalajara had resulted in the Italian troops, who were supporting the Nationalists, being defeated.

'*¡Gracias a Dios!*' he murmured. 'Let us hope that Franco's attempts to take Madrid will now stop.'

Charlotte was greatly relieved to see that the nurse was right in her prognosis as the wound looked much better once it was cleaned. The bullet had skimmed the flesh but not penetrated the bone, or damaged any vein or artery. Guillermo was out of bed in no time, going off to check that his mates were safe too, if staggering with a painful limp and doing his best not to show too much anguish in his face.

Many of the volunteer fighters had also been injured as a result of this latest attack, and some killed, just when they'd believed the worst to be over. Morale seemed to be low. The next morning at breakfast Guillermo glanced around, and with a frown asked if anyone had seen Fergus lately.

Startled by this question, Charlotte shook her head. 'No, come to think of it, I haven't seen him around for a day or two.'

'He's a yellow renegade and has run for it,' muttered a young man sitting opposite.

She was all too aware that although most of these brave young men had joined the International Brigade because they greatly wished to help the people of Spain exercise their democratic rights, some had failed to fully appreciate the horrors awaiting them. They'd nursed a naïve belief that they faced only a few months' fighting, then the battle would be over and they could return home. The reality was proving to be very different: the siege of Madrid, the battle in the Jarama Valley and the capture of Malaga had all taken their toll. And as this organisation was now a part of the Republican army, the volunteers were liable to the same terms and conditions of all soldiers. They would be released from service only when peace finally came. Feeling trapped as a result, defecting was becoming all too common.

'I never saw Fergus as a coward,' Charlotte protested. 'Why would he do such a thing?'

'He claimed to be suffering from some disease or other, or made out that he was. Just an excuse as he wanted to join his mate in Scotland.'

'Who would that be?' Guillermo asked.

'It must be Laurence,' Charlotte said, feeling stunned. Was he too suffering from homesickness? Or was there some other reason?

The young man nodded. 'They've been good friends ever since they met in the Pyrenees, apparently. Fergus persuaded a couple of the Red Cross workers to take him in an ambulance to the nearest railway station at Almeria.'

'Did he indeed?' Guillermo sternly retorted. 'Then we should seek to catch him before he gets on the train. I'll summon up a search party.'

Charlotte put a hand on his arm. 'It's too late, he'll have gone by now. Besides, he's a most courageous young man who has suffered badly and lost many friends. He may feel in need of a break. Let him go. I believe he'll be back soon, as will Laurence. Libby too, once she's fully recovered. I'm sure of it.'

Guillermo looked at her, a strange expression puckering his face. Charlotte could see how his mind was whirling by the way his eyes narrowed. He looked as if he was about to say something, but in the end merely gave a resigned sigh. '*De nada*. I hope you're right.'

TWENTY-FIVE
SCOTLAND – SPRING 1937

BACK IN SCOTLAND Libby was slowly beginning to recover. Confined as she was to her bed, it was good to look out of the window and see the rolling green hills again, bright with purple heather, not as glorious as it would look in September but still beautiful in her eyes. Feeling weary of the grey skies and constant rain, Libby was badly missing Spain, and Ray, of course. Laurence too was anxious to return, but he irritated her by constantly going on about how concerned he was for Fergus, as if his friend was more important to him than his own wife. But then they'd not been on particularly good terms since Laurence forgot to send her a Valentine's Day card.

The reunion of Nick, her beloved twin brother, with his parents had been good to see. Her mother had wept tears of joy, and her father too when no one was looking. They'd been spoiling and making a fuss of him ever since. Now Nick was saying to her that although he greatly appreciated their love and care, he was bored.

'Me too,' Libby admitted, as he sat by her bed with his chin propped in his hands.

'I miss having my go.'

'You canna be fighting all the time.'

'But ah've nae wish tae sit aboot doing nothing. The war isna over, so what am I supposed tae do?'

Libby thought about this for some moments. 'There's no much I can do with me arm in a sling, and I'm still feeling a bit washed out. But mebbe ye could give talks?'

Nick sat up, back straight, eyes bright with hope. 'Och, I could, aye. Ah'd love to tell local folk aboot what's happening in Spain, and remind them that if we lose the battle there, then it could happen here too. We might receive more donations as a result.'

Libby smiled. 'Aye, that'd be good. Ye could ask for support of the International Brigade in Spain, and for the families o' local volunteers.'

'I'll start wi' going round the churches, pubs and clubs.' He was on his feet in a second, and giving her a quick peck of thanks on her brow waved goodbye and dashed off to start making arrangements.

Feeling glad she'd helped, Libby called after her brother's rapidly departing figure. 'Let me know how ye go on.' She received no answer as he'd already disappeared, and giving a sad little sigh at finding herself again alone, slumped back down on to her pillow.

෴

Libby woke one morning to find Lady Felicity seated beside her bed. 'How are you feeling, dear Libby? I heard you'd been shot in the shoulder. What a terrible thing to happen.'

Flushed with embarrassment Libby struggled to sit up. 'I'm on the mend, milady, if a wee bit slow.'

'Careful how you move, dear,' Lady Felicity said, jumping up to adjust the pillows and make her more comfortable. 'Do tell me, how is my darling daughter? I believe she was injured too?'

Noting her anxiety, Libby gave a reassuring smile. 'Charlie is fine. She made an excellent recovery.'

Lady Felicity put a hand to her chest and let out a little gasp of relief. 'Thank goodness for that. I've been so worried, although I must say that Charlotte's request for me to do some fundraising has helped enormously, giving me something useful to do with my time.'

'How very noble of ye, milady.'

'Please call me Felicity. It's so much easier. And as I've known you since you were a bairn, Libby, you now feel like a daughter to me.'

'Thank you,' Libby said, making no comment on how Charlie used to complain of her adored mother's constant withdrawal. But she had been strictly controlled by the laird, so perhaps escaping into her own private world had been the only way she could cope. That now seemed to be changing.

'I've been working hard to raise more money for your cause,' she said, confirming Libby's thoughts. 'I held a garden fete for the local worthy and wealthy, and employed a pipe band to play at an outdoor festival, which was attended by people from the entire area. So many folk made donations, including those on the dole, while others gave tinned foods they could probably ill afford to lose. Amazingly generous.'

'Och, that's wonderful mi— Felicity. Charlie will be delighted as more medical equipment, medicines, bandages, and warm winter clothing for the Brigaders is on her list. Did the laird no object to yer efforts?'

'Phuff.' Felicity gave a dismissive little sound through the flutter of her lips. 'I've resolved to stop asking his opinion. It really is no business of his. This charitable good cause is on behalf of my daughter.'

'And the people of Spain.'

'Yes, of course, as well as all the volunteers involved in the war. At a dinner party I held, someone had the nerve to say that General

Franco is "the saviour of Christian principles and will rid the world of Communists". It's not quite as simple as that, I told him. Too many people are dying as a result of this philosophy.'

'Good for you, ma'am.' Yet again Lady Felicity reminded Libby to call her by her first name, which she found difficult to do. But her admiration for the lady was growing by the second.

'I told the fellow that my beloved daughter was acting as nurse for all those in need, irrespective of their politics, and asked what he was doing to help. I'm afraid he avoided answering the question by changing the subject, as men like him tend to do. They can be so arrogant and obstinate.'

At that moment Libby's mother appeared with a tea tray. Setting it on the side table she quickly poured two cups, handing one to her ladyship before speedily departing.

'How kind, thank you so much, Mrs Forbes. Oh, she's gone. I was about to ask your mother if she wished to join us.'

'Ma is a busy woman, with a lot to do on the farm as well as in the house.' And nervous of aristocrats, if not as irritated by them as she herself was, came the thought in Libby's head.

'I dare say. What about you, dear, do you think you'll be well enough to leave this bed soon and continue with your own labours?'

'Och, I do hope so,' Libby said with a groan. 'Although I'm no sure when I'll be fit enough tae return to a war zone. That could tak' a wee while.'

'I think it might, dear.'

Libby let out a sigh. 'Tae be honest, I'm bored sick of being stuck here, as is my brother.' She told Lady Felicity then of Nick's decision to give talks.

'Oh, what an excellent idea. I'm sure people will love to hear someone speaking from a personal point of view on what exactly is happening in Spain. It could bring in more money too. I was about to suggest that having raised a fair sum, to which I'm willing to add a sizeable contribution of my own, that we should rent a warehouse in which we could stock supplies. What do you think about that, dear? You would be in charge, of course.'

Libby almost choked on her tea. 'Are ye serious?'

'Never more so. This fundraising has given me a real purpose in life, one I've been in need of for some time to drag me out of my mental reclusion. I will continue to hold cocktail parties and play my piano at little musical soirees, but only in order to raise funds, not simply to socialise.' Leaning closer, her lovely blue-grey eyes bright, she said, 'I've found a disused old woollen mill, which I think might suit our purpose wonderfully. As soon as you feel well enough, we'll go and view it together.'

⌒○

Within days of Lady Felicity's visit Libby had risen from her bed, determined to begin living life again, despite her mother's protests that she should continue resting until the wound was fully healed and the sling removed. 'It'll be coming off any day noo,' Libby assured her. 'And I'm eager tae see this mill. Why don't ye come wi' us?'

'Nae, lass, it's naught tae do wi' me. But ye go, if it'll mebbe make ye feel any better.'

Libby, Nick and Laurence accompanied Lady Felicity to view the mill. It was a stone-built two-storey building with rows of windows overlooking a small branch of the River Dee. Alongside stood a huge water wheel that had once provided power for the looms back in the eighteenth century. Now the mill was empty and in something of a sorry state, with a few broken windows and piles of rubbish everywhere. As they stood staring into the dusty gloom, a rat scampered across the floor in front of them.

'I'm afraid it could do with a good clean. Windows will have to be replaced, some sort of heating and lighting installed, as well as shelving for the stock of goods we'll be storing here,' Lady Felicity said, looking slightly overwhelmed by the enormity of the task facing them.

'Aye, it's a manky mess, but nothing that a wee bit of effort canna resolve,' Libby assured her, wishing she could roll up her sleeves, grab a brush and start scrubbing the floor that very minute.

'You tell us what needs doing, old thing, and we'll do it,' Laurence said. 'That will be after we've killed the rat.' And they all laughed.

With the help of a group of local volunteers it took no time at all before the mill was cleaned and scrubbed, all vermin dealt with, and refurbishment commenced. Everyone worked hard, including Laurence, which helped to lessen the tension between them.

'Do ye still love me?' Libby asked one night as they climbed into bed back at the farm.

'Of course I do, sweetheart. Being a part of your life is ripping fun. Never a dull moment.'

'It's just been so long since we – well – since you showed me how much.'

'That's because of the war, and then your injury.'

'But I'm feeling much better now, my sling is off and the wound almost healed.' As she wrapped her arms about his neck, he gave her a quick kiss.

'But you must still take care. Good night, old fruit,' he whispered, before turning over to be snoring in seconds.

With a sad sigh, Libby slipped back into her lonely dreams.

It was the following afternoon as they sat discussing how to install electricity that the mill door opened and Fergus walked in, as always clutching a cigarette between finger and thumb.

'*Hola*, everyone,' he announced, grinning at their startled expressions. 'Your ma told me I'd find you here, Libby. It's so good to see ye all again.'

She stared at him in stunned disbelief. Laurence was on his feet in seconds, shaking Fergus's hand and slapping him on the back by way of welcome. 'Goodness gracious, it's good to see you too. How did you get here?'

'By train. Quite easily, in fact.'

'And how is everyone back in Spain?'

'Och, they're fine, if suffering from exhaustion, but settled in a safe place right noo.'

He began to tell them about *Casa Oliva*, but the conversation blurred in her head as Libby watched her husband pull up a chair close to his own so that he and Fergus could sit and chat. What good friends they appeared to be, as she and Laurence had once been. What on earth had gone wrong? His rejection of her the previous night reverberated afresh in her heart. Nick too joined in the conversation and began to ask questions, but Lady Felicity interrupted with a polite little cough.

'Could this discussion wait for a while?'

'Of course,' Laurence said, making an apology as he flicked a smile across at Fergus. 'We'll talk later, old sport.'

Lady Felicity graciously nodded. 'Now, as I was saying, water wheels once powered looms and all manner of machinery in mines and factories, as well as grinding corn at a flour mill. Although it's unlikely we'll be doing anything of that sort here, electricity to provide lighting would be useful, particularly on dark grey days like this. Otherwise we would have to resort to oil lamps, which is a bleak prospect. Does anyone know how the old system worked, and if it could be restored?'

'I do,' Fergus said, stubbing out his cigarette to wave his hands about in illustration. 'Water is taken from the river and channelled along the millrace tae the water wheel, which I can see is suitably big. Put simply, tae create the necessary energy the flow of water needs to be fast and with a high head, then is directed through pipes tae the blades of a turbine that passes it on to power the generator for electricity.'

'Didn't understand a word of that, old sport, but sounds absolutely topping!' Laurence said, clapping his friend's back one more time. 'Looks as if you arrived at exactly the right moment.'

Lady Felicity smiled. 'We are delighted to have you with us, Mr McKenzie, particularly if you're willing to help with our current project. Unless, of course, you're heading straight back to Spain?'

'Awa' wi' ye. There's nae rush. I'll be glad tae help.'

He set to work that very morning by investigating the ancient equipment still occupying the outhouses. Libby welcomed his support, but a part of her remained troubled about why this man was more important to Laurence than she was.

❧

To celebrate May Day they heard that a huge rally was to be held in Glasgow in support of Spain, which thousands of people were expected to attend. Inspired by this idea Lady Felicity arranged for one to be held in the grounds of the mill, albeit much smaller. Posters were put up around town advertising the event, many of them stating: *Spain's Danger is Ours* or *In Support of the Republic*. Libby, together with all the women helpers at the mill, practised the maypole dance for days. Laurence and Fergus happily joined in.

When the day arrived, a beautifully decorated maypole with ribbons attached was set up, and a piper played music as the dancers jigged around, weaving in and out, watched by flocks of people. Bluebells were blooming in the woodlands all around, and a blue cloudless sky lit by a bright sun smiled down upon them.

'What a wonderful day. I think we're going to make pots of money,' Felicity said, beaming with pleasure as she bustled off to help the housekeeper, Mrs Murray, prepare refreshments for their many guests.

Nell Forbes was running a small stall on which she was selling donations of bric-a-brac, pots and pans, old clothes not suitable for soldiers, together with some beautiful fans that Libby had brought back with her from Spain.

'What a treasure ye are, Ma. We seem to be doing really well,' Libby said, feeling proud of her mother for her sterling efforts to help, despite having more than enough work of her own to occupy her. She was so enjoying this treat of a day, even though her mind was still in a muddle over what had gone wrong with her marriage. But right now, that could wait. Raising money to help the International Brigade and the Spanish people was far more important.

'I think we've nearly sold out. Have we anything more we could sell?' her mother asked.

'Och, I'll go and rummage through the donations and see what I can find,' Libby said, and dashed off to the mill.

It was as she was packing some teddies and dolls into a box, which were rather sweet but of no interest to soldiers, that she heard a door slam and a voice roar behind her. 'What the *hell* do you think you're up to?'

'I beg yer pardon?' Libby turned to find the laird glowering furiously at her.

'Thanks to you, my stepdaughter went off to Spain and has not yet returned. In addition, you've now lured my *wife* away from home too.'

She blinked. 'I've done nae such thing. If ye're referring tae renting this wee mill, that was Lady Felicity's idea. As was this wonderful May Day celebration. I'm just helping her.'

'Nonsense, this was all your idea in the first place. My wife is giving away more money than we can afford, and has demanded that I hand over my fishing boat for transporting your damned goods. You also stole the man who was meant to marry my step-daughter,' he shouted, stabbing a finger inches from her face. 'How dare you keep ruining my life and involving my wife in this non-sensical enterprise?'

As Libby struggled to find the right response, the mill door opened and Lady Felicity herself walked in. 'Darling, I thought I heard your roaring voice. How lovely to see you. So glad you could come as we're having a marvellous time. Do come and listen to the piper, he's so good, you'll love him. Oh, and dear Libby is quite right when she says this was entirely my idea, but it does seem to be working.'

'I'm not interested in watching silly folk dance around a may-pole, drat you. Total waste of time and money.'

'Actually we're making quite a lot of money for the cause. I'm sorry if I've robbed you of your beloved fishing boat, dearest, but we do bring in coal from Whitehaven, as well as transport other goods to and from various places.'

'You should have asked my permission first,' he snapped.

Lady Felicity chuckled. 'Well, as I purchased the boat I didn't think you'd mind if I borrowed it for a little while.' Then her eyes narrowed into a firm grim line. 'Please don't blame Libby for my darling daughter going to Spain. Charlotte may never have thought to go had you not thrown her out of our home.'

'*My* home,' he snarled, and turning on his heel marched away.

With a sigh, she shook her head. 'How fortunate you are, Libby, to be married to such a sweet man. Keeping one's husband happy can at times be extremely difficult.'

Libby felt the urge to say that sweet as Laurence was, keeping him happy was also proving to be a problem, if for different rea-sons. But she managed to hold her tongue and keep these concerns private.

The day turned out to be a complete success. They raised so much money to add to that already collected at other events, including Nick's talks, that the storeroom was soon packed. They had boxes of medical supplies, first aid equipment, clothes, boots, tins of milk, beans, cocoa, sardines, cigarettes and beer. They'd also raised enough money to buy a truck in order to send everything out to Spain.

Nell Forbes, together with some of her friends, had spent weeks knitting balaclavas, scarves and gloves. A day or two later as Libby collected these together she thanked her mother for her efforts, giving her a warm hug. 'Bless you. Where is everyone?' she asked.

'The vehicle has arrived and Laurence and Fergus are packing it right now.'

'Ah good, I'll take these over, then.' Libby hurried off, carrying the parcel of woollens, to find the two men in the back of the lorry in a locked embrace, kissing.

TWENTY-SIX

LIBBY WAS SHOCKED by what she'd witnessed: her own beloved husband kissing a man in a way he'd never kissed her. Seeing Laurence in an embrace with Fergus explained everything. How naïve of her not to appreciate this was the reason for the problems between them. Heart thumping she quickly hurried away, not wishing them to see her, as well as requiring a little time to recover. Why had he kept his preferences secret from her? Anger and despair warred within, although as much at herself as him. She'd foolishly coerced Laurence into making a proposal not simply out of fondness for him, or a desire to improve her wealth and status, but because she was expecting. She'd felt desperate not to ruin her reputation. Then she'd lost the wee child, making the sacrifice of her freedom a complete waste of time. Libby had assumed that his suspicion about her condition was the reason for the growing distance between them; that he was jealous of Dunmore. She'd lived in hope that their marriage would improve, once they were free of the war. Now it seemed the problem was insurmountable.

But they were not free of war yet, and must go on, no matter what their personal problems.

Staunchly calming herself, Libby called out to them as she approached a second time. 'Ah, there ye are, Laurence,' she said, handing over the parcel of woollen goods, striving to appear as if everything was perfectly normal between them. She really had no wish to discuss the state of their marriage in front of his lover.

It was not until Laurence climbed into bed beside her, as usual kissing her goodnight and instantly turning away, that she challenged him on the issue. 'Why did ye never tell me who it is ye really want tae have here in bed with ye?'

'W-what are you talking about?' he asked, giving a slight stutter.

'I saw ye today with Fergus, engaged in the kind of embrace we have never enjoyed.' Silence followed this remark. Libby was aware that her tone of voice sounded oddly flat, and tears threatened to fall as they filled her eyes. 'Ye could have spared me so much anguish if ye'd taken the trouble tae explain.'

Wrapping his arms about himself as if in defence, Laurence bowed his head. 'You're right. I'm so sorry. I never meant to hurt you, sweetheart. I was only attempting to make you happy. I believed that telling you the truth would have upset you too much, and ruined our friendship.'

Libby gazed at him in bewilderment. 'Instead, ye've ruined our marriage.'

Dropping his chin he avoided her gaze. 'I accept that we probably never should have eloped, although it seemed like a good idea at the time.'

'Aye, as it would save ye from the threat of prison?'

'Something of the sort, yes.' Shame and embarrassment now pinked his cheeks. 'I do still love you, old thing, if not as you would like to be loved. But I have no problem with you finding romance elsewhere. You could divorce me, if you prefer, or we could carry on as we are, free to do as we please.'

'I think right noo I'll go tae sleep,' Libby hissed. 'I'll think aboot that.'

'Do you wish me to sleep elsewhere tonight?'

'I'm afraid there is nowhere else. This is but a small farmhouse, and my brothers and sisters are already cramped in their own rooms.'

'Goodnight then, sweetheart.'

No wonder Fergus had come to join them here in Scotland. He obviously couldn't bear being parted from Laurence. Libby had to admit that Fergus was a helpful, friendly man, having done everything he'd promised by providing the mill with electric lighting. He'd also cleaned the chimneys so they could light fires in the rooms where they were working. And he was quite good-looking, so how could Laurence resist him, since he was that way inclined?

Libby worked hard over the following week or two, doing her utmost to come to terms with reality. 'Does it bother me a wee bit,' she asked herself, 'if Laurence loves him? Ach, no, why would it?' She wasn't madly in love with her husband, although he would forever occupy a special place in her heart. He was still fond of her too, and as he had suggested, she could find romance elsewhere, so why make a fuss? Was Ray the man she truly loved? Libby really couldn't say for sure, but it was a possibility.

They were obliged to continue to share a bed, if sleeping side by side like old friends, not lovers. And Libby had no wish right now for all the expense and hassle of a divorce, even if one were easy to come by without risking jail for dear Laurence, which would be quite dreadful. His emotional ties to this man were not a crime in her eyes. Libby just wished he'd been open and honest with her from the start. But then perhaps she should have been with him.

'Noo we're ready tae return to Spain,' Nick announced one day, with which Laurence and Fergus heartily agreed.

'What about me?' Libby asked.

Laurence gave her a gentle hug. 'You stay here, old thing. You're not yet fit enough to embark upon such a long journey and go back to the war. Make a full recovery first.'

Feeling obliged to accept this truth, Libby agreed to remain in Scotland a while longer. 'I'll join ye soon,' she promised, kissing them all goodbye, and sadness clenched her heart as she watched them drive away.

~

Libby felt lost without her husband and beloved brother. How she wished she could have gone with them. Yet here she was, stuck fast in Scotland, still feeling fragile and with nothing now to occupy her and few friends left to keep her company. Loneliness and despair washed over her.

How long would she be stuck here with nothing worthwhile left to do, and no chance of ever seeing Ray? She could only hope that while she was away he wouldn't start making passes at other women, most of all Charlie. Leaving Spain was the last thing she'd wanted to do, but then she was a wee bit of a fool to be so obsessed with him. He may be exciting and good fun, but he was something of a woman-chaser.

That afternoon, as Libby and Lady Felicity cleaned out the empty mill, her mother came to help. The three women were sitting together enjoying the delicious shortbread Nell Forbes had made for them to have with their tea. It still seemed amazing that her ladyship was happy to drink from a pot mug instead of a china cup, not to mention being clothed in an apron with a turban tying up her golden fair hair. Her elegance and beauty were always very evident, as it was with her daughter, even when Charlotte was covered in mud. But Libby's fondness and admiration for the McBain ladies were still tempered with a slight tang of envy.

'So what do we do now?' she asked Lady Felicity as a wave of tiredness, or was it boredom, caused her to slouch in her seat.

'I'm sure we'll find something to occupy us, as well as help the cause. News from the front line is slow to arrive, and mothers anxiously wait for news of their sons and daughters for weeks or months, which can be quite agonising. Letters that do get through all beg for more help.' Turning to Nell, Lady Felicity smiled. 'I was hugely impressed with the support you gave by way of your knitting, Mrs Forbes.'

'Nae problem, and I'm happy to carry on if ye could provide the wool.'

'Of course we can, and we'll continue to collect donations of food and other goods. But I feel it would be good to do more. I was interested in how many people mentioned their wish to help the children of Spain.'

'Dozens of wee bairns handed over a penny or halfpenny out of their pocket money,' Libby agreed. 'Their generosity moved me to tears.'

'So many Spanish children have lost their parents, in particular as a result of the bombing of Guernica in April. Apparently over a thousand people were killed and almost as many injured. I believe this has left a lot of Basque children in dire need of care. A committee has been formed here in Scotland, which is searching for suitable homes willing to take them. Craiklyn Manor is a huge, largely empty property, and certainly not short of bedrooms. I thought that as we have the space, we could offer accommodation for at least twenty.'

Libby gazed at her in awe, startled surprise lifting her eyebrows. 'Goodness, I can see noo where Charlotte gets her vigour from. What an amazing lady ye are.'

'So are you, dear. Most courageous and hard-working.'

'She is, aye,' Nell Forbes said, smiling proudly at her daughter.

'Och, that would be wonderful, but what would the laird think?' Libby tentatively asked. 'As ye know, he's already vented his wrath at me for having encouraged Charlotte and now you to join us in this project. He would surely consider a house full of wee children likely to create more mayhem.'

Lady Felicity pursed her lips. 'There comes a point in life, and in one's marriage, when it is necessary to put the needs of others first, as well as one's own. These children could badly do with some help. Many are orphans, and although others do still have a family, they have no homes to go to. We cannot simply leave them to die with no shelter, food or water in a bombed-out city.'

'I do agree,' Libby said, deeply moved by her plan. 'But ye sound like ye're talking of completely changing yer lifestyle, one that could be quite demanding.'

'I am, yes,' Lady Felicity agreed. 'And why not? It will probably only be for a short time, till the war is over and the children can be returned to their families. Would you be happy to help?'

As Libby loved children, the idea brought forth a stir of excitement, instantly curbed by her desire to return to Spain. The feeling created a certain caution in her about becoming too involved. 'Do bear in mind that I'll be going back to Spain as soon as I am fit enough,' she warned, knowing in her heart she could barely wait to do that.

Apart from the work, which she greatly enjoyed, Libby still badly missed Ray. She'd written several letters to him but he hadn't responded to any of them. Not too surprising since he was bound to feel cautious about intruding upon her marriage. Yet as things now stood between herself and Laurence, and if Ray was the man she'd truly loved all along as he brought such joy and happiness to her life, there seemed no reason not to be with him.

And at least this latest project would give her something worthwhile to do for the cause until she was fit enough to return. At times Libby could barely allow herself to sit still for more than five minutes, she felt so desolate.

Both women were now smiling at her. 'We know that, dear,' Lady Felicity said. 'I'm sure we could get together some helpers to look after these little ones. It could be a lovely way for friends and relatives of Brigaders to show support for their loved ones who have volunteered to do their bit. And as I said, I've been in need of something worthwhile to occupy me for some time, so have no wish to cease working for a good cause. Would you be interested in assisting us to launch this plan by helping get the rooms ready?'

'I certainly would.'

'Ye'd have my help too,' Nell Forbes offered with a smile.

'Excellent. A great deal will have to be done. It'll take considerable effort to clean that shabby manor house, and get everything organised as well as pay for the children to be brought over. Our fundraising must continue for some time. So since we are in agreement, let's make a list.'

Libby couldn't help chuckling, as that was exactly what Charlotte had said when first they'd started on this project over a year ago. Lady Felicity's enthusiasm and vitality had sparked new energy in her. The prospect of helping children was making her feel better already.

'It has just occurred to me that now my brother has gone back to Spain, I could do the talks in his place. I still have a list of clubs and organisations hoping to hear him speak about the war.'

Nell Forbes gave her daughter a warm hug. 'What wonderfully clever bairns I have. Aye, lass, ye could tell folk all about how ye nurse and care for these soldiers. It might encourage a few more tae volunteer, or tae help us.'

'Oh, what a splendid idea,' Lady Felicity said, clapping her hands.

❧

The laird, as expected, reacted with fury to the very idea of handing over his home to a 'flock of peasants', as he termed them. 'I will not allow this,' he roared, stamping back and forth like a lion seeking its prey while the manor was invaded by a horde of village women. They marched in carrying mops and buckets, brushes and dustpans. Paying no attention to him they set about dusting, sweeping, mopping and polishing with great vigour, determined to restore this fine building to its former glory. His lady wife, too, happily donned an apron and turban in order to help.

'You can be responsible for making everyone a cup of tea at eleven o'clock, and bring the biscuits too, dear,' Felicity instructed him. 'Please don't forget, or we may not return the compliment come dinner time, and you could find yourself going hungry,' she said with a chuckle. Then she readily went off to work alongside them, ignoring his roars and shouts.

Libby quickly escaped through a side door to the scullery to help the housekeeper, who had already started laundering sheets that hadn't been used in years. 'Will she win him round, d'ye think?'

'She wouldna at one time.' Mrs Murray grinned. 'But as the laird has no a penny left in the world, he'll have to accept whatever dear Lady Felicity says. She is the one in charge noo, and the only one wi' money.'

It was such a lovely thought. Relationships could be awkward and difficult at times, both between friends and spouses, and apparently for the rich and wealthy too. How she'd enjoyed working with this lovely lady, and her daughter, of course. She sorely missed Charlie.

Peace at last settled within Libby, and the future suddenly seemed brighter. Hopefully, by the time she returned to Spain, Ray would be missing her. Although Libby felt some concern that he might have forgotten all about her and started an affair with Charlie. Her friend tended to assume that all men would drool over her and propose, whether it be Laurence, Ray, or now this Guillermo. Yet milady was far too independent-minded and full of herself to wish to marry any of them. Fond as Libby was of Charlie, a nub of jealousy yet again began to eat away at her.

TWENTY-SEVEN
SPAIN — SUMMER 1937

THE SUMMER HEAT was upon them, not a cloud visible in the bright blue sky. Charlotte had been granted a day off and made the decision to take a rest in the shade of the olive grove, as Guillermo had advised. She was seated with Rosita, happily chatting in Spanish as they so loved to do, her new friend also picking up quite a bit of English. Feeling the need to do something relaxing, Charlotte had begun to paint a poster for propaganda purposes. It had been so long since she'd picked up a brush that it felt a total delight to dip it in paint and start to dab pictures on canvas again.

'You are *muy bueno*,' Rosita said with an admiring smile as she watched her.

'I used to love painting flowers in our garden back home, but this is an entirely different project. Hope I can make it work.'

Dunmore, who had been sketching images of the Brigaders as they cleaned their guns, came over to see what she was doing, instantly dismissing the idea as dangerous drivel. 'It's a very risky thing to do and not worth the effort as it will do no good at all.'

'Nonsense! Rosita and I intend to stick these posters up on walls in local villages in the hope they'll encourage more women to take on war work, and men too, of course.'

'It's a complete waste of time,' he snorted derisively. 'In June, Bilbao fell to the Nationalists, and I read in the paper last week that the Vatican has officially recognised Franco's regime, so what is the point?'

'The Spanish are still fighting,' Charlotte calmly responded.

'But these posters are a complete mess. Absolute rubbish!'

'*Incorrecto*,' Rosita firmly protested, going on to speak in a mix of Spanish and English. 'I've seen many of her sketches. She's a very gifted lady and doing a great job.'

'And as this is a new enterprise – I've barely started,' Charlotte firmly added.

He let out a burst of mocking laughter. 'I tried my best to teach Lady Charlotte how to paint, but she never was much good. Always used a far too restricted palette, and couldn't paint people to save her life. I could repaint it for you and brighten it up.'

'No thanks,' Charlotte snapped. 'I don't require anyone's help. Rosita is quite right. It may take time, so have patience and stop bossing me.'

'You know full well that unlike the laird, I believe people should be free to do their own thing. I'm a joker, not a bully, milady.'

'But sometimes not at all funny, and don't start that milady business again. Call me Charlotte, or better still, Charlie.'

'Isn't that a boy's name?' Rosita asked with a chuckle when Charlotte translated bits of the conversation to her.

'Quite appropriate, really.' Charlotte grinned. 'You can see that women artists are considered to be just as insignificant as you Spanish ladies, certainly by men. So I thought I should pretend to be a man.'

'Much safer,' Rosita agreed, watching in awe as her new friend quickly painted a mountain, surrounding it with flags and guns held by images of soldiers marching across it. Then she looked at one Charlotte had painted earlier of a small child screaming as she stared up at a sky filled with aircraft, and gave a little sigh of respect. 'She is a brilliant artist, Mr Dunmore. Do not insult her. Charlotte is *estupendo*.'

'Oh, thank you, Rosita. I shall paint you a picture of your lovely *cortijo* and Taco the donkey next. I would enjoy that as I love doing something to take my mind off all the injuries and death that surround us.'

'Wonderful,' her friend agreed, giving her a kiss. 'I must now return to the kitchen and use my poor skills to make my husband's dinner, as a good wife is expected to do.' And pulling a wry grimace of displeasure, she hurried away.

Ray stood in silence for some moments after she'd gone, watching Charlotte paint. 'You are indeed a most charming lady, but then I've always thought so. And you are improving as an artist.'

'Thank you.'

'Don't mention it, or else you could thank me properly.' Reaching out a hand he twirled a lock of her hair, as he used to do back at his classes in Kirkcudbright. Charlotte attempted to pull away from his hold on a sigh of irritation, but he caught her by the throat and kissed her. Furiously slapping at him, she pushed him away. 'Don't you *dare* touch me like that! How many times have I told you to leave me alone?'

But instead of doing what she asked, he simply laughed, one hand roaming over her breast. 'Come on, I know you're being generous with Rosita's cousin, so don't I deserve a few favours too?'

'Damn you!' Charlotte cried, and as he pushed her up against a tree yet again she raised her knee to thump him. This time he caught it, sliding his hand along her thigh, and with his tongue in her mouth began to devour her. The thought resounded in her head that for once her stepfather might have been right not to trust this odious man. Frantically struggling to free herself she thankfully heard footsteps approaching, and a voice calling her name. Quickly letting her go, Dunmore stepped back, just before Guillermo appeared.

'Ah, there you are. Rosita told me what you were doing, and sent me to view your work. Oh, that's wonderful. *Excelente!*' And then, glancing coolly at Dunmore, he casually remarked, 'I'm so glad that I came to look. She's good, isn't she?'

'She's an amateur,' Dunmore snarled.

'Not so far as I can see. I suggest you leave her in peace to get on with it.'

And giving a snort of laughter, Dunmore walked away.

Charlotte drew in a steadying breath, smiling as Guillermo embraced her. But she chose not to tell him what had just happened, or that she'd felt in danger of being raped. There was quite enough happening in the world for him to worry about right now. She had no wish to add to it. As for Dunmore's opinion of her work, it was clearly defined by his desire to assault her.

TWENTY-EIGHT
SPAIN — 1986

COMING OUT of the shower following her usual swim, Jo glanced out over the sunlit garden, smiling at the glorious pink of a hibiscus, and a purple bougainvillea that spread its beautiful leafy flowers halfway up the wall of the small *cortijo*. Jo loved it here, and could quite understand why Charlotte and Libby too had fallen in love with Spain. Interestingly, in spite of their anguish and the danger they faced of being bombed or shot, they'd still found the time and energy to fall in love. It had no doubt given them something positive to focus upon. Right now, love was the last thing on her mind, Jo firmly told herself.

Slipping into a silk dressing gown, Jo was deciding what to wear for her day out at a fiesta with Anton, when she heard the sound of a car engine. Going to the window she was surprised to see a silver Peugeot that looked very like a rental car drawing up. Now who could that be? When the driver's door flew open and Felix himself stepped out, she jerked with shock.

'What on earth . . . ?'

He walked in with a jaunty step as if he had every right to be there. Realising she had no time to change, Jo quickly tightened the belt of her bathrobe and met him in the salon, tight-lipped, arms folded.

'Wow, you've got a tan already,' he said with a laugh, coming over to kiss her on the cheek. Jo turned her face away, so that he missed. Stepping back with a sigh, he said, 'Can't we at least be friends? Particularly as there's something I should tell you, or have you already spoken to your mother?'

'I have indeed. What the *hell* are you doing here?'

He gave a rueful grin as he set down his small suitcase and took off his jacket to drop it on the floor, clearly sweating in the heat. He was dressed in a dark grey suit, shirt and tie, as if he'd just stepped out of the office. 'Nowhere else to go right now, so thought I might as well take up your offer to enjoy a little sunshine.'

How stupid of her to tell Felix about this trip. In view of lingering feelings she'd been having trouble eradicating, she'd gone to see him to explain why she was going off to Spain with a perfect stranger. Possibly hoping that he would offer to come with her.

'How would you feel about a holiday in Spain?' she'd asked.

He'd been sitting hunched over his desk, and as usual barely lifted his eyes from the computer screen to answer her question. 'You are joking! Can't you see that I'm up to my ears in work?'

She'd longed to put her arms about him and kiss the top of his head, as she might once have done. Instead, she had held herself firmly in check and gone on to briefly explain about the accusation of forgery as a result of her displaying a picture without proper provenance.

'How very silly of you, but you always were foolishly impulsive. You really should learn to think before you act,' he'd caustically remarked.

At this point the telephone rang and Jo hadn't failed to notice how he'd instantly turned to answer it in whispered tones. It was perfectly obvious who he was talking to. She walked out the door.

Now, having banished him forever from her heart, Jo felt no desire for him to join her.

'So you're hiding from the bank, or the bailiffs,' she said, anger beginning to simmer within her.

'You could say that.'

She headed for the kettle, feeling the need to compose herself. 'I'll make you some coffee, but our relationship is over. You're now with this . . .'

'Shelley.'

'Whoever!' At that moment she heard a clattering of heels on the gravelled drive. To her utter amazement Jo spotted the familiar figure of a young girl wobbling towards them in ridiculously high heels. 'You've brought *Sophie* with you?'

'I could hardly leave her behind, could I, now that we have nowhere to live?' he said, grabbing the coffee mug she'd been in the process of handing him.

'You surely weren't imagining that you could both stay *here*? This isn't my house, it's merely a temporary holiday let, provided by its most generous owner.'

Felix snorted in disbelief. 'Maybe he hopes for payment in kind.'

Had the girl not tottered in at that precise moment, Jo might well have slapped his arrogant face.

Sophie presented herself in an ankle-length black silk skirt and skinny top, bright blue eyes ringed with black eyeliner and dark violet eye shadow. Was this a new gothic look she'd adopted? Stunned at the unexpected sight of this young rebel teenager, Jo struggled to think of something complimentary to say by way of welcome, even as her heart melted with fondness and pity for this poor girl. Because of the neglect she herself had suffered as a child, Jo had done her best to be a caring surrogate mother to Felix's daughter. It hadn't been easy as at fourteen the girl was going through a difficult adolescent age, and still grieving for the loss of her mother.

'You look gorgeous, sweetie, how lovely to see you, if something of a surprise,' Jo said, as she gave the girl a warm hug.

Glancing from one to the other to take in their angry faces, and no doubt having heard something of their raised voices, Sophie groaned. 'I *soooo* didn't want to come here. This is all *your* fault, Jo, for coming up with such a stupid idea. Dad doesn't give a hoot for *boring* holidays in the middle of nowhere. I don't either. I wish to stay somewhere much more *with it.*'

'That would be an excellent idea,' Jo said with a smile. 'Actually I like this quiet rural area, but I should think it holds little appeal for you, sweetie, or your dad. I'm just here for a rest, and to solve the riddle of a painting. I'm also learning more about my grandmother. But I agree you'd both be much happier in an apartment on the *playa*,' she brightly suggested. 'There's more going on down there, and you'd be able to swim in the sea as well as enjoy relaxing on the beach.'

Tossing back her henna-tinted dreadlocks, Sophie turned her back upon Jo to directly address her father. 'That might be a good idea, Dad. I certainly have no wish to spend an *entire* week listening to you two *arguing* the whole time! Or have to suffer *her* going on at me as if she were my mother, which she most definitely *isn't.*'

Jo considered it wise to make no response to this. It was certainly true that at twenty-five she wasn't old enough to qualify for such a role. But Sophie was so locked in her own misery that she obviously found it easier to blame Jo for whatever she found to be lacking in her life, rather than her own father, despite the fact that his neglect of her was pitiful.

Felix was scowling at them both. 'Sophie, fetch your suitcase. We can't afford to rent a beach hut, never mind an apartment.'

And whose fault is that? Jo thought, but bit down hard on her lower lip in case the words popped unbidden from her mouth. Had he not brought Sophie, she would have had no hesitation in turning him out to sleep on the streets. But how could she do that to this lovely young girl? Drawing in a calming breath she helped Sophie to carry in her bags, and led her to the small bedroom close to the back terrace.

'This is worse than a B and B in Brighton,' Sophie sneered, glancing at the whitewashed walls and single bed with only one sheet and a pillow. But then nothing more was necessary in this heat.

Jo laughed. 'It is pretty basic, although there's a built-in wardrobe and you do have your own tiny shower room.' Something of a relief considering how long Sophie spent titivating herself each morning. 'Plus access to a pool, so when you've unpacked why not put on your swimsuit and dive in.'

'No thanks, I've just had my hair done. I certainly have no wish to ruin it the first day we arrive.'

Teenagers could be so difficult. Stifling a sigh and wasting no further time on this fruitless attempt to please her, Jo left Sophie to unpack and locked herself in her own room to change. Then finding Felix idling by the pool, she coolly addressed him. 'I'm afraid this house only has two bedrooms, so you'll have to spend the night on the sofa.'

Felix glared at her, then a wicked twinkle melted his angry gaze. 'Oh, come on. We've shared a bed for nearly three years, what difference would a few more nights make?'

'The difference is that we are no longer a couple. We're separated, Felix, if you remember, and won't be getting back together. Not ever!' With relief Jo found she did not feel the usual bleakness in her soul at these words, having banished him at last from her heart. She certainly had no intention of being used for his sexual gratification when *his* heart lay elsewhere.

Felix gave a little chuckle as if she'd made some sort of joke. 'As you wish, assuming the sofa's big enough to take my six-foot torso.'

She'd once adored the tallness of him, and the well-muscled legs and thighs of this fit and active man. Now her response was icy cold. 'It won't be very comfortable, so find yourself an apartment or hotel. I shall be out for the entire day. You must be gone by the time I return.' Then she walked away without another word.

∾

Struggling to calm herself, Jo met up with Anton as they had arranged to do. Yet again Felix was attempting to mess up her life, completely obsessed with his own problems and giving no thought at all to hers. Maybe it was a family trait to be too trusting and naïve, as she seemed to have followed in the footsteps of not only her mother but also her very homely grandmother. Consideration for others was quite beyond him. But no matter how obstinate and difficult he might prove to be, she would not allow him to control her ever again. Hopefully he would have moved out by the time she returned.

Now she banished him from her mind and walked happily with Anton through the *pueblo*. The narrow streets were bustling with people, lined with row upon row of stalls. One was selling fans that were so beautiful Jo couldn't resist buying herself one, particularly in this intense heat. 'Are they holding a *rastro*?' she asked. 'Is this market day?'

'Today we are having a *fiesta*. You could call it a *feria del día*. A day fair. There's usually a procession later in the evening, not a religious one on this occasion, but where folk wear fancy dress and dance to celebrate the summer. Followed by fireworks.'

'Oh, great.' She looked up at him, loving the sparkle in his eyes.

A long table occupied the centre of the village square, laid out with plates of cheese, ham, chorizo and olives. In one corner two old men were stirring *migas* in a huge round pan over a fire. Many people were sitting at tables set around the square, helping themselves to the free food. The bars served wine while a band played and a group of young girls danced a flamenco. They were gorgeously attired in swirling gowns of crimson and white. Nearby a stall displayed a row of these lovely frilly dresses for sale. Jo was tempted to buy one for Sophie, but as the young girl was not present to give her opinion, she decided it was safer not to. In any case her taste in fashion was quite individual.

She'd agreed to go with her father down to *playa*, where hopefully they would find alternative accommodation as Jo had instructed him to do. Fond as she was of Sophie, she would find it a great strain to have Felix living under the same roof. Her feelings for him had completely evaporated.

The sound of singing and clapping, wonderful Spanish music, and children's laughter brought a smile of happiness to Jo's face as she watched families enjoying themselves. Even the church bells joined in the fun. How she loved this place. 'What a captivating, lively scene it is, no doubt entirely different to what must have been happening here during the war.'

'I'm sure you're right,' Anton said, refilling her wine glass. 'Those brave souls risked their lives for the sake of future generations, so let us raise a glass to their courage, and enjoy the life we now have.'

Clinking glasses Jo felt a warm glow in her heart as she gazed into his gorgeous dark amber eyes. Casually dressed in shorts and a T-shirt, Anton looked completely relaxed and content. He led a very busy life, not only working the land, but he also owned and ran the local olive mill. Yet despite that, he was prepared to find time to help with her research. So generous of him.

The day passed in a whirl of celebration, finishing with a wonderful evening spent watching a magnificent procession bright with beautiful costumes, bands playing, ladies dancing, little girls in frilly frocks and big straw hats, and boys dressed as matadors or soldiers. The horses pulling the carts were also gorgeously attired.

'I've never witnessed anything so glorious in my life. How clever and artistic you Spanish are.'

'They spend months preparing for these kind of events,' he told her with a proud smile.

After this came dancing for everyone in the square, and Jo found herself melting with happiness as Anton held her close in his arms. She felt his chin brush against her hair, the warmth of his thighs against hers, and the sweetness of him run through her like fire. She could no longer deny a growing attraction for him. He was such a handsome, resourceful and friendly man. They later sat together enjoying a nightcap as they watched the fireworks, laughing and cheering with delight.

When this wonderful day came to an end, his closeness as he walked beside her across the *campo* made her heart beat faster. The sky was radiant with stars, a soft breeze cooling her after a long, hot day. Was that the reason she could feel her cheeks glowing and a burning sensation inside her, or something else entirely? As they reached the door of the *cortijo* and he leaned over to open it, she found herself intoxicated by the scent of his aftershave and warm skin. He met her gaze with desire very evident in his expression, his mouth a mere inch away from hers, then a flash of uncertainty came into his eyes. Jo felt it too as she recalled how Libby could be Gregorio's real mother. If that were true then she and Anton would indeed be related. Disappointment resonated through her. Were it not for that possibility he might well have kissed her. And Jo knew in her heart she would have welcomed that.

It also crossed her mind that she'd made no mention of Felix's arrival, or her one-time relationship with him. Should she have done so, she wondered. Hopefully, her ex-boyfriend would have left by now, as ordered. It was then that the door opened and Felix appeared.

TWENTY-NINE

THE TWO MEN stood staring at each other in stunned disbelief while Jo felt her heart sink to her toes. The last thing she'd wanted was for Felix and Anton to meet. How embarrassing.

'I didn't realise you had a visitor,' Anton said, his tone a little cool. 'I thought you were here alone.'

'I am.' Glowering at Felix, she said, 'I thought you promised to find alternative accommodation down on the *playa?*'

Ignoring this question Felix winked at Anton. 'Jo and I have been together for some years, so I couldn't resist coming to join her on holiday.'

Jo gasped, his remark leaving her speechless with fury. Before she could think of a suitable response Sophie came to stand beside her father, her eyes glimmering with curiosity as she looked at their visitor.

'Is this your daughter?' Anton asked Jo, a small puckered frown on his brow as he politely smiled.

'Goodness, no,' she said, which brought forth a peal of laughter from the teenager.

Felix chuckled too. 'You could say she's her stepdaughter, as she's been a good mother to her.'

Sophie gave him a nudge with her elbow. 'You're a complete airhead! How can that be when you never married her?'

'We are a couple, though, and you are an important part of our family.'

'We most certainly *aren't* a couple. Not any more,' Jo snapped.

'I think I'd better go,' Anton tactfully remarked. 'I'll see you tomorrow, Jo, for our visit to the art expert when we'll hopefully get the results of the picture inspection. I wish you goodnight.' And turning on his heel, he walked briskly away.

Jo felt humiliated and deeply disappointed that such a wonderful day should end so embarrassingly badly. Yet wishing to avoid any further argument in front of Sophie, she stormed to her room and quickly locked the door. As she leaned against it with tears in her eyes, Jo couldn't help but wonder if Felix's presence had ruined her relationship with Anton, even if it was little more than a friendship. A part of her ached for it to be something more, despite all the reservations she felt.

❧

'I'm so sorry about last night,' Jo told Anton when they met up the next morning. 'Felix and I were together for a while but split up some weeks ago. He's here because of financial difficulties, nothing to do with me. And most definitely confined to the sofa.'

Was that a blink of relief she saw in his gaze, or a complete lack of interest? It was hard to tell. 'So you weren't sorry to see the relationship end?'

'Not in the least. Having discovered he was having an affair with a work colleague it was probably naïve of me to believe him when he said it had ended. I was stupid enough to forgive him.'

'You were probably just being a little too kind, but then I know that feeling well. It happened to me too.'

She looked up at him with deep sympathy in her eyes. 'Really? I'm sorry to hear that.'

'I too forgave her, and instantly regretted it as she then had a fling with someone else. Not something I would ever risk doing again. If you can't trust the person you love, who can you trust?'

'I do so agree.' Their eyes locked in complete understanding, and something more compelling. 'I've made it clear to Felix that he has to leave,' Jo said, taking a breath as she felt her heart start to race.

'*Excelente!* If that is what you wish.'

'It most certainly is.'

His smile in response to this comment was really quite heart-warming. 'Relationships can be a bit tricky at times,' he admitted.

'As it was with Charlotte and Libby,' Jo agreed. 'Close friends so far as Charlotte was concerned, but jealous rivals in Libby's screwed-up mind. Right now I'm really looking forward to hearing the results of the investigation of this picture.'

He nodded. 'Me too.'

'You'll be interested to hear that I found identical colours in both pictures: burnt umber, ultramarine, cadmium yellow, vermil-ion, titanium white and ivory black,' the art expert told them. 'The brush strokes, canvas, and style of painting are also the same, so I can confirm that both these pictures were painted by the same per-son. I checked for any touch-ups in the smaller picture, and there are a few but I'm still convinced it's genuine. In addition I did a further x-ray which revealed matching fingerprints on each.'

Jo breathed a sigh of relief, feeling a swell of excitement within. This was the result she'd been hoping for all along. 'Thank goodness for that. So they were both painted by this Ramón Peña Barros.'

'They were indeed. Unfortunately, as well as being a political activist, it is believed he was involved in the theft of a painting taken from a local museum.'

'Really?' Having been about to reveal the artist's true name, Jo stared at him in dismay. Would that now be the right thing to do? Sharing a quick glance with Anton, she got the impression from the warning in his eyes that he thought not.

'Is there any evidence that he was guilty as charged?' Anton asked.

'None that I can find. But there is little, if any, information available about this man's life. He clearly kept well hidden, perhaps in order to save himself from prosecution, as so many did in those days.'

'Well, that is none of our concern. Thank you so much for your help,' Jo said as she quickly settled the bill. It was a considerable sum and she doubted the director of the gallery would repay her, even when she explained that she'd been right in her judgement. 'I'm so glad we didn't reveal that this Ramón Peña Barros was actually Charlotte,' she told Anton as they walked back out to the car. 'The thought that she was accused of theft is quite terrifying.'

'It is indeed, but as this art expert did not seem to know who Peña Barros truly was, she may have managed to evade prosecution.'

'We could ask Rosita if she knows anything about the rumour,' Jo said, as they drove home, both pictures safely stowed away in the boot of the car.

'I would love to find an answer to that too, Jo. I'm really enjoying helping you investigate this matter.' When again his gaze collided with hers, she felt a huge relief that their friendship still seemed quite vibrant, despite Felix's invasion.

'I very much appreciate your help too,' she softly told him.

'You should be aware that Rosita lost many friends who were either killed, or fled the country because they were threatened with arrest, whom she never saw again. It was a devastating time for her. I once asked if her husband had been taken to prison, thinking that could be the reason she never mentioned him. A question that was met by her usual stony silence.' Anton gave a little sigh. 'There's a limit to what she's prepared to speak of.'

'We can but ask,' Jo said, feeling a sudden desire to smooth her hands through his dark curly hair, and touch the tempting smoothness of his mouth as they'd almost done last evening. There was something intoxicating about this man. But as her breathing started to quicken, she reminded herself they could be related so must keep their distance.

'To discover the true identity of this artist is one thing,' she said to Rosita. 'But we still don't know if this charge against him, or rather her, is true.'

'I can tell you how that charge came about,' Rosita said. 'All thanks to my Fascist husband.'

Intrigued, Jo and Anton settled side by side to listen.

⁶〜⁹

One night in the autumn of 1937 Demetrio told me with a smirk that he had a plan to make us rich. 'I've heard that the authorities in Madrid have transported pictures from the Prado to a safer hiding place. We're not sure where that is, but the local art gallery has decided to do the same. They will be moving their stock of paintings over to Almeria city. With Ray's help I intend to hijack the van and help myself to some of this collection.'

I stared at him in disbelief. 'You cannot be serious. Why would you run the risk of being arrested for a criminal offence?'

'Dunmore will do all the dirty work, as he knows which pictures are valuable and which are not, while I shall keep well hidden in the driving seat. I have it all carefully planned. I mean to store the pictures in the caves on our land, a place no one will think to look. Then after the war we can sell them and become rich. This will enable you to give up working and devote yourself entirely to me and our future children.'

I felt my heart sink with fear. Fortunately, I managed to hold my lips tightly shut, otherwise I might have said something I would live to regret. Had Demetrio gone completely mad? This was entirely the wrong thing to do. Desperately afraid of the consequences for my mother and sisters, I could think of no way to stop him.

As Nick had returned, I decided to tell him. He seemed to be constantly at my side, eager to help with whatever I was doing. And he was most attractive, a sweet, caring man who treated me with complete respect. We'd become quite good friends. The touch of his hand set my senses soaring. But much as he excited me I did my utmost not to become too close to him, all too aware that Demetrio could be watching.

'I really have no idea how I can prevent him from committing this crime, wrong though it undoubtedly is,' I explained, as I told him what I'd learned. 'This scheme is madness, and Demetrio fully intends to involve me by using our caves. Living with my husband is like being confined in a straitjacket. He has unrealistic expectations and power is everything to him, so whatever he tells me to do, I must obey, which in this instance will surely be most dangerous.'

'I'm sure we can put a stop to his plan,' Nick said, putting his arms about me and giving me a hug, no doubt in an attempt to offer comfort. But within seconds, quite unable to resist as my heart raced at feeling the warmth of his body against mine, I was kissing him, and he responded with fervour. I confess it was a moment I'd longed for. I adored him, and it was quite clear that he felt the same way about me. Fortunately, Demetrio was not around to see what we were up to, but we both realised we'd overstepped a boundary and quickly broke apart.

'I'm so sorry. I should no have done that,' he instantly apologised.

'It was my fault,' I said, giving him a shy smile, while in my heart I longed for him to kiss me again.

He was tactfully backing away. 'Ye can safely leave this matter wi' me. Ah, but ye're a lovely wee lady.' Then stepping close once more he captured my face between the palms of his hands and kissed me again. I knew by the sad regret in his eyes when he finally released me and walked away, that it would be the last time.

How I wished that I could turn back the clock. Rushing into marriage had been entirely the wrong thing to do, but I could see no way out of it. I was completely under my husband's control.

When I explained to Charlotte what Demetrio was planning to do, my new friend was utterly appalled. 'What kind of a fool is this husband of yours?' she asked.

'A dangerous one,' I calmly responded. 'I did try to point out the risks he would be taking, but nothing I said would make him change his mind. And as he plans to store the stolen pictures on *my* family's land, I too could be considered complicit in his plan and equally guilty.'

'Is this anything to do with attempting to defeat Franco?'

I gave a shake of the head. 'Demetrio is very much a believer in fascism.'

'I have little understanding of Spanish politics,' Charlotte said, 'although, as you know, I believe in democracy and the rights of an individual, in particular those of women. So despite this man being your husband, he has no right to involve you in a crime.'

'Because he's turned into a thief.'

'Exactly. And why involve Dunmore? I agree he is an idiot of the first quarter who does not take life seriously, and very anti-establishment. But he's no criminal. He's also a gifted artist, so why would he take such a risk? It could ruin his career. All these magazines, newspapers and companies who have bought his sketches of the Civil War would instantly drop him.'

'Demetrio may not have told him the whole story, in order to save his own skin. Apparently, Ray will be the one handling the artwork, not my husband,' I said, going on to explain how Demetrio had boasted he would keep out of sight and leave Ray to do the dirty work.

Charlotte frowned. 'That's dreadful. I'll speak to Guillermo. See if he has any ideas what we could do.'

I was all too aware there was a love developing between the two of them, which pleased me. My cousin clearly occupied the heart and soul of her. 'Good idea. I have spoken to Nick, but I agree we should also tell Guillermo. We need all the help we can get.'

We discovered that Nick had already told him about Demetrio's plan, and the two men were attempting to devise a scheme to prevent it. 'We'll first ask Dunmore if he's aware he could be the one held to blame,' Guillermo said.

Nick frowned. 'We need tae approach him wi' caution. The fellow can be a wee bit stubborn, and Rosita must be kept out of it.'

'*Muy importante*,' Guillermo agreed, giving my hand a gentle squeeze before going to find Ray.

Charlotte had described him as a philanderer, a bohemian devil and a real womaniser. Seeing him approach, I felt it best to protect myself so hid behind a tree to keep well out of his way while they talked.

'We'd no advise ye tae do this,' Nick was saying, having tactfully outlined the rumour they'd heard without revealing my name. 'It could be highly dangerous.'

Ray Dunmore laughed. 'Not at all. It's important that we save these famous works of art. The Prado is doing that, so why shouldn't we help the local museum and art gallery to save their collection? Do you want Franco's men to come and steal that too?'

'Of course not,' Guillermo firmly responded. 'But we're concerned that Demetrio may have plans to steal the pictures for himself.'

'Nonsense. His aim is to protect and save them.'

'We believe he's planning to bring them here, which is risky for my cousins and aunt.'

'Why, if the work will be safely hidden?' Ray scoffed. 'It's as good a place as any.'

The argument continued for some time. Realising they were getting absolutely nowhere, and utterly failing to persuade him to steer clear, I felt a certain depression close in upon me. They too exchanged glances of despair. Ray just laughed and walked away.

'We cannot stand by and do nothing,' Charlotte said, looking quite cross.

Guillermo gave her a quick kiss. 'You're quite right. I'll make every effort to protect my family and put a stop to this stupid plan.'

'I'll be glad tae help,' Nick said.

'Me too,' Charlotte agreed.

'Are you sure?' Guillermo asked. 'You're a woman, not a soldier.'

'Fancy that, and there's a war on, which many women are involved with, including the fighting.' She met the loving pride shining in his dark eyes with a smile of deep gratitude in her own. 'And I do care about paintings. I'm working on one at the moment for Rosita.'

'She is indeed,' I said, going to join them and linking my arm with hers. 'She's a talented and brave lady, and a good friend.'

Guillermo grinned. 'She can drive us, then. But we must keep absolutely silent about this. Not a word to anyone.'

'Aye, it's just between us,' Nick agreed.

Later that evening I watched Ray and Demetrio drive off together, that arrogant artist presumably still believing he was doing a good thing for the sake of those pictures while my husband fully intended to line his own pockets. My cousin and his friends followed on behind, Charlotte driving the truck, all determined to foil Demetrio's plan. I spent the evening locked in fear over what might happen next.

THIRTY

SILENCE BLANKETED the countryside of La Colina de Arboledas, the night sky bright with stars as Charlotte drove along the winding road down the mountain towards the coast. A grey fox scampered across the road in front of her, causing her to brake and slow down, which was just as well for as she turned the next bend she saw the main coastal road stretching ahead. A huge lorry was parked to one side with its doors open, a small farm truck blocking the road in front of it. Drawing to a halt some safe distance away, she quickly switched off the sidelights as Guillermo instructed.

'Stay here,' he ordered her, and he and Nick climbed out of the vehicle.

'I'd like to come with you,' she whispered.

He shook his head. 'Reverse back around this bend, then turn the truck ready to depart. We may be in need of a quick getaway.'

How could she argue with that?

Charlotte watched, heart pounding as they gathered their weapons. Guillermo led the way round the edge of the mountain towards the main road. She could hear the sound of men shouting in the distance, one issuing orders and another valiantly protesting. She struggled to decide whether she recognised the voice. Was that Demetrio or Dunmore, she wondered, finding it impossible to decide as she quickly changed gear to turn the vehicle around. Parking the truck by the side of the road and leaving the engine running, Charlotte slipped from the driver's seat to trot a little way down the road in Guillermo and Nick's wake, desperate to see what was happening.

It was then that she heard shots being fired.

Fear escalated through her, the memory of the bomb flashing across her mind. But the prospect of losing Guillermo was so terrifying that without a thought for her own safety Charlotte ran as fast as she could till she reached the area where the hijack was taking place. Crouching down in the rough grass behind an oleander bush, she saw Dunmore standing in the middle of the road holding a picture in his arms. He seemed to be in the process of handing it over to Demetrio, who stood by the smaller farm truck, not hiding in the driving seat at all. The process had been halted by the arrival of two men clothed in black, balaclavas covering their faces. Charlotte couldn't be certain who was who, and it was all too evident that the two would-be thieves had no idea who their attackers were either.

'¡Basta!' came the order from a loud commanding voice. 'Deje de hacer lo que están haciendo.' Was that Guillermo issuing the order, telling them to stop what they were doing? She couldn't be certain as he sounded much more harsh and aggressive than usual.

The pair did indeed stop, fear evident on both their faces.

'Tengo un arma,' he told them, waving his gun in the air. He'd obviously fired it previously to demonstrate his power.

More rapid Spanish followed, some of which Charlotte didn't quite catch, but she watched in awe as the paintings were returned to the lorry, which was meant to be transporting the collection to Almeria city. The driver looked beside himself with joy, and when waved back into his seat quickly shook his rescuer's hand then jumped aboard and drove away at speed.

It was only as she stared at the clouds of dust left by this racing exit that Charlotte realised the men in black had vanished. Dunmore stood in the middle of the road looking utterly bewildered, while Demetrio roared at him in fury. She didn't hang around to listen. Racing back, almost wishing she'd done as she was told and stayed in the truck ready to depart, she was panting for breath by the time she arrived. Nick was already in the passenger seat. Guillermo stood waiting for her, a wry grin on his face as she quickly apologised.

'Success! Well done,' she cried, giving him a quick hug.

'Only if we manage to get back to *Casa Oliva* before Demetrio. So start driving, girl. *Now!*'

'On our way,' she laughed, slamming her foot down on the accelerator.

By the time Dunmore came to join the Brigaders for his usual nightcap, Guillermo and Nick were already seated along-side Laurence and Fergus. Charlotte settled beside Rosita, happily chatting as if they'd not moved all evening, a secret smile passing between them.

୭

The next morning as the sun was rising above the mountains, Charlotte reported the full story of their adventure to Rosita as she helped her feed the hens and goats. Her friend sighed with relief. 'Thank you so much for your help.'

'I was only acting as driver; it's your dear cousin Guillermo you should thank, and Nick, of course. The two of them saw to it that the theft was halted and every painting replaced and dispatched to safety, as they should be.'

Later, Charlotte did not fail to notice that it was Nick whom Rosita thanked first, giving him a big hug of gratitude, after a quick glance over her shoulder to make sure Demetrio was nowhere around. They did seem to be good friends, Charlotte thought, and growing ever closer. If only they weren't in the midst of a war then this young girl could perhaps achieve her freedom from this rogue of a husband and start life afresh, as she so deserved to do. Who knew what the future might hold for her, or for any of them.

Charlotte wondered when she would be able to return to Scotland and see Mama again. She could, of course, stay in Spain with Guillermo. An interesting but fascinating decision to make. She made a private vow to think positively. The war must end eventually, and life would then surely get better. And was her old friend feeling any better? How she missed dear Libby.

A day later, as if in answer to her concern, a vehicle drove in and amazingly, there she was.

'Libby, I don't believe it. Oh, I'm so pleased to see you again,' Charlotte said, hugging her tight. There followed a joyful reunion between brother and sister, then Laurence swept his wife up in his arms to give her a big hug and a kiss.

'Missed you so much, old thing. So glad you're now well enough to join us.'

'I'm fine and dandy,' Libby said, looking so pink-cheeked with happiness that Charlotte found it lovely to watch how they welcomed each other. Was all well with their marriage after all? Although Libby kept glancing over towards Dunmore, who very sensibly kept his distance. 'Did ye really miss me?' she asked.

'Absolutely. I've been busy arranging for the deportment of orphaned children to Scotland. Not easy, so could really do with your help.'

'Oh, I'll be happy to give it. Lady Felicity is now offering accommodation to refugee children.' And she proceeded to explain how the good lady had carried out this plan despite opposition from the laird.

Charlotte listened in amazement, fascinated to hear what her beloved mother was doing for the cause, and how she at last seemed to be building a life separate from her husband. 'I'm so delighted to hear this news. Is dear Mama finding confidence in herself again?'

'Aye, she is. Quite a lively lady now. Here's a letter Lady Felicity has sent ye, with all her love.'

Charlotte clasped it to her heart with delight. 'Thank you. I'm thrilled to have you back with us, Libby darling. I was only thinking of you yesterday as I've missed you so much, and here you are. Wonderful! So how is our beloved Scotland?' she asked with a bright smile.

'As beautiful as ever,' Libby said with a smile. 'Missed you too, milady.'

'Oh, don't start that again, we're not in the milking parlour now', and they both giggled.

Dunmore ambled over at that moment to peck Libby on the cheek and whisper something in her ear. It obviously didn't go down well as all colour drained from her pretty face, glaring at Charlotte in fury.

Charlotte blinked, feeling slightly baffled. 'What was all that about?' she asked.

Ignoring her completely, Libby turned back to Laurence and launched into a tale about how she'd travelled with a band of eager volunteers in a small ambulance packed with yet more first aid equipment. 'We drove it from Scotland to Dover, then through France to Marseilles where we caught a steam boat to Cartagena.'

Feeling her presence was unwanted, Charlotte went to sit in the shade of an olive tree to read her letter. The heat of the sun was already high and Laurence was insisting that Libby join her to take a rest. 'I'll take this suitcase to your tent, old thing, then bring you each a cup of tea.'

'A glass of lemon juice would be more appropriate in this heat, I think, Laurence,' Charlotte suggested, and off he dashed to do as she asked. 'Your dear husband is always so anxious to please,' she told Libby with a fond smile.

'He certainly is, and prepared tae marry a woman when that's the last thing he wants, bearing in mind his proclivities.'

The smile faded from Charlotte's face and the letter sat unopened on her lap as she stared at her friend in dismay. 'Ah, then you know.'

Libby blinked. 'So do you, by the sound of it.'

'I'm afraid so.'

'*How* did ye know, and *why* did ye never tell *me*, his wife?'

Charlotte found herself blushing. 'To cut a long story short I spotted him on the beach in a clinch with his friend Gowan. It felt quite a relief at the time as it spared me from accepting his proposal. However, Laurence made it very clear that I was not to say a word to anyone. He could end up being arrested for what to him is perfectly normal behaviour. I made him that promise, and as you eloped and told no one of your coming marriage, how could I warn you in advance?'

'You've had plenty of opportunity since!' Libby snapped.

'Not without breaking my promise, which Laurence insisted I mustn't do. Besides, you told me you were happy and that all was well between you.'

'I lied.' Libby was glaring at her with a wide, furiously cold gaze, her fists clenched. 'Despite all my efforts tae be a loving wife, he's rarely touched me.'

'I'm sorry to hear that,' Charlotte said, 'if not particularly surprised. Did he finally admit the truth?'

Libby shook her head, quickly explaining what she'd seen when he and Fergus were packing the truck. 'He's offered me the choice of a divorce or tae carry on as we are. I shall probably go for the latter as I'm no against enjoying a wee romance. Neither are you.

From what I've heard ye're having an affair with both Guillermo and Dunmore.'

'Utter nonsense! Who on earth said that?'

'Dunmore. He said ye'd happily kept him company as he was missing me so much. I'm no stupid and understand exactly what he's telling me.'

'Then he's lying. That man lives in a fantasy world. He loves nothing more than to crack jokes and say whatever might win him favours from a woman. I assure you I've done nothing of the sort,' Charlotte hotly retorted, then went on to explain his attempt to seduce her.

'I dinna believe ye,' Libby protested. 'He clearly knew ye wanted him, as much as he wanted you. But since ye already have a lover in Guillermo, leave Ray alone. He's *mine!*'

'You are welcome to him, Libby, but would that be wise?' she asked, feeling deeply angry at this accusation. 'As you know perfectly well from the way he behaved back in Scotland, and since, Dunmore loves to flirt with every girl he sees, many of whom happily respond. He's a bohemian type who believes in free love. I've seen him chatting up Rosita too, even though she's married and wisely resists him, as well as many of the nurses. Yet he doesn't care about any of them, being interested only in his own satisfaction.'

Libby was on her feet, a crimson sheen of fury blighting her face. 'He certainly does care about me. He always has.'

'I wouldn't be too sure about that. How can you trust that fellow when he's such a philanderer?'

'So are you! How you love to keep every man's attention for yerself, which you feel ye have the right to enjoy, being such a fine lady.'

Making a valiant effort to calm herself down, Charlotte sighed. 'Don't start all that nonsense again. We are friends, Libby. Can't you see that I'm just attempting to protect you? And you know very well that all the attention and proposals I used to receive drove me mad. Now I have met Guillermo and he is everything to me. I am not at all interested in that bohemian libertine.'

'Why would I believe that when you didna care enough aboot me tae save my disastrous marriage? But I too have the right tae happiness, so damn you, Lady bloody Charlotte.' Whereupon Libby stormed off, bumping straight into Laurence and sending the glasses of lemon juice spinning out of his hand.

⁓

Charlotte found it utterly heart-rending that relations with her old friend now seemed to have dipped to an all-time low. Libby was deliberately avoiding her, and refusing to speak to her. Striving to block these concerns from her head, she was packing an ambulance in preparation for her usual first aid duty for the day when Nick came over. 'We didna have quite the success we imagined the other night. I've been keeping an eye on Demetrio, for Rosita's sake, and he seems tae have visited the cave quite a few times lately.'

Charlotte stared at him in horror. 'Oh no! Are you saying that he may have succeeded in stealing some pictures after all?'

'I get the impression he could have something secreted away, aye. He's oot today so I intend to tak a wee nose aroond.'

'Please do that.'

Nick returned to say that he'd searched the cave but found nothing. 'Mebbe I was wrong.'

'Then why does Demetrio keep visiting it?' Charlotte asked with a puzzled frown.

He shook his head. 'Dunno, but I'll continue tae keep an eye on him and see if I can find oot what he's up tae.'

Glancing across the *campo*, Charlotte saw Dunmore chatting to Rosita as he set up his easel. Was he about to paint her? She was beaming at him as only such a lovely young girl could do. A memory of her own experience of having her portrait painted by Dunmore brought a quiver of shame to Charlotte's soul. It had felt like fun at the time, exciting her by the way his looks had skittered her senses, but it had come at a cost. She'd achieved freedom and was doing something useful with her life but she had lost her home and contact with her mother. By coming to Spain she'd also found love, but danger was present each and every day. Libby had been less fortunate. Not finding the love she'd hoped for, she'd become obsessed with Dunmore and put herself in danger as a result. Charlotte had no wish to see Rosita suffer in the same way. Neither had she any wish for her to be coerced into doing something she may regret as a result of being flattered by Dunmore's attention.

Feeling some concern for her new friend Charlotte slid the last box of bandages into the ambulance, then strolled over. 'Is painting Rosita your latest project?' she asked him.

He chuckled. 'Why do you ask? Are you jealous?'

A ripple of anger brought a flush to her cheeks. 'Don't be ridiculous. Why would I be? I'm concerned that you might offend Demetrio by painting his wife, which could make things difficult for her. I'm in the process of painting a picture of her house, so maybe you should do something similar.'

'It's perfectly all right,' Rosita said with a smile. 'It is my dear friend Taco the donkey he's painting.'

'Oh, I'm sorry, didn't realise.' Charlotte's flush now changed to one of crimson embarrassment. Interfering in this way had made her look extremely foolish.

Dunmore snorted with laughter. 'This old burro works hard and deserves to have a place in history. Rosita would love to have his picture adorning her wall, would you not, my dear?'

'*Sí, por favor*,' she agreed. 'I'm sure Demetrio would have no objection to that.'

Giving her friend a hug, Charlotte whispered in her ear. 'Do take care to protect yourself, Rosita. He's ruined my friend's life, and is now doing his utmost to spoil mine. Don't let him interfere with yours too.' Then raising her brows, she locked Dunmore in a stern gaze. 'See that you treat this young girl with absolute respect and courtesy. You'll answer to me if you don't.'

'Ah, so you really are jealous, milady?' he chortled, and Charlotte stalked away, unable to think of a suitable retort. This man seemed hell-bent on creating problems.

❧

'Did Dunmore behave himself?' Charlotte asked a few days later as she and Rosita were stripping leaves off the pruned olive branches in order to produce some kindling for the stove.

'Why would he not?' Rosita said with a smile. 'He was just painting Taco, although he has expressed a wish to paint me too.'

Carrying the basket of kindling over to the outhouse, Charlotte piled them upon the rest of the stack, then returned for the next load. She and Rosita worked well together, a close friendship having developed between them. She felt the need to warn her about him yet again, but before she could find the right words, Libby came over to join them. Charlotte felt relieved to see her, and when they'd finished this task they set about preparing breakfast together.

The three of them chatted about the weather, Taco the donkey, the state of the crops, anything but the war as they sat enjoying a *café con leche* and *tostadas* with tomatoes and olive oil, a typical Andalucían breakfast, as they so loved to do.

'Look at us in our scrubby work overalls. Do ye think we'll ever be normal females again?' Libby asked with a grin.

Charlotte laughed. 'Goodness, do you remember all those fancy gowns Mama used to buy for me? What a fuss she would make if she saw me like this. I've quite forgotten how to look glamorous.'

'Ye always look perfect, milady Charlie, even when ye have mud all over you.'

Libby might never understand how status and money were of no importance to Charlotte, but their friendship most definitely was. Relations between them did seem to be improving a little. 'I'm not convinced of that but have always been an outdoor person, as you know. Much more fun than talking to the ghosts in Craiklyn Manor. Look at my hair. It falls halfway down my back whenever I unpin it.'

'Still dark and glossy, but I could trim it for ye,' Libby offered.

'Really? That would be wonderful.'

'Mine needs cutting too,' Rosita said. 'It blows all over my face whenever I'm digging.'

Moments later they were all happily washing their hair in the jars of water Taco brought for them, then giggling as chunks of hair fell to the ground all around as Libby clipped away. 'Not too short,' Charlotte said. 'Just reaching my shoulders would be perfect. Do you remember that time when the three of us tried our hand at sailing on the River Dee, with Laurence in charge, of course?'

'Och, aye, and you nearly got knocked into the water when the sails came spinning round,' Libby said with a chuckle.

'Thankfully saved by you shouting at me to duck, which I managed to do just in time.'

'Had you fallen in ye could well have turned into a duck, flapping about.'

'I might have drowned, as I wasn't a good swimmer at that stage. You saved my life, darling, and what fun it was.' The two friends' gazes locked in memories of the jolly times they'd enjoyed together over the years. 'Now I love the fact I'm doing something useful with my life.'

'Me too,' Libby agreed as she brushed and tidied Rosita's hair, having trimmed it to a more practical and elegant length too. 'There ye are. Right, now that ye're both looking a wee bit more respectable, I'm off to help Laurence with these refugee children.'

'Before you go, I've been warning Rosita not to be too trusting of Dunmore. As we know, he is a man filled with problems. He wishes to paint her – what would you advise?'

Gazing at Rosita now with anguish in her chocolate brown eyes, Libby shook her head. 'Dinna ever allow him tae do that.'

'Why ever not?'

Sitting herself down on the bench again, she gave a little sigh. 'Mebbe there's something ye should both know. Ray and I have been involved for well over a year.'

'So you did have an affair?' Charlotte quietly asked.

'Aye! It began when I first modelled for him, which got me with child and was the reason I persuaded Laurence tae wed me. I knew marriage would never be on Ray's list.'

'Oh, my goodness! Now I understand everything', and Charlotte put her arms about her old friend to hold her close.

Then she and Rosita listened in silence as Libby told her heart-rending tale, including how she lost her child, and still found it hard to resist Dunmore. 'I believe he loves me. It's no easy to be sure, or that he's faithful to me,' she said, carefully avoiding meeting Charlotte's gaze. 'But he makes me happy. Laurence and I have come to an agreement that I can do as I please. So now ye know, Rosita, ye'd be best to avoid him. No matter what, he's mine.'

THIRTY-ONE
SPAIN – WINTER 1938

IT WAS PROVING to be a bitterly cold winter and people on all sides were dying as a result of freezing temperatures, many from frostbite. According to reports Franco was again seeking to attack Madrid with the continued support of Hitler and Mussolini, although hampered by the bad weather. The Republicans, assisted by the International Brigade, had launched a counter-attack in Teruel hoping to distract the Nationalists from their advance. But by the end of January it was not looking good. The Nationalist artillery was making steady progress and bombing the city, forcing the Republican army to retreat.

'Things are not too good in our own area either,' Rosita told Charlotte. 'Republicans and anarchists are seeking to attack people from the right, while Nationalists dispose of anyone they consider to be of the left. Will this war never end?'

'It does seem to be growing worse by the day,' Charlotte agreed, all too aware that bombs were still dropping on Mojacar, Cartagena and Almeria. Here in La Colina de Arboledas, villagers were valiantly attempting to protect their own, but some people were regarded with open suspicion. Anyone who had acted as an agent at an election, or whose loved ones had been arrested, felt in fear for their lives. Claiming to be a moderate and not in any way an extremist was no guarantee of safety.

'People dread the sound of heavy footsteps approaching, and of hammering on the door,' Rosita pointed out. 'Houses have become fortresses with *rejas* guarding the windows and huge iron bars locking the doors. Some villagers feel trapped, as if they are prisoners in their own homes. They often hide away in an attic or secret room. Priests too live in fear for their lives. One in a neighbouring town, dressed in ordinary clothes as a means of protection, was still captured and beaten. And many have been killed.'

The very thought of all these terrifying problems, the sound of exploding bombs and shells being constantly fired, would set Charlotte's heart pounding. Droning aircraft again filled the skies, and the air was putrid with revenge. She remembered too well the terror she'd felt at being buried under bombed-out rubble, and had no wish to experience that ever again. Her sympathy went out to these people.

'Is there anything more we can do to help these village friends of yours?' Charlotte asked, thinking Rosita must be equally troubled by the increasing dangers of the situation.

'Some are vanishing overnight to hide in the mountains,' she said. 'The trouble is that if the authorities do not find the man they are seeking they will take his wife, or children, arresting them simply because they can't find him. Just threatening a man with that possibility will cause him to surrender. And tragically, family differences can result in revealing where a fugitive is hiding.'

'Heavens, that's terrifying if you can't trust your own family.'

'It is hard to trust anyone in this world. I can't say I trust my own husband, but don't tell Demetrio I said that.'

'Of course not! You can most definitely trust me,' Charlotte assured her with a hug.

Rosita smiled. 'It feels so wonderful to have friends living here.' Then glancing over her shoulder, she lowered her voice to a whisper. 'Lorena, another dear friend of mine, is in need of help. Her husband was threatened with arrest simply for being a Republican but managed to escape. Having heard he's safely arrived in Mexico she is desperate to join him. She's turned up with her children and is hiding in our cave.'

'Is that why Demetrio keeps visiting it? Has he found her?'

Rosita looked blank. 'I do hope not. What are you saying?'

Charlotte quickly explained what Nick had told her about Demetrio visiting the cave.

'No, no! Fortunately, he left on one of his campaigns early yesterday morning, and she only arrived late last night. I'm about to take Lorena and her children some food. But I wondered if you'd come with me, as she does seem to have another problem.'

'Of course, I'll be happy to help.'

༺༻

The cave was quite small and dark, but Rosita led her through to another smaller cave tucked away in a corner at the back, deep beneath the hill. It was darker, the only light coming from a small candle burning, but not as cold. A young woman sat on a rug in a corner with two children cuddled up beside her. Charlotte crouched down to examine her, noticing how she was shivering and groaning as she rubbed her swollen tummy. 'Are you in pain?' she asked.

The woman nodded. 'I think my baby is coming.'

'I'd say that might well be the case. And you are Lorena, yes?'

'*Sí.*'

Moving the candle a little closer, Charlotte carefully examined her cervix, a nervousness flickering inside her as she recalled only assisting a midwife a couple of times to deliver a baby. 'I'm not an expert but you seem to be fully dilated. It shouldn't take long.' There wasn't even time to walk her around as Lorena suddenly began to push, an urge she clearly couldn't resist as she must have been in agony for some time.

Moments later Charlotte was fully engaged in delivering the baby, while Rosita took care of the children. 'Try not to make a sound,' Rosita warned her friend. 'We don't want anyone to know you're here.'

As the contractions became longer and more painful, the woman bit down hard on her lower lip, desperate to remain silent as advised. Blood oozed down her chin from her bitten lip, but only the sound of her breathing echoed in the hollowness of the cave.

'Now push one more time,' Charlotte urged her. 'That's good, Lorena. Well done. I see the head. Now start panting.'

The baby gave a loud cry as it came sliding out into the glow of candlelight. 'It's a girl,' Charlotte said, quickly wrapping the infant up in a towel she'd brought in her first aid bag. 'You have a daughter, Lorena. What a little sweetie she is. Beautiful.'

As the baby's siblings came to hug their beloved mother, she began to weep as a smile lit up her tired face. Rosita was still fidgeting and looking extremely anxious. Lowering her voice, she spoke quietly so that the little family couldn't hear her. 'In view of what you've just told me about my husband, we should find Lorena somewhere safer than this cave.'

Charlotte met her gaze with a knowing look. 'I agree. Nick suspects Demetrio may have hidden something of value here.'

Looking startled Rosita glanced around, as if fearing he might walk in upon them at any moment. 'He could be back any time soon. Can we move her?'

'I think so, once the placenta has appeared,' Charlotte said, carefully massaging Lorena's stomach. 'Ah, here it comes. I could do with some warm water if that's possible, *por favor*.'

Rosita rushed off to fetch a small bowl, soap and a fresh towel, plus clothes for the baby, which Estela was able to provide, her mother never being one to throw anything away. Once the patient had been washed and dried, and was happily propped up against the wall with the baby tucked in her arms, Charlotte took Rosita to one side. 'Where do you suggest we move her to?' she asked.

'Follow me, and I'll show you.'

When Charlotte saw a hidden part of the cave that her friend had in mind, she firmly shook her head. *'No es possible.* Besides which, it would be far too cold for a new baby in there.'

'But we must do something. I know of one woman accused of helping her husband to escape, who was later found shot through the head.'

A shiver of fear rippled down Charlotte's spine. 'Don't worry. Nick can help me lift her into the ambulance. I'm sure she'll be safe there for the night—'

It was then that they heard the clump of footsteps approaching. 'Oh, my God, he's back already.'

Quickly extinguishing the candle, and gently holding a hand over each child's mouth, Charlotte sent up a silent prayer that the darkness would protect them. Rosita walked out into the main cave carrying the bowl, now empty of water, if still a little streaked with blood.

'What the hell are you doing here?' Charlotte heard Demetrio roar.

'I was told a fox had attacked a rabbit and it was lying here wounded,' Rosita lied, obviously saying the first thing that came into her head. 'Unfortunately, the poor animal was already dead and half eaten. I've buried it and cleaned up. How lovely to see you back early. Are you hungry? Can't be rabbit stew, I'm afraid, but I have some paella waiting.'

'I have things to do first,' he snapped.

'Oh, not right now, *amor mío*. Surely it can wait.' She pleaded in such a luring tone it filled Charlotte with admiration for her friend, knowing how she truly hated this man. 'You must be so tired, and I haven't seen you since early yesterday. Let's go and eat, or do something more exciting first, if you like.'

Charlotte winced as she heard him groan with desire, then slaver a kiss over her. The sound of his boots gradually faded as he led his wife away.

'Try to keep the baby and children quiet. I'll be back in a moment,' she told Lorena.

'*Muchas gracias*,' she said, squeezing Charlotte's hand with a grateful sigh.

'*De nada*.'

So many lives had been ruined by this war that Charlotte always felt ready to help, and desperately hoped this family would remain safe. Wasting no time, she ran to find Nick, who liked to help too, being so kind and caring towards Rosita. The pair of them lifted their patient, together with her precious baby, onto a stretcher and carried them to the ambulance, where the young mother and her children spent the night. Just before dawn Charlotte drove them down to the port at Garrucha, where they boarded a ship to Lisbon to start their journey to join her husband in Mexico, hoping to begin a new life.

Throughout February, Charlotte and her comrades were working in Mojacar in a worn-out school hall that stank of vomit and decaying flesh, tending to the wounded. It was heart-rending to watch mothers weep over their lost children, to see young men with their stomachs, brains or limbs blown to bits. How could war be a good thing, Charlotte would think in anger as she valiantly helped the doctor in the operating theatre. And why wouldn't the British government help these people?

When she wasn't engaged in nursing and caring for patients she spent hours cleaning up blood, scrubbing filthy floors, and trying to find food and water in a town rapidly losing all of its resources.

It was always a relief after a spell of hard work to return to the Olive House for a much-needed rest, however short that might be, and sit and chat with Rosita. Wishing to take her mind off the horrors of war she'd spent hours painting a picture of the *cortijo*. Now it was finished and Charlotte showed it to her friend. 'What do you think? If you don't like it then I'll toss it away.'

'Oh, it's beautiful. It so wonderfully depicts the *cortijo*, olive grove and flowers, and my dear Taco. Is this really for me?'

'Of course it is.' Carefully hanging the large picture on the wall of the *cortijo*, they stood back to admire it, tears of happiness in Rosita's eyes.

'Thank you so much, I shall treasure it always.'

Touched and flattered by her reaction, Charlotte accepted her friend's hug with great happiness. What a joy it was to give people pleasure just by painting a picture, which she so loved to do. She then made a suggestion. 'Since I'm done painting for now, why don't we go and search the cave, just in case Demetrio has indeed stolen a picture.'

'Let's hope we don't find one,' Rosita said, again revealing to her the secret section of the cave that Nick had obviously been unaware of. They had to carefully climb up a rocky section of the inner cliff, struggle through a hole quite high up, after which to her utter amazement Charlotte found herself in a long dark tunnel.

'Goodness, what's this?'

'It used to lead to the mine but not any longer,' Rosita told her. 'It was blocked off some years ago.'

Here they did indeed find a picture, hidden away tucked up in a blanket. 'Oh, dear, it looks like he did steal one,' Charlotte grimly remarked. 'We must return it to the museum.'

'But how can we do that without Demetrio realising what we've done?' Rosita said, staring at it in shock.

'I have an idea,' Charlotte said. 'A bit risky, but worth a try.'

It took her several days but she carefully painted a replica of the picture, working in this secret section of the cave. Rosita worked equally hard on the land close by, ready to distract Demetrio were he to approach. Fortunately he was absent for much of the time, as he so often was, and they remained safe.

Finally satisfied with her efforts, Charlotte deliberately aged her copy with dirt, ground leaves and rusty water, making scratches and little holes in the back just like the original. She even managed to replicate the frame by adapting one that Rosita already owned. 'That's the best I can do. Let's hope it works,' she said.

Late in the evening when darkness fell, they stowed the forged picture inside the mining tunnel, replacing the original, which they carefully wrapped in a sheet Rosita had brought along for the purpose. Then they placed this in the back of the ambulance in preparation for returning it to the museum.

'We'll park it by the *cortijo* then I'll take it back tomorrow and claim that I found it lying among the pine trees near the road where the attempted hijack took place,' Charlotte said. 'We can but hope Demetrio accepts my copy as the original.'

'He's no art expert, so I'm sure he will,' Rosita said.

Her husband might not be, but Dunmore most certainly was, Charlotte thought with a tremor of nerves.

∾

From beneath an olive tree where she lay in Ray's arms, Libby watched as her two friends came out of the cave on the hill opposite, wondering what they were up to. Were they carrying something tucked up in that sheet, and where were they taking it? Now they were driving away in the ambulance. That was odd, considering the cave was within easy walking distance of the *cortijo*.

Dunmore's tongue flicked over her nipple, burning a tantalising trail over her breast. Then cupping her buttocks he lifted her against the hardness of him. Libby instantly forgot what she'd seen as he thrust himself inside her, the rhythm becoming so powerful that she cried out in ecstasy as an exquisite sensation cascaded through her. Didn't this prove how much he loved her?

He laughed when eventually he flung himself off her. 'For a moment I thought you weren't interested.'

Struggling to catch her breath, Libby smiled. 'How could I not be? Don't I love ye tae bits?'

'So what was capturing your attention?'

'Nothing important. I was just watching Charlie and Rosita over by the cave. I think Charlie must have been doing another of her posters as she was carrying her box of paints.' Libby laughed. 'She's still addicted to painting. Have you seen the one she's done of the *cortijo*? It's beautiful, with aircraft filling the skies, of course.'

Dunmore was scowling. 'An artist doesn't paint at night, so what is she up to now?'

'No idea. Kiss me again.'

'I'm done for now. Let's go and investigate.'

'Why would we do that?'

'I'm curious.'

Lighting one of the candles that Rosita stored in a box just inside the cave, Dunmore held it up high as he led the way. He looked all around but could see nothing. Then walking through to the small cave at the back he quickly scrambled up the side of the rock and through a crevice in the upper corner. Libby watched in stunned silence, completely unaware that it was there. Seconds later he'd slipped back down, holding a picture in his arms.

'Damn and blast her,' he snapped, but got no further as a beam of light fell upon them. Spinning round, Libby found herself face to face with Demetrio holding a torch in his hand. For some reason a chill ran down her spine. Had he been watching them all along? Why would he do such a thing? It was surely of no interest to him if she was cheating on her husband? And why was he visiting the cave at this time of night?

'*¿Qué diablos hacen ustedes aqui?*' he snarled in furious Spanish, a language they were all accustomed to by now, if not swear words.

'This is a fake,' Ray snapped, flinging the picture down before him.

'No doubt painted by you.'

'No, it has nought to do with me.'

'I don't believe you,' Demetrio shouted. 'We all know *you* are the art expert, so it appears that you've robbed me of the original and replaced it with this rubbish.' Kicking the picture to one side he lunged at him with a knife. Dunmore ducked, lashing out a fist in defence.

Libby stood frozen in terrified disbelief as the two men wrestled together, Ray struggling to hold Demetrio off by grasping his wrist while ducking and dodging to avoid further blows.

'Stop this at once!' she screamed, but neither of the men took the slightest bit of notice.

Desperate to deflect what could be a devastating thrust, Dunmore was kicking and pummelling his attacker. Putting up one arm in defence, with his other hand he gripped Demetrio's elbow in an attempt to disarm him. But yet another stab was made, this time slashing him across the arm. Blood poured out. 'It's not me who painted this bloody awful picture, it's Charlotte.'

Fear spiralled inside Libby at these words. 'Don't say that, Ray. Charlie would never do such a thing.' Yet a part of her guessed that he might be right. Why else would she and Rosita be in the cave at this time of night? Demetrio obviously believed him as he pulled back, calling a halt to the fight.

'We'll see what she has to say on the matter.'

Libby spent the next hour applying pressure to Ray's cuts to halt the bleeding, then cleansed and bandaged them. By then it was almost dawn, far too late to go looking for her friend. Charlie was not in their tent and Libby didn't have the nerve to go to Guillermo's. Besides, it was unlikely Demetrio would speak to her until tomorrow, so there was surely no rush. Shaking with relief that at least Dunmore was safe, she fell into her own sleeping bag and was asleep in seconds.

∽

Charlotte was taking a siesta in her tent the next afternoon, feeling relieved that when she'd earlier delivered the original painting to the museum, the warden had been delighted and had not accused her of being the thief. Now she was anxiously waiting for Guillermo to safely return from the latest conflict when one of the nurses brought her a message. 'Sorry to disturb you, dear, but you're required to go up to the *cortijo*,' she said. There was something in the woman's expression that chilled her. Had Guillermo been injured yet again? The prospect that this time it could be worse, or the fear he might have been killed, escalated within her.

Quickly pulling on her boots Charlotte hurried up the hill and along the farm track. She found the door to the *cortijo* wide open. To her astonishment the kitchen was filled with men she didn't rec-ognise. Looking frantically around, desperate to see some sign of the man she loved, she saw instead Demetrio leaning against the empty stove with his arms folded. His sense of superiority was all too evident in his stance. Rosita, her mother or sisters were nowhere to be seen. Neither was there any sign of Libby, Laurence or Nick. Never had Charlotte felt more alone. Then one of the men approached her.

'Your papers and passport, *por favor.*'

Feeling slightly stunned by this request, Charlotte quickly apologised. 'Sorry, they're in my tent. I'll go and fetch them.' Who were these strangers? Falangists, said a small, terrified voice in the back of her head, and she felt herself start to shake.

'No need, we will search it.' The man in charge nodded at one of his comrades, who quickly marched out.

Charlotte made a move to accompany him and show him the way, but she was held back by one of the other men. 'Please let me go, he won't know which tent is mine.'

The sergeant, if that's what he was, gave a dismissive grunt. 'He can check them all if necessary. We've already searched the Olive House and, as reported, found papers linking you to associating with anarchists and counter-revolutionaries. Now it is necessary for me to see your passport.'

'She is also guilty of stealing a picture from the museum,' Demetrio said.

Charlotte stared at him in shock. 'That's not true. Most definitely not a thief. I'm here as a volunteer with the International Brigade. We care for all the wounded, no matter what their political persuasion. I have no politics of my own.'

There was no response to this beyond a snort of disbelief. Moments later the man sent to search her tent came rushing back. He handed over her passport to his leader, who flicked quickly through it. 'Ah, as expected. This is illegal. You are now under arrest.'

'I assure you it is not illegal,' she cried, sounding very like the Lady Charlotte she'd once been. But no one seemed to be listening.

With horror she found her hands pulled behind her back and her thumbs tied together with wire.

'Do not say another word,' the man shouted. 'Not until you reach prison, when we will question you closely.'

As she was led away Charlotte glared across at Demetrio, to see a knowing look and satisfied smirk light his face.

PART FOUR

THIRTY-TWO
SPAIN — 1986

SUNDAY SHOULD BE a restful day, Jo thought, spent languishing in the pool and relaxing in the sun. But she felt far from relaxed. Breakfast passed in a frozen silence, then Felix took himself off for a long walk, leaving Sophie in her care, as he had done on countless occasions in the past.

'I need time to think,' he said, when Jo asked where he was going.

The young girl was at least no longer fretting about her hair, devoting her time to swimming in the pool and lying on a lounger in her bikini. Jo produced a salad for lunch, which they ate on a table set beneath the shade of an olive tree on the pool terrace. 'Did he say when he'd be back?'

Sophie shrugged. 'Nope.'

Jo gave a sigh of frustration. 'The problem I have is that Anton has arranged for us to continue my research this afternoon. But I don't feel I can leave you on your own.' She'd expressed a strong desire to explore the caves where Rosita's husband allegedly hid those stolen paintings, hoping to find more evidence of why and when this particular picture was painted.

'I'll be okay on my own,' Sophie said.

'But it's not a good idea to lie about in the heat of the afternoon sun. You mustn't risk getting sunburnt or suffer from heatstroke.'

Pushing her plate aside with her lunch hardly touched, Sophie gave a snort of disapproval. 'Stop telling me what to do, we aren't *family*, as I pointed out to that guy.' Following this remark she stormed off to park herself back upon her lounger in the centre of the terrace in full sunshine. 'If it gets too hot I can always watch TV.'

'Sorry, there isn't a television set.'

'Oh, I forgot. That's so *boring*! What on earth are we going to do with ourselves for an entire week? Is there a disco or nightclub of some sort, perhaps in a nearby town?'

'No idea. But even if there were I doubt your father would give his permission. You're only fourteen, far too young for such activities.'

Sophie gave a little pout. 'I can talk him into letting me do anything, I kid you not. And if this Anton bloke is trying to win you over by taking you out, I should maybe warn Dad that he has competition.'

Jo rolled her eyes in amusement. 'I doubt he'd be interested, even if it were true. This outing with Anton is purely business.' The voice in the back of her head said that was definitely not true. The thought of spending another afternoon with him was making her stomach churn with excitement. At this point she heard the front door bang, but it was Anton, not Felix, who had arrived. She at once leaped to her feet, and quickly offered an apology. 'As Sophie's father is not back from his walk, I'm afraid I can't leave her on her own, so must cancel whatever you were planning for this afternoon.'

Anton smiled at them both. 'Pleased to meet you again, Sophie. *¿Qué tal?*'

'*Muy bien,*' she said with a grin. '*¿Y tú?*'

'I'm very well too, thank you,' he said, giving a nod of approval at her Spanish. 'I was hoping to show you the cave, Jo, as requested, and since it's Sunday I have the whole day off. Would this young lady care to join us?'

'Fantabulous! I love caving,' Sophie said, much to Jo's surprise.

'Really?'

'I've been on quite a few school trips, if you remember?'

'Yes, I do, but didn't realise you actually enjoyed them. It's very kind of you to let her come with us,' Jo said to Anton as they set out to walk over the *campo*.

'Why would there be caves in these mountains?' Sophie wanted to know.

'Nature has created them, and as mining has been a part of life here in La Colina de Arboledas since the Bronze Age, many miners chose to live in the small caves close to where they worked, as it cost them nothing. I can't imagine they provided much in the way of comfort, if warmer inside than out on cold winter days. Some caves are connected to the mines by tunnels, chiselled out underground to accommodate donkeys to carry the lead or copper ore, and later fitted with rail tracks.'

'So what are we looking for?' the young girl asked as they stood in the small cave cut into the hill.

'Evidence of where some stolen paintings might have been kept years ago,' Jo explained. 'Not that we have any proof they were ever here, and looking around I can't see it being possible. Where on earth could anything be hidden in a small cave like this?'

Anton led them through to a smaller cave beyond, but still they could find nothing. 'Doesn't look very likely, does it? Although I confess I've generally avoided visiting these caves as goats tend to be kept here now. These animals have no wish to be constantly out in the sun, any more than we do,' he said with a laugh. 'But they do leave their fleas behind, which are not pleasant.'

'Ugh!' Sophie said, giving a little shudder.

They searched the second cave, deeper underground, but found nothing there either. 'So, there we are, then. No nearer to an answer,' Jo remarked with a resigned sigh.

Sophie was still looking around, rubbing her hands over the surface of the rocks, and peering into every nook and cranny. 'Whenever I went caving with the school we were told that most people don't look up, and if you were ever to be trapped in a cave that's what you should do.' Then shining the torch upwards, she said, 'See, there's a crevice tucked in that far corner of the roof, which might be worth looking into.'

Following the beam of light, they both gasped. 'Heavens, I've lived here all my life and never noticed that before,' Anton said, looking stunned. 'But then, as I say, I'm not interested in caves.'

'Me neither,' Jo said, 'being into art and bright, open places.'

'I reckon I could climb up these rocks if I had the right boots on,' Sophie said.

'It would be easier if I fetched a ladder as we don't want you to take any risks.'

Anton quickly brought one over from the olive grove and Sophie happily volunteered to climb up and investigate.

'Rightio. Back in a tick.' Sprinting up the ladder Sophie quickly disappeared into the hole head first, her feet kicking out behind her only for a second before they too vanished.

The glow from her torch was soon no longer visible and Jo was suddenly filled with trepidation. 'Are you all right, Sophie? Do take care.' No answer came. Beginning to panic she called again.

'I'm sure she'll be fine. She seems to be a very resilient girl,' Anton kindly remarked.

'Oh, she most definitely is, and she does seem to know what she's doing.'

'We're lucky she's here.'

How could she argue with that?

The silence continued for some moments and then her face peeped out at them from the narrow dark hole. 'Guess what I've found?'

'A picture?'

Sophie gave a grim shake of her head. 'Nope, a skeleton.'

⁂

Jo had found the discovery quite traumatising, although she felt hugely impressed by this young girl's resilience and skills. The skeleton would never have been found without her, as Anton had quite rightly stated. They had climbed the ladder and followed Sophie through the mining tunnel, under her instructions, and stood looking down upon it in horror.

'Awesome! I wonder who it might be,' Sophie said, a tinge of excitement and puzzlement in her young voice.

'I dread to think,' Jo said.

'Something we will carefully investigate, so don't touch it,' Anton told her.

'Course not,' Sophie said, wrinkling her nose in distaste. 'So scary. Feels a bit like a Stephen King movie.'

They all agreed to say nothing until Anton had spoken to his family on the subject. Now, with Sophie tucked up in bed having enjoyed a most thrilling day, Jo yet again confronted Felix, determined this time to be rid of him for good. Seated in the cane chairs on the front terrace, she could but hope that the teenager wouldn't creep out to eavesdrop on their conversation, as it would not be an easy one.

The temperature in the late evening was softly warm, the heat having finally dissipated. This was a favourite time for the Spanish to be eating out and enjoying themselves, not something Jo felt she could associate with in her ex-boyfriend's unwelcome presence.

And she had no idea how to deal with the financial problems he'd created for her.

Silence hung between them. Felix sipped his wine with the usual sour expression on his face. Eventually Jo summoned up the courage to broach the subject occupying her mind, feeling inspired by the bravery of those forgotten women. 'Would you care to explain this financial problem of yours? Is it true that you've gone bankrupt, and that the bank has taken possession of our apartment?'

'I'm afraid so.' He talked at some length about losing clients to his competitors, deals cancelled, and a great deal of stuff about the poor state of the financial market, none of which made any sense to her. In the end, Jo's mind going fuzzy with too much information and perhaps the wine she was drinking by way of consolation and comfort, she called a halt.

'Since I am not involved in your business, either as a partner or an investor, how do I get back my share of the flat?'

'I'm not sure you can.'

'That doesn't sound right. We aren't married so why should I be robbed of my life savings?' she asked, anger beginning to erupt within her despite her efforts to remain calm.

'Your name is not on the deeds. The mortgage is in my name.'

'But I made a sizeable contribution when I moved in with you. Are you saying that I should appoint a lawyer to get it back?'

He gave a casual shrug. 'That would probably be a complete waste of time and money, as I haven't a penny to my name. Your name can be added to my list of debtors, but you'd have to take your chances in getting your money back along with them. It all depends on what price the bank gets for the apartment when they sell, and I'm afraid I have no control over that.'

Any more than I've had over you, Jo thought, a bitter pain stabbing like a knife in her heart. 'What a complete fool I was to trust you, to believe that your suggestion I move in with you was motivated by love, not money.'

He let out a heavy sigh. 'I didn't ask for your money, Jo, you offered it. But I didn't expect to ever go bankrupt.'

'That's not true, you kept casually hinting at it, as you were spending like there was no tomorrow. Meals at the Ritz and the Savoy, a box at the opera, holidays in the Seychelles? And I had assumed we would soon be married, since I was pregnant.'

He made no reply to this, silence again falling between them. Jo poured the last of the white wine into her glass, furiously mulling over all that he'd told her. How dare he treat her with such contempt! He was the most demanding, self-indulgent man. 'So why did you come here?'

'I felt in need of time to work out some solutions, and could think of nowhere else to go.'

'Why didn't you move in with this Shelley, assuming you're still an item?'

He gazed at her with a bleak expression in his eyes. 'She rejected that proposition. Shelley decided it was not quite appropriate since we aren't married and I have a young daughter. She claims to have no desire for a family of her own, or to take on someone else's. I'm afraid she's not as tolerant and kind-hearted as you, certainly so far as Sophie is concerned.'

'Are you saying that is why you hooked up with me in the first place, because you wanted someone to look after your daughter?' Jo felt mortified by this notion, one that had never occurred to her before.

'Sophie had lost her mother, so why would I not?'

The pain was instantly flushed away by yet another wave of hot anger. What a fool she'd been. Finishing her wine, she got to her feet. 'I believe I will take the same stand Shelley has. The problems you are facing in life are no more mine than they are hers. And fond as I am of dear Sophie, I'm afraid she's no longer *my* responsibility. She's *your* daughter so stop being so neglectful of her. It's long past time you learned to be a good father. She's a lovely girl in sore need of your care and attention. Tomorrow I'll be out all day working. This time when I return, I expect you to have found alternative accommodation and be gone. This will be your last night here. Goodnight.'

And Jo walked away, not waiting to hear his response. She'd had quite enough emotional traumas for one day.

THIRTY-THREE
SPAIN — SPRING 1938

CHARLOTTE FELT as if the prison walls were closing in and suffocating her, stifling her breathing and making her want to choke and vomit. It was like stepping back in time to when she'd been locked in her room by the laird simply for wishing to attend Glasgow School of Art, or refusing to marry the man he'd chosen for her. Only far worse. Being closeted had always had a bad effect upon her, but however furious and terrified she'd been at the time she at least had been able to enjoy the glorious beauty of the River Dee.

Here the window was barred, and so high up in the wall there was nothing to see but a small blot of bright blue sky as the days grew ever warmer. The cell itself was fuming with heat, alive with fleas, mosquitoes, cockroaches, spiders, lice, bedbugs and vermin. Picking bugs from her skin, crushing and stamping on them had become an obsession. There was not even a proper bed to sleep in. The conditions were dreadful. At night the hundreds of women prisoners packed into the prison slept on a filthy old rush floor mat, listening to the high-pitched squeak of rats as they scuttled about. And rarely more than three times a day – morning, noon and night – were they allowed to visit the lavatory, which stank to high heaven. Other than that they had no choice but to pee in a corner.

But all of this was as nothing compared with the day she'd first arrived. Held alone in a cell, her thumbs still wired tightly together behind her back, she'd sat on a stool while questions were fired at her for hours on end. The Falange official began his interrogation by asking the usual one of why she'd come to Spain. It became much more difficult after that, every response Charlotte made leading to a punishment of some sort, followed by yet more questions.

'When did you first join the anarchist movement?' was the one that shocked her the most.

'I am not an anarchist, or a member of any political party,' Charlotte firmly retorted.

He slapped her face, so hard it made her brain go fuzzy. 'We are aware you're anti-Fascist. Give us the names of those you've worked with.'

'I've worked with none!'

'Do not lie to us,' he yelled, this time striking her across her shoulders with a stick.

Gritting her teeth against the pain Charlotte made a private vow not to cry. 'I'm telling you the truth,' she answered, stubbornly damping down the names of several village women she'd saved from persecution, including Rosita's dear friend Lorena, now safely in Mexico with her husband. Nothing would make her reveal who these poor souls were as that might risk them being captured and brought back to Spain to be imprisoned too, or worse.

'Write down all the names you know, whether you worked with them or not,' he roared, tossing a pad of paper and a pencil across the floor to her. The police officer standing behind her untied her thumbs, which was a huge relief, but Charlotte chose to ignore the order.

'I've already told you, I know none.'

'Take off your dress.'

Charlotte glared at him in shocked apprehension, all too aware that many prisoners died simply as a result of torture or rape, or were shot without trial. Terror made her go weak at the thought. 'No,' she firmly responded.

Reaching over he ripped open the buttons of her dress with both hands, and yanked it off her. She was then made to stand on the stool dressed only in her petticoat. 'You're a pretty woman. A red whore, I'd say.'

Charlotte could feel herself start to shake as fear and rage shot through her. She had to bite down hard on her lower lip in order to prevent herself from yelling at him. He made her turn round and round, then sit with her legs open as he and his comrades peered at her, chortling with laughter.

'Would you like to "work" with us?' he said, curling his tongue around the outside of his mouth.

'Never! I thought Spain believed in treating women with respect.'

'Only if you are a virgin or a mother, and not anti-Fascist.'

'I've already told you . . .'

She never got to finish the sentence as he began to slash at her bare legs with a riding whip, over and over again until they were scarred with red weals. So traumatised was Charlotte by the pain that, despite her valiant courage, she could no longer stop herself from crying out in agony. Tears flooded her eyes. Was this the beginning of the end and he would gradually beat her to death?

'Do you now repent your decision?'

'I don't know what you're talking about. I've done nothing wrong,' Charlotte insisted through gritted teeth, fearful she would pass out at any moment. It was then that the policeman behind her began to cut and shave off her hair. Chunks of dark curls fell all around her, tearing her heart into shreds. After that, still sitting in her underwear and now with a bald head, she was given a glass of cod liver oil to drink. Charlotte knew it would purge her system but had no choice but to do as she was told and drink it. She'd been warned that the Fascist attitude to women often resulted in them being made to walk naked through the streets, as witches had been forced to do back in the dark ages. But no matter what they did to her, somehow or other she must focus her mind entirely on survival.

༄

Following the interrogation Charlotte spent a month in solitary confinement. She knew that it was exactly thirty lonely days as she'd kept track of every single one by scratching a mark on the wall with a small scrap of stone she'd found in a corner of the cell. Judging by similar marks, it would seem it had been used for that purpose on many occasions before. At least it had given her something to do each morning as dawn broke. The weals on her legs swelled and festered as she was allowed only a small jug of water to drink and wash herself with each day, the pain at times overwhelming. She filled the rest of her time by doing exercises, reciting all the poems she could remember, and nursery rhymes her nanny used to sing to her when she was small. Charlotte wondered if returning to her childhood meant she was going completely mad.

One day, using the scrap of stone, she began to draw faces and figures on the wall. It brought a smile to her own face as she recalled her lack of interest in drawing portraits when attending art classes in Kirkcudbright, despite Libby acting as a model. But however badly done her efforts might be, she told herself that at least such activities helped to keep her mind occupied. It stopped her from obsessively worrying over what might be about to happen to her.

She desperately missed Guillermo, and was anxious about him too.

When her solitary confinement was finally over Charlotte was once again put through another lengthy interrogation as painful as the first, yet she gave the same answers to the same questions.

When at last she was released and moved into a cell with other women, they quickly gathered around her to help save her sanity. They held her, nursed her, fed and soothed her, and lent her a small bar of soap and bowl of water for her to wash herself properly, which after a month of grubby filth felt utterly blissful. In no time at all she'd made friends with her fellow inmates. These wonderfully brave Spanish women hugely impressed her. Their sense of solidarity clearly helped them to cope not only with the dreadful conditions they were living under, but the torture and beatings they too had suffered, the loss of their loved ones, and in many cases the fear of their own possible demise.

'You were fortunate not to be raped,' said one woman, introducing herself as Consuelo. 'So many are, no matter what their age, old or young. And it has nothing to do with sex and desire, only power and control.'

'I'm sure that is the case.' Charlotte winced as the woman applied a tiny sliver of olive oil to the open sores that had broken out again on her legs, hurting so badly she could barely walk. 'The guards seemed to imagine I'd be willing to submit to them in order to stop the beating. I declined.'

'Good for you, as that would mean they'd won,' Consuelo said. 'Why were you arrested?'

'I believe I was denounced.'

The other woman nodded. 'Ah yes, anyone can do that. Thousands of women have suffered in this way simply for helping a member of their family or a friend to escape from a village under attack.'

'I know. So what were you arrested for?'

Sadness came over her face. 'I was working in the rear guard helping to support our men by looking after their health, nursing and feeding them, doing their laundry and many other dirty jobs. I, of course, wore an overall for ease, which was the reason given for my arrest. Women are not permitted to dress like men, or be *miliciana*.' She laughed. 'I should have chosen to wear my flamenco gown instead, although that would have confirmed their belief that I was there only to offer sexual favours. Women to them are all deemed to be prostitutes.'

Charlotte managed a smile. 'I too was accused of being a red whore.'

Consuelo sighed. 'Are you married?'

'No, but I have a boyfriend.'

'Good. My family has been destroyed. My husband was killed, and now that I am in prison my children have lost both their parents. I know that it is common for children to lose their father in a war but they should not lose their mother too simply because she went to help with the militia laundry, or wore supposedly inappropriate clothes.' Tears filled her eyes. 'When my children visit me here, I'm not allowed to touch them. Have these guards no heart?'

'They don't seem to have.'

As Consuelo began to weep Charlotte put her arms about her in a warm hug but the woman quickly pulled away, looking over her shoulder to check they weren't being watched. 'We must not let the guards see that we have become close friends. They could then transfer one of us to another prison. Relationships are not allowed as they assume such things lead to plotting and intrigue. Women are treated like dirt. I dream of my release but we all live in fear of being beaten, tortured, raped or executed.'

'I fear I might be too old to have children by the time this war is over,' said another woman, coming to join them. 'I may not be able to even now, since they gave my private parts a number of electric shocks.'

'Oh, my God!' Charlotte struggled not to hug this lady too, as she looked sorely in need of comfort. 'Let's hope you can.'

The woman gave a smile of defiance. 'Their torture of men is even worse, so no matter what they threaten us with, we must remain strong and survive. That's all that matters.'

The Spanish resilience filled her yet again with admiration.

Each evening the women would sing or dance, and perform little plays. Sometimes one would read from a book she owned, Charlotte would recite her favourite poetry or tell them a story from *Doctor Dolittle*, which always brought forth a smile.

Those women unable to read and write were eager to learn, not only to occupy their minds with something beyond fear, but also so they could send letters home. Remembering how hard Rosita worked educating her village friends, Charlotte gladly offered to help with that too. She felt extremely disapproving of this nonsensical belief that reading would rob women of their innocence and virtue. She fully understood their needs, as smuggling a letter out to Rosita was important to her too.

Charlotte felt desperate for news of Guillermo, and ached to know that he was safe. She worried too about all her other friends. Would they be safe?

᠗

'What are you saying, Laurence, that this little one might never return to Spain?' Libby asked, staring at him in stunned disbelief. She'd been helping the next group of refugee children heading for the sanctuary of Scotland to board a small truck when she'd heard him warn one weeping mother that she might not see her child ever again. 'Are you suggesting it would be too dangerous for the child to return home?' she asked him softly in English, so the woman wouldn't understand what they were saying.

He gave a sad nod of his head. 'I'd say if Franco wins this war that's a real possibility, if these children are to remain safe. He is already removing children from families who have had one of their members assassinated, imprisoned, or refused to accept the beliefs of fascism. I believe he's handing them over to families who do follow him.'

'Oh, that's terrible. Why should a child lose its parents over stupid politics?'

'I agree, old thing, but the Fascists see themselves as superior. They are being assisted in this enterprise by the Catholic Church, who believe it's the right thing to do if a family leans towards communism. That aside, who knows what will happen to these parents while their children are gone. But at least they can be kept safe, far from the war.'

'Lady Felicity is already doing a wonderful job in that respect,' Libby agreed. 'As are many other generous souls.'

Libby watched with heart-rending sympathy as a young mother said goodbye to her five-year-old daughter. She clung tightly to her, striving to hold back her tears and remain strong, assuring the child she would see her again soon. Stepping forward, Libby smiled. 'She'll be well taken care of, and I'm sure ye will see her again one day.' She could but hope that would be the case, seeing the grief already etched in the woman's face.

'*Muchas gracias.*'

Libby sat the little girl on her knee as they prepared to leave. Fergus was driving and Laurence seated in the back with the refugee children, all waving, screaming or crying. Her heart bled for them. How she loved children and still grieved for the loss of her own, despite the problems that pregnancy had created. She dreamed that one day she might have another.

Libby and Laurence saw the refugees safely on board the train, two of the volunteer nurses returning with them, then stood on the platform waving as it pulled out of the station.

'I know you'd love a child of your own, dearest. Maybe we'll manage it one day.'

Libby looked at her husband in astonishment that he seemed to have read her thoughts. 'Don't let Fergus hear you say that. He might be jealous.'

They exchanged a smile, proving they were still close friends, and linking arms walked back to the truck where Fergus was waiting for them, a cigarette clamped in his mouth, as always. 'We have quite a long drive, so why don't you take a rest?' Laurence kindly suggested to her.

Agreeing that she would welcome a little sleep, Libby settled back and closed her eyes, smiling to herself as the two lovers chatted happily together. But she had Dunmore, so what did it matter?

They must have been travelling for almost an hour when Libby was woken by the vehicle suddenly slowing down. She heard Laurence swear, which she'd never heard him do before. 'Bugger, there's a patrol ahead, flagging us down.'

'We're going to have to stop,' Fergus agreed.

When ordered to do so, Libby climbed out of the truck with some trepidation, her heart pounding as she fully expected to be arrested or attacked. Instead two Falangist guards began to search each of their pockets, robbing them of the few pesetas they had left. They also took Laurence's watch, Fergus's Mosin rifle, and Libby's wedding ring. As the thieves examined their spoils Laurence and Fergus exchanged a nod, then reaching forward banged the guards' heads together.

'*Run!*' Fergus ordered them, as he dived forward to pick up his gun.

Grabbing Libby's hand Laurence started to race back to the truck. They'd almost reached it when they heard a shot fired. Ducking down, Libby leaped into the passenger seat and looking back saw Fergus stretched out on the ground, blood oozing from a wound in his neck. 'Oh, my lord, they've shot him.'

Laurence jerked with shock. '*No!*'

Without pausing to consider the consequences he rushed back to save his friend. As he lifted Fergus over his shoulder to carry him to safety, Libby too ran to help. By a miracle they managed to get him back to the truck as bullets sprayed the air all around them. Seconds later Laurence drove away at speed while Libby frantically attempted to halt the bleeding.

Back in the hospital tent at the Olive House she helped one of the nurses remove the bullet from Fergus's neck. Not easy as it was buried deep, close to his spine. When dawn broke Libby found she had to inform Laurence that, having lost too much blood, his dear friend had passed away.

THIRTY-FOUR
SPAIN — SUMMER 1938

IT WAS ONE day in June that Charlotte was told she had a visitor, and there Rosita was. How delighted she was to see her. They sat facing each other across a table, it having been made very clear that they could not touch.

'I can't believe you're actually here,' Charlotte said, her heart racing with excitement.

'I've been asking to come for months, but they've only now given permission.'

'It's so good to see you. *¿Qué tal?*'

'*Muy bien, ¿y tú?*' Rosita asked, giving her gentle smile.

Charlotte pulled a face, saying nothing as she slid a bundle of letters across the table towards her. 'I hope you received all the ones I sent to you via the women who have been released? And thank you for forwarding Guillermo's letters to me. It's so wonderful to receive them. I read them over and over again till I nearly know them off by heart. Is he well too?'

'I'm glad to help. It takes some time for the letters you send to reach me, as they are passed around from hand to hand. But it's always lovely to hear from you. Guillermo too sends his letters through friends.'

When she paused Charlotte's heart sank, for Rosita still hadn't answered her question. 'Tell me what's happened to him. Where is he? He never says.'

Rosita took a breath. 'He was arrested too, on charges similar to your own. We think he may have been sent to Jaen, but can't be certain. If I discover exactly where he is, I'll let you know. At least he is still alive and well, as this latest letter from him thankfully indicates.'

Charlotte could find no words to express the fear that escalated through her at this news. She'd believed her own arrest had simply been an act of revenge on Demetrio's part for forging that picture, no doubt revealed to him by Dunmore. Not for a moment had she expected Guillermo to be charged too. Had Demetrio realised who the two men were who'd prevented the success of his hijack?

As Rosita slipped an envelope across the table Charlotte quickly slid it into her pocket, and wiping tears from her eyes managed a tremulous smile. 'Thanks, and how are dear Libby, Laurence, Fergus and Nick? And Dunmore, of course.'

The silence this time lasted even longer before Rosita responded. 'I'm afraid Fergus was killed a couple of weeks ago while he was helping Laurence and Libby transport refugee children to the station. They were halted and attacked on the way home.'

'Oh no, poor Fergus! And poor Laurence. He must be utterly devastated. Are he and Libby safe?'

'Thanks to Fergus, they are. Laurence is dealing with the grief of losing his friend by working harder than ever for the refugees, ably assisted by his wife. As we know, despite the problems in their marriage they are still close. But since my husband attacked Dunmore, Libby has not been at all herself. She refuses to speak to either of them, not even to me.'

'Why?'

'I really can't say, unless she believes I should have stopped my husband from charging you with this nonsensical crime. You know I would have done so had that been possible, but I have no power over what Demetrio does.'

'Of course you don't, darling girl. I'm fully aware of that. But it sounds as if I was right in assuming that Dunmore did accuse me of forging that picture. Was Libby with him when he discovered the painting?' Charlotte asked, suddenly desperate to know more, but the guard was already at her side. Grasping her arm he marched her away, the short visit over.

'Don't worry, I'll come again as soon as I can,' Rosita called after her.

᨞

Prison food was proving to be a nightmare. A bowl of brownish hot water in which floated a few lentils, peas or onion with perhaps a drop of oil, *rancho* as it was known, was the best they could hope for. It would also contain bits of dirt, weeds, flies or maggots. The women ate every part of it because these creatures were the nearest to meat they were likely to have. Why would they complain, Charlotte told herself, when the entire city of Madrid, and no doubt other areas of Spain, were also facing starvation? Sometimes the stew contained rotten fish and an epidemic of food poisoning would break out. Many children would die as a result.

These little ones also died of dysentery and malnutrition, not to mention rat bites. Children had to endure ringworm, scabs, fleas and clothes that stank of urine and faeces. Judging by their sunken eyes and lacklustre expressions, revealing they no longer had the energy to cry, it tragically looked like many more would die. To have a child in prison was a woman's worst nightmare. If the infant was fortunate enough to survive the birth it would often be taken from her, and their emaciated mothers could do nothing to save them.

The depth of everyone's starvation was so bad that the women loved to sit and remember the good times. They would talk about parties and fiestas, their favourite food such as *Roscón de Reyes*, a large ring-shaped cake decorated with candied fruits to represent the jewels on the robes of the three kings, and eaten on their special day, 6 January.

'Hidden inside are *sorpresas*, surprises as you would call them,' Consuelo told her. 'The one who finds the lucky prize is king or queen for the day. But the person who finds the bean is not so lucky as they must provide the Kings' Cake for the next year.'

'And they are not easy to make,' laughed another woman. Then silence would fall as everyone's minds began to recall Fiesta de Los Reyes and Christmases past with loved ones now gone, till someone started singing again to cheer them up once more.

Charlotte felt so desperately hungry that she bought essential food on a number of occasions by handing over a few pesetas, a ring, and even the bracelet her father gave her, in payment to the guards as so many of the women had been forced to do. The agony of losing this precious treasure almost broke her heart, but she knew her father would want her to survive. At least the rest of his gifts to her were safe in Scotland.

But once she had nothing of value left, her condition worsened. Starvation brought endless aches and pain to her belly, causing her to vomit, although she scarcely had any food in her stomach to throw up. Fortunately, Rosita was now helping her to survive. She would bring her food, if only a few strawberries or oranges, and occasionally a small loaf of homemade bread, for which she and her fellow cellmates were profoundly grateful. Whenever she visited, Charlotte would hurry back to the cells and split up the fruit or whatever she'd brought to share with her friends, which was what they all did to help each other.

'My children have brought me a tin of sardines,' Consuelo said one afternoon with great excitement. By the time it was divided up between a score or more of the starving women they barely had a mouthful each. Oh, but it was so delicious, Charlotte thought, savouring every morsel. The next morning she was again sick, when Consuelo approached and with a frown asked, 'How far gone are you?'

Charlotte looked at her in puzzlement. 'What do you mean, far gone with what?'

Her face softened. 'Did you not realise that you must be expecting?'

'Oh my goodness, am I really?'

'I think you may be.'

'I just assumed I was starving hungry. Obviously my periods ended months ago, due to lack of nutrition, and I've put no weight on.'

Consuelo chuckled. 'On this diet, how could you? But we must try to find you some extra food to feed this little one.'

Wondering if what Consuelo had told her could be true she thought back to the start of the year when she'd spent most nights with Guillermo throughout January and much of February, just before she was arrested. If she was indeed with child then she could be three or four months gone already. Oh, how she longed to share this news with him, but revealing it might only increase his concerns for her. Should she tell him or not?

∾

Libby was offering her husband all the support she could as he grieved for his beloved friend.

'Sorry you lost your ring, sweetheart, but at least we saved ourselves, or rather Fergus saved us.' His tone sounded low and drained, and a wave of compassion washed over her.

'That's no important. Fergus was such a brave man, as are you too, Laurence. Ye always manage tae protect me.'

'Why would I not? We're a team.'

'We are indeed,' Libby said with a warm smile.

Despite the improvement in the state of their relationship, Libby's first instinct following Fergus's death had been to run straight to Ray to tell him what had happened, and how they'd nearly been captured. The desire to feel her lover's arms around her had been so strong that she'd been willing to block out the resentment she felt towards him for charging Charlotte with the forgery of that dratted picture. Fortunately, common sense prevailed and she'd managed to resist the temptation. The death of this young man was far too upsetting for Laurence, so he needed her by his side right now.

Libby also felt devastated by Charlotte's arrest, guilt still echoing within her whenever she recalled how she'd given in to Dunmore's pleas not to say a word to anyone about what he'd done. Had she refused to keep it secret and admitted to her friend that she'd witnessed Dunmore blaming her for that picture, dear Charlie might well have managed to escape before the Falangists came for her. But not for a moment had Libby believed that would happen. At the time she'd thought only that she was protecting Dunmore from Demetrio. Her feelings for him had not gone away. She was missing him more than ever.

Today, having returned early from hospital duties, Libby saw him sitting with his easel in his favourite spot in the olive grove. Her desire for him surged within her yet again. Ray Dunmore had been the love of her life for so long, why should she not at least listen to his side of the story? Charlie's arrest was surely Demetrio's fault, and not Ray's at all. There was no reason to assume he'd expected that to happen any more than she did. Guillermo too had been arrested and he'd had nothing to do with that picture, so far as she was aware. She could ask Ray if he'd be prepared to help her make a plea for Charlie to be released, as the charges against her were ridiculous.

Quickly taking off her Glengarry bonnet and tidying her hair, Libby smoothed down her kilt and strolled slowly over. But as she approached she noticed that he was not alone. Rosita was seated opposite him. This time he was painting her, not Taco the donkey, that picture now proudly on display in the *cortijo*.

Getting to his feet he stepped over to Rosita to smooth the dark tresses of her hair, then slid the palm of his hand down her cheek and neck. Remembering how he used to do that to her, Libby felt a sick pain churn in her stomach. He'd always been so loving and exciting, constantly telling her they were soul mates, an important part of her life for so long. Was Rosita attracted by him too, just as Charlie had been, despite Libby making it clear that they were a couple? She saw her Spanish friend suddenly bounce to her feet. They seemed to be discussing something quite passionately. Slipping behind a tree to hide, Libby couldn't hear what was being said. Was Rosita begging him to kiss her? A jealous rage yet again pulsated through her.

Dunmore's arms closed around the girl and, not wishing to see any more, Libby spun around and stormed away.

∽

As summer slowly changed into autumn Charlotte counted the days to Rosita's visits, once every two or three weeks. Libby, who looked gaunt, pale and subdued, often accompanied her. Her old friend seemed reluctant to discuss personal matters. She had little to say to Rosita either, although they may have been keeping some personal issues private because they knew she had enough to deal with in prison. Nevertheless, Charlotte felt deeply grateful for their visits. Seeing her friends gave her a reason to go on.

By September, much to her satisfaction, Charlotte was beginning to feel better. By then she'd finally admitted her condition to Rosita and Libby, and they helped by bringing her more food.

'Have you told Guillermo?' Libby asked one day.

Charlotte shook her head. 'Not yet.'

'Is that because you're no certain it's his child?'

Charlotte felt shocked by this question. 'Of course it's his. Who else could be the father?'

'As ye had a wee fling with Dunmore, it could be his, couldn't it?'

Charlotte glared at Libby, feeling a tide of anger wash over her. 'Oh, for goodness' sake, you aren't still rattling on about such nonsense? I thought I'd made it clear that I would never allow Dunmore to touch me in such a way.'

As the two old friends glared at each other Rosita quickly interrupted, anxious to change the subject in order to prevent them quarrelling. 'As a matter of fact Dunmore has vanished. Defected or deserted, however you care to describe it.'

'Goodness, why would he do such a thing when it's quite safe and comfortable for him living at the Olive House?'

'That's because ye're no longer around,' Libby snapped, tears filling her tired eyes. 'Not that I care so much aboot him as I do for my brother, who has gone too.'

'Gone where? Dunmore may be something of a coward but Nick certainly isn't. He hasn't been falsely arrested again has he, like that time in Madrid?'

Libby shook her head in despair. 'We've no evidence o' that. Laurence and I have searched everywhere, but canna find any sign of him.'

'You should be aware that news of the war is not good,' Rosita put in, gently patting her friend's hand. 'My husband informs me that the battle of Ebro, which started back in July, is still ongoing. It could be that as both sides are suffering from the worst casualties so far, they've gone to help.'

'Why didna Nick tell me?'

Silence fell for some time before Rosita answered. She had such problems in her marriage that silently shutting out pain seemed to be the only way she could cope. 'They were not allowed to, as they were obeying orders,' she said at last. 'Demetrio told me that the Republicans are trapped in the hills without shelter, and very little in the way of food or resources with the Nationalists firing at them day after day. Franco has increased his numbers to such an extent, together with the assistance of Italy and Germany, that they are now in serious danger of defeat.'

'If that's true then Nick and Dunmore could also be in danger,' Charlotte said. As Libby began to sob, she broke the rules of the prison to put her arms about her friend, sharing her anguish and mentally dismissing the accusation hurled at her earlier. 'If all hopes of a victory for democracy don't come about, then I could well end up serving this five-year sentence imposed upon me.'

'I'm afraid that could be true,' Rosita agreed, and the three friends sat gazing at each other in bleak despair.

Their visit so depressed her that for once Charlotte was greatly relieved when her friends left. If the International Brigade had transferred these two men into yet another battle, she could but hope they'd be safe. She felt considerable resentment towards Dunmore, but had no wish for anything dreadful to happen to him. Charlotte recalled the story he'd told of how he'd been abused as a young boy, and felt a certain pity for him. Had this ill treatment made him self-destructive? Did he tell these lies in order to gain her compassion? She rather thought the latter. He saw himself as highly desirable and most sexually attractive. But having made her lack of interest in him quite clear, why would Libby believe she would ever involve herself in an affair with that bohemian rake?

More importantly, she worried about Libby's brother. What dangers would Nick be facing now?

The sound of singing that evening managed to raise her morale a little. But as she sat scribbling a reply to Guillermo's latest letter, which Rosita had brought her that day, Charlotte's secret wedge of happiness over the child she carried did battle with the fear she might be stuck in prison for years. Would this precious child she carried inside her survive?

Glancing across at the woman sitting opposite rocking an empty shawl in her arms, she sighed with pity. The poor lady tended to nurse something all day and every day, whatever she could lay her hands on. And by the loving smile on her face as she sang to the cup, plate or woolly cardigan she was holding, she must truly believe that it was her child, the loss of whom had clearly destroyed her.

Many of the women were cradling their babies or children on their laps, no doubt praying too that they would survive. Charlotte gazed upon them with a mix of sympathy, admiration and hope in her heart. What could be more wonderful than having Guillermo's child? She still longed to tell him her news, but had so far resisted, as she feared she might lose the baby due to the malnutrition she was suffering from, although there had been some small improvement in her health. Better to wait until she too was holding her child safely in her arms. The birth couldn't be too far off, surely no more than a month to six weeks at most.

As this joyous thought warmed her, she realised the singing had stopped as the guard began to read out names of the latest victims.

Charlotte was about to write that she hoped to have some good news to share with him soon when she heard her own name called, and realised her moment had come.

Shocked to the core, she quickly handed the unfinished letter to Consuelo, who looked utterly devastated. They'd agreed to forward any last letters to loved ones were this ever to happen to one of them. A strange numbness came over her, as if her brain had stopped working. Aware she was about to face death, the fear she'd been living under for months seemed to slide away as she thought of her dear Papa waiting for her in the next world. Without a word Charlotte fell into line with the other women to walk stiff-backed, chin held high, out to the courtyard. Had she suspected this was about to happen she would have put on a prettier dress instead of this scrubby mess, so that she looked her best. Not a single sound could be heard from the thousands of women held in the prison. Silence clouded the air as darkly as the night sky. Charlotte gazed up at the stars, her last thoughts and prayers as she took her place before the firing squad being of her beloved mother, and Guillermo.

THIRTY-FIVE
SPAIN — 1986

SO THAT WAS the moment Charlotte had faced the firing squad, Jo thought. How dreadful! Did Rosita learn all of this from Consuelo, Charlotte's prison companion, when she was handed her friend's last letter? If she truly had been killed, no wonder they had never managed to find where she was buried. As always the trauma of the tale had exhausted Rosita, so there'd be an agonising wait before this frail old lady found the strength to tell what happened next. Jo spent a largely sleepless night, knowing the end was not going to be easy to hear. Finally falling asleep around dawn, she woke late to discover that Felix had gone off alone somewhere, leaving his daughter behind yet again. He'd obviously ignored all she'd said to him the previous evening. What a selfish, arrogant man he was. Why wouldn't he leave her in peace, she thought in silent fury. And why on earth had she ever been attracted to him in the first place? He was so different to Anton.

'Looks like you're stuck with spending the day with me yet again,' she said to Sophie with a smile, and was surprised to receive quite a happy one in return.

Today Anton was taking her to see the nuns in the hope of finding some answers. Jo had written to the convent, explaining how she wished to speak to someone who might have memories of babies born there during the Civil War, and thankfully had been offered an appointment.

'I can see why you find this man attractive,' Sophie whispered, as they climbed into his large black Panda car. 'He's much kinder and more thoughtful than my egghead of a father.'

Jo made no comment, feeling very wary of saying the wrong thing. Besides, the young girl seemed much more relaxed, actually taking an interest in what they were researching and asking a whole string of questions.

The convent sat on top of a hill at the far side of town, its white walls gleaming in the sun. Anton rang the bell and spoke to the nun who opened a small window, giving her their names. Sophie offered to remain by the car, saying she'd take a little meander around if it was too hot to sit in.

A small wooden door opened and Anton and Jo were shown into the courtyard, where they waited for some time. Eventually a nun appeared, walking slowly towards them with the aid of a stick and certainly looking old enough to have lived through the war. She led them into a small office, and, taking the seat offered, Jo explained why she had come.

'I wish to clear my grandmother's name of the charge of tossing away her baby, and wondered if you had any record of births at that time.'

Not understanding her attempt at Spanish, the woman looked at Anton, who repeated the question more clearly.

With a firm shake of her head she declined to answer. 'We have no wish to speak of the war as we prefer not to remember it. We leave that to God.'

'It must have been a difficult time but you surely cannot live within these cloistered walls and not face the effect of what happened during that period? The war created so much mayhem and trauma,' Jo politely pointed out. 'As I explained, I'm seeking information about Libby, my grandmother. Did she truly have a child, and if so what happened to it?'

'You must ask her that question. Or God.'

Jo felt a surge of frustration. 'And what of her friend, Charlotte McBain? In a letter of hers that we found she speaks of being imprisoned, and of the dreadful conditions she had to cope with. I would like to know what happened to her after that. Do you remember her at all? Was she shot by the firing squad? Did the nuns offer any help to women in prison on death row?'

When the nun's expression tightened but still no answer came, Anton politely intervened. 'We fully understand the fear that must have been instilled within the religious community, both in the war and during the Franco regime that followed. But we would welcome any snippets of information you could give us regarding these two ladies. My father too would greatly appreciate a little help on discovering the facts of his own birth.'

Rising from behind the desk, the old nun hobbled over to hold open the door. 'I'm sorry I can't help. Good day to you,' she calmly replied.

It appeared they had no option but to leave.

Sophie was waiting for them by the car, and as Anton opened the doors to cool it before they climbed in, Jo watched in despair as the convent doors were closed and firmly locked behind them. What a secret world these nuns must live in. And despite them generously agreeing to see her, she'd learned nothing.

'You wouldn't believe what I have to tell you,' Sophie said in excitement, when finally they drove away.

Jo stifled a sigh, expecting some tale of how she'd found another cave, or perhaps seen a *tortuga* ambling by. Instead, Sophie explained how a young nun had seen her waiting in the heat and invited her inside. 'We sat in the shade of the terrace in the courtyard and I asked her why anyone would give a child away during the Civil War. "Because that was the Fascist rule," she said. "All children born to unmarried mothers had to be handed over to a proper family, one who was a true supporter of the Nationalist regime." Isn't that shocking?'

'That's how it was back then,' Anton said with a sigh.

'But imagine losing your child just because it was illegitimate, or your political beliefs didn't suit. Dreadful. I gave her the two names you mentioned and she admitted to hearing a conversation between the nun you spoke to and another sister before you arrived. Apparently Sister Joseph Mary, the one with the stick, admits that she lied because she'd helped her, but then lived in fear of being found out.'

Jo stared at Sophie in stunned disbelief. 'That's amazing! So that's why she refuses to speak of the war?'

Anton was equally surprised by this news and quickly drew the car to a halt on a quiet country road so they could listen to the rest of Sophie's tale.

'The nun I was speaking to was young and obviously hadn't yet taken her vows as she was dressed differently. Do you call them a novice? Anyway, she didn't sound at all approving of the nuns' silence, and was warm with sympathy for us. She admitted the nuns do speak to each other on the subject occasionally, as if they still suffer guilt over all that happened back then. But they refuse to reveal any of the facts to the families concerned, probably out of fear, which she doesn't think is quite right. She told me that it was not Libby who tossed a baby away, as she was never in prison or present at the convent. It was her friend Charlotte who gave birth.'

'Really? So she was spared by the firing squad, probably because of her condition. We learned she was pregnant in this latest part of the story Rosita told us.' She glanced at Anton and he met her gaze with a lift of his eyebrows. Was Charlotte then Gregorio's mother? Jo wondered, which would mean they weren't related after all.

'I asked what happened to the baby but she'd no idea whether it survived the birth or was given away. She said Sister Joseph Mary was not prepared to say. Sorry, but that's all she could tell me. We did enjoy a good natter.'

Jo gave Sophie a big hug of gratitude. 'Thank you so much for your help once more. What a star you are.'

'Actually, I felt I owed you a favour as you've been so kind to me these last years, despite all my problems.'

'I do hope you can put those troubled emotions behind you now and move on to enjoy life, sweetie, as your mother would wish you to do. And do remember that I'll always be there for you, should you ever need me. Even though I'm no longer with your father.'

'Thanks, I will, although I've every intention of training Dad to pay more attention to me,' she said with a giggle.

Jo laughed. 'Don't bank on that, although I've urged him to do so. He too should move on in life. Whether these ladies managed to do so is still a bit of a puzzle. I understand more fully now the reason for silence on the part of the nuns. But why did Gran refuse to speak of such matters? There are still several unanswered questions. Did this child survive and if so, what happened to it? And what happened to Charlotte after giving birth?'

Sophie shook her head. 'That was a question she couldn't answer either. She did explain that the nuns were often held responsible for keeping activist women confined, behaving as jailers when they were about to give birth.'

'That is most certainly true,' Anton said. 'Although whether that was willingly done on their part or under duress from the religious hierarchy, is hard to say. If Charlotte was charged with being an activist, then even today she would be looked upon as dishonest or unclean.'

Sophie nodded. 'This novice did say something of the sort, that women were supposed to confine themselves to domestic work, not politics. And respectable women were not allowed to go to a café or bar without an escort. Yuk!'

Jo chuckled. 'Can't quite see you being happy with such a prospect, sweetie. But it seems we're no nearer to knowing Charlotte's fate. Did she die or not? We've tried and failed to find where she was buried.'

'Quite a difficult task,' Anton agreed.

Sophie looked sad at the thought, perhaps remembering her own mother's funeral. 'She also said that some prisoners took their own lives sooner than face the firing squad. I wonder if that's what this Lady Charlotte did in the end.'

Jo felt depressed by such a prospect, although if her baby had been stolen by the Fascists and she was facing possible death, who could blame Charlotte if that was what she chose to do. Yet a part of her was unconvinced. 'I don't believe she would do such a thing. She seemed to be a lady of great courage, desperate to see her lover again. So what happened to Guillermo, I wonder. Other questions that still require answering are: When did she paint that picture? And how did it come to be in Gran's possession?'

'And whose was the skeleton in the cave?' Anton added. 'I think we should speak again to *mi abuela*.'

⌒◯

When Jo woke late the next morning, to her immense relief she found that Felix had at last gone. Sophie had left her a little note stuck on the fridge door. '*Thanks for this lovely break. Really enjoyed Spain. Be happy and let's stay in touch. Love, Sophie.*'

Tears came to her eyes as she read it. If only her own child had lived. How she would have enjoyed being a mother. But Jo was immensely relieved that Felix had finally seen sense and departed. As to whether or not she could find happiness that was very much open to question. Was Charlotte Gregorio's mother, or did Rosita indeed have an affair with Nick? If she and Anton truly were related, then their relationship could end before it had scarcely begun. Not that she had any memory of this great-uncle Nicholas. What happened to him when he went missing, she wondered. That was another question needing answering.

As she drank her morning coffee Jo began to scribble out her family tree, of which she realised she knew very little. Then she drove down to the nearest telephone kiosk to ring her father. They chatted for a while before she finally asked him if he had any memories of Laurence, or Nick. He claimed not to recognise either of their names. As Libby had been a single mother until she married Robert Hendrick, he'd always assumed himself to be illegitimate.

'Isn't there any mention of your father on your birth certificate?' Jo asked him.

'My birth was never registered,' he answered with a caustic little laugh. 'So I don't have one of those things.'

Could her father be Charlotte's child, or was it Gregorio? As Anton had stated, they must speak to Rosita and beg her to tell them the truth of Gregorio's birth.

THIRTY-SIX

'THERE IS SOMETHING I should tell you before I go any further with Charlotte's story,' Rosita said to Jo as they sat together on the terrace, carefully shaded from the blazing sun, and with Anton seated alongside them. 'It concerns Dunmore and why he disappeared. Not an easy story to tell. Charlotte had explained to me how he loved nothing more than to take advantage of vulnerable young girls. "Do take care to protect yourself, Rosita. He's ruined my friend's life, and is now doing his utmost to spoil mine. Don't let him interfere with you too." And as you know, Libby warned me to keep well clear of him.'

'He does sound an extremely selfish man who cared only for his own pleasures in life.'

Rosita gave a wry smile. 'He was indeed, and of no interest to me. I saw him as eccentric, unconventional, and really full of himself. I'll admit I was attracted to good-looking men, even if I was a married woman, in particular to Nick, who was a lovely, kind man. I was always cautious because of Demetrio, but being young and vulnerable I didn't pay enough attention to what Charlie said. I felt flattered when Dunmore said he wished to paint me because I was attractive, never having thought of myself as a beauty.

'Seating me on a chair beneath an olive tree he arranged me like a model, stroking my face as he tilted my chin up and fluffed out my hair. "You are very pretty. *Muy bonita*. I shall so enjoy painting your portrait."

'"I really don't have time. I have work to do," I protested, still feeling rather awed by the way his gaze was devouring me.

'"Oh, but you must," he insisted. "I've admired you for so long I'm burning with desire. Please let me kiss you." Had I fully understood what he'd said to me I would have left, but as always he spoke to me in a mix of English and bad Spanish, which I didn't find easy to understand. Then sliding his thumb softly over my lips, his mouth opened as it hovered close above mine.

'Instantly panicking I jumped to my feet, not wishing him to touch me and terrified of what would happen if Demetrio suddenly appeared. "*No hagas eso*, don't do that. I'm a married woman. My husband would attack you yet again if you were to touch me."

'"He's not here, so how will he know? I'm desperate to make you mine," he murmured, and instantly began to devour me with kisses.

'I did my best to push him away, but there was no one around to protect me. Charlotte was in prison, Libby and Laurence on hospital duty some kilometres away, as were many of the other Brigaders. The camp was largely empty save for a few nurses tending the wounded. *Madre* and my young sisters were out on the *campo* busily working the land. When I finally managed to get him to release me, insisting that was what I should be doing too, he laughed. "No more fussing, girl, I know you're as desperate for me as I am for you." Then thrusting me down on the ground he started to caress me, running his hands over my breasts, neck and thighs. He was like an octopus with feelers everywhere. I vehemently protested but within seconds it was as if I was in bed with my brute of a husband as he thrust himself inside me.'

'He *raped* you?' Jo asked, appalled.

'He did, yes.'

'What did you do? Did you hit him, punch his belly, scream?'

Rosita shook her head.

'I tried to shout at him to stop but he pressed his hand over my mouth to silence me. It happened so quickly, and I was so scared, I was unable to do anything to protect myself. I admit that as a young girl with no experience of true love, I accepted that many men believed they had the right to violate women. You have to remember that I did not have a good marriage, or a loving husband; partly the reason I could never afterwards speak of what happened, not to a living soul. I was also fearful of Demetrio finding out, as he would be sure to blame me. Later, there were other reasons for keeping silent.

'When finally he rolled off me, I was struggling to get to my feet and make my escape, heart pounding and feeling utterly ravaged, when Nick suddenly appeared. He'd arrived back from duty early and came looking for me, if unfortunately too late to save me. But he guessed what had happened and struck out at Dunmore. "You bastard," he shouted. Seconds later the two men were punching, kicking and fighting each other. It was terrifying to watch. I made a desperate attempt to stop them but completely failed. Then realising that, as Nick was a fighting soldier, and he was nothing more than a cowardly artist, Dunmore turned on his heels and ran away.

'Nick came to me at once to gather me in his arms and offer comfort. I was sobbing but could not resist hugging and kissing him. To our ill luck it was then that my husband found us and naturally assumed we were having an affair. Dunmore might well have seen him approaching and that was why he ran.'

Rosita fell silent for some moments, as was her way. Anton and Jo exchanged an anguished glance. When her grandson slipped a comforting arm about her, she continued with the story in a quiet, heart-rending voice.

'The pair of them stood glaring furiously at each other for some long moments, then Demetrio ordered me back to the house. I tried to protest that I'd done nothing wrong but he wasn't listening. I quickly explained that it was Dunmore who'd assaulted me, not Nick.

'"Then I'll deal with *him* later," Demetrio roared.

'"Don't worry, you go home, Rosita, I'll be fine," Nick assured me. "I'll explain to your husband exactly what happened."

'So I left and hurried to join my family. How I wish I hadn't, as I never saw Nick again.'

'Are you suggesting that your husband killed Libby's brother?' Anton asked, looking shocked.

'I have no proof, but it could well be the case.'

Jo took hold of the old lady's hands, gently stroking them. 'That might explain why my grandmother never spoke of him. But may I ask you a personal question?'

'Whatever you like, dear. My silence is over at last.'

'Did you find yourself pregnant as a result of that assault?'

'I did,' Rosita quietly admitted, meeting Jo's sympathetic gaze with a sad smile.

'So now we know who Gregorio's father was. It was not Nick.'

'No dear, it was definitely Dunmore. A most shocking thing to happen to me, which is why I've grown accustomed to keeping silent about all that took place back then. I once attempted to tell my son, then decided it would be dreadful for him to discover he was the result of rape. I again fell silent and let him believe he was adopted. Now I appreciate that it is time to tell him the whole story.'

Looking up, Jo met Anton's gaze, which seemed alight with relief and hope as he tenderly smiled at her. It was as if he was saying, thank goodness, we can enjoy a romance after all. Jo found herself returning his smile, her heart racing with joy.

But again feeling overwhelmed by sadness at hearing this tragic tale, she wanted to know more. 'What happened to Charlotte, was she killed by the firing squad?'

THIRTY-SEVEN
SPAIN — OCTOBER 1938

LIBBY LISTENED in horror as Demetrio informed them that Charlotte was dead. 'No, no, she canna be,' she protested, utterly devastated by this news. 'We only saw her the other week and she looked fine.' Laurence looked equally upset, and Rosita began to quietly weep.

Puffing out his chest Demetrio regarded them all, stony-faced. 'She was taken out and executed by the firing squad for plotting against the Falange party, who will soon be running this country.'

Libby felt a strong desire to punch him in the face. 'She would never do such a thing. Charlotte is no interested in politics, only in fair democracy for the Spanish people. And she's a Lady, dinna forget, so if this is what they've done tae her they'll have Lady Felicity and worse, the laird, tae answer to.'

'That could be interesting,' he smirked.

Libby felt her gut harden with pain and anger, as well as guilt. Her relationship with Charlie had not always been easy, the class difference between them breeding jealousy within her. But having worked so well with Lady Felicity, that was a reaction she should have banished from her mind long since. She'd foolishly envied Charlotte for being pregnant because she'd lost her own child. Yet now, Libby's heart filled with anguish over the loss of her old friend. How she wished she'd been less intolerant of her, and she and Rosita had found a way to save her. Now she'd lost her for good. 'Whatever happened over that picture, ye lied about Charlotte in order to tak your revenge. This is all *your* fault.'

'And Dunmore's,' Laurence gently reminded her.

Feeling a flush of embarrassment Libby had to concede this to be true. Hadn't she personally seen the way he'd accused Charlie, obviously in an effort to protect himself when Demetrio had attacked him? It was just as well Ray had absconded, wherever it was he'd run off to. But the disappearance of her beloved brother was another matter altogether. 'Mebbe ye're right, but noo he's gone. Nick too. Where are they?' she yelled at Demetrio. 'Tell me what has happened tae my brother. Did ye attack him too, as ye did that time wi' Dunmore?'

'If you make such a charge against me then I'll beat you to a pulp, you little whore,' he snarled.

'Don't you dare touch my wife, or call her by such names.' Quickly stepping forward, Laurence put his arm protectively about her.

'No more lies. I wish tae know the truth,' Libby demanded, unmoved by this threat. 'Nick would never leave without telling me, *so where is he*? If ye've done something tae him, dinna imagine for one moment that we'll allow ye to get away with it.'

Demetrio snorted with laughter. 'Your role in this war is over. It's time for you all to leave. The Republican prime minister, Juan Negrin, has announced to the League of Nations that all foreign volunteers will now be withdrawn. He foolishly believes that Franco will also dispose of foreign support.' He chuckled yet again. 'That isn't going to happen. This civil war is almost over and Franco will win.'

'I'm afraid he's speaking the truth,' Laurence quietly remarked. 'We received word from the International Brigade headquarters yesterday.'

Libby stared at her husband, feeling utterly bereft. The three of them had come to Spain to fight for democracy and help the Spanish people and volunteers. They'd faced the constant danger of bombs and shooting, suffered serious injuries, done battle to locate her missing brother and get him released from jail, and endured long working hours under difficult conditions. They were joined by Ray and Fergus, and had been taken care of by Rosita and her family. The friendships that had developed had given them the strength to battle on, despite difficulties in some of the relationships. Now she and Laurence were being forced to leave, having lost all of their dear friends and her brother yet again, possibly for good this time. The prospect of life without him was unbearable.

Rosita too was clearly heartbroken at the prospect of losing her friends and wept all the more. After a degree of silence between them, Libby now gathered her close in a warm hug. 'Dinna fash yerself, we'll keep in touch.'

'Never attempt to contact my wife again,' Demetrio coldly commanded her. 'Once this war is over she will return to her role of wife and mother. Now I must go about my own business. I shall expect you all to be gone by the time I return.'

Since they had no choice but to obey, they said a sad goodbye to Rosita, her mother and young sisters, then quietly returned to the *campo* to take down their tents and pack, along with the other Brigaders.

It was as they were loading the lorry that Rosita suddenly came running over, waving a letter in her hand. 'Look at this, look at this,' she cried. 'I've just been delivered some good news. Charlotte is *alive!*'

Laurence let out a loud cheer of joy, and filled with excitement Libby ran to take the letter from her to quickly read it.

Dear Libby and Rosita,

This is a short note to let you know that at the last moment instead of executing the prisoners the guards took a photograph, which they sent to the British press. As I was expecting, they then transferred me to this convent. It's now being used as a prison so I'm still trapped. I gave birth but the child died, which did not surprise me considering what I'd been through. I fear I may now be returned to the main prison and again face the firing squad. Is there any way you could get me out of here? Here's a sketch of where I believe I am.

All my love, Charlie.

Libby gazed at Rosita in stunned delight as panic ricocheted through her. 'We must go tae the convent noo, this minute, and beg for her release.'

'I'll come with you,' Laurence said.

'Better not,' Rosita told him. '*We* might manage to persuade the nuns to let us see her, but they'd never let a man in.'

'So be it,' he said with a sigh. 'As there isn't enough space on the lorries for everyone and I've no wish to drive, I thought we'd go home by train. There's one arriving late this afternoon that will take us north to the border, so why don't you borrow the ambulance. You'll have to return it, but you can do that when we meet up at the railway station.'

'What time does the train leave?' Libby asked.

'Around five o'clock. Don't worry, I'll do my best to make sure it waits for you. But do try not to miss it.'

Libby briskly nodded. 'Let us hope that we are not too late to save her.'

❧

Charlotte could hardly believe it when Rosita and Libby appeared, feeling quite unable to put into words how delighted she was to see them. She could not remember what day it was, or how long she'd been held in prison. Charlotte did recall being brought to the convent in a blacked-out truck with several other women. No food or water had been provided, despite the heat, and no stops made for the toilet. Even now she still felt as if she was being treated worse than the cows on Libby's farm, only too aware she was but one small step away from death. Waiting for it to happen felt a far greater ordeal than the event itself and she valiantly attempted to block the fear out. What did it matter if she did die? Knowing her child was dead she felt a strange urge to join it in that other world. Now Charlotte embraced her friends with joy.

'We had some problems persuading the nuns tae let us in as it's no a visitor's day,' Libby said, as they sat together on the narrow cell bed to chat. 'But when we explained the situation, a friendly nun did at last open the door for us. Thank God ye're still with us, Charlie. I can hardly believe it.'

'Neither can I,' Charlotte said, the knot of fear inside her uncurling a little. 'But I may not be for much longer. The prison authorities are threatening to take me back to prison any day, no doubt once more to face the firing squad.'

'I've just explained tae the nuns that ye were falsely accused, that ye've worked as a volunteer nurse for all sides during the war and are guilty of nothing.'

'I fully translated for her, and echoed that,' Rosita agreed. Glancing across at the cell door where two nuns were engaged in conversation, she quietly added, 'I think they are discussing the problem right now.'

'They'd never risk putting themselves in danger by letting me go,' Charlotte said, her ash-pale face creasing with fresh anxiety.

Libby took her friend's hands in hers to give them a gentle squeeze. 'Ye dinna look too good, dear Charlie. I'm so sorry ye lost yer child. That must have been dreadful for ye.'

Charlotte felt her heart plummet, yet again feeling a dark pit opening up beneath her. 'It was a most painful birth, probably because of my poor state of health and the fact I was so exhausted. I remember very little about it, except that they told me the baby was stillborn.'

'Was it a boy or a girl?' Rosita tenderly asked.

Silence enveloped Charlotte as she struggled to relive the moment in her head, tears streaming down her cheeks. 'I do not know. They whisked it away and said what did it matter, as it was dead.'

'Are you saying that you didn't see or get to hold your baby?' Charlotte gave a sad shake of her head as Rosita and Libby exchanged a startled glance.

'So what proof do ye have that it did dee?'

Charlotte jerked, finding herself staring at her old friend in wonder. 'Are you suggesting they might have lied to me?'

Libby nodded. 'Laurence has discovered that handing babies over tae Fascist families is considered the right thing tae do, particularly if the child is illegitimate or the birth family is believed tae be Communist.'

Charlotte felt her heart start to pound at this news. 'Could that be what happened?'

'I'll ask,' Rosita said, going to the young nun who now stood alone by the door, patiently waiting. 'Sister Joseph Mary, could we have a word? As I explained, my dear friend has suffered a great deal being locked in prison for no good reason. Now she is grieving for having lost her child, and we wonder if you could tell us what happened.'

'I can't say anything. I was not in charge, only helping as a novice,' she hastily remarked, giving a slight shake of the head.

'But never having seen her baby, she doesn't know whether it was a boy or a girl, simply told it was a stillbirth. Could she at least visit the place where he or she is buried?'

'Stillbirth? Buried?' The young novice looked shocked by this remark. 'This lady gave birth to a perfectly healthy son.'

Charlotte felt as if her insides were falling apart. 'I had a *healthy son*? Does that mean he's alive?'

'He is indeed,' the nun said with a gentle smile, which quickly faded. 'Whatever you've been told is because of the orders imposed upon us by the Nationalists.'

Rosita frowned. 'You mean those orders to hand babies over to Fascist families? Is that what happened?'

Glancing over her shoulder to check there was no one around, she quietly closed the door then quickly returned to whisper to them. 'The baby has been handed over to a young man who came to collect him just a short time ago.'

'What was his name?' Rosita snapped.

The nun pulled a slip of paper from the pocket of her habit. 'Señor Quintana López.'

Rosita put her hands to her face in horrified silence for some seconds. 'That is my husband. He is very much a Fascist and disappointed in me for not giving him a son. Of course, I always made sure I was protected as I'd no wish to have his child. This is all my fault,' she said, turning to Charlotte with agony etched on her lovely face.

'No, no,' the novice protested. 'The fault is not yours, or ours. As I said, this is a rule we are forced to obey. The man – your husband – left just half an hour ago. If this is a family problem you might manage to claim the child back. And as you've assured me this lady is innocent of all charges, I'd like to help, as this law is not something I agree with.'

'Won't that be dangerous for you?' Charlotte tentatively asked, new hope reverberating within her.

'I believe in the presence of God to stand by me when doing the right thing,' she said with a smile. 'Come with me. I can get you out of here. But don't make a sound,' she said, helping Charlotte to her feet.

Leading them out of the cell she took them quickly down a narrow back staircase. At the bottom she unlocked the door and, giving them all her blessing, opened it up onto the wooded countryside.

Breathing fresh air into her lungs felt like a miracle to Charlotte. The last time had been while she stood facing the firing squad. This time she could be facing freedom.

'You must promise never to tell anyone that I helped you. Ever.'

'We won't say a word.'

The young novice nodded. 'Thank you, and don't worry. I will name no names. If any officials notice you're missing, which they hopefully won't, I'll tell them someone called to take you back to prison whom I assumed to have been sent by the prison authorities.'

'I'd prefer it if you told them I died in childbirth. If they believe I am dead they will not come looking for me,' Charlotte said.

Falling silent for a moment, the nun gravely nodded as she let them out the door. 'Very well. I'm sure God will forgive me that lie.'

'God bless, and thank you,' Charlotte said, kissing her on each cheek. Libby hugged her too, as did Rosita. Then the three of them slipped away into the dusk.

THIRTY-EIGHT

A S THEY MADE their way through the woods in search of Demetrio a cold sweat came over Charlotte, her mouth turning dry with fear. How would she manage to reclaim her child, if and when they found him? And how could she do battle against this man with no weapon to defend herself? Not only that, but she felt so weak and exhausted. She'd once had every confidence in her own strength and courage. Did she have any left? She at least had her friends' support, and began to listen to what they were saying.

Libby was telling Rosita how a cheering crowd in Barcelona had thanked the International Brigade when they'd marched in a final parade. 'I heard that La Pasionaria gave a farewell speech filled with sadness, but mentioning their bravery. She told them: "You can go with pride. You are history. You are legend." She went on to say: "We will not forget you." And told them to think of Spain as their homeland. Isn't that wonderful?'

'They were indeed brave, and so many have risked their lives,' Rosita agreed.

Charlotte gave a sad shake of her head. 'I can't see many wishing to return to Spain, not if Franco comes to power and it looks as if he is about to do so. His philosophy seems to insist that everyone must agree with him, or they will be disposed of. Yet the other side are almost as bad. All parties are so filled with hatred and the desire for revenge it's unlikely the conflict will end any time soon, war or no war.'

Libby nodded in agreement. 'So many people have already died, or suffered dreadful wounding, and I suspect there'll be more losses to come. At least now the volunteers will soon be able to make their journey home.'

'They may go into exile,' Rosita pointed out. 'Not everyone will find it safe to go home. If they come from Germany or Italy and are against the regime growing in their own country, they will have to find someplace else to live. Just as some Spaniards are fleeing their homeland.'

'They could always try coming to Scotland,' Libby said with a smile.

'It's such a scary world. How do *we* get home?' Charlotte asked.

'There's a train coming late this afternoon for those of us not wishing to drive, and Laurence says we must . . .'

She got no further as they suddenly heard a baby crying and all three of them stopped in their tracks.

'Shh!' Rosita said, putting her finger to her lips. Hiding behind a pine tree, they all three peeped out across the woodland. 'There he is. He's not an easy man. How do we deal with this?'

Ignoring the sight of Demetrio slumped on a log smoking a cigarette, Charlotte's gaze was focused exclusively upon the basket set beside his feet from which emanated the sound of a baby's cries. That was *her* child, *her* son. How could those nuns be forced to lie and claim a child was dead simply in order to give it away without the permission of its mother? Not pausing to think further, or listen to the whispered discussion her friends were engaged in, she stepped out from behind the tree and marched towards him. 'I believe that is *my* baby.'

He jerked with shock, his dark eyes narrowing as he glared at her, then stamping out his cigarette, he smirked. 'Not any longer.'

'I will not allow you to steal my child.'

His eyes and mouth twitched but he said nothing. Charlotte found his silence disconcerting, the only sound that of the baby crying and a rush of feet scuffling in the grass as her two friends rushed to join her.

Rosita grasped her arm as she nervously whispered in her ear. 'My husband is not in a good mood right now, so take care not to enrage him further.'

'I'm not afraid of him.' Gently brushing her hand away, Charlotte addressed him in her most imperious tone. 'Hand my son over now. He is not yours and never will be.'

'What makes you imagine you can exercise any power over me, you foolish girl? He's *mine!*' Demetrio chuckled as he picked the basket up, holding his arm outstretched to rock it back and forth.

'Don't do that, you fool. He might fall out.'

'Tut, tut, that would be a shame if he really did die, wouldn't it? I admit that getting this child was something of a bonus, after managing to rid myself of you and your dirty plots. So maybe it is best to keep him safe.'

Charlotte sighed with relief as he set the basket back down on the ground, instinctively moving closer as the baby screamed all the louder. She was so concerned for him that it didn't occur to her what this man was about to do. He suddenly lurched forward and punched her in the face, sending her flying. Rosita ran at once to help her while Libby grabbed a stick and struck him across his shoulders.

'You divil! How dare ye do that tae her! You're a tyrant who beats his wife, attempts to steal valuable pictures, and lies all the time just to suit yer own greed. And I believe ye killed my brother.'

Wobbling back on his heels Demetrio only just managed to maintain his balance. Avoiding meeting her gaze, he sneered. 'Wouldn't you like to know the truth about that?' Then pulling his Colt pistol from his pocket, he aimed it directly at Charlotte. 'Take this woman back to the convent prison where she belongs, or I'll kill her too.'

It was Rosita this time who hit him from behind; striking him on the head with a much larger stick she'd found lying on the ground beside her. Falling forward on to his knees he almost dropped the pistol but somehow managed to keep hold of it and recover.

Within seconds Charlotte too was on her feet, the sound of her baby's screams ringing in her ears as she kicked Demetrio in the stomach. Swinging round he aimed another punch at her, but managing to duck and avoid it she grabbed his wrist and began to grapple furiously for his gun. Failing to find the strength necessary to retrieve it, fear escalated through her that at any moment it might go off. Giving a sneer of satisfaction as he kept a tight hold of the weapon, he finally broke free of her hold and pointed the gun straight at the child. Rosita and Libby at once fell upon him to hit him with sticks, fists, boots and stones. This time when Charlotte grasped his wrist she turned the weapon into his chest and pressed the trigger. Only when a pool of blood poured from him, and he lay unmoving with his eyes wide open, did they realise he was dead.

All three women stood staring at his body for some long moments, each of them panting for breath but not a single tear being shed.

Picking up the pistol, Charlotte tossed it furiously away as far as she could into a distant clump of sage bushes. Then hurrying over to her screaming son she lifted him from the basket to cuddle him close in her arms. Sinking to her knees in tears she opened her blouse and, as her breasts were fortunately still leaking milk, began to feed her precious child.

It was some time later, as the three women sat together watching the baby contentedly sleep in his mother's arms, that it became clear this was a secret they must keep forever.

'We must never speak of this to anyone,' Libby said, and they each nodded in agreement.

'We must also go our separate ways, otherwise we'll be caught and executed. I really have no wish to go through all of that agony ever again,' Charlotte said with a shudder. 'You two must stay safe too. La Pasionaria might not wish us to be forgotten, but I do. Go home, Rosita, and express surprise or alarm when your husband does not return.'

'But say nothing.'

'Not a word. There's a war on, so simply assume that is what killed him. Few people know where members of their family have been killed, or why. As for you, Libby darling, we'll go and meet Laurence at the train. Then as we have to return the ambulance, I'll get a lift in the truck. With the help of members of the Brigade, I hope to find Guillermo. I have no intention of leaving Spain without the father of my child,' Charlotte said, gazing with love at her son as she gently rocked him in her arms. 'But I will miss you both,' she said. And the three of them held each other close with tears in their eyes for several long minutes, making a pact of silence between them that must last forever.

THIRTY-NINE
SPAIN—1986

'**N**OW I UNDERSTAND why my beloved grandmother has kept quiet all these years,' Jo said, feeling a heart-rending sympathy for these three women. 'What a terrible situation to find yourselves in.'

'It was indeed,' Rosita quietly agreed, her eyes filled with tears. 'Not something we had planned. It just happened.'

'But a perfectly understandable response,' Anton agreed. 'To threaten to kill a woman and a child, having already killed one or possibly two men, how could you not defend yourselves against him? The fellow had no heart.'

'None at all. He was a brute of the worst order,' she stoutly responded.

'May I ask what you did with his body?' her grandson quietly asked.

Drawing in a deep breath she gave a resigned little nod. 'We felt we had to move it as far away from the convent as we could, so dragged it back along the path, dumped it in the ambulance and drove out to the coast, where we tossed it in the sea. The body was washed up some days later and his colleagues tried to find his killer, but fortunately didn't succeed. I nevertheless lived in fear for some time in case they did come to charge me with my husband's murder.

'Silence was our only means of staying safe. Even after the war ended many people were still afraid to discuss what had happened during those dreadful years, out of fear of reprisals. Some women spent many more years in prison, but after their release were urged by their families to keep quiet and not admit to whatever beliefs or political persuasions they'd held at the time. It became a taboo subject.'

'And wasn't a pact of silence imposed in the Amnesty Law of 1977 after Franco's death, to prevent investigation into war crimes?' Anton said.

Rosita nodded. 'Even photos of missing loved ones are kept hidden and unnamed. I wish I possessed a picture of my friends. I missed them so much, and Nick, of course. I never saw them again, which is why I so longed to see some of them one more time.'

Jo gently held her hand. 'I take it that the skeleton Sophie found in the mine tunnel is likely to be Nick?'

Rosita's eyes looked bleak. 'I'm afraid that must be the case, or else Dunmore. Demetrio was in such a rage and so controlling of me that I'm quite sure he killed both men in revenge. They could both be in there, or else tossed down a mine shaft.'

'We'll have it searched and arrange for any remains to be properly buried,' Anton told her, giving his grandmother a gentle hug.

'Thank you,' she said with a faint smile. 'Now I shall take my siesta.'

'Yes, that's a good idea after the trauma of telling us such a tragic tale,' Jo agreed, and gave the old lady a kiss before Anton escorted her to her room.

'What a story,' Anton said when he returned half an hour later. 'Not at all what I expected, but it has its good points as well as bad.'

Jo shyly nodded as they gazed into each other's eyes, which seemed to be saying more than they could find the words to express right now. She was still struggling to come to terms with the horrors of what she'd heard; yet they now seemed to have all the answers, at least almost all. 'What about your father? You'll have to explain this to him.'

'I've just quickly done that, and *mi abuela* has agreed to fill him in with the fine details later, once she's rested.'

'Was he upset or angry?'

Anton shook his head. 'Really quite sanguine, just relieved to know the truth at last, I think.'

'I was so fearful that his belief he was Libby's illegitimate son might be correct. Then I thought your father might be Nick's son, but it seems they were not lovers, after all, so we are not related.'

'Thank heaven for that,' he said, at last kissing her softly. 'I've been wanting to do this for so long, only I, too, feared we were cousins,' he murmured as he smiled into her eyes.

A tremor of excitement stirred within her. 'Thank goodness we aren't', and with a chuckle of happiness they kissed again, much deeper this time.

'I do feel a wonderful closeness between us. I shall miss you when you leave, Jo. Is your flight on Friday or Saturday?'

'Thursday.'

'Oh no, even worse. I wish you didn't have to go.'

She smiled at him, wondering if he could sense the slow beat of her heart. 'I could always postpone it. My life back in Scotland is in something of a mess, so I did wonder about staying on in Spain for a while. I thought I might start my own business here, teaching art. There must be plenty of ex-pats around who'd love to take up painting as a hobby.'

'I'm sure there are. That would be a splendid idea. And I'm certain *mi abuela* would be happy to let you stay on at the *cortijo* for as long as you like. She would miss you too, if you left.'

'That would be wonderful, but I do insist upon paying a proper rent.'

Pulling her closer, he gazed into her eyes with deep feeling in his own. 'Let's say only when you've got the business going, till then it can remain rent-free.'

Thanking him with more kisses and joy in her heart, Jo could no longer deny that she was falling in love with this wonderful man, and hoped he was feeling the same way about her. Sitting close in each other's arms on the bench beneath their favourite olive tree, she couldn't help but express her sympathy for his grandmother. 'How awful that Rosita lost Nick, the man she truly loved. She must have led a lonely life.'

'I fear so, except that despite the dreadful way she found herself pregnant she adores Gregorio, and has been a devoted mother to him. They are actually very close. Even now in Spain, being illegitimate or having an affair is not considered respectable or proper.'

'The only question we still haven't found an answer to is what happened to Charlotte after they went their separate ways, which is sad,' Jo admitted. 'Did she ever find Guillermo and manage to escape Spain, or was she re-arrested and shot, as many were?'

'Let's look again at that picture she painted, just in case we've missed something,' he suggested.

They spent some time going over every detail of it. Then suddenly Jo stared at the flag. 'This isn't a flag of Spain, it's Cornwall, which is where Charlotte originally came from. And look here, this could be her family coat of arms. Why didn't I notice that before?'

'I suppose because we assumed she was dead.'

'Yes, but as Charlotte survived, that could be where she went to live, and she put clues into this picture so that whenever it felt safe for them to do so, her friends could find her.'

'That's amazing!' Anton said with a grin. 'How clever of you.'

'I need to ring Mum. She lives in London close to various archives and libraries, so might be able to help.'

Jo went to the phone and made the call immediately. She chatted with her mother happily for a little while, quickly filling her in on how she'd finally banished Felix from her life, although remained on good terms with Sophie. She then went on to explain all they'd discovered about Libby and her friends, and what they still needed to know about Charlotte. Her mother promised to do some investigating. A day later she rang back to say she'd found her.

'I visited the archives and when I could find no mention of her, searched instead for this Laurence Cunningham, and there he was. He's a Member of Parliament, would you believe?'

'Ah, that makes sense. He always did express an interest in politics. Well done.'

'I contacted him and, being told where she was now living, he managed to get in touch with her. He and Charlotte have agreed to come to Spain.'

'Oh, my goodness, I must ring Gran and tell her.'

'I've already done that,' her mother said. 'I hope I've persuaded her to come to Spain too. They've all promised to be there on Thursday, but I don't recommend you tell Rosita yet, in case Libby changes her mind. She may not manage to find the courage to leave the house. You know how she prefers to confine herself indoors.'

'I fully understand now why she has that problem, but do hope they all come, including Gran. How wonderful that would be,' Jo cried. And hanging up the phone she instinctively flung herself into Anton's arms as joy cascaded through her. Within seconds his mouth closed over hers, kissing her with increasing passion.

❦

The next day or two dragged slowly by, but when finally Thursday dawned, Jo and Anton sat waiting in the olive grove with excited anticipation. Around midday they heard a car turn into the drive and, exchanging a delighted grin, hurried to welcome their visitors.

Rosita was seated on the terrace reading when Jo casually strolled towards her. 'You told us that you longed to see your friends again,' she said with a smile. 'Well, I have a surprise for you. Here they are.'

Looking up, Rosita gave a cry of disbelief to find herself face to face with Charlotte, Libby and Laurence. Tears were shed in abundance as they all hugged each other, ecstatic with happiness at being together again at last, and all talking at once.

'How did you find them?' she asked, wiping the tears from her eyes with her lace handkerchief.

'Would you believe with the help of that picture?' Jo said.

'I can't believe this is happening.'

'Neither can I,' Libby agreed. 'Having suffered from mild agoraphobia for years, rarely going further than local shops, this is the furthest I've travelled since I returned from the war. But I found the courage to come surprisingly easy as I so longed to see you all again.'

'Do please make yourselves comfortable, everyone,' Jo said. And as the group of old friends all settled themselves close together on the wicker chairs, still chattering away like mad, she happily started to hand round coffee and cakes, assisted by Anton. 'It's wonderful to meet you at last, but there's so much I would still like to know about you all. Charlotte, can we begin with you? Did you find Guillermo again, and how did you escape from Spain?'

'Ah, quite a story,' she answered, reaching for a small piece of madeleine cake.

FORTY
SPAIN — NOVEMBER 1938

THEY'D BEEN DRIVING for some hours, having passed Valencia and Zaragoza, aiming for the Pyrenees, when it began to feel as if winter was closing in. Charlotte sat squashed in the lorry with a score of Brigaders, her baby tucked in a sling close to her heart. A bitter cold wind was blowing, the mountain roads quite slippy with ice. But even as she shivered and shook, the further north they went the easier she felt inside. Charlotte lived in hope that those responsible for arresting her would be convinced she'd died in childbirth. She desperately wanted her beloved child to remain safe. The sensation of his warm little body and gentle heartbeat filled her with a happiness she'd never expected to feel ever again.

Thankfully, Libby had managed to dig out some essentials for the baby, including nappies, milk and a bottle. Charlotte carried them stuffed in a knapsack, so at least the little one was provided for, although she had nothing of her own. Her dear friend had even shown her how to change a nappy, of which she was an expert, having younger siblings.

When one of the old Brigaders, watching her clumsy efforts to do that, said, 'Och, he's a lovely wee bairn. What's he called?'

Charlotte felt stunned. Goodness, there'd been so much going on that she hadn't got around to choosing a name. But now the answer came to her. So obvious. 'Oliver,' she answered.

'Ah, what a sweet name. I assume ye're going home. Do ye have a passport or papers of any sort?'

Charlotte shook her head. 'It was taken from me while I was held in prison. I lost everything, including most of my clothing.' And almost my child too, she thought, but held on to the silence they'd agreed upon.

He grinned. 'Yer looking a bit cold, but if you dinna mind wearing an old man's overcoat, I can gie you one o' those. As for the passport, ye could write home for a new one, or ask the police for a pass. Otherwise ye might have problems getting oot of Spain.'

This wasn't something Charlotte had taken into consideration, and she certainly had no intention of speaking to the police. Her one thought was to find Guillermo. She could but hope the prison authorities would have released him by now. They'd made a pledge to each other a while back that were they ever to lose contact by the time the International Brigade were ordered home, they'd meet up again at the cathedral in Pamplona. Charlotte fully intended to keep that promise as she had no wish to leave Spain without him.

She said as much to this helpful old man as she gratefully pulled on the overcoat he gave her. It stank of beer, cigarettes and sweat, but what did that matter as long as she and her child could keep warm within it? He also wrapped a scarf about her neck and set a Glengarry bonnet on her head.

'There ye are, dearie, now ye're fit to travel,' he said with a soft chuckle.

Charlotte gave him her heartfelt thanks. She'd forgotten how generous and helpful these Scotsmen were, and it was with some degree of sadness that, when they reached Pamplona, she had to say goodbye to this friendly old soldier.

'I do hope I can find him,' she murmured.

'Dinna fash yerself, I'll send word out that ye're looking for this Guillermo Abana Martínez, with a reminder where he can find ye.'

❦

There were so many churches in this busy city that locating the cathedral did not prove to be easy. But Charlotte quite enjoyed exploring the narrow streets, if now in something of a shambled mess thanks to the war. She was aware that Pamplona was famous for its Running of the Bulls, not that Charlotte had any wish to see that, as it was an extremely dangerous event and she felt she'd suffered enough perils and danger to last a lifetime. Fortunately this was the wrong time of year, even if such activities had continued during the war, which she very much doubted. But she kept a wary eye out, just in case there were any bulls around.

Asking for directions she finally found the *Centro Histórico*, and suddenly there it was: *Catedral De Santa Maria De Pamplona*, tucked away in a corner off the main street. In a strange way this beautiful gothic building with its pillared entrance and twin towers reminded her a little of Craiklyn Manor. She felt a sudden urge to paint it, using her favourite colours. Oh, how she missed those days.

Smiling to herself, she walked through the courtyard and slipped inside to seat herself with some relief on one of the wooden pews. It felt quite dark, probably not looking its best as no doubt its precious sculptures, carvings and paintings had been hidden away to protect them.

Despite not being a Catholic, Charlotte felt the urge to light a candle in honour of the valiant heroes who had fought in the war. Then going back to her seat she knelt and sent up a silent prayer for them all, including Sister Joseph Mary, the young nun who'd helped her to escape prison and been prepared to lie for her. Charlotte could but hope that she too would be safe. It wasn't long before her eyelids began to droop and she fell asleep out of exhaustion, the baby safely tucked in her sling.

She was woken some time later by the sound of footsteps echoing on the flagged floors behind her. Panic resonated within her as for a moment Charlotte couldn't remember where she was. It was as if she was back in prison and the guards were coming for her again. Then she remembered. Dare she turn around to see if this could possibly be Guillermo? It was highly unlikely he would arrive so soon, and it didn't sound like him. Had she made a dreadful mistake by sitting in full view? She should have tucked herself away in a corner out of sight. Keeping her head down and thankful for the disguise of the overcoat, scarf and Glengarry bonnet, she prayed the baby would not cry and reveal himself.

A man's voice softly remarked, '*Hola*, are you in need of a bed, young lady, or help for your child? Night is almost upon us.' Looking up, Charlotte found herself facing the kind smiling face of a priest.

'I'm waiting for a friend,' she said, feeling strangely comforted by his presence.

Giving a slight nod of his head to indicate she should follow him, he led her down some steps into a small room hidden deep within the crypt. He laid out a straw-filled palliasse for her to sleep on, provided her with a blanket and small pillow, brought her food and water, and asking no further questions informed her she was welcome to stay as long as she wished. He was clearly accustomed to helping people escape from Spain.

The days passed so slowly that boredom soon set in and Charlotte asked if there were any tasks she could do in return for her keep. 'Although I've no wish to be on view to the public,' she admitted. 'But I can knit, sew, mend, paint pictures. Is there anything of that nature I could do for you?'

'A picture of the cathedral would be wonderful, but then you'd have to sit outside.'

'I could paint one of the altar, a statue or window. This is a beautiful building.' And that is what she did. The priest brought her canvasses, a box of oil paints and brushes, all the necessary equipment she needed. Settling her child on the bed, and filled with gratitude for the priest's kindness, she devoted hour upon hour to painting, as she so loved to do. Being busy helped to keep her fear in check as she waited in agony for Guillermo. Would he ever be free to come and find her?

In addition to painting several pictures of the cathedral from various angles, she could not resist painting a small one of *Casa Oliva*, in memory of the much larger picture she'd done for Rosita, which was still strong in her mind. She added an image of herself carrying her child to this one, as well as planes and soldiers to illustrate the war. It was one day when she started to paint a small portrait of baby Oliver that she again heard footsteps approaching, much heavier this time.

'I was told to look out for that bonnet, and there it is.'

Spinning around Charlotte gazed up at him in unbelievable joy. 'Guillermo!'

Seconds later she was in his arms, sharing their son with him as they kissed. 'Thank you, God. You've sent him back to me, and we're together at last.' They each lit another candle and made a silent prayer.

ᙡ

They slowly crossed the Pyrenees into France without worrying about a passport but taking the small picture of *Casa Oliva* and the portrait of their son with them. They walked for hours in the darkness, led by a woman with a dog they'd met en route. Her name was

Felisa and she'd offered to take them as she knew the mountains well and was happy to help people escape. Felisa insisted that no talking was allowed, silence being essential as sound echoed in the mountains, particularly at night. They were also ordered to keep to the rocks in case any dogs were following, as they could easily pick up their scent on grass. Together they scrambled over crags, one climb leading to another, and yet another, hill after hill, rock upon rock.

The weather remained bitterly cold and windy, and, close to exhaustion, they were constantly lashed by rain and sleet. Charlotte felt her feet were so frozen they must be in danger of frostbite. Guillermo now held baby Oliver slung safely across his chest, and readily helped Charlotte to keep a steady hold of the rocks with her hands and feet. Panting for breath and needing to take frequent rests before reaching the summit, there were times when she feared she might never make it. Not surprisingly, she no longer felt as fit as when she'd first arrived in Spain.

They lived rough and remained fearful of being caught, terrified that at any moment a Falange guard might appear, and then she'd be captured and sent back to prison. Fortunately, Guillermo had been officially released so was reasonably safe. Although, recalling what she'd learned from Fergus back at the start of the war, Charlotte had some doubts about that. As he was a Spaniard, the Falangists could deny him the right to leave.

When finally they reached the border, Felisa confirmed this fear with a final warning. 'As you have no papers, take care not to get caught as you cross into France or you could be held in a concentration camp, or returned to Spain.'

Paying her what they owed and thanking this kind lady for her help, that night as they huddled together in a tin shack they went over the various possibilities open to them.

'We could find a railway station and try to catch a train,' Guillermo suggested. 'Although we'd still require papers. I heard that many International Brigaders have had to wait weeks for the right paperwork to allow them to leave, but are expecting to be transported soon.'

'Where from?'

He shook his head. 'No idea. Do you wish to return to Scotland?'

'No.' Charlotte firmly shook her head. She felt far too nervous of going back home as that would be the obvious place the Fascists would come looking for her, which could endanger Libby's life too.

Explaining to Guillermo how the young novice had agreed to claim that she'd died in childbirth so that everyone would think she was dead, Charlotte made no mention of the events that had followed her escape. Her silence was absolute, as she had no wish to put his life in danger any more than that of her child.

'We could write to Mama, but then we'd have to name some place to which she could send the papers, and wait weeks for a response. The trouble is that would prove I am still alive, which would put my friends and the nun in danger, as well as myself.'

'I agree that since your escape from prison would be viewed as illegal, we have no wish for anyone to know that.'

They slept badly that night, turning the problem over in their minds, but by dawn Charlotte had devised a plan. 'Now could be the moment to take advantage of my status, and for me to play the Lady that I once was, and Libby keeps accusing me of still being,' she suggested with a giggle. 'I can speak French and if we could borrow or buy some decent clothes, I could do that easily. But I'm afraid you would have to act as my servant.'

Guillermo burst out laughing as he hugged her. 'That could work, so long as we used different names.'

It cost them most of the money Guillermo had left, but dressed in a black suit and bow tie, Guillermo naturally became William.

Charlotte, clad in a rabbit-fur coat she'd bought at a market that looked far more expensive than it actually was, called herself Lady Adélaïde Montague. These were her mother's second and maiden names, so seemed entirely appropriate.

'Sometimes it's a good idea not to be a Charlie,' she said as they found the railway station at Canfranc, high in the Pyrenees not far from the French border.

Throughout the train journey into France she spoke entirely in French, sounding extremely noble, and constantly ordering her servant William to fetch this or do that. When asked for her papers she gave the guard her most charming and appealing smile. 'Oh, my dear man, how very foolish of me. I only crossed the border to visit a friend and forgot all about my passport. I'm Lady Adélaïde Montague, and this is my manservant; I do so hope that will be enough for you. And please don't upset my darling child, who is asleep at last in this dreadful cold weather.'

Her charm and imperious tone were such that he tenderly stroked the baby's head, politely bowed, and assuring her that all was fine, bustled away. So it was that they crossed the border into France without any difficulty at all, and caught the next train to London.

FORTY-ONE
SPAIN — 1986

'I LATER secretly wrote to Mama, but we didn't meet up until after the Second World War was over,' Charlotte admitted to her friends.

'She was such a generous lady,' Laurence said. 'She took excellent care of all the children I sent her over the years. Once the war was finally over and the Spanish refugee children were returned to their families, or else adopted if they were orphaned, she happily took in Jewish refugee children during World War Two.'

Charlotte nodded with a proud smile. 'So I believe. Mama did tell me a little about that. Of course, the laird did not approve and tended to hide himself away in the east wing. When that war too was over and the refugee home closed, she left him and went back to live in Cornwall, where she'd been born. They never had enjoyed quite the happy marriage she'd hoped for. We went to join her. By then Billy and I, which is what I called Guillermo once we were settled in England, had two more children: Peter and Margot, Oliver's beloved siblings. Sadly, Guillermo died of a heart attack just two years ago, but we were blessed with a happy marriage right to the end, and enjoyed a wonderful family life in Cornwall. Just before Mama died, at her suggestion I added the Cornish flag and her family coat of arms to the picture. I also tucked the last letter Billy had received from me into the back of the frame. She believed this would give hints of where my friends could find me, were it ever to become safe to do so.'

'That is so like dear Lady Felicity,' Libby said. 'To want us all tae meet up again. I did love working with her.'

'It was indeed, which is why, after she died, I sent it to you, darling.'

Libby gave a sad little chuckle. 'Tae think if I'd examined it properly, instead of locking it away with blocked-out memories, I could have found the answer to where ye were years ago. So sorry I failed tae do that.'

Charlotte smiled as she hugged her old friend again. 'I can fully understand your reluctance to look back, Libby, and why you've been so badly affected by fear. Haven't we all felt that way for so long?'

Libby nodded. 'I kept hidden away in case the Fascists came looking for us, were they ever to work out who had killed your husband, Rosita. That is the reason I denied you and I were ever friends, instinctively knowing I must protect us all. It was a deliberate lie I told ye, Jo, because of our pact of silence.'

'I kept silent for the same reason,' Rosita agreed. 'I've led something of a quiet life, never having got over losing Nick, your lovely brother. Living under the Franco regime was not easy but I loved my family and home, and at least I was free of that devil of a husband. But I decided that before I move on from this world I needed to see you all one last time, which is why I sent my grandson to that exhibition. As I had no idea where you all lived, that picture has proved to be extremely useful in finding you.'

'So it was no a foolish mistake for me tae allow Jo to put it in the exhibition?' Libby asked with a wry smile.

'Of course not. It's just wonderful to be together again.'

'Oh, I second that,' Charlotte agreed. 'It's absolutely amazing to see everyone once more, my darlings, after all these years.'

'Aye, it is, although Laurence and I did manage tae remain in touch,' Libby said. 'He disappeared off tae London following our divorce, but we found each other again back in the fifties, didn't we, laddie?'

'Yes, when as a Member of Parliament I was able to help banish the law against homosexuals, which finally ended in the sixties.'

'That's wonderful. So you not only achieved your dream but were able to do your bit to resolve that stupid problem,' Charlotte said with a warm smile.

'He was indeed,' Libby agreed with pride in her voice. 'I learned aboot what he'd achieved from his parents. Surprisingly they became quite friendly towards me, despite their initial disapproval, so I naturally wrote tae Laurence to offer him my support. We've kept in contact a wee bit ever since, if only to exchange Christmas and birthday cards. Although I was always careful never tae speak o' the past.'

'She kept absolutely silent about what happened to Demetrio,' Laurence added. 'But a card can say all that is necessary in such circumstances.'

'There's something else ye should know,' Libby said, smiling across at Jo. 'As I found I couldna have any bairns of my own, I fell for one o' the orphaned children and brought him up as my own son. He is noo yer father.'

'You're saying that Dad was adopted, and is Spanish?' Jo asked in astonishment.

'He is, aye. He was a sweet wee laddie who took a shine to me when he was but two years old, and me to him. He's seen me as his mum ever since, and I never told him otherwise, for his own safety as well as mine. I mebbe did keep him a bit tied tae the house, oot of fear of losing him tae the Falangists. They would come looking for their lost children and tak' them back tae Spain, so I was very protective of him. I largely stayed indoors meself because of the fear that remained within me, and ended up suffering from agoraphobia. Your father and I still get on well despite his stubborn independence and determination to be free tae roam wherever he pleases. But now we're in a safer era, and our silence is finally over, I can explain everything properly to him.'

'That is the reason I at last told my own son,' Rosita admitted. 'The time for truth is upon us.'

'Oh, I'm sure Dad will be as fascinated to hear your story, as am I. And you're still my gran,' Jo said, giving Libby a warm hug.

'I am indeed, lassie.'

'I feel I understand everything about my family so much better now.' Then, smiling with delight, she turned to Anton. 'I must be half Spanish.'

'Welcome,' he said with a grin.

Rising from her chair Jo beamed around at everyone. 'It's been good to hear all your stories too. You were such brave young women, I'm proud to know you. Now we have finally sorted all this out, I think Anton and I will go for a little walk and leave you in peace. I'm sure you have a great deal still to talk about and catch up on with all those missed years.'

'That could take a while,' Charlotte said with an impish grin.

'Not to worry,' Anton said. 'Take your time. We have quite a lot to talk about too, not least making plans for our future together.' And, smiling into each other's eyes, they happily walked away with his arm warmly wrapped around her.

ACKNOWLEDGEMENTS

La Colina de Arboledas is fictional, but all other places mentioned are real. We first had a village holiday home in Spain but in the late nineties bought an olive grove and built a house upon it, where we happily spend our winters. Here we enjoy a relaxed and reasonably stress-free lifestyle. We have space to breathe and enjoy the wonderful climate and a lovely outdoor life: walking, swimming, and working on the land. The Spanish are delightfully friendly people, making ex-pats feel very much a part of the community. We do now spend our summers in the UK. But having lived here so long, I couldn't resist the ideas that came to me when we visited the Salvador Dalí museum in Figueres, and the Prado in Madrid. I've also read many books and articles on the subject of the Civil War, my favourites being: *A Concise History of the Spanish Civil War*, and *Doves of War*, both by Paul Preston. He is very much an expert on the subject. Other books included: *Memories of Resistance – Women's Voices from the Spanish Civil War* by Shirley Mangini; *Malaga Burning* by Gamel Woolsey; *Homage to Caledonia* by Daniel Gray; *Tales of the Kirkcudbright Artists* by Haig Gordon. Thanks also to Maria Dolores Castro, a Spanish friend who checked the Spanish language for me, and to my brother-in-law, Michael, who checked the historical facts. I am most grateful for their help and support, and of course to my husband David, who as well as keeping me well fed and cared for, helps with proofing and other admin tasks. My wonderful agent, Amanda Preston, and the excellent Amazon editing team: Victoria Pepe and Sammia Hamer. I would also like to thank all my readers who follow me on Facebook: www.facebook.com/pages/Freda-Lightfoot-Books/149641371839646 or Twitter: @fredalightfoot.

For more details, or if you wish to sign up for my newsletter, please visit my website: www.fredalightfoot.co.uk.

Kind regards,

Freda

ABOUT THE AUTHOR

Sunday Times bestselling author Freda Lightfoot hails from Oswaldtwistle, a small mill town in Lancashire. Her mother comes from generations of weavers, and her father was a shoe repairer; she still remembers the first pair of clogs he made for her.

After several years of teaching, Freda opened a bookshop in Kendal, Cumbria. And while living in the rural Lakeland Fells, rearing sheep and hens and making jam, Freda turned to writing. She wrote over fifty articles and short stories for magazines such as *My Weekly* and *Woman's Realm*, before finding her vocation as a novelist. She has since written over forty-five novels, mostly historical fiction and family sagas. She now lives in Spain with her own olive grove, and divides her time between sunny winters and the summer rains of Britain.